PRAISE FOR ELMER KELTON

"Kelton's characters jump off the page, they are so real. This is another fine title from the man named the greatest Western writer of all time in a 1995 survey by the Western Writers of America."　　—*American Cowboy* on *The Smiling Country*

"Elmer Kelton, a wily old cloudburst, imbues his Westerns with ancient myths and modern motifs that transcend cowboys and cattle trails."　　—*The Dallas Morning News*

"One thing is certain: As long as there are writers as skillful as Elmer Kelton, Western literature will never die."
　　—*True West* magazine

"Kelton, like fine wine, just keeps getting better and better."
　　—*Tulsa World*

"Elmer Kelton is a Texas treasure, as important for his state as Willa Cather is for Nebraska and Badger Clark for South Dakota. Kelton truly deserves to be made one of our immortals of literature."　　—*El Paso Herald-Post*

ELMER KELTON

THE RAIDERS

SONS OF TEXAS

A TOM DOHERTY ASSOCIATES BOOK
NEW YORK

This is a work of fiction. All of the characters, organizations, and events portrayed in this novel are either products of the author's imagination or are used fictitiously.

THE RAIDERS: SONS OF TEXAS

Copyright © 1989 by Tom Early

Originally published in 1989 by the Berkley Publishing Group as *Sons of Texas: The Raiders,* by Tom Early, a pseudonym of Elmer Kelton.

All rights reserved, including the right to reproduce this book, or portions thereof, in any form.

A Forge Book
Published by Tom Doherty Associates, LLC
175 Fifth Avenue
New York, NY 10010

www.tor-forge.com

Forge® is a registered trademark of Tom Doherty Associates, LLC.

ISBN-13: 978-0-7653-4898-2
ISBN-10: 0-7653-4898-5

First Edition: May 2006
First Mass Market Edition: August 2007

Printed in the United States of America

0 9 8 7 6 5 4 3 2 1

PART I

THE

ALIEN LAND

1

YESTERDAY NATURE had been quarrelsome. Dark and chilly clouds had scudded ominously inland from the Gulf of Mexico, threatening a drenching cold rain across the gently rolling prairie land and dense forests that stretched westward beyond the flat coastal plain of Texas. An angry wind had lashed the trees, whipping away new leaves still the pale green of early spring. Michael Lewis had pulled his bay horse into the deep woods in search of protection, but the trees had offered only partial shelter from winter's final revolt against the changing of the season.

He had slept fitfully last night, for an old nightmare he hoped he had finally put behind him had crept back like a thief in the darkness. He had awakened wide-eyed to the sound of his own voice crying out. Afterward he had lain cold and trembling, trying to rewrap his thin woolen blanket around his shoulders in a way that would shut out the chill. But the chill came more from within than from without, and no blanket was thick enough to shield him from a memory too cruel to die.

Today Nature smiled. The skies had cleared. The sun was pleasantly warm, and he had taken off his old woolen coat, remnant of another time back in Tennessee. The wind had dropped to a soft and kindly breeze that carried the hopeful scent of new grass, the sweetness of wild flowers coming to blossom, and at times the slightest salty hint of the Gulf many long miles eastward. Michael had lived close to Nature all of his twenty-five years; he accepted her blessings with the same equanimity that he endured her torments. Nature had to be taken as she was, for nothing a man could do would change her. The works of men, however, need not be accepted without question, and Michael never had. So now he wandered here, far west of the American settlements, hoping the solitude would give him peace, would help him put down old angers, old ghosts.

Michael Lewis was a tall man, with strong arms and shoulders, though he had a gaunt and hungry look about him, as if he seldom had enough to eat, seldom got a full night's sleep. Comfort was but an occasional acquaintance, and plenty was a stranger. From the hills of Tennessee to the first American colony in Texas, his next meal had often depended upon the long-barreled rifle he carried. He seldom failed to hit what he saw over the sights, but there were times the rifle stayed cold when game was scarce and he found nothing at which to aim. The shadow of want was often upon him when he left home and hearth for the challenge of unknown lands.

Days behind him waited his French-Spanish wife Marie and a young son Michael had named Mordecai after his father, long since buried. By now Marie probably worried that he might have met with misfortune, for the few days intended had stretched to many. He knew he should be turning back. But the devils which had driven him here had come along with him, and he did not know how to shake free of their torment. It had to do with this land, this Texas, which he had visited with the first Mordecai Lewis almost a decade ago. It had been a forbidden land then, property of the Spanish crown. No longer forbidden, at least by law, it could still at times be forbidding.

This was a Texas which belonged to a newly independent Mexico but had guardedly opened its doors to limited numbers of American settlers under a young Missouri *empresario*, Stephen F. Austin. An older Austin named Moses, who had lived under Spanish rule when Spain had owned Missouri, had appealed to colonial authorities in San Antonio de Bexar. He had argued that despite its great size and potential, the interior of Texas had attracted only some two thousand Spanish inhabitants. Even these few were constantly endangered by Indian depredation. As bad or worse were nagging incursions by illegal land seekers who relentlessly pushed across the boundary from Louisiana. For a century or so these had been mostly French. Now that the Louisiana Purchase had transferred a vast region to the United States, they were American in the main. How much better it would be, Austin had reasoned, that legal immigrants be allowed to establish a deterrent to the filibusters and illegal squatters, as well as placing a buffer between the few isolated old Spanish settlements and the Indians who roamed wild and free to the west and north. To that argument he found Spanish ears receptive. If Indians had to kill someone, let it be Americans, the authorities decided.

To Austin, once wealthy but broken by a national money panic, Texas had seemed a promised land. Like an earlier Moses, he had not lived to see his promised land become reality. His son Stephen, frail in body but possessed of a dogged patience and steely determination, had taken up the lantern lighted by his father's dream. It had been a twisting, thorny path. Just as the colony was driving its first stakes into the ground, Mexico had thrown off the domination of the Spanish crown and declared itself free, as the United States had severed its ties to England two generations before. The young Austin had faced the formidable challenge of doing over with the new government of Mexico all that he and his father had accomplished with the old colonial leadership. Through nerve, statesmanship, and a stubborn refusal to accept half a loaf, he had gradually established a friendly, if sometimes uneasy, relationship with at least some of the powers in Bexar and Mexico City. He had been granted a region some one hundred twenty miles square, extending northwestward from the Gulf of Mexico. His Old Three Hundred colonists were firmly entrenched in this new land, mostly along the two major rivers, the Brazos and the Colorado. Others were gradually coming in overland and by sea, breaking the prairie sod, chopping away at the forests, transforming the wilderness into some resemblance of the places they had left behind them in the old states.

Texas was accepting more and more newcomers, some under Austin, many under other *empresarios* who followed the path Austin had blazed.

Part of what troubled Michael Lewis was this, for he had seen the same forces at work during his youth back in Tennessee. He had loved the woods and the wild open spaces where a man afoot or on horseback could travel for hours, even days, and see no mark of another human. Little by little he had watched the woods hacked away, the open spaces surrendered to the plow, the game decimated or driven off. Now those forces were here, repeating in this virgin land the pattern of the whole western migration. And Michael, though he did not like it, had been a party to the process.

Back yonder, many days' ride behind him, he owned a grant of land, guaranteed by a paper which carried the flourish of Stephen F. Austin. Over the last three years he had gradually enlarged his field, turning under the ancient prairie sod, bringing up the rich black soil built through untold ages of nature's annual cycle: growth, decay, and regrowth. He should be at home now, plowing out the winter weeds, planting the seed for a new year's crops. He knew many would call him an idler, a shiftless leatherstocking tramping in the woods when good Christian men were at work in their fields, living up to their responsibilities.

But in Michael's veins pulsed the blood of a father who had been a leatherstocking in his own time, a product of the canebrake and wood, a man whose hands fit more easily upon the rifle than upon the plow. Mordecai Lewis had grown fitful when he spent too many days in the fields, too many nights within the confines of his cabin. His eyes would turn west toward new lands that lay somewhere beyond sight. His westering ways had brought him finally to a violent death and an unmarked grave in an alien country far from home.

Yesterday Michael had bent down over a clear-running

stream for a drink of water. The angular, bearded face he saw reflected back at him did not appear to be his own; it was his father's.

That, as much as the oppressive weather, had been at the root of his nightmare; that and a small company of Mexican soldiers who had innocently ridden by Michael's farm. Their unexpected appearance had swept his mind back to another time, other soldiers. After a fruitless inner struggle to put down the ghosts, he kissed Marie and the boy good-bye and rode west up the Colorado River, looking for he knew not what. He was not sure he would even know when he found it.

He was at the edge of the wood when he saw the wolf, working a zigzag pattern through the old winter-dried grass, sniffing at the ground for scent of a rabbit or other prey. Michael's hand tightened instinctively on the long rifle that lay across his lap. Then it relaxed, for there would be no point in killing the wolf. It was too far west to be any threat to Marie's priceless little flock of chickens, or even to Michael's few calves. Here it could do no harm beyond that which Nature had appointed as its duty, controlling the increase of prey animals that otherwise might multiply beyond the ability of the land to sustain them. So Michael felt no threat from the wolf and saw no reason that he should be any threat to it.

He drew gently on the reins and stopped, his attention riveted to the graceful movement of the gray predator, its coat still winter-rough, its ribs spare of flesh because food had been scant through the cold months. The wolf caught his scent and jerked its head up, holding its nose into the breeze. Finding Michael, it stood still as a stone for a full minute, perhaps more, watching him. This was a region in which men—white men, anyway—did not often invade. The wolf was probably accustomed to wild horses, so it saw the bay as no threat. It exhibited caution but no particular fear. Curiosity satisfied, it went on about its business of searching for a meal.

Michael felt an instinctive kinship to the wolf, for at heart he was a hunter, a creature of the wild. Circumstances forced him to take on the trappings of the civilized man, to build his cabin and farm his land, to try to be a husband to his wife and a father to his child. But beneath the surface, fighting for escape, was a man who would be grateful to live in a state of nature if circumstances would but allow.

The wolf moved on. Michael watched, hoping to see it scare up a rabbit, for he could feel its hunger, its need. He had a hunger of his own, a hunger civilization would not allow him to satisfy.

He saw the wolf pull up short again, two hundred yards away, and he thought for a moment it had found the scent it sought. But the animal watched something hidden from Michael by a jutting edge of the forest. It crouched, retreated several paces, then halted to look again.

Michael saw them as they came around the outer edge of the irregular wood; half a dozen men on horseback. At a glance he knew they were Indians. He had no idea of their tribe, for he had not seen enough of Texas Indians to have any clear notion of their tribal characteristics. It would not matter anyway if they were of violent intent. Tawakoni, Karankawa, Waco, or Tonkawa: one could kill a man as dead as another. Comanche—perhaps these were Comanche. He was far enough west to be in their hunting grounds. That horseback tribe preyed mercilessly upon the Mexican settlers around Bexar and beyond but so far had professed a wary friendliness toward the light-skinned new American invaders, perhaps still trying to figure out just what manner of human they were.

It was too late to escape discovery. Michael was fifty yards beyond the forest, and a sudden movement back to cover would only draw their attention that much sooner. Any defensive advantage the trees could give him would be temporary at best. He might just as well stand his ground.

They had seen the wolf, for they drew their horses into a line and halted, watching the animal move through the grass. As it had done for Michael, it stopped and stared at them for a moment, then changed course just enough to angle past them without going into actual retreat.

Proud little bastard, Michael thought. *It ain't just about to turn tail and run.*

It had no reason to run. Michael had heard it said that most

Indians held the wolf in some reverence. Many thought it a guiding spirit. Few would do it harm, fearing they might run afoul of some supernatural malevolence.

The Indians watched the wolf until it had moved well past. Only then did one of them notice Michael, sitting on his horse some three hundred yards away. The warrior raised a hand, and the others turned their heads. Michael trembled to a chill that ran down his back. It was a struggle not to turn and run. To do so would only insure that they would come and take him. To stand defiant would require all the nerve he could muster, from as deeply as he could reach, but it might also save his life.

The warriors clustered together, holding a quick council, then surged forward, pushing their horses into a trot. They were a wild, barbaric sight, bows in their hands, feathers in their hair jiggling up and down to the rhythm of their horses' movements. Michael lifted the long rifle enough that they would surely see it. He checked the pan to be certain it held powder to set off a shot. One shot was all he would have time for.

The Indians slowed and spread a little as they neared him. He continued to hold the rifle high but forced down a strong impulse to aim at one of the riders. He pointed the muzzle over their heads.

They halted at perhaps thirty paces. Their horses were curious about his bay, as the riders were curious about Michael, but the Indians did not move closer. They studied Michael with keen eyes, so keen that he had a feeling they knew he had eaten squirrel for breakfast. He could hear their voices as they talked about him in low tones, though he had no sense of the words or their meaning. He could not tell whether they intended to declare friendship or to kill him.

After a few tense minutes they decided to do neither, exactly. A young warrior in the center, who carried himself like a leader, rode a few feet beyond the others. He spoke words Michael had no way of understanding. It took all of his resolve not to lower the muzzle of the rifle and center it on a small leather pouch the man wore about his neck. At length the Indian raised his bow to arm's length, shouted and pulled his horse about. As he rode through the ragged line, the others turned and followed.

Michael suspected they had intentionally put him through a test of nerve, and he had passed it to their satisfaction. After a moment he felt his lungs ache and realized he was still holding his breath. He expelled it, then took several long, deep breaths to compensate. He lowered the rifle and found his hands wet, his mouth dry.

The wolf circled back toward him. Watching, he felt that kinship again. He knew the Indians had felt it too.

Brothers to the wolf. It struck him that kinship to the wolf gave him a kinship to the Indians as well.

He turned back, finally, and pointed his horse toward the settlement, days to the east. He would follow the river, and it would lead him home.

He had been far enough west, this time. There would be other times.

2

THE BLUE-SPECKLED ox plodded with stolid patience to the end of the row, then stopped, waiting for Andrew Lewis to give the command to turn. But Andrew laid the wooden plow over on its side and stood a moment wiping his brow, smelling the dampness of freshly turned earth, looking off across the rolling prairie toward a faraway log cabin. At this distance he could not see whether smoke curled from the stone chimney or not. It was getting on toward time for his brother's wife Marie to be cooking supper. He wondered if Michael had come home yet to eat it. He did not have to look toward his own cabin, just up the long slope from the field, to know that its chimney yielded no smoke. No one was there to build a fire or to cook anything for him.

He pondered the irony of it. Michael had somebody but would not stay home to enjoy the warmth of her company. Andrew, twenty-three now, wished for someone like Marie but had nobody. What was more, he saw no prospects. Marriageable women were scarce as gold coin in Austin's colony, and those few had bachelors lined up at their doors, handsomer and richer than Andrew Lewis. Well, richer, anyway. As to handsome, that was a matter of a woman's taste. It had been a while since one had given him any indication that he qualified, at least one who measured up to his notion of a partner

for bed and board. She would need to be somebody much like
his brother's wife, and he had never met anyone quite like
Marie. Maybe someday, if he ever got time, he would take
himself a long ride beyond the Sabine River to the old
Louisiana French town of Natchitoches. That was where
Michael had found Marie. Perhaps there was another like her
at home, as yet unclaimed.

At least Andrew never had to worry about getting fat, eating
his own cooking. Texas had lots of lanky bachelors.

Now and again when he was *really* hungry he would find an
excuse to ride over to his brother's cabin and debauch himself
on Marie's cooking. Being of both French and Spanish extrac-
tion, she had ways of fixing food unlike anything he had
known in old Tennessee. She could make squirrel stew taste as
good as roast beef, pretty near, and do things with simple garden truck that even Andrew's mother back home had never
thought of.

The ox took a notion to shake itself, trying to ease the chaf-
ing of the heavy wooden yoke. Andrew said, "All right, Blue,
we've plowed a right smart of ground today. We'll go to the
house."

He looked around for his dog, which had wandered away in
search of a rabbit and had not come back. The fool dog would
trot behind him back and forth across the field all day, watching for the ox and plow to scare up some edible prey like a
rabbit or a wood rat, then disappear just when it was time to
send him off to bring home the milk cow. *He'll wander into a
hungry Indian out in those woods one of these days, and he'll
wish he'd paid a little better attention to business,* Andrew
thought.

Actually, Andrew had never run into an Indian in the woods
himself, though through the years since he had taken up this
piece of land on the Colorado River side of Austin's colony,
he had halfway expected to. Austin's people had been fortunate so far not to have had much serious Indian trouble beyond some nocturnal taking of horses and mules or the
occasional ransacking of a cabin. Murder had been rare. But it

was probably only a question of time. It didn't hurt for a man to have a rifle always within reach.

The dog came panting up to the cabin about the time Andrew finished unyoking the ox and giving the big beast a forkful of hay. The ox would wander off presently in search of fresh green grass, but it would be waiting here in the morning for another modest bait of dry prairie hay. Andrew had conditioned it that way to structure its habits and give him control. He saw the reddish milk cow plodding in from the edge of the wood, where the wide river ran deep and cold. The bell around her neck clanked softly to her measured steps. He had tried to condition her like the ox, but she possessed a more independent turn of mind, as if she knew how much he had had to pay for her. He called her Boss, for good reason.

At least he would not have to send the dog to fetch her this time. Boss hated the dog, which nipped at her heels when she tried to defy him. She would run at him, tossing her head and trying to dig him in the ribs with her short, curved horns. She had succeeded only once. That experience had had a salutary effect upon the dog's attention to duty. The dog and the cow eyed each other warily as she approached the pole pen where Andrew milked her morning and evening. The dog would end up getting half the milk, because Boss gave twice as much as Andrew needed for drinking or cooking. That seemed not to mellow the dog's narrow opinion of her, however. He nipped once at her heels as she entered the open gate. She quickened her step, and the bell clamored in protest.

Andrew scolded him. "Hickory, you come back away from there!" He picked up a stick as if to throw it. The dog trotted off toward the cabin, totally happy with itself. Andrew chuckled at the show of bravado and forked the cow some hay to keep her in place until he could get back from the cabin with his milk bucket.

He stopped a moment to look with a warm surge of satisfaction at his pole pens, his single-unit log cabin, his field which he had expanded bit by bit, year by year. Everything here had been built or bought with his own sweat, along with some help from his older brother Michael. He and Michael had often traded labor when one or the other had a job too large or too urgent to do by himself. Michael, being a married man, had been granted a larger tract of land than Andrew, but that was all right. Andrew's was more than large enough to meet his present needs. If he should ever find himself a wife the terms of his contract with Stephen Austin were that he could acquire more land. What he already had was far more than he could have expected to acquire in a lifetime had he remained in Tennessee instead of running off from home to tag along behind his brother. He could not imagine willingly giving this up and returning to the old country, ever. He had been gone too long for Tennessee to be home again. This was home now. He had put his sweat and blood, his heart and soul into this bit of new land. He would live here and he would be buried here. God and the Indians willing, he would be an old man when that happened.

Finished with the milking, he found the bucket nearly three-quarters full, far more than he could use or the dog needed. He remembered that Marie's best cow had dried up pending her freshening with a new calf, and the young heifer serving in her stead probably gave only about enough milk to fill a fair-to-middling coffee cup. If Andrew started now he should reach Marie's cabin just ahead of suppertime. He did not particularly relish the idea of eating his own cooking tonight anyway. A man took his excuses where he found them.

His brown horse had ambled up to the pens just behind the cow and stood waiting in the hope that Andrew might be generous with the hay kept tantalizingly out of reach behind a sturdy rail fence. Andrew slipped a bridle over the brown's head and got a sad look of betrayal. "I'll feed you when we come back, Brown," he said. "Right now you've got a little job of work to do."

He had never given the horse a better name than simply Brown, for its color. The animal was strictly utilitarian, lacking any strong individuality that might give rise to a more imaginative appellation. He did what he had to, and no more. He had even less personality than that blue ox.

Andrew saddled up. At the cabin he cut down a quarter of venison that was likely to spoil before he could get around to eating all of it anyway, and he picked up the bucket of milk. He wished he had something more practical to carry it in that would not allow half of it to slosh out on the way. But the necessities were hard to come by in colonial Texas, and luxuries like a good metal container were out of his reach. He had seen Mexicans and Indians carry water in goatskins and the paunches from cattle, but he feared those were not the proper vessels for milk. At least not if he was taking it to Marie. Though she had learned to be a good pioneering woman, able to do with a little and make it seem a lot, her Louisiana upbringing had been more refined than that.

The brown horse had an easy gait, so Andrew managed to keep most of the milk in the bucket. He lost a little of it crossing an arroyo and a little more when the brown horse took it in his head to jump a fallen tree rather than go around it.

A black and white spotted dog barked as he approached. A young woman stepped out into the open dog-run that separated the two sections of Michael and Marie's log cabin. One hand held a rifle; the other shaded her eyes. A small boy clung to her floor-length homespun skirt, peering around her in shy curiosity. Andrew felt his heart rise as he rode toward her. He had always thought Marie an uncommonly handsome woman. He always wished he had seen her first.

A glimmer of disappointment showed in her dark eyes. She said with a noticeable accent, "From the sun you came at me, and you looked like Michael."

Impatience tugged at Andrew as he thought of his brother leaving this woman and boy here alone. If Marie were his, he would never leave her. "Hasn't he come home yet? I'd've figured he'd be back by now. Field over yonder needs to be gettin' seed in the ground."

"He was in something of—what you say?—a state when he left here."

Andrew frowned. He assumed Michael and Marie had argued. But she went on, "It was the soldiers riding by. That is what did it, I think."

"Soldiers?"

"Mexican soldiers. Their horses, they watered at the river. They were friendly; they did not seem to want anything. But just to see them, Michael was much nervous. Soon then, he was gone. We know, you and me, what is his trouble."

Andrew nodded grimly. Brother Michael displayed little fear of the world's traditional hazards. Man, beast, or weather, he took them in stride. But Andrew could remember times, when they had lived and traveled together, that Michael would awaken in the night in a cold sweat, trembling from a dream. He would seldom talk of it, but Andrew knew where its roots lay. Years ago, when Michael had been but fifteen, he had followed his footloose father Mordecai on a horse-gathering trip west of the Sabine River at a time when Texas belonged to Spain. Grasping adventurers and power-seeking filibusters had made Americans extremely unpopular, subject to summary justice. When a troop of Spanish soldiers caught up with the little party of horse hunters, a vengeful lieutenant ordered them slaughtered like cattle on the open prairie. The officer had blown Mordecai Lewis's brains out. Michael was wounded and left for dead.

That Michael was back in Texas a decade later, and settled down to stay, seemed remarkable to Andrew. The political climate had changed. The Mexican government was at least guardedly hospitable to American immigrants so long as they minded their own business, pledged allegiance to their new hosts, and showed no inclination toward lawlessness or rebellion. Itself having been born of rebellion, the government of Mexico was particularly sensitive to any sign of discontent among its subjects lest history repeat itself.

Michael had seemed to have no qualms about embracing that government. He held Spain, not Mexico, responsible for the killing of his and Andrew's father. But the sight of dark-skinned soldiers in uniform still opened old wounds unlikely ever to heal.

Marie smiled tentatively as she looked up at the bucket in Andrew's hand. "For strawberries, it is much too early."

Her smile could turn a man's heart to butter. "Milk," he

said. "My old Boss cow is fairly spillin' over because of all this new spring grass. Thought you and the button might have some use for it, if you don't mind a little weedy flavor."

"It will taste fine. Get down. I will fix the supper."

"I wouldn't want to put you to no trouble."

"No trouble. Maybe Michael will come."

Andrew smiled. He had always liked to listen to Marie talk. Her speech betrayed her French and Spanish heritage. The accent was not enough to get in the way; it was just enough to play arrestingly upon the ear.

Leaning from the saddle, he handed her the bucket, then swung to the ground and untied the venison. She told him to put the brown horse in the pen and give it some hay while she set a pot over the fire. He took a little time, feeling awkward about being here alone with Michael's young wife when Michael was gone. It was not as if anything untoward was going to happen. Even though he was strongly drawn to Marie, to act upon those feelings was unthinkable. It was the appearance that bothered him, however innocent the reality might be. Michael would think nothing of it, but some people in the colony were given to talk. There were people everywhere who would talk, whether there was anything to talk about or not.

Little Mordecai stood on the dog-run and watched his uncle with big and curious eyes that reminded Andrew of his own small brother named Jonathan, left behind in Tennessee. The Lewis stamp had always been strong. Andrew suspected that as this boy grew older he would take on his grandfather Mordecai's gaunt and rangy look. All the Lewis male offspring did. He tousled the boy's long hair. "Another year or two, young'un, and you'll have to learn to follow a plow."

"Plow," Mordecai said, pointing toward the field. The boy was always initially shy when Andrew came over, but he never remained that way for long. He warmed quickly to company.

Andrew said, "I may have to come plow that field if your daddy don't find his way home pretty quick."

It was in his mind that some misfortune might have befallen Michael, but he regarded that possibility as remote. Their father had been an outdoorsman, never so happy as when he tramped the woods, preferably alone. Michael was in many ways his father's image and unable to change the legacy. Their mother often had taken the responsibility of organizing the farm work and parceling out the tasks to her young sons when Mordecai forgot to come home from the forests. Now Michael's Marie was following the same pattern. But little Mordecai was several years shy of being able to take on the work.

Before entering the cabin Andrew walked to the woodpile out back. The stack was large; Michael had dragged up deadfall timber from the forest during winter's lull. But only a little of it was chopped into short lengths for the fireplace. Andrew picked up the ax, looked around to be sure the boy was not in harm's way, then set to work. He took out against the ax and the wood the anger he felt against Michael. A few chips bounced violently off the log wall of the cabin. He did not stop until Marie called him for supper.

She had sliced a little of the venison he had brought, had made some cornbread and warmed up a pot of beans. He would have liked coffee, but that was a luxury. Texas settlers often parched grain as a substitute for coffee beans. To Andrew it had always been a poor replacement. He'd as soon drink plain water, and did.

After sating his first hunger he paused to tell her, "It's awful good, Marie."

"*Your* venison," she said. "For some days we are out of meat, except for ham in the smokehouse. That I take only a little, to make it last."

"If I'd known, I'd've fetched you somethin'. I'll make a little sashay out into the woods tomorrow."

"You should do your plowing while the weather is good. You should not bother about us."

No, he would agree, he shouldn't. And he wouldn't have to if Michael stayed around like a good husband. But that was Michael's way, and nothing would keep him from roaming except a crippling accident, or worse. He said, "You don't need to be worryin' about the weather. Old Man Willet is somethin' of a weather prophet. He says we're fixin' to have a good spring."

Marie wrinkled her fine little nose. "The Old Man Willet always says it will be good weather. When it is dry he says soon it will rain. When it rains he says soon the sun will shine."

Marie pushed away from the table and walked out the door to the dog-run. She stood with arms folded, brow furrowed, and stared toward the dark line of forest that lay to the west, as Michael remembered his mother doing many a time. Marie had eaten but little. Andrew was mildly ashamed for having eaten so much. One piece of cornbread remained on the plate. The boy Mordecai looked longingly at it but was too well trained to reach for it so long as someone older sat at the table. Andrew pushed the plate toward him. "You better eat this before that spotted dog comes in here and steals it." He walked out onto the dog-run and joined Marie.

Dusk was gathering. Marie's sad eyes indicated that she knew Michael was not coming.

Andrew said, "Maybe he'll be back tomorrow."

"Perhaps." Her frown deepened. "I did not want to tell you, but I should, I think. Three men came yesterday, looking for him."

Andrew had been trying to dislodge a rough-ground piece of corn from between his teeth by probing at it with his tongue. He stopped abruptly. "What men was that?"

"They did not say their names. They said they knew Michael back in Tennessee. They were a rough-looking lot of men."

Andrew began digging at the wedged corn again. A lot of men in these colonies would look rough by the standards of other places, but Marie was used to that. "Did they say *how* they knew him?"

"They said only that they were old friends and neighbors. They kept asking which way he had gone. I told them west of here is a very big country. They said they would be back."

A dark suspicion began rising in Andrew. "If they knew Michael in Tennessee, they knew me too."

"They talked about Michael only. They said they were his friends, but they made me nervous."

"What did they look like?" He was afraid he already knew.

Marie shrugged. "Tall men, thin, bearded. About the age of you and Michael."

His eyes narrowed. "Was a one-armed man amongst them?"

She blinked, remembering. "Yes, it is true. One of them *did* have a sleeve pinned up."

"Blackwood!" He spoke the name like a curse.

The name brought a flicker to her eyes. She had heard Michael and Andrew speak of them. "You think so?"

He nodded bleakly and stared toward the dark woods, wishing Michael were here. He had not thought about the Blackwoods in a long time. He and Michael had assumed they put the Blackwood trouble behind them years ago, when they left Tennessee. But that kind of trouble seemed to follow a man like a hungry wolf sniffing out tracks. "Whichaway did they go when they left?"

"East, toward San Felipe. They said they look for land. They said soon they will be Michael's neighbors again."

"Like hell they will!" Andrew muttered. He picked up his rifle and started toward the pen where he had put the brown horse.

Surprised, she asked, "Where do you go?"

"To San Felipe, to see Stephen Austin. If I start now I'll be there in the mornin'." He turned to face her. His voice was grim. "If Michael gets back before I do, you tell him about the Blackwoods first thing. *Then* you can take time to kiss him."

Riding in the darkness, he startled some wild animal, which broke for the nearby brush, crackling branches as it plunged into the protective cover. Deer, he thought, though he never got a clear look at it. He found his heart thumping, his hand slick on the stock of his rifle.

It could as easily have been the Blackwoods, setting up an ambush.

That would have been their style.

3

GENERATIONS LATER, Texans would know them as blue-bonnets, but these blue-and-white wild flowers had not yet acquired the name. Riding his brown horse toward the village of San Felipe de Austin on a trail not yet old enough to be deeply beaten-out, Andrew Lewis knew only that they were one of the most striking sights he had ever seen. Even in his weariness from riding all night, he was able to appreciate their beauty. Their early-spring splendor was like a reflection of the morning's open sky, a brilliant blue carpet spread almost solidly across the hillsides and down into the valleys, broken here and there by newly leafing trees and bushes, some of which had blossoms of their own to provide a counterpoint in color. Now and again the blue weave was interspersed by yellow buttercups and by blazing orange skeins of another wild flower similar in height. In a sense, these blue flowers were like Texas itself, new and fresh and unspoiled. They would run their course much too soon, the blossoms drying and dropping away, leaving a coarse and nondescript weed, like a beautiful, smiling girl who turns much too quickly into a nagging and unappealing old crone. But while they lasted they lifted his spirit and made him glad he had followed his brother Michael westward into Texas. It was a raw country yet, long

on hardship and privation, short on prosperity and comfort.
But if its weeds could bring forth such blossoms, even for a
little while, then surely this stern and still-rugged land should
be capable of a gentle and generous side to its nature.

It had, up to now, been generous with its wildlife, its bounty
of fresh meat to help put food on families' tables until they
had time to break out their land and lay by a crop or two. Were
it not for deer and squirrel, fish and wild fowl, Andrew and
Michael might not have survived their first two years. But
now, as more and more people took up parcels of land in the
region the Mexican government had allotted for Austin's
colony, Andrew sensed that the game was thinning, killed off
or scared away into remote regions not yet familiar with the
strike of the ax, the bite of plowpoint into primeval sod.

Most settlers, including Stephen Austin, seemed to feel that
this was the way it was meant to be, that destiny called for the
wilderness and all that went with it to be pushed steadily westward until it ran out of room and out of existence. Andrew
found himself partially inclined toward Austin's view, that the
land was meant to be tamed, that the wild forest was to be
converted to fruitful fields, that the wild animal was to give
way to the domestic beast, that civilized man was meant to
live from his own cattle and hogs and chickens, not by the
hunt for the native white-tailed deer that multiplied and con-
sumed the land's bounty and too often contributed not to the
welfare of man. Nature was not to be accommodated, it was to
be overcome, for only thus could the multitudes be fed.

Andrew had no fear of the multitudes. It was his nature to
be gregarious, to enjoy company and laughter and song.

But another side of him felt sympathy with his brother's far
different view. Michael was uncomfortable wherever there
were many people. He loved the forests, the unaltered
prairies. He had a respect that bordered on worship for the
wild things of the earth and sky, while he had what amounted
almost to contempt for the cud-chewing cow, the rooting pig,
the ever-dependent sheep.

Andrew saw futility in that view, even while he acknowledged the validity of it. Like it or not, people would keep

coming. Their ever-expanding numbers would need fields to provide them sustenance, homes for shelter, roads to grant them passage, grass and water for the domestic livestock which provided their walking commissary. The Indian had made little demand upon the land, had altered its face virtually none at all. But the white man's way was to take whatever he found and restructure it, to bend it to his own needs, his own dreams. The Michael Lewises of this world would never stop that process of constant change. They might as well try to stop the wind.

Andrew's stomach growled, for normally by this time he had eaten his breakfast and had been at work in the field for an hour or more. He had paused only once in his journey, at the cabin of the Willet family some miles east of his own. There he had shared a quick cup of parched-corn coffee and a story or two with Old Man Willet before traveling on. Given congenial company such as that, he would have been happy under normal circumstances to have spent a day or two. It was in Andrew's nature to laugh, to sing, something Michael had never learned.

San Felipe de Austin, some seventy miles inland from Galveston Bay, could hardly claim to be a town, not in the sense of towns Andrew had known in Tennessee. Village was more like it, though if one counted the many farms which clustered close around, the total population would have amounted to much more than the small settlement revealed at first glance. In the Mexican style it boasted a small square bearing a high-sounding name, Constitutional Plaza. But the plaza had far more huisache trees around it than buildings. Most of the stores and houses were strung in a random manner along a road that paralleled Palmito Creek. Timber was plentiful here, so most were constructed mainly of logs, American-style. A majority were built on about the same rough utilitarian plan as those Andrew had known in Tennessee; double cabins like Michael and Marie's, with an open dog-run in the center and a single roof joining the two sections, or a single cabin like Andrew's own, which could easily be expanded into a double cabin if the right girl ever smiled at him. There was little about San Felipe to indicate that this was part of Mexico. It was totally unlike the town of San Antonio de Bexar, which he had found to be in sharp contrast to anything he had seen elsewhere. Bexar was unlike even the northernmost Mexican town of Nacogdoches, Texas. And Nacogdoches was different in many ways from its sister city Natchitoches, across the Sabine in Louisiana, despite the similarity in names. Each had a personality uniquely its own.

San Felipe, except for the Spanish name and what passed for a plaza, appeared to be simply an extension of the old states, an American island in an alien sea. To the occasional Mexicans who visited, it must have seemed as strange as Bexar had been to Andrew. But he had found something intriguing about Bexar, almost magnetic. Perhaps Mexican visitors to San Felipe knew the same feeling. The new and unknown tended to have two sides like a coin, one bringing apprehension, the other an exotic and compelling attraction.

There was nothing about Stephen Austin's office to mark it as different or better than other structures in this village on a bluff above the wide and muddy Brazos River. There was little about Austin himself to mark him as wealthier or living any better than the colonists who depended upon him for leadership except that he had the general look of a tradesman or merchant rather than the rough and weather-worn appearance of a farmer. He customarily wore homespun to avoid giving an impression that he felt himself above those in his community who could afford no better. His double log cabin, shaded by a huge moss-strewn oak, served as both residence and working quarters.

Andrew dismounted and tied the brown horse, then walked up the foot-packed path toward the cabin. Two men burst angrily through the door and down from the dog-run. A burly young man was a step or two in the lead, a dour, gray-bearded man behind him. The young man in his haste bumped hard against Andrew, causing Andrew to falter and fall back. The man turned with blazing eyes. "Why don't you get the hell out of folks' way?" he demanded. "You seen me comin'."

He acted as if he intended to pursue the matter with his

fists, and Andrew raised his own in self-defense. But the older man gripped the younger one's arm. Andrew saw thunder and lightning in the creased old face as the bearded man said, "Come on, son. Let us begone from this place." The younger one seemed inclined to stay and pursue his grievances, whatever they were, but the old man hustled him toward two tied horses.

Andrew watched them ride away. He thought the old man's back was straighter than the young one's. Whatever had made him angry had done a thorough job of it. When the pair had traveled fifty yards or so and he was sure they were not coming back, Andrew walked to a well in the yard, rocked up to about waist height. "Help yourself," a pleasant voice said. "Water is the one thing which we have in plentiful measure." Stephen Austin stood on the dog-run, watching him.

Andrew turned the windlass and studied the man as he filled the community dipper from the wooden bucket. Austin looked older than his early thirties. He was thin, almost emaciated-looking, betraying in his spare frame little of the inner strength that had enabled him to build this American outpost in the midst of an untouched wilderness, that had made it possible for him to deal on the one hand with leather-clad frontiersmen who in some instances could not write their own names on the deeds he prepared for them, and on the other to fit into the highest courts of Mexico, fighting his colonists' cause with the vigor and resolve of a missionary zealot. Andrew and Michael had met him in Natchitoches on the brink of his first great adventure into Texas. Other would-be land *empresarios* had tried to duplicate what Austin had done. Most had fallen by the wayside. Austin's eyes burned with a fire that said he would die before he would retreat.

Andrew measured all men by his brother Michael and by the memory of his father Mordecai. Physically, Austin stood in their shadow. But in spirit and determination he would have put them to severe test.

Austin shook hands. "It is good to see you, Andrew Lewis. But I would think you would be at home, taking advantage of this fine spring weather to get your planting done."

"Been workin' on it," Andrew acknowledged with a nod. "But somethin' come up." He frowned.

Austin said, "Whatever it is, it will look better over a cup of coffee."

Andrew followed the *empresario* into the office side of the cabin, where the coals of a burned-down fire still glowed beneath a blackened pot. Austin poured coffee for Andrew and refilled his own cup. Andrew blew the coffee and savored its aroma. Real coffee was an indulgence he reserved for special days, and there were not many of those.

He said, "Them fellers that just left here, they weren't in too good a humor."

"I just refused them land in this colony. I do not believe they are the sort we want."

"Who are they?"

"The old one is named Tolliver Beard, from Louisiana. The other is his son. Their reputation has preceded them. Beard is a contentious old man who would bring nothing but discord into this colony. His son Jayce is just a brutal lout with no sense of propriety. I told them not to come back."

"I'd as soon not see them again," Andrew said. He studied a hand-drawn map stretched across part of the log wall. Idly he ran his finger from San Felipe past several dozen other land holdings to the pair which bore his name and Michael's. They were among those farthest west. That had been Michael's doing, a legacy from their father Mordecai. Mordecai's eyes had always been set on something farther west.

Austin said speculatively, "You indicated trouble. I hope no one is ill. Perhaps your sister-in-law is with child again?"

Andrew blinked. Such a thought had not occurred to him. "Not that I know of. I'm already an uncle once. But in a way this concerns her. There was three men come by my brother's place while he was gone. Caused Marie a mite of worry. I wonder if you've talked to some fellers named Blackwood?"

Austin pondered a moment, his eyes narrowing. "As a matter of fact, I have. Three brothers. From Georgia, they said— no, Tennessee. They asked me about taking up land." He paused, contemplating darkly. "And yes, they asked about your brother Michael. They said they knew him."

Andrew nodded solemnly. "They know him sure enough."

Austin seemed to sense Andrew's mood. "I would surmise that it is not a friendly acquaintance?"

"They're a shiftless family. Only thing they ever broke a sweat at was mischief. Reason Michael come to Texas in the first place was, he knew if he stayed he'd sooner or later have to kill one of them, or they'd kill him."

More than that, though he saw no need to burden Austin with details, had been Michael's fear that the Blackwoods in their determination to get at him would hurt others in his family. Finis Blackwood had wounded Michael's Uncle Benjamin by mistake, trying to hit Michael. Andrew thought it best not to mention that. Austin had gone to considerable lengths to avoid accepting violent men and leatherstockings among his colonists. He had probably suspected more than once that Michael belonged in that class. By extension, Andrew would also fit the category.

Andrew said, "I hope you're not grantin' them land."

Austin shook his head and almost spilled his coffee. "I made up my mind almost on sight that I would find reason to pass them by. They did not appear the sort to fit in with my Old Three Hundred. And the fact that they said your brother was a friend of theirs gave me some pause about *him*. That he is not their friend comes as a relief."

"It'd be a relief to *me* if you could chase them plumb back to Tennessee."

"Under Mexican law I am the *alcalde* here. I have considerable police and military power. But that power extends only to the borders of this colony. That is as far as I could push them. And even then I probably would not have authority to do so until and unless they break the law."

"They will, sooner or later. It's born in them, I reckon, like it's born in a fox to steal chickens."

Austin's face was creased with concern. To him, this colony was his life and the people in it were his family, even if a few became errant now and again, or resented him out of a false perception that he was becoming rich on their labor. "One of my requirements for land claimants is that they bring proof of good character, letters of reference or recommendation. The Blackwoods had none. If they appear again in San Felipe I will request that they depart this colony forthwith."

Request. Andrew wondered what Austin could do if they refused. This colony was so law-abiding that as yet there had been no necessity even to build a jail. The nearest he knew was a Mexican *calabozo* in Bexar, a long way for anybody to be obliged to ride with the Blackwoods as reluctant company.

Austin said, "If these men appear again, tell them I wish to consult with them. The problem will be out of your hands."

"They may not want to come."

"I have always suspected that your brother possesses strong powers of persuasion. I suspect that some of his determination runs in your blood as well." Austin drained his cup and smiled. "Just see that you do not spill any of that blood in the process, will you please? Violence disturbs the Mexican authorities in Bexar. And it does my digestion no good, either."

Austin did not invite Andrew to stay for dinner. By the thin look of him Andrew suspected the man might not be eating regularly anyway; the work and worry of the colony overrode his sense of comfort, or even of physical need. He was one of those people who stopped to eat only when the notion struck him. Other matters took priority, even over concern for his own health.

Andrew could put aside considerations of comfort when the need arose, but he was not immune to fatigue. The coffee had temporarily overcome his hunger, but he felt the weight of the night's long miles bearing heavily upon him. More important, he knew the brown horse did also. He followed the wagon road down to the bluff and lingered to watch the ferry which operated between the two banks of the wide and silt-laden Brazos. Sleepiness soon overcame his curiosity. He rode up-river away from the noise of human endeavor, staked the brown horse on new grass, and lay down in the benign shade of a towering oak from which the moss dangled like an old man's long beard.

He was awakened, finally, by a snuffing sound around his face. He opened his startled eyes and found himself the object of interest for a couple of lean hounds of a bluish hue, a kind favored by coon hunters back in Tennessee. One of them backed away cautiously, but the other continued to sniff at Andrew's legs, probably picking up the scent of Andrew's dog Hickory. A man's voice hailed him. "Sorry if my hounds woke you up. They got no more manners than a brush hog."

Andrew rose up and stretched, facing a farmer probably ten or fifteen years his senior. The man rode a black mule. Behind him, astride an old plow mare, came a boy of ten or twelve. He drove half a dozen cows, three with calves trotting beside them. Andrew had seen the man around San Felipe. This was probably his land.

The man said jovially, "We come out to gather up our stock. Didn't figure to gather up no company. Your name is Lewis, ain't it?"

"Andrew Lewis." Andrew extended his hand. "Rode all night. Just lettin' my horse rest a little before I start home."

The man smiled. "I always like to see a man who watches out for the welfare of his animals." He pointed upriver with his chin. "Time we get to the barn with our cows, the woman'll have dinner ready to put on the table. We'd be pleasured to have you join us."

It would have been impolite to refuse, even if Andrew had not been so hungry. "I'd be tickled." He rode along beside the man, complimenting him first upon his strapping son, then upon the fruitfulness of his cows. Besides the three which had already calved, two more would obviously yield their increase before the bluebonnets lost all their blooms. The farmer acknowledged that five out of six wasn't bad. But the dry cow had cost him the most. A man didn't always get just what he paid for, he lamented with good humor.

The man's fields were well plowed, the rows straight as a rifle barrel, and they were pole-fenced to keep the cattle from getting in. The log house was long, three rooms at least, with a sturdy clapboard roof. The whole place showed the mark of a good and industrious manager, the kind Austin had sought for the nucleus of his colony. As they drove the cows and calves into a pen and closed the gate behind them, the woman of the house rang dinnertime by hammering a broken piece of wagon wheel against a dangling iron ring on the dog-run.

The fare was simple, all home-raised, but it was plentiful and filling. Andrew sensed the contentment of the farmer and his wife, and watching them reminded him of the missing element in his own life, of the empty cabin to which he would return. When he remarked upon the fact that the farmer had a handsome family—there were three children younger than the boy who had ridden the plow mare—the farmer replied, "That's what makes the work a pleasure, Andrew, havin' somebody to share the fruits of it with. Can't be much in it for a man who don't work for nobody except himself."

Andrew's mind drifted to Marie. "Not what there ought to be," he agreed.

The farmer said, "We've done well here in Texas. Got more land here than we could ever've gotten back in Georgia. There it was mostly all took, and too high for a man ever to buy and pay for. We've only broke out the smallest part of this so far. Time the boys come of age they can each parcel off for their own needs, and we'll still have plenty. Austin's been real good to us."

"The Mexican government's been good to us," Andrew remarked.

That was the first time he had seen the farmer frown. The man said, "But it's a foreign government, and we're Americans. That's the only thing which don't set quite right with me. They're good to us now, sure, but what if they come along some day and see what we've built and decide they want it for theirselves? They ain't our people, and we ain't theirs. They won't have any deep compunctions against tryin' to take it away from us, I'm thinkin'."

Andrew said, "They've promised us, solemn."

"The bunch that's *in* has promised us. But them people

down in Mexico, they're everlastin'ly fightin' amongst theirselves. What if someday a bunch takes over that won't honor
the promises? What'll we do?"

This was not the first time Andrew had heard that question
asked. He had no answer.

The farmer said, "We'll fight. That's all we *can* do."

Andrew shrugged. "Maybe it'll never come to that."

The farmer slapped the flat of his hand against his stomach.
"I've got a feelin' in my gut, and it's a fair-sized gut as you can
see. It will come to that. Maybe not tomorrow, maybe not next
year. But someday. And not even Mr. Austin will be able to
stop it."

Andrew started toward home after the best meal he had
eaten in days, his stomach satisfied but his mind in turmoil.
The farmer had started him thinking about questions that had
risen periodically from his subconscious and that he had
forcibly put aside.

It was a long way south to Mexico City. Who here could really know what was happening there, and how many men
were harboring the same suspicion of the American colonists
as the colonists harbored about them?

4

LIEUTENANT ELIZANDRO Zaragosa sat gun-barrel straight on his finely curried, shiny black horse and stared down in painful resignation at the line of ragged men slouched before him, a dozen half-starved new recruits, all but barefoot after their long march to San Antonio de Bexar from somewhere south of the Rio Grande. The indifference in their dark and unshaven faces did not lead him to hope they would be better than the last set, now mostly scattered: deserted; jailed; killed in fights over women, whiskey, or games of no chance. He wondered from what prisons in Monclova or Monterrey these had been dredged up. It made no difference. Brilliant military minds in the interior had sent them. It was his duty to do the best he could with what he was given.

The mentality of the central government was supposed to have improved when Mexico wrested its independence from Spain, but some things never changed. The lower-level bureaucrats who sat comfortably at their desks and exacted their bribes under the benign name *mordida,* or little bite, were mostly the same men who had always been there. The outer trappings had changed, but the inner machinery of government was as corrupt as under the Spanish king. Painting the house did not rid it of the termites hidden within the wood.

He shrugged and commended the recruits to the dubious

mercies of a heavyset noncommissioned officer whose generous black moustache made his dark scowl look even fiercer
than it was. Sergeant Isidro Gomez had a man's work ahead
of him. Zaragosa could sympathize. Now in his early thirties
and looking a world-weary forty or more, he himself had once
been a sergeant in this same garrison, when all of Mexico including Texas had been but an outpost of Spain. He had
whipped his share of unlikely recruits into some semblance of
military discipline and had suffered through his share of fail-
ures. He might still be doing so had it not been for the revolution. Or, and this was by no means unlikely, he would be dead.
God knew how close he had come.

His left arm was still a little stiff and gave him pain at times
when the weather changed, all because of a vengeful royalist
officer's bullet. It had been Zaragosa's considerable pleasure
to put a better-aimed bullet through that son of a goat and send
him to his everlasting punishment in a place far hotter even
than Texas.

He turned in the saddle and saw some passing citizens giving the recruits a baleful study. Soldiers were a bane of their
life. Supposedly sent to protect them from Indian depreda-
tions, the soldiers themselves all too often became the predators. Underpaid, underfed, many of them taken from the
prisons of Mexico, they had on occasion burglarized homes
and businesses and even openly robbed people at the point of
a gun or a knife, knowing that the citizens' well-justified fear
of the military would probably prevent their ever being called
upon to pay for their crimes. Most citizens looked upon the
soldiers as they looked upon taxes: a curse to be avoided
where possible but endured with stoical resignation when cir-
cumvention was not to be.

At least, he thought, the situation was less harsh under the
government of free Mexico than it had been under the royalist
aristocrats. The *gachupínes* had looked upon the common
people as little more than chattels, their only purpose to make
life richer and more comfortable for those who possessed the
power. There had been disappointments. Despite the revolution, many of the *gachupínes* remained in high positions. By

and large they were more careful now in the way they wielded their power. The new government took a more benign view and exhibited some regard for the rights of even the lowliest. So far, at least. But time had not dulled Zaragosa's suspicions. Resentments still smouldered beneath the surface, both with the *gachupínes* who had lost power and with the common people who had but a tenuous hold. News drifted to Bexar from time to time about power struggles in the capital far, far to the south. First one and then another politician or military leader pushed to the fore with his own concepts of the proper way to govern Mexico. Zaragosa feared it was only a matter of time before the common people again were forced to take up arms to fight for their rights and their dignity against those who had known absolute power before and were determined to have absolute power again.

In the crowd which watched the recruits he saw two light-skinned *americanos,* one wearing a blondish beard which reminded him uncomfortably of the blue-eyed pureblood Spaniards who so long had lorded it over the mixed-blood people. He could not restrain a frown which set itself deeply into his dark features, or a sour feeling of dislike that arose. His mind told him these foreigners had nothing to do with those who so long had oppressed the majority of Mexican citizens, that the only similarity was their appearance. But appearance was enough to arouse old angers in his heart. He was glad most of the American settlers lived far enough away that he did not often have to look upon them.

A light-colored beard, a pair of blue eyes, always made him remember Lieutenant Armando Rodriguez, a pureblood, a *gachupín* of the most hated sort. It had been Rodriguez's bullet which had stiffened Zaragosa's arm, and Zaragosa's bullet which had sent Rodriguez to a watery grave in the Sabine River. But that bullet had not laid the memory to rest. Though long dead, Rodriguez still lurked in the dark corners of Zaragosa's mind, appearing unexpectedly, as now, to disturb the peace of his soul.

How many times must I yet kill him before he is finally dead? Zaragosa wondered.

From the tail of his eye he caught movement as Captain Emilio Sanchez appeared in the doorway of the *comandante*'s office. Sanchez stared a minute at the recruits, then beckoned Zaragosa with a silent jerk of his head. Zaragosa pulled the black horse around and walked him to the front of the building, dismounting and handing the reins to an orderly who stood waiting at stiff attention. The orderly saluted, and Zaragosa gave him a slack response that betrayed his weariness with the military regimen.

Captain Sanchez was a pureblood Spaniard, but Zaragosa had found him a generally tolerant man as *gachupines* went, not disposed to flaunt his power or his station, an officer firm but generally fair in dealing with his subordinates. He was a portly gentleman, his dark brown eyes rimmed with angry red veins, testimony to his frequent excesses with wine. Zaragosa did not know whether this was a cause or an effect of Sanchez's being exiled to the isolated northern province of Texas, an obscure outpost far from the captain's old home in the interior of Mexico. He pitied Sanchez in his afflictions, the principal of these being periodic seizures of painful gout and constant harassment by a shrewish wife who felt he had betrayed her by not earning a prestigious station in Mexico City.

Each time Zaragosa encountered the vitriolic *Señora* Sanchez, he became more grateful for the quiet temperament and warmly loving attention given him by his own wife, Elvira. Captain Sanchez had a great deal more money and the command of this post, but Zaragosa would not trade places with him for as much as a minute. At night Zaragosa could look forward to going to sleep contented in the tender and willing embrace of Elvira. Sanchez could sleep only in the sodden embrace of a quart of poor wine.

Not all the *gachupines* were favored.

Sanchez returned his salute with an indifference to which officers of his rank seemed addicted, and he seated himself behind a heavy, hand-carved wooden desk. He gestured for Zaragosa to sit in a high-backed chair he suspected was designed to be so uncomfortable that visitors would quickly state their business and be gone. Sanchez's expression was pained. Zaragosa suspected he was still under the attack of last night's wine. The captain asked, "What do you think of the new recruits?"

Zaragosa shrugged. "They look like just about all the others. We will probably get two or three decent soldiers from the lot. The others should never have been let out of jail."

The captain covered his mouth as he burped gas from last night's indulgences. Pain crossed his face, and he ran his tongue over his lips. That wine must have a sour taste indeed, the tenth time it came up. He said, "Recruits are a nuisance, but they are not the heaviest cross we are called upon to bear in this life." He burped again and made a considerable noise in clearing his throat. He asked, "How do you get along with the American settlers in our midst?"

Zaragosa was not sure how he was expected to answer. "I have no problems with them. I avoid them whenever possible."

"Would that we could all do so," Sanchez said. "How long has it been since you have visited their colonies?"

Zaragosa thought back. "I made an inspection through Austin's colony last fall. I found it peaceful and prosperous."

Sanchez nodded. "Austin's Americans have never given us much cause for concern. They apply themselves diligently to their own business and leave politics alone. But there are problems around Nacogdoches."

Zaragosa had heard rumors. "Of what sort, sir?"

"Squatters, illegal settlers, thieves, and brigands of all sorts. They steal across from the neutral strip between us and the Americans in Louisiana. They harass our people and cause unrest among the Indians. They are breaking out farms where they have no right and taking land from our own people. They seem to think that because they are Americans they are a superior race."

Zaragosa remembered. As a sergeant in the Spanish army, serving under the late Lieutenant Rodriguez, he was stationed for some years in the northern outpost of Nacogdoches. He had spent much time in the saddle, rooting out and expelling smugglers and illegal immigrants who seemed constantly working to extend the borders of the United States westward and confiscate Texas lands that were a part of Mexico. Many of these were lawless and defiant men who knew no authority except that which came at the point of a sword or from the muzzle of a rifle.

The late Lieutenant Rodriguez had taken special pleasure in obliging them with either or both, to the point of bloody excess which had sometimes turned Zaragosa's stomach. The courts were slow and overly lenient, Rodriguez had contended. On the other hand, there was no appeal from the grave.

Sanchez said, "The situation appears beyond the control of our few soldiers in Nacogdoches. You know that region, lieutenant. Therefore I am dispatching you northward with enough troops to make our presence felt. I want you to seek out those who have no legitimate purpose on our side of the Sabine River and send them back where they belong. How soon could you start?"

"Whenever you say, sir. I await your orders." He hoped he spoke with military correctness and that his misgivings did not betray themselves. Nacogdoches and its region held many unpleasant memories for him. Even more important, he knew that to take Elvira with him was out of the question. He had no idea how long this mission might require him to be separated from her.

Sanchez said, "Tomorrow, then. I will issue orders to the quartermaster to see that your troops are properly outfitted."

"Properly outfitted" meant little in the Mexican army, certainly not at this level and in such an isolated post. His men would be given little beyond arms and a modest supply of ammunition, horses, and castoff equipment that no other army post between here and Mexico City had wanted. Their rations would be of the most meager kind. For the most part Zaragosa and his men would be expected to live off of the land. As a practical matter, beyond whatever wild game they could manage to bag, that meant taking from the settlers whose lives and property it was supposed to be their duty to protect. To be sure, they would issue army scrip or requisitions in payment, but these usually were worth no more than the paper they were written upon. Small wonder then, that settlers—Mexican or American—tried to hide whatever they had that was of value when they saw soldiers.

Sanchez said, "I would expect that you will want to go home early and have time for a proper good-bye to that beautiful wife of yours, and your children."

"I would be grateful, sir." Zaragosa saluted and started for the door.

Sanchez called after him. "One more thing, lieutenant. I want you to go by the Austin colony, just for a look around."

Zaragosa frowned. That would add much distance to the trip, for Austin's colony was east of Bexar. Nacogdoches was far to the northeast. He commented, "Austin's people are quiet, sir."

"Seeing a few soldiers once in a while should help keep them that way." Sanchez frowned under a fresh attack of biliousness. He asked, "Do you speak English?"

"Here a word, there a word. My English is poor."

"Then take Corporal Diaz with you as interpreter. He contemplates matrimony to a most devious young woman. Perhaps some time away from Bexar will afford him the opportunity to reconsider his error. He will thank me someday."

ZARAGOSA FOUND little Manuel at the front of his modest adobe house, throwing a stick for a small spotted dog to run and fetch. Manuel, six, appeared surprised at seeing him, for it was still early in the afternoon, but he came running as Zaragosa stepped down from the black horse. "Papa!" he called. Zaragosa knelt for the boy to hug him. He asked, "Is the baby asleep?"

Manuel shook his head. "No, she is crawling everywhere. I came outside to get away from her for a while. Why are children such a nuisance, Papa?"

Zaragosa smiled. "That is simply their way. We just have to suffer them until they grow up like you and me." He turned to look for the dog. "You had better keep him away from the heels of that black horse. It does not like dogs."

Manuel ran off in a direction away from the mount, luring the dog after him with the stick. He joined several neighbor boys with whom he often played. Zaragosa watched a moment, taking pleasure in the laughter of children, then pushed the heavy wooden door inward. The thick adobe walls made the room dark and cool.

Elvira stood in the kitchen doorway, her eyes wide in surprise. They were beautiful eyes, large and dark, set in a face he found so beautiful that he could never stop with kissing her upon the lips. He had to kiss each smooth cheek, the high forehead, the tip of her perfect nose. As he held her body against his and she responded by clasping her arms tightly around him, he felt the upsurge of a wanting that was never satisfied for long. Glancing toward the bedroom door, he wondered if this was a proper time to surrender to such an impulse. The baby girl crawling on the floor would pay no attention, but the boy might return to the house.

They would have the night, all of the night, if he could wait.

When they pushed to arm's length, Elvira caught her breath. "Why are you home so early? Is anything wrong?"

He knew no easy way to tell her, but it was a thing to which a soldier's wife had to become accustomed. "I must leave for Nacogdoches in the morning."

Her large black eyes looked downward, trying to hide their dismay. "I hope it is not for anything dangerous." She always reacted badly when he had to leave her for any length of time.

He said, "It is only routine." He saw no reason to tell her everything. It was the lot of a soldier's wife to accept without question, just as the soldier himself accepted without question. "But I thought while I am gone it might be well for you to go out to the farm and stay with your father and mother so you will not feel alone. It would be good for the boy to be away from this town for a while too."

Her family, the Galindos, had land holdings north of town along the Nacogdoches road. They were considered wealthy, as wealth was measured in a community like Bexar where no one had any excess of the world's goods. Their wealth, if such it be, was tied up in land and horses, cattle and sheep, not in coin of the republic.

Elvira could not hold back a couple of tears. Tenderly he caught them with one finger as they trailed down her soft cheek, and he wiped them away with a gentle gesture. "I will be back before you have time to miss me," he promised.

She nodded but turned her face away from him, leaning her head against his chest. "I wish you never had to go anywhere again. I wish you would accept what Papa has offered you."

They had talked about this many times. Old Mauro Galindo's proposal had been generous. He said, "I am a soldier, not a farmer."

"You need not always be a soldier. There are other things."

"Someday, perhaps. But let me save a little more money first. Let me say that I had something of my own besides just a kind and generous father-in-law."

"You have too much pride, Elizandro."

"If I had no pride, you could not love me."

She turned her face up toward him and pressed her lips against his. Her kiss was first warm and soft, then turned fierce and demanding as a flush rose in her cheeks. Her hands roamed, and he let his roam in response. She said, "I love you so much I never want you to leave me. Not for a day, much less for a night."

She gave the baby girl a concerned glance and found she had dropped off to sleep on the floor, peacefully clutching a small glove. The child often ignored toys but could entertain herself for hours with something as lifeless as a shoe. Elvira turned toward the bedroom, tugging at her husband's hand.

He gave her no resistance. The boy would probably remain outside, playing with his friends. Even if not, there was a small wooden bar on the inside of the bedroom door.

5

MICHAEL LEWIS felt his backside prickling with anxiety as the bay horse carried him closer to home. He had been gone now more than two weeks, probably close to three; he had lost count of days after ten or so. He had not told Marie where he was going or how long he would be gone for the simple reason that he had no real idea himself, except that he would ride west. It was a legacy from his footloose father, who had never known a place he did not want to go, so long as it was westward, and never found a place where he wanted to stay. Marie would have every right not to speak to him, he thought. She would have every right to bar the bedroom door and make him sleep on the dog-run, or out in the pole-walled shed. But his mother had endured the same treatment over and over during the long and often taxing years of her marriage to Mordecai Lewis. Michael had seen her resentment rise during Mordecai's extended absences, anger enough that she attacked her housework with a determination bordering on violence. Unlucky was the hound that strayed upon the dog-run when she held a broom in her hands. But the anger usually vanished when Mordecai finally appeared. She would welcome him home like the prodigal son rather than the errant husband.

Marie had maintained the same tolerance with Michael. He

had warned her before their marriage that he was his father's
son and that wedlock was unlikely to cure his wanderlust. Before that, he had even vowed that he would never marry because he did not want some woman to put up with the
loneliness and hardship his mother had endured. But that vow
had melted like ice in July when he looked into the dark eyes
of Marie Villaret. His desire for her overcame his best intentions. Each time he tested Marie's endurance with a long trip
away from home, he half expected her to meet his return with
an explosive release of pent-up resentment. God knew she had
reason enough.

It was not just his encounter with the Indians that had
turned him homeward. It was his need and hunger for her, his
guilt over leaving Marie and the boy Mordecai for so long, the
firewood not cut, the fields not planted. Each time he returned
from one of those solitary sojourns, he promised himself he
would never do it again. He avoided making that vow to
Marie, however. It was forgivable to break a promise to one-
self, but he would not give Marie a pledge he knew his nature
would probably prevent him from keeping. Whatever his
other shortcomings might be, he would not lie to her.

He could have reached home last night had he pushed to do
so, but he had held back. He remembered times when his father had come in the middle of the night, as if he were sneak-
ing in. However Michael's conscience might punish him, he
would not use darkness to hide his homecoming. He would
ride up to the front of the cabin in broad daylight like a man
who knew who he was and what he was about. If Marie had a
dose of bitter medicine waiting for him, he would stand
squarely on both feet and accept the punishment due him. He
had not run from the Indians. He would not turn and run from
a little French-speaking woman who probably weighed no
more than a hundred pounds wearing all the clothes she
owned and had a waist so tiny he could reach most of the way
around it with his two big, rough hands.

He brought a peace offering of sorts, meat in the form of a
doe he had shot just at daylight as she edged into a clearing in
search of forage.

Following the general course of the Colorado River but remaining up out of the heavy timber that bordered it, he found he was leaning forward in the saddle as if this would help him see his home sooner. He settled back and took a deep breath to steady himself. For two days he had been composing the first words he would say to Marie, speaking them aloud to himself for practice, honing them until he had given them the right combination of contrition and male authority. The trees fell back to his left, and he touched his spurs gently to the bay horse to put him up the final hill. He said the words one more time to be certain he had them down firmly. As he topped over, he saw at a glance that all was not just as he had left it. Someone had been plowing his field. Row after row, the earth had the dark look of fresh turning. His first thought was that Marie had done it. Conscience came rushing back with a vengeance at the thought of that little woman struggling with the big red ox and heavy wooden plow. Then he saw a man at the far side of the field, carrying a large stone the plow had turned up. The man dumped it a couple of paces beyond the end of the row and faced around. Michael knew him by the way he walked, the way he stood.

His younger brother Andrew was doing the work that should have been Michael's.

Aw, hell, he thought, *he didn't have to go and do that.* But that was Andrew's way. He had inherited their father's strength without so much of his wandering nature. Like their older brother Joseph, who had remained on the old farm back in Tennessee, Andrew tended to business first.

Michael pulled the horse to a stop and gathered all his resolve. He took one last long look back over his shoulder at the timber which lined the broad Colorado River. He had no idea how far west he would have to travel to find its source, how far out into mysterious lands known only to the Indians. Someday he would know. Someday he would go—

He angrily clenched his fist. *Damn you, you haven't even got home yet, and you're already thinking about going again. When're you ever going to grow up and take hold of your responsibilities?*

The morning sun was halfway to noon as he pushed the horse down the long slope and out upon the flat where he and Marie had chosen to build their cabin, within easy water-toting distance of the river. Life was tough enough for a woman on the outer edge of the settlements in a newly developing land without her carrying water in a heavy wooden bucket a step farther than necessary. In Natchitoches, where Marie had grown up, she had enjoyed some of life's little luxuries, within the limitations of a river town itself not far from the western frontier. By the standards of the time and place, her father had been relatively well-off, for he operated a mercantile business that served a wide and developing region. Some of his trade was clandestine, reaching far into Texas when it had still been Spanish and continuing now that it belonged to Mexico. Old Baptiste Villaret had provided well for his family.

Marie's life was far different out here. Sometimes Michael wondered how she stood up to its challenge. He could truthfully declare that she had never actually gone hungry. One way or another, he had always provided food for the table. There had been times at first when the next meal had been highly in doubt, and only his keen eye over the sights of the long rifle had brought them through. But she had strengths of her own; Baptiste Villaret had seen to that in her upbringing. Natchitoches was enough of a frontier town that it taught its children self-sufficiency. She had put in a log-fenced garden, enlarging it every year they had lived here. From the time of her first crop, she had seen to it that their dugout storage had a stock of food always in reserve against the lean days when no game presented itself to Michael's good aim. She and the child could subsist for a considerable time if he never came back.

He saw her in the garden, bending over a hoe, chopping the early spring weeds out of her first emerging plants. The boy Mordecai played nearby with the protective dog, which never failed to place itself between the boy and anything unusual that arose. Once last year Michael had seen the dog dragging the baby by its shirt while little Mordecai howled in protest.

When Michael hurried out to reprimand the animal, he had seen that it was pulling the boy away from a coiled rattlesnake.

The dog was the first to see Michael. It moved in front of the boy and started barking. Marie turned and looked up, dropping the hoe as recognition came. The dog stopped barking and bounded forth to meet Michael, while little Mordecai turned quickly toward his mother, unsure who the horseman might be.

Marie waited outside the hip-high garden fence. A wide slat bonnet shaded her face so that he could hardly see the fine features, but memory filled them in for him. She looked little enough that he could pick her up under one arm and carry her into the cabin. But not against her will, for she had strength that did not show.

He stepped down from the horse, looking at her, trying to remember the words he had so carefully rehearsed. They had left him like brown leaves swept away by the west wind. She stood staring at him as he stared at her, then pulled the slip-knot in the string that bound the bonnet beneath her chin. She slipped the bonnet from her head and took a long step toward him, her arms outstretched. He hurried into them and crushed her with joy and wanting. They held together in silence for a minute or two. Little Mordecai clung to his leg and talked rapidly in words the dog might have understood but Michael could not.

He asked Marie finally, "Ain't you teachin' that boy English?"

She smiled up at Michael. "*You* teach him English." She spoke with an accent that never failed to delight him. "I will teach him French and Spanish. Then he can talk to anybody who comes."

Michael lifted the youngster into his arms and hugged him. "You been a good boy?" he demanded. "Been helpin' your mama?"

Mordecai nodded vigorously, arms clasped around Michael's neck. "You stay home now, Papa? You stay home?"

"I'll stay home. Got lots of work to do." He turned and

looked off toward the field. "Marie, I hope you didn't ask Andrew to start my plowin' for me. He's got work enough of his own to do."

"I told him that. But he said he thought the corn should be planted, at least. We cannot eat cotton, but we can live on corn."

"I ought to've been here," he admitted ruefully. That was as near as he would come to an apology. Even that was further than his father ever went. Apology was an admission of error.

Marie took his free left arm; he held the boy in his right. She said, "You are hungry?"

He nodded toward the doe tied across his horse. "I brought meat. I could eat half of it myself, here and now."

"Hang it in the dog-run, and what you want to eat, cut it off. I will go to build up the fire."

He looked back again. "I ought to go speak to Andrew first."

She blinked. "I almost forgot. Andrew said I should tell you. Some men came—the Blackwoods."

An old cold, sick feeling spread from the pit of Michael's stomach. Blackwood. The name itself was enough to spoil his hunger. He set the boy down upon the ground and clenched his hands into fists. He glanced back at his saddle, where his long rifle hung. "You sure it was the Blackwoods?"

"Andrew said yes, they were."

"They do anything, say anything?"

"Said you were old friends. Said they wished to see you."

"Over the sights of a rifle is the way they would like it best. I thought Texas would be far enough—" His face twisted to the sour taste that rose in his mouth. His eyes narrowed as he studied her. "They didn't do nothin'—didn't touch you or nothin'?"

"They stayed on their horses. They only said I must tell you they will see you soon."

"I just hope I see them first." He turned to the horse, lifting the doe's carcass down from behind the saddle. "I'll quarter this and hang it up. Then I better go out and talk to Andrew."

"You will not eat first?"

"I've lost my appetite." He looked at the boy, then at Marie, feeling an apprehension akin to that which had come to him when he had faced the Indian hunting party. "Till we know for sure what their intentions are, you and little Mordecai better not go farther than the garden. If you see anybody comin' besides me or Andrew, skin out for the cabin and bar the door."

Her eyes widened. "They are that bad?"

"They're bad, them Blackwoods, and they're cowards. That's the most dangerous combination I can think of."

ANDREW HALTED the big ox and laid Michael's wooden plow over on its side. Michael had built the plow himself out of timber near at hand, as he had built most of the other accoutrements on this farm. A steel plow made by a blacksmith cost more money than he could spare. From what he had read, folks had used a plow like this since Bible times. If it was good enough for the Bible, he figured it was good enough for him. Anyway, some folks argued that a steel point might somehow poison the ground.

Andrew stood with hands on his hips, frowning darkly as Michael rode up. That took Michael aback a little, for a smile fitted his brother much better than a frown. Usually he was so cheerful that Michael was now and then tempted to choke him. Sweat soaked Andrew's homespun shirt and made dirty rivulets down his dusty face. Farming was not a clean job. Michael thought he saw relief in Andrew's eyes, but it did not endure. Censure took its place. Andrew said accusingly, "You been gone long enough."

Michael saw no point in argument. "Too long, I'm afraid. I didn't figure on you doin' my work for me."

"It needed doin', and you wasn't here." Andrew gave him a moment to absorb the rebuke, then added, "Anyway, I thought I'd better stay pretty close for Marie's sake. She had company while you was off yonder roamin' around."

"She told me it was the Blackwoods."

"It was. I rode over to San Felipe and talked to Stephen Austin. He says they'll get no place in this colony, but that don't mean they can't take up in some other, or just squat somewhere the way so many do."

"They didn't come to Texas just to get land. They've come to get even. What I don't figure is why they waited so long."

"They had to work up the nerve. Sooner or later they'll come lookin' for their chance. I hope you've got eyes in the back of your head, because they'll likely be comin' from behind you."

"I don't reckon they can help themselves. It runs in the blood, like a family disease. Their old daddy Cyrus never was worth his own hide and tallow."

Andrew's gaze went to Michael's rifle. "You better keep that with you everywhere you go."

"I always do."

"Might even be a good idea if you had two rifles. We can work together; finish your field, then go finish mine."

Michael looked toward the red ox, standing stolidly in the field where Andrew had stopped him. "You'd do that? You gave me a strong notion that you were mad at me."

Andrew's voice cut like a blade. "Hell yes, I'm mad at you, goin' off the way you done, leavin' a woman and a boy that need you. But you're the only brother I've got this side of Tennessee. Be damned if I want to lose you to the likes of them Blackwoods."

6

MARIE AWAKENED earlier than usual, and she felt the warmth of her husband lying in the narrow bed close beside her. She turned slowly toward Michael, careful not to wake him. In the near darkness that preceded the dawn, she stared into the freshly shaved face that only in sleep looked totally at peace. The bed had seemed large and empty those many long nights he had been gone. She resisted a strong desire to caress his cheek. She supposed she had a right to feel hurt and angry that he had left her here with the baby, and perhaps there had been times during his absence when she had allowed herself the luxury of brief self-pity. But she had known how he was when she married him; he had made no effort to convince her he would change. If anything, she had been attracted by that sense of adventure, the hint of danger that seemed always a part of him. She would not acknowledge it now as a threat to the life they shared.

Even so, she remembered her Spanish mother's dire warnings about the trap she was setting for herself, tied to a foot-loose *americano* frontiersman. That her mother had married a once-footloose French frontiersman was beside the point, the older woman argued. There was half a world's difference between Baptiste Villaret and Michael Lewis. Marie's mother had been happy and, after a time, enjoyed a relatively comfortable life in the old Louisiana town of Natchitoches. Marie was confident that a similar future was in store for her, eventually. She was young. What other people might consider hardship she counted as but inconvenience. It was a small price to pay for being able to live with a man she had loved since she had been twelve and he fifteen, brought back from Texas gravely wounded by a Spanish bullet. She had spent long hours at his bedside then, watching anxiously as he pulled back gradually from the dark precipice and regained strength enough to return to his old home in Tennessee.

His leaving her behind was nothing new. That time, he had not returned until he was a grown man.

She felt a peaceful glow as she lay looking at his quiet face. Dawn's light began to push back the darkness. It was time to be getting up and going about the day's work. She gave in to a wish and softly kissed his forehead.

He awoke instantly, his eyes wide in momentary confusion. She raised up on one elbow and kissed him again, on the end of his nose. She whispered, "It is too late for you to go out and wake up the rooster. I have heard him already."

Michael raised a big hand gently to her cheek, and she felt a stirring at his touch. She placed her hand over his and touched her lips to the tips of his fingers. "I will start a fire for breakfast," she said.

He caught her arm and held her. "I don't feel like I've had a full night's sleep yet."

She smiled wickedly. "You have not. It was not for sleep that you came to the bed."

His face turned red, and her smile broadened. She said in mock accusation, "You are embarrassed."

He brought both arms around her. "You have a shameless mind."

"Where is there shame in it? We are properly married."

"Some things a woman ain't supposed to talk about."

"It is only for men to talk? If it is all right to do something, why is it not all right to talk about it? Everyone knows what we do. Little Mordecai is the evidence."

"I've got no answer for that." Michael raised up on his elbows and looked across the room to the boy's small bed, set in a corner. The youngster had not yet stirred. "He's pretty soon goin' to have to start sleepin' someplace else. He's gettin' big enough to notice things."

"He is too small to climb a ladder to the loft. He might fall."

The cabin had only two rooms, the kitchen on one side, the bedroom on the other, with an open loft beneath the roof of the dog-run that separated the two parts.

Michael said, "I may have to build us another room. Like as not Mordecai won't be the last young 'un."

She smiled to herself. She had not told him yet. She wanted to wait until the mood was proper. Right now he had enough on his mind, getting the crops planted, worrying about the three brothers named Blackwood.

He lay back on the bed and stared up at her, his eyes soft. "By rights, Marie, you ought not to even speak to me, much less love me like you done. I'd've understood if you'd sent me out of the house to sleep in the shed with Andrew."

"But I wanted you in the house. I wanted you here, where you are."

"I ain't done right by you; I know that."

"You have made a home for me here. We have land that is ours. We have a son, and—" She checked herself before she gave the rest of it away. "With you, Michael, I am happy. No, I do not like it when you are gone from me. But when you come home, all is good again." She leaned down and kissed him.

He said, "I didn't mean to be gone so long. But you know how it is with me."

She leaned her face against his. "You do not have to say more. I know." She felt a flood of warmth as she lay against him, and she nearly gave herself to it before she pushed back. "We had better get up before Andrew comes in."

"He could as well have gone home."

"You know he stays because of those men. Come on, we should get up."

He held her arms for a moment. "Can't say as I'm ready."

"You will be ready when you smell breakfast on the hearth."

He lay watching her as she removed her gown and slipped a plain homespun cotton dress over her head for the day's work. "Seein' you thataway, I don't know how I can ever leave."

"You see me like that every morning and again every night."

"Not when I'm gone from you. Except I keep seein' you in my mind. That always brings me back."

She gave him a pleased smile. "Then never forget."

"I just wish I could provide better clothes for you. You had good clothes when you lived in Natchitoches."

"Not many women in Austin's colony have more. And no other woman in Austin's colony has you. I do not complain."

She went into the kitchen and began to stir the coals and ashes from last night's fire, slowly kindling a new fire with small pieces of straw and thin strips of pine, adding larger pieces as the flames gained strength. Michael took a wooden bucket and went out to milk the red cow Andrew had brought over so there would be plenty for little Mordecai. Marie promised herself she would also start drinking more milk, too, now that she was again providing for two bodies instead of one. She wondered if Michael would be perceptive enough to guess for himself. Probably not. Men could tell when a cow was going to calve, but they did not know half so much about women.

Andrew stood in the door, his arms full of wood cut to the proper length for the fireplace. He seldom failed to bring something when he came to a meal, even if no more than a little wood so Marie would not have to carry it herself. She smiled at him. "Good morning, Andrew."

"Mornin'." He had a shy way about him, at least around Marie. But always when she was not looking in his direction she sensed his eyes following her. Sometimes she wondered if in his own way he might not be in love with her. Or perhaps not her, exactly, but what she stood for: a home life, someone with whom to share. The thought aroused ambivalent feelings in Marie. On the one hand she was flattered that she could still attract the interest of a man other than her husband. On the other she felt a vague stirring of guilt, a fear that she might have done something to encourage his feelings. She could offer Andrew nothing except the love of a sister.

She stole a glance at him and saw him cut his eyes quickly away. It was amazing how much he resembled Michael. Even a stranger seeing them together would recognize that they were brothers. She could remember in a general way how their father, the old Mordecai, had looked the time he had stopped in Natchitoches before he made his fatal trip into Spanish Texas in search of wild horses. The two brothers had the same rangy build, the same deeply carved features. Where there was a major difference was in their blue eyes. Andrew's were lively and questing, where Michael's were often stern and troubled, haunted by terrible sights Andrew had been fortunate enough not to see.

Andrew apologized as he watched Marie bend over the hearth. "I'm sorry to be a burden to you. You got family enough of your own to feed."

"You are part of this family, Andrew. You have no one to cook for you except me."

"I do for myself most of the time."

"But you are here to help Michael finish his planting. We owe you much more than food. And to cook for one more is no extra work."

For a moment she considered the extravagance, then decided to put coffee on to boil. They took coffee as a luxury on special occasions. She decided Andrew deserved to be treated as a special guest. That finished, she turned and gave him a long, speculative study. "It is not good that you live alone. When the crops are finished this year you should make a trip. Go to Natchitoches. Go even back to Tennessee. Somewhere there must be a girl who watches for someone like you to come and carry her away."

Andrew shook his head. "I'm afraid I'd be hard to suit. I'd not want to settle for less than my brother has got, and I doubt there's another one like you anywhere around."

A pleased warmth rose in Marie's face. She watched Andrew pick up Michael's rifle and walk outside for a cautious look around. Neither he nor Michael had spoken much of the

Blackwoods, but she knew the thought was never out of mind. She knew, though no one had told her, that Andrew was staying here not to help plant the field so much as to help protect his brother should the Blackwoods come again.

It would be nice if Andrew found himself a wife. It would be good to have a woman so close by that they could visit every day. But that woman would have to be special to be worthy of a husband like Andrew, she thought.

Michael brought the fresh milk, then checked the water bucket and found it nearly empty. He walked down to the river, swinging the bucket as if he had no cares. Marie noticed that he stood a long time at the bank, looking down into the water. When he returned, he set the bucket on a rough table he had built with his own skilled hands.

She said, "You were gone so long, I had some fear you had fallen in."

Michael shook his head and turned to Andrew, who had walked in behind him and set the rifle on its pegs over the fireplace above another rifle that was Marie's. "I was just lookin' at that runnin' water, thinkin' where-all it's been before it got all the way down here to us, thinkin' I'd like to go someday and see the place where it comes from."

Marie caught the look that flashed for a moment in Andrew's eyes and knew it mirrored her own. Michael had just come home yesterday. Already his mind was beginning to turn toward the next leavetaking.

"Breakfast is ready," she said, and tried to make her voice cheerful. But her mind was beginning to prepare itself for the next time Michael left her.

7

ISAAC BLACKWOOD kept turning in the saddle, looking back in disappointment at the wheel-worn ruts that were the main street of San Felipe de Austin. Wild flowers lined either side in great profusion and variety of color, their sweet scent heady. He thought this region could match beauty with the prettiest places he had ever seen in Tennessee. That made his regret even deeper, for he had not wanted to leave home in the first place. It had seemed expedient, however, perhaps even crucial. At twenty-three he could no longer plead youth as an excuse for following his two older brothers where none of them should go and into deeds none of them should do, keeping them constantly crossways with the authorities.

Finis, the oldest, rode three lengths ahead, with next oldest Luke beside him. Finis's angry voice demanded, "Spur up, Isaac. Ain't no use us wastin' any more time around this Goddamned place."

"Goddamned place," Luke echoed.

Isaac drummed his bootheels against his horse's ribs in an effort to catch up. He knew there was little to be gained by arguing with Finis when anger so crimsoned that part of his face which showed around a long, ragged growth of black beard. There was nothing to be gained by arguing with Luke at any time, because Luke looked to Finis for The Word, and Luke was sure Finis was never wrong. But Isaac contended, "Austin didn't say right out that we *couldn't* take up land around here. What he said was, we'll need to put up some money, and we'll need an endorsement of good character."

Finis's eyes had the fiery look that might have come from a jug of bad whiskey, but the whiskey had played out far back up the trail. The color was from outrage. When his temper was running loose he usually flapped his stump of an arm up and down like a rooster flapping its wings. "He'd just as well've asked us to drag the moon up to his doorstep for him. We ain't got no money, and from the looks of this place there ain't none to be had. I'll bet there ain't five hundred dollars in honest-to-God specie between here and the Sabine River.

"As for an endorsement, where the hell you think we'll get that? Ain't nobody here knows us, and if they did they wouldn't walk across the road to help us none. They never would back in Tennessee."

Luke came in like an echo, "Not in Tennessee."

Isaac said, "The Lewises know us."

Finis looked at Isaac as if he considered him the village idiot. "The *Lewises*." He spat. "Them's the last people on earth that'll give us a helpin' hand."

Luke echoed. "The last people."

Finis said grittily, "The only thing they ever gave *me* was the losin' of this arm." He raised the stump again. "I owe Michael Lewis for that. And before we leave this country, I swear I'll pay him good and proper."

Luke nodded solemn agreement. "Good and proper. Remember what we promised Maw."

Maw. Isaac grimaced, an ugly memory rising like poison. Charity was their mother's name, but she had precious little of it in her character. Charity Blackwood had spent most of the last thirty years trying to whip her sons into the men her husband never was. She had promised them, threatened them, cajoled them, beaten them. That her own people had forced her into a loveless marriage to a man without spine had festered in her soul like an open sore until it had become an obsession with her to make the Blackwood name feared.

"If we can't make them respect us, we can by God make them afraid of us," she had declared many a time. She had drilled it into her sons from the time they were old enough to understand: *Let no man laugh at you, let no insult go unavenged.* Isaac, like his older brothers, had followed her teachings, though it had exposed him to many a fight, many a brutal beating. And for what? he had begun to ask himself. It had earned him no one's respect, and certainly no one's liking. Fear? People feared a snake. For a hundred miles in every direction of their Tennessee home, people knew the Blackwood name and spoke it in deprecation. There was not a sheriff in twice that distance who did not have a Blackwood name scribbled in his little book of men to watch for and arrest if they chanced into his jurisdiction. Eventually the three oldest brothers had no choice but to leave Tennessee in the dark of night and seek new country where they were not known. It had been older brother Finis's decision to come to Texas, for Michael Lewis was here. Finis had pledged to Charity Blackwood that one way or another he would finally settle a blood debt long deferred.

Times like now, Isaac wished he had let his two older brothers go their own way. He wished he had chosen another direction to travel, up into Missouri, perhaps, to make a new start where Finis and Luke would not hang like a millstone around his neck. But he was a Blackwood. Blackwoods stood by their own.

That lesson Charity Blackwood had taught him well, even if she had driven herself crazy doing it.

Isaac said, "There's other colonies besides Austin's. And there's Louisiana. We seen a lot of good country comin' through Louisiana, country that didn't have nobody on it."

"We come to Texas," Finis said, with a strong tone of rebuke. "We'll stay in Texas!"

Isaac declared, "Not if you go and kill Michael Lewis."

Finis only grunted in reply.

Isaac had a pretty good notion where Finis was headed, but he asked anyway.

Finis grunted. "What difference does it make to you? You'll go where we go."

"Looks to me like this is the direction to the Lewis place."

"I do believe you're gettin' smarter as you get older, little brother. By God, Luke, maybe there's hope for him yet."

Luke grinned, his teeth crooked as they showed through matted whiskers that had not felt scissors or razor in months. "Yeah, there's hope for him."

Their mother had said Luke was born two months too soon, and he had come up cheated on mental development. Isaac's suspicions confirmed, he said, "I'd like to know what you figure on us doin' when we get there."

"I ain't set in my mind yet. We'll just draw the cards as they come up. Whatever we do, it won't be somethin' Michael Lewis is goin' to like."

"I don't want no part of a killin'."

"I don't see you got any choice, if that's what me and Luke decide to do."

"If it comes to a killin', don't you be figurin' on me."

"You're a Blackwood. If we're in, you're in."

Several times on the long trip to Texas Isaac had felt sorely tempted to go off and leave them to ride into hell in their own good time without his company. He was confident he could make a better place for himself without them. He was a tolerably good farmer, when he set his mind and his shoulders to it, something Finis and Luke would never be. He was a better than average hunter and trapper. Just give him woods where he could find game, some decent pelt-bearing animals; he would make a living. If it hadn't been for his skill with the rifle on the way here from Tennessee, Finis and Luke would have starved down like a gutted snowbird. They could talk big and cuss the bark off of a stump, but neither had ever shown an ability to make a living on his own. Like Paw, they had leaned on Maw or Isaac. Now Maw was too far back east to help them any. They were Isaac's responsibility.

That was the reason he had not left them on the trail, and why he knew he would not leave them now, though the urge was so strong it fair made a fever rise in him sometimes. A man could not travel far enough to get completely away from Maw. The lessons she had drilled into him, sometimes with sugar and sometimes with a whip, would be with him to the grave.

The grave. That could be nearer rather than farther if he stayed with Finis and Luke, for they hated fiercely and never gave a moment's thought to consequences until after the deed was done. Then their main thought was to run like hell.

He shivered. After Texas, where could they run? They had already reached the end of the earth, seemed like.

THE TWO older brothers shut Isaac out of their deliberations as they sat on their horses and looked across a gently rolling prairie toward a field and a double cabin. Luke said, "I see two fellers workin' out yonder, Finis. Didn't you say we'd catch Michael all by himself?"

"That's the way I'd figured it. It's probably that younger brother of his, that Andrew. They was always close."

Isaac frowned. He remembered one time he and his two brothers had fought with Michael over the rightful possession of a deer both Finis and Michael had shot at. Andrew had waded in fiercely, taking his brother's side with a chunk of wood as big as a man's arm. Isaac still remembered the pain.

Finis turned his narrowed eyes to Isaac. "You're the best shot, little brother. You reckon you could hit him from here?"

Isaac shrugged. "Maybe. But I ain't a-goin' to."

Finis's eyes narrowed even more. "And why the hell not?"

"Because I don't cotton to shootin' a man that ain't even lookin' at me. If a man's worth killin', he's worth killin' with me standin' there lookin' him square in the eye."

Finis snapped, "He'll look at you right enough, right over the sights of his rifle. Way I remember it, he's a hell of a good shot."

Isaac glanced at Finis's stump of an arm. Dryly he said, "He sure is."

Finis swallowed a few times in anger and made threatening motions toward Isaac as if he intended to do him injury. But Isaac knew it was all show. If Finis ever came at him with real hostile intent, it would be from behind. What Finis usually did when he was out of sorts with Isaac was to sic Luke onto him like a dog. Sometimes Isaac could whip Luke and sometimes he couldn't. He had lost count of the occasions when they had fought each other to exhaustion, with Finis standing there cussing them both. What they should have done, Isaac sometimes thought, was to turn and whip Finis. But they both had pity for a poor one-armed man.

Isaac said, "I won't ambush him for you, so you'd just as leave forget that. But if you'll ride down yonder and face him man to man, I'll go and see that him and Andrew don't get no unfair advantage."

He could tell that Finis was not strong for such a notion, but Luke was not one to read minds and faces very well. Luke declared, "And I'll be with you too, Finis. Ain't much they can do with three of us standin' together."

Isaac grunted, remembering the long-ago fight in Tennessee. The two Lewises had won.

Finis was caught between his two younger brothers. With obvious misgivings he said, "I ain't afraid of him, if that's what you-all are thinkin'. I ain't afraid of nobody. I reckon it won't hurt nothin' to go down and talk to him. When the talkin's done, we'll see what happens."

Isaac smiled inwardly but did not let Finis see it. Chances were that nothing would happen, for the Lewis brothers would be too much on their guard to allow Finis the kind of advantage he would want before he would make any attempt on Michael.

Finis seemed to be stalling for time, licking his lips nervously as he looked down toward the field where the Lewises worked, each following a plow behind a large ox. "Now, don't you-all lag behind. You stay right up beside me, because we ain't go no idee what them Lewises are apt to do."

Isaac said, "One thing they *won't* do is to shoot first. So you don't have to worry unless you fire at them. Then you probably won't have *time* to worry."

Finis gave him a look of anger, tinged with fear. "I swear, little brother, sometimes you just don't sound like a Blackwood."

If Finis had any hope of catching the Lewis brothers by surprise, that hope was quickly dashed. Long before the Blackwoods reached the field, Michael and Andrew Lewis had walked to the end of the freshly turned rows and stood waiting, rifles cradled in their arms. Isaac chilled a little, looking at those weapons. He hoped Finis or Luke would not do something stupid, for he would be forced to try to defend them.

Finis halted a dozen paces from the Lewises. Luke went a little farther, then backed his horse nervously as he realized he had put himself in front of his older brother. Isaac reined up a little short of both. He felt Michael's gaze touch him for a brief moment before returning to Finis. It was clear that Michael regarded Finis as the spokesman and, if it came to that, the primary target. Michael said, "Finis." Not *howdy,* or *hello,* or even *what the hell do you want here?* Just *Finis.* A man could put any meaning he wanted to that, or no meaning at all.

Andrew did not speak. Clearly, Michael was the spokesman for both Lewis brothers.

Two hundred yards away, Isaac saw a movement at the double cabin. A slender woman stood in the dog-run, the breeze gently moving her long skirt. She also held a rifle. He remembered their brief conversation with her several days ago. She had shown them no fear, he remembered. She had remained on the dog-run the whole time, not more than a single step from a rifle she had brought outside and leaned against the log wall. He remembered too that she had an odd way of talking, some kind of a foreign-sounding way of speaking her words. Isaac wondered if these foreign women had been taught to shoot. He wondered if she was a good enough shot to hit a man at this distance. Maw could. Inasmuch as this was Michael Lewis's wife, he thought it likely that she could too.

Finis said, "We already come once. You was gone."

"I'm here now," Michael replied flatly. "If you've got business with me, let's get it done."

Finis glanced fretfully at his brothers, one on either side of him, as if he were half afraid they might not be there.

Luke blurted, "Your damn right we got business. Tell him, Finis."

Finis gave Luke an irritated look that said to keep his mouth shut. "We come a long ways, Michael. You-all with them guns, you look like you're afraid of us."

Michael's voice had a cutting edge. "I'm never afraid of a Blackwood as long as I'm lookin' at him. I just don't want him gettin' behind me."

Isaac had learned years ago to tell when Finis was lying. His voice shifted to a higher than normal pitch, and he talked faster. He began talking faster now. "We never come to do you no harm, Michael. The things that happened, they was a long time ago. We just come here lookin' for a new home."

"It's Stephen Austin who parcels out the land. I got nothin' to do with that."

"He says we got to have a recommendation. You could give us a recommendation, Michael."

Isaac frowned, wondering about the direction of the conversation. Finis had already given up on obtaining land in Austin's colony, and surely he entertained no hope of an endorsement from the Lewises. Isaac suspected Finis was stalling for time, hoping for some opportunity to grab the upper hand. From the determined look in the cold blue eyes of the Lewis brothers, Isaac judged that they could stand here until the snow fell and never give up any advantage.

Michael's voice kept its edge. "I couldn't give *you* a recommendation to old Scratch himself, Finis. If that's what you come for, you've put some good horses to a long trip for nothin'."

Finis muttered a little. He raised the stub of an arm. "It was you done this to me. Crippled me for life, you did. I figure you owe me somethin'."

Michael's hand tightened on his rifle. "Mine wasn't the first shot. And I fired from the open. You fired from ambush."

Isaac remembered that Michael had boldly faced the whole Blackwood family later the day of the shooting and delivered the same declaration. It had made no difference to the Blackwoods then. It made no difference to Finis now.

Finis said, "This is a nice-lookin' place you got, Michael. Good-lookin' woman over yonder, and I seen a young'un too. I ain't got none of that. I ain't likely to ever have none of that.

I can't work the land like a man that's got two arms. And you have any idea how a woman looks at a man that's just got a stump of an arm? Turns their stomachs, it does."

Michael said nothing. But Andrew challenged, "It ain't the arm that turns their stomachs, Finis. You ever take a bath? You ever shave so you can get a good look at yourself?"

Isaac could see his brother's ears reddening, a twitch beginning around his eyes. When that happened, Finis sometimes lost what good sense he otherwise had. Isaac said nervously, "We're gettin' nothin' done here, Finis. Let's be goin'."

When Finis showed no sign that he had heard, Isaac reached out and gripped his good arm. "Come on, Finis. Let's git."

Finis angrily shook loose. "Shut up, Isaac. We ain't leavin' here till we've took care of business."

Michael said, "We've *got* no further business, Finis." He shifted his rifle from a cradled position to the ready.

Finis was seething. "There's a lot of things could happen to a man, Michael. That fine cabin of yours, it could burn down some night with you in it, and that woman, and that button too. Your stock could all turn up dead, and your fields could burn off just before the harvest. There's lots of things could happen to an unlucky man."

Andrew had followed Michael's lead and had his rifle aimed loosely somewhere between Luke and Isaac. Michael's was pointed straight at Finis. Isaac felt a deep chill and wondered if Finis was so enraged now that he could not see what was fixing to happen to him—to all of them.

"Finis," he pleaded, "for God's sake—"

Luke declared, "We can git them both, Finis."

Isaac's lungs ached from holding his breath. His hands were slick and wet on the stock of his rifle. He felt death in the air, strong as the tingle he sometimes got from an electrical storm. If firing erupted, he had no choice. He had to try to defend his brothers. A protest stuck in his throat. He wanted to cry "No!", but it would not come out.

He saw a movement in the timber down by the river. Horsemen, a lot of them. He tried to tell Finis, but his throat was too tight.

Luke saw them too, turning his head abruptly in their direction. "Finis," he shouted, "looky yonder! Indians comin'!"

It was not Indians, Isaac realized. It was soldiers, fifteen, no, more like twenty of them.

Finis tore his attention from Michael, but Michael's gaze never left Finis for an instant. He asked his brother, "What is it, Andrew?"

Andrew turned. "Mexican soldiers, Michael." He showed a semblance of a smile. "The officer in charge, I think maybe he's our old friend Zaragosa."

Isaac looked at his oldest brother. He saw rage turn to consternation and consternation to fear in Finis's eyes. Finis swallowed hard. He lowered the rifle to his lap. Defeat was in his voice. "Them soldiers is friends of yours, Michael?"

Michael's gaze was still riveted to Finis. "One of them, anyway."

Luke was near panic, for he had heard stories from Paw about Spanish soldiers shooting American prisoners ten years ago. Spanish—Mexican—to him they were all the same. He pleaded, "Let's run, Finis, before they git us."

Relief helped Isaac find his voice. "They'd catch up to us before we went a mile."

Finis mustered a semblance of nerve again. His voice scolded. "Michael, what kind of an American *are* you? You got a wife that talks funny. Now you got some Mexico soldier friend comin' to save you."

Isaac would not tell his brother for fifty dollars in United States gold, but he had a strong notion it was not the Lewises those soldiers were fixing to save.

8

MICHAEL LEWIS decided finally that the Blackwoods were no longer a threat. Dread of the soldiers was plain in their eyes, especially Luke's. Michael remembered from old times in Tennessee that Luke had never been very fast in the head. He had a streak of cruelty broader even than Finis's, but he was easier to scare. Michael was a little surprised to see relief in Isaac Blackwood's face. He had always considered Isaac the smartest of the bunch but badly misled by his older brothers. He would like to give Isaac the benefit of the doubt, but he could not overlook the fact that he was, after all, a Blackwood. The taint in the blood might be diluted some—maybe his mama had met a traveling man—but it was still there.

Michael turned half around to see what the soldiers were doing. They had paused at the cabin. Marie stood in the open dog-run, pointing toward the field and gesturing with both hands. Her easy command of Spanish had been handy on those rare occasions when soldiers or Mexican officials came around. Michael had learned enough Spanish that he would not starve to death for want of communication should he somehow become stranded in Mexican territory, but he doubted that he could hold down his end of any complicated conversation. Andrew had been an easier learner when it came to languages. Michael attributed that to his being more sociable. Andrew could horse-trade more easily with the occasional Mexican entrepreneurs who came through the colony to buy or sell livestock.

Zaragosa doffed his hat, bowed in the saddle, and turned away from Marie. He started toward the field, his troops following. Michael felt the old chill that uniformed soldiers always gave him, even though this time they had come at a most opportune moment.

Luke's voice trembled. "They fixin' to shoot us?"

Michael thought that might not be a bad idea. But Andrew seized upon the moment as a chance to guarantee the Blackwoods' good behavior. "Not if you do just what they tell you. But raise an eyebrow wrong and they're liable to blast you right off of your horse."

Michael doubted that. However, the Blackwoods seemed to accept it as gospel fact. Michael would not give them comfort by denying his brother's words.

Zaragosa rode directly to Michael and Andrew, reining his shiny black horse up beside them, facing the Blackwoods. He held a long flintlock pistol that looked heavy enough to club a man to death if the shot missed. It was not pointed directly at any of the Blackwoods, but it might as well have been for the fear it put into Luke Blackwood's eyes. The soldiers fanned out in a ragged line on either side of the lieutenant as if to cut off any notion of flight by the three brothers. Zaragosa spoke a greeting to the Lewises in Spanish. Michael brought himself to answer, "*Buenos dias,* Zaragosa." He liked Zaragosa the man, but the uniform aroused chilling old memories that could easily get in the way of friendship.

Andrew said something a little more complicated than *Buenos dias*; he enjoyed using his Spanish.

The officer turned to a young corporal who sat on a bay horse beside him. He talked rapidly. The young soldier in turn translated into a clipped, strongly accented English while Zaragosa fastened a stern gaze upon the Blackwoods.

"My lieutenant says you will dismount from the horses. You will place your rifles upon the ground."

Finis did not comply. His brother Isaac said curtly, "Better listen at him, Finis. Or ain't you counted them?"

Finis swallowed and pulled his gaze from the officer. "Damn you, Michael, you've always had the devil's own luck."

Michael replied, "I don't know if it was our good luck or yours, them comin'. Either way, you'd best listen to what the soldiers say. I've seen what they can do. So's your old daddy."

The young soldier translated Michael's words for the lieutenant's benefit, though Michael sensed that Zaragosa understood most of it. The lieutenant nodded gravely as if to reinforce Michael's dark warning.

Isaac dismounted, laying down his rifle and gripping Finis's reins with his big-knuckled right hand. "Come on, Finis. Ain't no show for us now but to do what they tell us."

The young soldier listened to the officer a moment, then asked of Finis, "You have land in Esteban Austin's colony?"

Finis sat slumped in defeat and did not reply. Isaac did it for him. "No, we just now come out of Tennessee."

The soldier translated, then came back with, "The lieutenant, he says it is better you *return* to Tennessee. People who make trouble, there is no room for them in Texas."

Finis grumbled, "We got a right."

The soldier's face flushed with sudden anger. He did not wait for his officer to reply. "You are *americano*. You have no rights in Texas but those our government gives you. Here, the lieutenant is the government. He says you do not stay."

Finis lost what little momentary bluster he had managed. He dismounted as ordered and laid his rifle carefully on the green grass. Luke followed his example, trembling. The officer spoke, and a soldier gathered up all three weapons, carefully blowing the powder out of the pans as a precaution.

The officer turned back to Michael and Andrew, taking time now to shake hands. Michael steeled himself a little and looked directly into Zaragosa's friendly brown face, trying to see only an old acquaintance and not the uniform. It was difficult to shut out the other soldiers. Their presence, welcome though it was, rekindled the painful memory of the day Span-

ish troops had killed his father and the other men who had ridden with him. Michael felt his mouth going dry. He was not
much of a whiskey-drinking man, but at this moment he could
have done good service with a jug of Kentucky squeezings.

Andrew evidenced no such reservations. He grinned like a
fox stealing grapes and said how glad he was to see Zaragosa
and his men. Andrew asked, "Whichaway you headed,
amigo?"

The young interpreter answered, "We go to San Felipe de
Austin, then up to Nacogdoches. The lieutenant says we will
take these men with us and see that they leave Texas."

Isaac Blackwood asked carefully, "You sayin' we're your
prisoners?"

The lieutenant replied through the interpreter, "Let us say
you are our guests. We would be most hurt if you did not remain our guests all the way to the Sabine River."

Luke glanced woefully at his older brother. "The Sabine?
Ain't that the one we swum over gittin' out of Louisiana?
That's a powerful long ways."

Andrew put in, "A long ways. Too far for you to be
a-comin' back." He narrowed his eyes. "Was they to catch you
tryin', they'd shoot you like as not, and throw you into a bush
belly-up like they'd do a snake."

Andrew had always been one to spread the butter good and
thick, Michael thought. Michael's own inclination would have
been to tell them that if they came back *he* would shoot them
like snakes. But in the stifling presence of the soldiers he kept
his mouth shut.

He was gratified to see fear stark and cold in Finis's eyes.
Cruel, cold-blooded though he might be, Finis Blackwood
was a coward, like his daddy before him. Old Cyrus Blackwood had betrayed his fellow Tennesseans to the Spanish military to save his own skin. He bore the stain of Judas. Finis
was cut from the same shoddy piece of cloth. Michael did not
think Finis would try anything foolish now, not with so many
Mexican soldiers ready to cut him down. And Luke would not
do anything unless Finis put him up to it. He had no initiative
of his own.

Isaac? Michael was not sure what to make of Isaac. He saw no fear in Isaac's eyes; only an odd sort of relief that left Michael puzzled. He surmised that Isaac's heart had not been totally committed to this little sashay in the first place.

Finis grumbled, "We still ain't settled nothin', Michael."

"There's nothin' left to settle. Looks to me like the soldiers have taken care of it all."

"Maybe. And maybe you'll see us again sometime. Me and you still got us an accountin'."

"You better write it *paid* and forget about it, Finis."

Andrew invited Zaragosa and his soldiers to camp and be the Lewises' guests. Michael flinched. He would be pleased to host Zaragosa, but all those troopers, looking so much like the men who had slaughtered the Tennesseans on an open prairie so long ago—He closed his eyes and tried to shut out the insistent image that kept coming back.

Zaragosa eased his fears. He had never gotten down from the big black horse. Through the corporal he said, "I much regret that I must decline. Many hours remain of the daylight, and we would wish to be much nearer San Felipe before night. We would visit Esteban Austin in the morning. It is yet a long way to Nacogdoches."

Michael did not give Andrew a chance to argue. He said, "We understand. It's probably best that way. The farther you take the Blackwoods away from this place, the better we'll feel."

Zaragosa spoke for himself. "There is old trouble here?"

Michael gritted his teeth, glancing at the Blackwoods, then at Zaragosa. "You remember the wretch who betrayed my father to the soldiers?"

Zaragosa nodded grimly. "I remember." The royalist zealot Lieutenant Armando Rodriguez had ordered Zaragosa to shoot both the wounded boy Michael and the cringing old Cyrus Blackwood. Zaragosa had disobeyed at considerable peril to himself.

Michael pointed his chin toward the Blackwoods. "That was the daddy of these men here. The blood ain't improved a bit."

Zaragosa's interest quickened as he studied the three brothers. He acknowledged the family resemblance.

Isaac Blackwood appeared saddened. "Then it's true. Paw always swore that what you said was a lie."

Michael replied, "Ol' Cyrus swore a lot."

Isaac pondered. "Then this here soldier saved Paw's life, and yours."

Michael shuddered, remembering how close it had been. "He did."

Finis raised his stump of an arm. "It's a damn shame he didn't kill you. I'd still be a whole man."

Michael gritted, "You never was a whole man, Finis. Even before you made me shoot you, you was a moral cripple."

Zaragosa drew the conversation to a close. He nodded affably to Michael and Andrew. "Now we must go. *Adiós, amigos*." He touched spurs to his black horse and reined him eastward. His troopers closed around the Blackwoods and followed.

Finis turned in the saddle and shouted back. "It ain't over, Michael." A soldier prodded him with the muzzle of a musket.

Michael heard Isaac say, "Better hush, Finis."

He thought there might be hope for *one* Blackwood.

NEITHER MICHAEL nor Andrew spoke until the soldiers and the Blackwoods had gone several hundred yards along the tree-lined river. Andrew gave an audible sigh of relief. "Not to complain about your shed, Michael, but maybe now I can afford to go home and get a good night's sleep in my own bed."

Michael lowered his rifle to arm's length. He had not realized he still held it cradled in his arms as if for quick duty. "Surely you wasn't afraid of them Blackwoods. The worst day we ever had, we could've taken care of ourselves against such as them."

"I expected them to sneak up and try to shoot you in the back."

"They never could shoot very straight."

Andrew shrugged. "Even a blind hog'll find an acorn once in a while." He looked back toward the cabin. Marie still stood in the dog-run, watching, though she had put her rifle away.

With a touch of regret he said, "I only regret that I can't stay around here and eat at Marie's table. It's back to my own cookin'."

Michael thought his brother had put on a few pounds in the days he had spent here, helping watch for the Blackwoods. Like just about every bachelor Michael had known, Andrew had done himself proud when he had a chance to eat in a woman's kitchen. "No use bein' in a hurry about it. We'd just as well finish the day in this field, and let Marie fix supper for you."

Andrew was still looking toward the cabin. Michael saw something in his brother's eyes that bothered him. It appeared there every time Marie was in sight. If it had been someone other than his brother—Michael said, "You know what's the matter with your cabin, don't you?"

"The matter? Ain't nothin' the matter with it. The roof's tight, and the walls are chinked good and proper."

"It's too empty. Needs a woman in it. There's bound to be a likely young lady someplace, just waitin' for you to fetch her a bouquet."

"Marie's been tellin' me the same thing. But women are even scarcer around here than money."

"If a man can't catch fish on his own side of the stream, he goes where the fish are hungry and bitin'."

Dryly Andrew replied, "It's a long ways from here to anywhere. And I got mighty little for bait. You can't swap a bundle of winter pelts for a woman like you'd swap for coffee and beans. Even if you could find one."

"You've got a land claim. You've got a future. That's all I had when me and Marie got married. It's still all I've got, except for her and the baby. She don't complain."

"She never would; Marie's special. You could hunt for ten years and not find another like her."

Michael frowned. He had long sensed that his brother was drawn to Marie. He was convinced it was not a personal thing, especially. It was just the natural attraction of a man to a woman, any woman, when he lived alone. Michael told himself it was nothing that need ever worry him. The situation would resolve itself when Andrew found a woman of his own. If he found a woman of his own.

Andrew seemed uneasy with this subject and changed the conversation's direction. "This was one time that seein' soldiers didn't seem to upset your liver too much."

That was easy to say, Michael thought; Andrew couldn't see the tension they had aroused within him. "Zaragosa was with them. Anyway, if they hadn't showed up we might've had to kill that whole bunch of Blackwoods. They wouldn't be worth the aggravation." Michael looked up at the afternoon sun. "Let's see how many more rows we can get planted before sundown."

He fed the animals in the fading light of the spring evening before seeing to his and Andrew's own supper. It had always been a cardinal rule among the Lewises that the welfare of their livestock was the first order of business. A man could miss a few meals without dire consequences, but if his animals went hungry he might find himself afoot, or with nothing to pull a plow.

Andrew went to the cabin to fetch the wooden milk bucket, carrying an armload of firewood in for Marie as he went. Michael frowned, watching. It was a good thing Andrew didn't stay here all the time; he would have Marie too spoiled to live with.

Returning with the bucket, Andrew said, "I'll leave Ol' Boss with you till your cow freshens. That boy needs the milk a lot more than I do." He put some feed in the trough and sat on a handmade wooden stool, setting the bucket beneath the cow's udder. The cords bulged on the backs of his hands as he rhythmically set about the milking. It was a job Michael had never found to his liking, though he had done it often enough. It was like following the ox and the plow, a necessity but hardly a pleasure. He would rather be out in the forest, hunting fresh meat. By contrast, Andrew seemed to enjoy the task. They were brothers and had been close all their lives, but there were some things about Andrew that Michael would never understand.

Michael observed, "Ol' Boss always stomps at the bucket when I try to milk her. She gets along a lot better with Marie."

Andrew shook his head. "That's just an excuse so you don't have to milk her yourself. You'd better take good care of Marie. You'd never find her like again."

"I don't intend to ever look."

ZARAGOSA GLANCED back once before the Lewis cabin dropped out of sight behind him. He had been tempted to accept Andrew's offer and camp the night on the river. It would have been pleasant to spend a few hours in the glowing company of Michael's wife Marie, for she reminded him considerably of his own Elvira. He found himself missing his wife terribly, though he had been away from her only three days. He would be fortunate if he got back to her within three months. When he returned from this mission he would give serious thought to her father's offer of a place on the family farm. Soldiering was all right for a bachelor, but it involved too much traveling for a man who had a family. This trip made him realize how much he was tiring of it.

He would have liked to have listened longer to Marie Lewis's lively version of Spanish. It had a little of the intriguing accent that came from the relative isolation of her forebears in northern Texas and Louisiana, and perhaps just a trace of the French influence imposed by her father. Marie and Elvira would get along nicely, he thought. But it was unlikely they would ever meet, for the social and cultural division between the Mexican town of Bexar and the American colonies to the east was like a great stone wall that could be climbed from neither side.

He felt this same alienation even from the two Lewis brothers, though he had known and liked them for several years. It was a pity, for he would prefer to be a closer friend. Language was just one of the barriers that stood between them.

The three Blackwoods seemed, by the tone of their voices, to be quarreling among themselves. The young Corporal

Diaz, the interpreter, dropped back to listen discreetly. Presently Zaragosa nodded for him to come forward. He asked, "What is the disagreement between them?"

"The two are blaming the young one. They say he could have shot Miguel Lewis from a distance and spared them all this trouble. He is saying they were wrong to come here at all."

"So long as they quarrel among themselves perhaps they will not give us trouble."

"I do not think they will give us trouble anyway. They are frightened of us, especially the two. They speak of their father and what happened to him."

"Perhaps I should have followed my orders ten years ago and killed him. The world would not have mourned the loss."

Diaz considered a while before he asked, "Those two named Lewis—they are really your friends?"

Zaragosa shrugged. "I once saved the life of the one named Miguel. Years later, he and the brother did me a great service in return. Yes, they are friends, as much as any *americanos* can be friends to one of us."

Diaz frowned. "It is hard to see *any* of them as friends."

Zaragosa was a little surprised. "You have lived among them, have you not? I understood that is how you learned to speak English."

Diaz nodded. "My family had a farm not far from Nacogdoches. The Lieutenant Rodriguez decided my father was disloyal to Spain. We had to flee into Louisiana. We lived among the *americanos* until Mexico freed itself from the tyranny."

"Surely you must have made some friends among them."

Diaz pondered darkly. "We lived among them. We worked among them. But friends? Never. We were much too different."

Zaragosa thought he understood, but he asked, "How so?"

"The language, the customs. And the Americans never seemed to have enough of anything. If they had one horse, they wanted two. If they had two horses, they wanted four. If they had a hundred hectares of land, they wanted twice as many. I never could understand their hunger."

"Whether we like it or not, they are among us now."

Diaz shook his head. "Not if the choice were mine. We

have made a mistake, sir, letting them come into Mexico. Wait. Watch. They remain Americans. How long do you think they will be content to live under Mexican laws instead of their own? Even Miguel Lewis who is your friend—did you see how he looked at the rest of us? He does not like us."

Zaragosa said, "That is your imagination." He knew it was not; he had seen the look in Michael Lewis's eyes. But he thought he knew the reason for it; he thought he knew the memories that haunted the Tennessean, for at times they haunted Zaragosa as well.

Diaz turned and looked back with a dark frown at the Blackwoods. "These and their kind will keep coming no matter what we do. The day will come when we will regret that we ever let the first American stay in Texas. The day will come when we will have to go to war with them and take Texas back. Or we will lose it."

Zaragosa turned his gaze back toward the river. Diaz had struck a painful nerve, for the same thought had troubled Zaragosa from time to time. He changed the subject abruptly. "As I remember, there is a nice spring a few miles farther on, which affords fresher water than we can get from the Colorado. We will find it and camp there tonight."

PART II

THE

PRICE

OF

HORSES

9

ANDREW HAD observed with misgivings that Michael was becoming increasingly ill at ease, confined since spring and into the summer to cabin and field and the limited distance which his cattle roamed in their casual grazing along the river. Michael betrayed his restlessness in the way he would sometimes halt whatever he was doing and stare off into the distance, usually westward. One day Andrew found him standing beside the river, the empty wooden bucket in his hand. Michael gazed wistfully upstream, toward the unknown land where the Comanches roamed free. Andrew felt a jolt as he realized how much Michael resembled their father Mordecai, and how often he had seen this look in Mordecai's eyes. Usually it was just before he left on an extended trip to God knew where.

Andrew deemed it prudent not to speak of it openly, but he thought Michael would understand his meaning. "You got a wife here that needs you, and a baby on the way."

Michael stiffened, as if surprised that Andrew had read his mind. He tried to deny what had not even been said. "The corn and the cotton are hoed out good. Marie's been needin' some stuff. I been thinkin' about ridin' down to San Felipe."

San Felipe was to the east. Michael was looking westward. Andrew pondered the possibilities. On the one hand it might relieve some of the pressure if Michael did go to San Felipe and get away by himself for two or three days. But on the other Andrew suspected he would not be content with a trip so short. The limitless and mostly unexplored land that was Texas spoke to men like Michael in ways other men would never hear. Two or three days could stretch into two or three weeks, even two or three months; it often had with Mordecai. And a trip started eastward toward San Felipe could easily turn back upon itself, ending up to the west instead, perhaps even to search out the headwaters of the Colorado River. Of late, Michael had spent a lot of time contemplating the swift-flowing waters.

Many things could happen to Marie while Michael was gone, and few of them good. Andrew lied, "I been thinkin' about goin' to San Felipe myself. Whatever Marie needs, I can fetch it back."

Michael's narrowed blue eyes flashed with quick resentment. "You don't trust me to come home?"

Andrew's voice took an edge of its own. "You'll come home. The only question is: when? I know you, Michael."

"No you don't. You're a farmer at heart. I've had to force myself into that mold, and it's a damned tight fit. You don't know how it binds on me to be tied to one place and not be able to move around free."

"What about Marie? She's tied down too. How long since she's been any farther off this farm than over to the Willets'?"

"She don't have the need. She's a woman. It's in her nature to build a nest and stay there."

"But not by herself. You ain't a free man anymore. You've got a responsibility here." Andrew squared his shoulders. "If anybody goes to San Felipe, it'll be me."

Michael's eyes were narrowed almost to the point of being closed to conceal his full resentment. "When I started to Texas from Tennessee and you tagged along after me, I had a good notion to chase you back. Maybe I ought to've done it."

"Maybe you could've done it then. You couldn't do it now. You need me here to keep you pointed in the right direction."

"I don't need you tryin' to mind my business," Michael declared sharply. He turned away from Andrew and stepped off several angry paces before he stopped. He stood a minute, his back to Andrew. Then he turned again, grudgingly resigned. "Marie'll have to tell you what she's needin'. Can't be much because we got mighty little money to buy anything with."

In Austin's colony, most negotiations were done through barter rather than in coin. All the honest coin for seventy miles along both the Colorado and the Brazos rivers probably would not fill a demijohn.

Andrew tried to smooth over the bad feelings. "I'll bring Ol' Boss down here before I leave. Marie and little Mordecai could probably use the milk."

"No need," Michael said stiffly. "Our cow's givin' more than enough."

Andrew shrugged. "Then I'll just turn her calf out with her till I get back." He paused, then said hopefully, "No hard feelin's?"

"I wouldn't go so far as to say that." Michael walked back to his shed, picked up a hoe and strode stiffly off toward the field, leaving the water bucket empty. Regret weighed heavily upon Andrew as he watched, but he contented himself in the conviction that what he had done was best for Marie. He could only hope that Michael would eventually realize it was for his own benefit as well.

Andrew had always considered Marie beautiful, and she had never been more so than now, her dark eyes sparkling with the anticipated joy of another birth. Her stomach, normally small, was beginning to expand some, but she managed to move with a certain ease and grace. If she had slowed any in her work routine, Andrew was unable to discern it. Watching her bustle about the kitchen, trying to keep up a busy show of normalcy, he felt a melancholy longing to take her into his arms and hold her protectively. This made him cautious about getting close. As much as possible he kept a nervous distance, at least half the width of the room. If she knew, she gave no sign. But he wondered, how could she not know?

He told her, "Michael asked me if I'd mind goin' to San Felipe. Said there's some things you're needin'."

"*You* are going?" She seemed a little surprised. "I thought

Michael—" She smiled thinly then, and the smile said she knew. Andrew had never been a good liar. "Thank you, Andrew. I have much dreaded the day he would go."

Andrew felt some repair was needed. "He wasn't hard to talk out of it. He knows he belongs here with you."

"I would not tell him he should not go. That he must know for himself."

"He knows. Otherwise I couldn't've convinced him so easy."

"I suppose," she said, though her eyes betrayed doubt. "He tries, but he cannot help being as he is. And I would be much wrong to try to force him."

Andrew was eager to change the subject, for discussing Michael's restless nature was as futile as complaining about the hot, humid summer winds that forced their way inland from the Gulf and sometimes left him gasping for a good breath. "What all you needin' from San Felipe?"

"Very little. A Mexican woman is there, a midwife. She puts together a mixture they say helps ease a woman who is"—she searched for a modest way of saying it—"in the hope. I think she would trade some of it for a ham from our smokehouse. It should cost no money."

It pained Andrew to see Marie do without most of life's conveniences. He wondered sometimes what Marie's father, old Baptiste Villaret, would say if he could see how his daughter lived in this rough cabin of oak logs, hands raw from hard work, her few clothes patched and faded from wear and washing. She shunned little niceties that she once had taken for granted, protecting her precious little money for those few things that were absolute necessities. If he knew, the prosperous old French merchant would probably drive a team of good horses to death getting here from Louisiana as quickly as he could. But then, he and his wife had pioneered in their own time; they had not always had the comfort they enjoyed now. Each generation made its own way, invented its own life.

If Andrew were in a hurry, unmindful about the welfare of his mount and the pack horse that carried some winter-cured hides for barter, he could reach the seat of Austin's colony in less than half a day. He took his time, however. He could sympathize with Michael's cooped-up feeling. He had some of the same symptoms, if considerably less severe. Both men had spent many long weeks getting the crops up, properly hoed, and on the way toward harvest. He watched for any new arrivals who might have broken out their first land this spring and summer while he had been too busy with his own place to know what anyone else was doing. The sight of a new farm, of a new chimney sending its friendly smoke skyward, always brought him a sense of satisfaction. It pleased him to see the land becoming populated. He liked knowing he had neighbors close by. The more the better.

By contrast, Michael fretted helplessly when he saw the prairie sod broken and trees cut down. He had favored this land the way it was the day he had first arrived. Sometimes Andrew wondered if Michael did not begrudge even the trees downed for the cabin he shared with Marie and the boy Mordecai. It was certain that Michael saw his field as a necessity and not a joy.

They were brothers, but on this basic issue they sometimes argued. Given his chance, Andrew sometimes thought, Michael would probably move to the moon. There nobody would crowd him.

It was in his mind to spend the night at the cabin of the Willet family, a few miles east of his own place. Old Man Lige Willet could talk the bark off of a tree, and that was what Andrew needed right now, some congenial socializing with people he liked, people beyond just family. They called him Old Man Willet, though in truth he was probably no older than his middle forties. That was old by the standards of the Texas colonies, for this was a young man's province. Breaking out new land, opening a new empire, was young man's work.

The Willet place was larger than either Michael's or Andrew's, for Willet had a sizeable family and qualified for a larger block of land. One of his sons had come of legal age, expanding the family holdings. For a man who loved to talk and played the fiddle better than anyone Andrew had ever heard, Lige Willet was nevertheless about as hardworking and knowledgeable a farmer as Andrew had ever known, perhaps as good as his own Uncle Benjamin back in Tennessee. His fields were clean, his rows straight as a new pine plank fresh from the sawmill. He had even found time to set out an orchard. Willet was going to be a most popular man in two or three years when those trees began bearing fruit enough to make a neighbor's journey worthwhile. Andrew suspected that was the main reason for the orchard in the first place; Willet loved company.

He expected to find Lige in his field, for it was just midafternoon. Several hours of daylight were left for righteous labor before the farmer put the day's due behind him to go in for supper and a leisurely hour or two of talking and fiddle playing to pass the evening. That was the Lord's reward for a day's work well done, Willet always said.

However, Andrew found only the oldest son Zebediah in the field, hoeing out a fine stand of corn. One of the youngest boys, a towhead named Daniel, leaned against the fence. At his feet was a wooden bucket with a tin dipper floating in it. The boy had brought fresh water to his older brother.

Andrew raised his hand and spoke jauntily to the older Willet boy. "You're doin' the work of two mules, Zeb. That'll make an old man out of you."

Zeb was always a serious one, in strong contrast to his jovial father. He nodded and leaned for a moment on the hoe, wiping his sleeve across his forehead. The sleeve was almost the only part of his shirt not soaked with sweat. "Good day to you, Mr. Lewis. If you're lookin' for Papa, he ain't here. He's gone over to help some new neighbors raise them a cabin."

"New neighbors?" Andrew's interest was immediately aroused. "Whichaway?"

Zeb pointed eastward. "Couple of miles down the trail toward San Felipe. Ain't hardly no way you can miss it. Folks' name is Nathan."

Andrew dismounted and walked up to the boy at the fence. "You got enough water to spare me a drink, Daniel?"

The boy, about seven or eight, had a grin that looked wide as a barrel hoop. "If I ain't, I'll go fetch another bucket." He was like his father; the more people around him, the better he felt.

Michael took a long drink of water from the dipper, then sipped a little more while he admired the standing corn and told Zeb what a good job he and his father were doing. Young Daniel pointed enthusiastically. "Papa traded and got me a pony. He's out yonder if you'd like to see him."

Zeb said with mild rebuke, "You oughtn't to pester everybody who comes along about that pony, Daniel. They ain't all as interested as you are."

Andrew caught disappointment in the boy's eyes. "I'd be tickled to look at him. I been thinkin' about findin' a pony for Michael's boy Mordecai. He'll pretty soon be gettin' big enough to learn how to ride."

He tied the pack horse to the fence and motioned for the boy to swing up behind his saddle. They rode off in the direction Daniel pointed. A little east of the family's sprawled log cabin they came upon half a dozen horses grazing. Daniel said proudly, "That there is him, the sorrel one."

The pony was of a nondescript nature, looking like a scrub out of a wild mustang band. Andrew praised him nevertheless, and the boy beamed proudly. Andrew said, "I didn't know you-all had this many horses."

"Papa done some tradin' with an old man who come down from Louisiana. Him and the old man went over to the new neighbors' place this mornin' to see if they'll be needin' any horses."

"What old man was that?" Andrew asked.

"I disremember his name. Just an old man with gray whiskers. Papa traded him some pelts and stuff. You ever seen a prettier pony?"

"Don't reckon I ever did."

He returned the boy to the field and retrieved the pack horse. He waved his hand at Zebediah, who had worked his way far down a row. Andrew then set out eastward in an easy trot that would not tax the animals. It was in his mind that if he came across the old man from Louisiana he wouldn't mind trading his brown mount for a better one. Trouble was, he probably had nothing much to offer for boot. Texas was big and fresh and beautiful and new but almighty stingy with its material blessings.

In a place where last spring he had ridden across an open grassland prairie, he found a family just starting the raising of a log cabin. They had evidently lived out of their wagon until they got their field broken and planted, which showed they had their priorities in order. Their crops appeared late, however. That meant they would go into fall praying for a late frost so they would not lose the corn before it could reach maturity.

Andrew knew the people had spotted him when he was still three hundred yards away, for a man stopped chopping and trimming a pine log that lay on the ground. He waved his hat as a sign for Andrew to come on in. There had been times and places when the first thing a man did upon seeing a stranger was to fetch his rifle, just in case. Andrew surmised that these folks came from a civilized country.

He recognized Old Man Willet a hundred yards or so before he reached the cabin. Willet, a broad-shouldered, broad-hipped man of some two hundred pounds, walked out to meet and greet Andrew. "Come on in here, Andrew Lewis, and meet these good folks. We need one more strong back, anyway, to help us lift them logs up where they're needful."

Like his young son Daniel, Lige Willet had a grin wide as a barrel hoop. Andrew could not conceive of his having an enemy anywhere in the world. Willet was a red-faced man with an unruly shock of rust-colored hair curling out from under an old black hat that had probably been new twenty years ago. Andrew swung down from his horse. He endured the crushing grip of the man's ham-sized hand and the breath-taking slap of that same hand across the middle of his back. "Miles Nathan," Willet declared in a happy voice loud enough to carry back to his own cabin, "I'd like you to meet Andrew Lewis. Him and his brother Michael are your neighbors a ways on up the river."

"Howdy," Nathan said. He drove the blade of his ax into the end of a log and left it there. Like Willet, he was a large man with a ruddy, deeply creased face that easily broke into a broad smile. He wiped the back of a big hand across his sweaty face and walked forward, extending the other hand. "If Willet vouches for you, you're mighty welcome at our house. I can't say *in* our house because we ain't got it finished yet."

If any bones in Andrew's hand remained uncrushed after Willet's grip, they fell victim to Nathan's, strong enough to choke a bear. This was a lonesome country where no man remained a stranger long.

Nathan made a broad sweep with his hand. "This here is my family."

Andrew took off his hat in deference to a bonneted woman in her thirties. Nearby stood a girl. He guessed her at twelve to perhaps fourteen. Some shy of marrying age, he thought, then wondered why such a notion had even come into his head. He said, "My sister-in-law Marie'll be tickled to hear we've got some new neighbors."

Nathan said, "We knowed there was folks up thataway, but we been too busy to come callin'. Didn't get our seed planted till late. If we don't make a crop, we're apt to have us a mighty long, thin winter."

Andrew nodded, remembering. The same thing had happened to him and Michael and Marie their first year. They had managed to survive largely on wild game. Now the hunting had already been compromised because the land was becoming more densely settled. What the Lewises had done, these people might not be able to do. Well, he and Michael would not let them suffer. Nor would the Willets. They would share if the need came; that was the way people did in a pioneer country like this. Andrew looked at the children, ranging in age from two or three—about the size of little Mordecai—up to the girl. By the time they got grown, this land would see a lot of changes.

Andrew had to stare wishfully for a moment at the wagon. The Nathans were fortunate to have it, for wagons remained a luxury in Austin's colony. They were difficult to transport the long distance overland and prohibitively expensive to ship to the Texas coast by sea. Most people packed their goods on horseback or on mules, or they built a log sled, like a raft on skids, often difficult for horses or oxen to pull. Andrew and Michael had little hope of acquiring a wagon for a few years yet.

He figured the Nathan family would be mighty popular around these parts. Sharing with neighbors was like an eleventh commandment, and a lot of people would want to borrow that wagon.

Mrs. Nathan's face was half hidden by the long bonnet that cast a shadow over her features, but her rough hands bore ample evidence of a life of hard work. Her eyes betrayed no complaint, and her smile was broad. "I'll fix you men some coffee," she said, and turned back toward the canvas-covered wagon. "Come along, Birdy, and stoke up the fire a little."

Andrew decided to bide a while with this good company. He pitched in to help shape the logs for the cabin wall, answering Nathan's urgent questions about the land, the seasons, the best ways of coaxing a good crop out of the soil. Andrew assured him that Willet was the best man to advise him. "He's the best farmer on the Colorado River," he said. "Me and Michael, we come over to his place and take lessons from him."

Willet beamed, enjoying the kind words.

Andrew stopped once to catch his breath. He could hear the ring of an ax somewhere in the woods. Someone out there was felling more trees for the cabin.

Nathan said, "Willet tells me you've had very little Indian trouble."

"None, really," Andrew replied. "We been lucky. The folks down on the Gulf've had some bad dealin's with the Karankawas. Some I know up this way have been visited by the Wacos and the Tawakonis. Mostly they just steal horses if they get the chance. But I wouldn't much like them to catch me out all by myself, with no rifle."

Willet shrugged off the discussion of Indians. "I ain't even seen one the whole time I've lived here. The only rifle I've got stays at the house where my wife can use it to defend her layin'-hens from the varmints. Was I you, neighbor Nathan,

I'd worry more about wolves than about Indians. They'll make short work of your chickens and then go after your calves."

Nathan nodded in satisfaction, watching his wife pour part of the contents of a pot into three cups. "They told us in San Felipe that this'd be a good place to put our roots down, but it's a comfort to hear it from people who've lived here a while."

The "coffee" was, as Andrew suspected, a substitute made from parched corn. It occurred to him to wonder if anybody had ever planted coffee beans here. He thought he might try. There were probably twelve good reasons why it wouldn't work, but he would find them all before he gave up. Parched corn made a poor drink, though he assured Mrs. Nathan that it was the best he had had since leaving Tennessee. It was not always a sin to lie to one's neighbors.

He saw a movement at the edge of the wood, in the direction from which he had earlier heard the ax at work. He saw a big workhorse dragging a log. Behind, holding to the long reins, trudged a rail-thin man whose stride bespoke considerable age. Andrew squinted, trying to see him better, for something in the man's movements seemed familiar.

"Who is that?" he asked.

Willet turned to look. "That's an old feller who come down with some horses to trade for whatever we might have that he could sell in Louisiana. I swapped him some of last winter's pelfry catch for three horses. Ain't very good horses, but they can all walk."

Andrew nodded. "Daniel showed me his pony. What's the old man's name?"

Willet glanced at Nathan. "Eli's his first name. I disremember if I even heard his last."

Andrew's heartbeat quickened. "Pleasant?"

"Yeah," Willet said, "he's a pleasant old feller, for a horse trader."

"That too, but is his name Pleasant? Eli Pleasant?"

Miles Nathan nodded. "That's right. I remember him tellin' me. You know him?"

"I'd know his hide in a tanyard."

Willet remarked, "A skinny hide it'd be. Ain't much body inside it."

"Maybe not, but there's a heart in it as strong as a lion. I've told you about him, Lige. He was a friend of my father's, and he brought my brother Michael back from the gates of hell."

He walked out toward Eli Pleasant, then in his eagerness broke into a run. The workhorse pulling the log shied away. Eli Pleasant sawed on the lines and commanded, "Whoa there! Whoa now!" To Andrew he shouted, "You, farmer, don't you know better than to run at a horse thataway?"

"And you, old man, have you plumb lost your eyesight that you don't know me?"

"My God!" exclaimed Eli Pleasant. He dropped the lines on the ground and strode forward to meet Andrew. They threw their arms around one another and danced a jubilant little jig.

When they were done, Andrew stepped back for a good look. "I swear, Eli, you ain't got a day younger."

"And you, little brother Andrew, you ain't learned a damned thing about horses."

10

ANDREW PICKED up the lines and started the plowhorse to pulling the log again. Eli walked alongside him, more than willing to yield the heavy work to a much younger man. He asked eagerly about Michael and Marie and how many children they had. "Always thought the world of your brother," Eli said warmly. "And I promised Ol' Man Villaret that I'd visit his daughter and his grandchildren if I was to find the place where you-all had settled at."

"They could easy have told you in San Felipe," Andrew pointed out. "Austin has a map on his wall."

Eli shook his head. "Me and Mr. Austin, we got a difference of opinion. The Mexican government has some kind of a notion that I ought to pay duty on whatever I bring into Texas. Austin, he'd see that I went to a Mexican *calabozo* if I was to let him lay hands on me. So I taken roundance on San Felipe."

Eli Pleasant was by trade a smuggler. Long ago he had begun making a career of smuggling trade goods into Spanish Texas from Louisiana, defying the customs officials, and had smuggled Spanish goods back into Louisiana. When Mexico became independent, he had seen no reason to change his occupation, for it was regarded as a necessary and honorable one by the settlers who benefited from it. This ancient trade was condemned only by the officials. Eli had never been particular what government he cheated out of its revenues.

Andrew decided there was no hurry about his getting to San Felipe and back home. The longer he took, the more time Michael would have to get over his resentment about the spoiling of his plan to travel. Andrew found himself enjoying the company, the easy camaraderie that went into cutting and shaping the logs and raising the walls of the cabin. And Mrs. Nathan knew her way around the cookfire. The Nathans were Alabama people. Mrs. Nathan's cooking reminded him of his mother's.

She voiced her anticipation of being able to move into the cabin and cook on a real hearth after all these months living out of the wagon. "It'll be a blessin'," she said. "Almost like we'd never left home."

The American colonists who had come into Texas had brought their old ways with them and had tried to duplicate in this new land the customs and the atmosphere they had left behind them in the old. Thus Texas had as yet developed few characteristics that were specifically its own. It was, in the main, still a rough copy of the Southern states.

Mrs. Nathan said, "The only thing lackin' now is a preacher to help us offer proper thanks for all the Lord has given us. Been a long time since we've been to proper services."

Ministers were about as scarce as real money in the colony, but Andrew said, "If I happen across one, I'll send him to you."

At night they sat around the dying fire and talked of old times back in Tennessee and Alabama and, in Lige Willet's case, Kentucky. After listening to Willet relate for an hour all the glories of the bluegrass country, Andrew wondered how he had ever brought himself to leave it.

Eli Pleasant related his dark memories of the trip he had made to Texas with Andrew and Michael's father and an eager group of Tennesseans, seeking wild horses to take back and sell to farmers. Michael, fifteen then, had followed behind, joining the group when they were too far from home for his father to send him back. After they had captured a sizeable bunch of Texas mustangs, the chronically quarrelsome Cyrus

Blackwood defected in anger. Captured by Spanish soldiers, he betrayed the rest of the band to save himself. Eli missed the slaughter because he had ridden out to recapture some runaway animals. Finding Michael lying wounded among the many slain, he carried him to a Mexican family for first treatment, then spirited him out of Texas to recover in the Louisiana home of the Villaret family. It was then that Michael and Marie had begun a friendship that years later led to marriage.

"Mean times they was," Eli said gravely. "I hope we never see their likes again."

Andrew observed, "We're under Mexico now instead of Spain. It's different."

The dancing light of the fire made the age lines look terribly deep in Eli's bewhiskered face. "Maybe."

They raised the walls the second day with the help of two bachelor neighbors to the east who came drifting in. The roof was well along when Andrew decided on the third day that the Nathans had more help than they needed. "I reckon I'll get on down to San Felipe," he said to Eli. "You just follow the river west and you'll come to Michael's place. Him and Marie'll be tickled to see you."

Eli shook his hand. "If you happen into Mr. Austin, I'd as soon you didn't remember me to him. I ain't as fast on my feet as I used to was."

Andrew promised the Nathans that he would stop by on his way back from San Felipe and perhaps eat the first meal cooked on the hearth in their new cabin. Then he set off to complete the trip he had started three days earlier. He was two hours on the trail when he encountered a trio of settlers, a father and two sons who said their name was Mann. Their home was up on the Brazos River. Quenton Mann, the elder, rode a mule. Harlan, the older of the sons, rode a young gelding that seemed not yet well broken. The other rode a black mare Andrew thought was old enough to have carried George Washington. They were looking for some lost horses, they said. They showed Andrew a set of tracks they had been following. The tracks led southward.

"Looks pretty clear to us that they was stole," said the father. "They ain't never showed any inclination to leave home. All we got left to ride is these three. They're just one notch better than bein' afoot."

For a fleeting moment Andrew thought of Eli and the horses he was trading in the colony. He quickly dismissed that notion and felt a little guilty over entertaining it at all. Eli skirted along the edge of the customs laws, but he had never been regarded as a thief. The Austin colony had suffered little from thievery, thanks to Austin's careful selection of the people he accepted as settlers. This was the sort of thing Andrew would have expected from the Blackwoods, but they had been escorted out of Texas. Another thought occurred to him. "You-all ever have Indian trouble up your way?"

The father glanced uneasily at his sons. "That possibility has crossed our minds."

"If it was Indians and you found them, what would you do?"

The father shrugged. "See how fast a mule and a wore-out old horse can run."

Andrew wished them luck and watched them for a few minutes as they proceeded southward, following the tracks.

His first move in San Felipe was to find the Mexican midwife and trade her the ham he had brought from Michael's smokehouse for the preparation Marie hoped would ease her pregnancy discomforts. He rode then to the store and traded the proprietor the hides from his pack horse for a few supplies.

He seldom visited the settlement without paying a courtesy call upon Stephen Austin, without whose self-sacrifice and sometimes painful negotiations with the authorities none of these Americans would have been allowed to settle in Mexican Texas. He found Austin looking harried and overworked as usual. After some casual small talk about Michael and Marie and crop prospects up on the Colorado River, Andrew mentioned his encounter with the horse-hunting Manns. It was the first Austin had heard. He said, "It is possible that some of those blackguards who have illegally settled the redlands up against Louisiana have come down here to see what they can steal. Or it could be Mexican outlaws from the south.

But most likely the horses simply strayed. I will make some inquiry and see if anyone else has had losses."

He gave Andrew a moment's frowning study. "I realize you are isolated and do not see many people out where you live. But I wonder if you have heard of any discontent, any stirring against the government?"

It was a question Austin asked almost every time Andrew saw him. "Nothin' of any consequence."

"If any should arise, I hope you will do what you can to stifle it before it spreads. Such a thing is very dangerous for our position here in Texas."

As Andrew prepared to go, Austin said, "If you are not in a hurry, I hear a rumor that there is a minister about, and he plans to hold services tonight out at the Hawkins farm."

"Are you goin'?"

"I cannot. Under the laws of Mexico, only Catholic services are allowed to be conducted here. As *alcalde* it would be my duty to take legal action should I witness any violation."

"But if you know about it—"

Austin smiled. "I know nothing. One hears rumors about many things. One cannot waste his time running after every rumor." It was not always the letter of the law that counted in colonial Texas; it was the appearance of law.

It occurred to Andrew that he might talk this minister into riding out to the Nathans' place. A visit from a man of the cloth would please Mrs. Nathan almost as much as moving into the new cabin. Marie would probably enjoy such a visit as well, though her French and Spanish upbringing had given her the faith officially sanctioned by Mexico. "I believe I'll go. A little churchin' wouldn't hurt me too much."

He stopped a while to share some catfish at the invitation of the village blacksmith who, when not busy, liked to walk down to the river and cast a line into the deep waters. Andrew asked directions to the Hawkins farm. It was west and a little south, not far off the trail he customarily used. On the way he met several settler families, some afoot, some on horseback, a couple in wagons, all traveling in the same direction. The Catholic church periodically sent a priest into the settlements to do marryings, baptisms, and conduct mass, and occasionally Protestant ministers clandestinely made the rounds, but these happenings were irregular and unpredictable. Given any notice at all, they usually drew a large and grateful crowd.

It was dusk when Andrew arrived. He estimated that close to a hundred people were gathered around a double log cabin. Because the summer weather was beneficent, and the cabin much too small for so many, the services were being conducted outdoors. The minister stood in the open dog-run, his back to Andrew. A large gathering crowded in front of him. Andrew could see that he was baptising several babies of varying sizes, born since the last clerical visitation. A large black-bound Bible sat on a chair beside him, but he did not need it. He was reciting the Scriptures at length by heart. The voice was deep and strong and reassuring. It also sounded somehow familiar.

Andrew tied his horses out away from the services, among those of the earlier arrivals, and strode around toward the front of the cabin to join those already in place. He heard the minister declaring, "Now we have come to join these couples in holy matrimony in the presence of the Lord and the sight of this company." Andrew wondered idly if any of the babies belonged to one or more of the three couples he saw standing before the dog-run, awaiting marriage ceremonies. Probably not, but such a thing was by no means unknown in isolated settlements where the Lord's messengers seldom came. The minister now had the Bible in his left hand and his right hand uplifted. "You will repeat after me—"

Standing on the far edge of the crowd, Andrew could not see the minister well. The man was shrouded in the gloom of the roofed-over dog-run and the gathered dusk. But he felt he had heard that voice before, or one very much like it. The minister exhorted the couples to be true to one another and to the Lord's covenants, to go forth and multiply and fill this pagan province with true believers. "It is your mission, and that of your descendants, to take this new land and bring it to full blossom, to make it an empire that will shine forevermore in the glory of Him who sent us here."

Andrew thought Mrs. Nathan would enjoy hearing that message.

The marrying done, the minister gave a short prayer, then told the congregation, "If you good people will forgive me, I must pause for a bit of supper to rebuild my strength so I may properly deliver the urgent message of salvation I have brought for you tonight. May the Lord's countenance shine upon you and bless you, and now let's eat."

Most of the people had brought food, and they began carrying it forward, placing it on a long, crude table assembled from split logs in front of the cabin. This would be a community supper, the participants contributing because few farmers in the colony could afford to host so many people out of their own limited resources. Andrew felt a little guilty that he had nothing to put on the table. The little stuff he had bought at the store was for Marie, not for himself. It mattered little, though. He knew he was as welcome here as if he had brought a side of beef. As a whole, the Old Three Hundred and those who had followed them were a gregarious and generous lot.

This, he thought, might be his chance to get close to the minister and ask him to visit the settlers out on the Colorado. He awaited his turn, for many people had crowded around. The man's back was to Andrew. When the well-wishers momentarily thinned, Andrew called, "Preacher, could I talk to you?"

The heavyset minister turned. Andrew sucked in a surprised breath and held it. A chill shuddered through him when he saw the black patch over one eye. He declared in revulsion, "Fairweather!"

The minister's jaw went slack as he stared at Andrew. He tried to speak, but in his surprise no words came. He grabbed at the big black Bible to keep from dropping it to the ground.

Andrew became conscious of several people staring at him and the black-clad minister. He said, "Maybe we'd better walk off out yonder a ways where we can talk in private."

Fairweather looked him over suspiciously. Andrew said, "I'm not armed. My rifle is on my horse."

Fairweather stammered to the people who watched, "If you

will excuse me, please, this young gentleman and I have some unfinished matters to discuss."

When they were out of earshot, Andrew said, "I thought they were finished a long time ago. I figured by now somebody had killed you."

"The Lord has been kind to me since our last meeting."

"Kinder to you than to them around you, I would imagine. What kind of swindle are you tryin' to pull off here? You're no more a minister than I am."

"I am no longer the same man I was when last you saw me."

Andrew gave him a dark study, trying in vain to read whatever was behind the man's one good eye. "You look the same to me. You were nothin' but a trail pirate. You used that preacher disguise to put us off our guard so you could rob and murder us on the road to Texas. If you ever worked for anybody besides yourself it was for Satan; it sure wasn't for the Lord."

He knew that the man's name was not even Fairweather. He had assumed that name, taken from a real minister he had robbed and very possibly even killed. But Fairweather was the only name Andrew knew him by.

Fairweather said, "I will admit that in those evil days I was not what I appeared. But I underwent a great revelation after my parting with you and your brother. Like Saul on the road to Damascus, I was blinded by a miracle, and then I could see as never before."

"You was blinded by a bullwhip in the hands of a woman you turned over to your gang of cutthroats to be raped and killed."

"And a just retribution it was. It took the loss of one eye to open the other to the path of righteousness."

Andrew sniffed. "Righteousness! You've just figured out a new way to rob people, is all. Your words are as bogus as them weddin's you just performed. Nobody ever ordained you to be a preacher."

"I need no man's ordination. I took mine from the Book, wherein reposes all truth."

Andrew began to wonder. He put little stock in sudden reformations, but it was just barely possible that the old fraud had used the Bible so long as a device for larceny that he finally had come to believe his own preachings. "If you're lookin' to take up a big collection from these folks, you're in for an awful disappointment. There's not enough cash money in this crowd to buy a demijohn of Kentucky squeezin's."

"There are rewards far greater than money could buy. I carry the Word so that I might earn that great reward for my soul when it comes time to depart this world of care."

It's a damned shame you didn't depart it a long time ago, Andrew thought. But he saw that these people believed. It would be cruel to rob them of their pleasure in a rare opportunity to hear someone deliver the Word in tones as persuasive as Fairweather's. "Tell you what: I'll stay around and listen to your preachin', and maybe I won't tell anybody what you really are. But there's a catch to it."

"And what might that be?"

"I want you to tell them before you start that you don't want any of their money, that you ain't goin' to take up any collection."

"That, young gentleman, is a heavy test of my sincerity."

"I can't offer you any better. If you won't do it, I'd advise you to leave right now. Otherwise, they just might stone you to death, like in the Book."

"Money is the root of all evil, my young friend. I have no need of it. I shall take up no collection."

"Fine. Go get your supper and then give these good folks the best sermon you ever preached. I'll be listenin'."

"Do that. You may find yourself uplifted."

Andrew watched with a frown as Fairweather turned away from him to the warm reception of the crowd. Either the man had truly reformed or he had become an even bigger fraud than Andrew remembered.

Andrew ate skimpily, not wishing to abuse hospitality when he had brought nothing to the table but his appetite. He noted that Fairweather suffered from no such compunctions but ate heartily and enjoyed the attention of the people who thronged around him. Andrew wanted to give him the benefit of the doubt but remembered all too well his and Michael's encounter with the bogus minister on their way to Texas. Twice the man had tried to kill them. He had also tried to appropriate two wagonloads of whiskey belonging to a woman teamster named Sally Boone. But her prowess with the whip had been his undoing. The skill that enabled her to knock a fly off the nigh leader's ear let her take out Fairweather's eye.

The supper done and the crowd quieted, Fairweather offered a prayer, then launched into the Biblical story about Saul and the road to Damascus. Andrew suspected that was for his benefit. Fairweather talked about the blinding of Saul, who had been a scourge to the Christians, and his redemption as a true believer under his new name of Paul.

Fairweather's name change had come long before his conversion, if indeed there had been one.

Andrew saw that the people were swept up in the glory of Fairweather's message, and after a while he began to feel the magnetism himself. Some of the doubt still clung, but he began to feel that the weight of evidence was swinging over to Fairweather's side. If he was not sincere, he was the best play-actor Andrew had ever seen.

The meeting broke up, finally. Some of the crowd began leaving for home. Others would camp the night and go home in the daylight. Fairweather, of course, was offered the Hawkins' bedroom in the double cabin. Andrew sidled up to him just before the minister retired.

"That was a pretty powerful load you dumped on the folks."

"It is written that the good shepherd always feeds his flock."

"You got any other flocks to tend in these parts?"

"Where the spirit beckons, I follow."

"There's some folks up on the Colorado River that would appreciate hearin' you. I'll take you tomorrow."

Fairweather was surprised again. "I thought you were the doubting Thomas."

"I am. I still got my doubts that you know the Master, but you do know the Word, and that's what the folks want to hear."

"I shall be ready."

Andrew lowered his voice. "Just one thing, Fairweather. One false move and I'll do to you what you tried to do to me and Michael. I'll shoot you, and tell God you died."

11

As was his custom, Andrew left his blanket at first light, but he found the Reverend Fairweather not inclined to early rising. Fairweather said, "The Lord provided the night so we could sleep. It is still night."

"That rooster yonder don't agree with you."

"Man was given more reason than a rooster. When the good folks start fixing breakfast, I shall be up and giving praise for the new day."

In fact, Fairweather gave praise several times. Many people who had camped set about building small fires and fixing their own meager breakfasts rather than impose upon the hosts. Fairweather arose when the first smell of frying ham reached him. He went from camp to camp, fire to fire, blessing the food, partaking liberally as it was offered to him. Andrew judged that he had eaten enough to kill an average man. But when the farmer Hawkins walked out onto the dog-run and bade the minister come in to breakfast, Fairweather obliged him.

Andrew itched to be saddled up and gone, but Fairweather had a parting sermon for those who had stayed over. He would not be rushed. He exalted the glory of sharing. He spoke of the angel who visits unaware and promised to be back on this circuit before long. Everybody pressed around, wanting to shake his hand one more time. Andrew despaired of their ever getting started. But eventually they set out upon the trail. Fairweather looked back over his shoulder at the people behind him, preparing to return to their homes refreshed in the spirit.

"There is a great joy in such fellowship."

"And some possibility of a bellyache."

It felt strange to Andrew, riding with a man who once had sought to rob and kill him and Michael. He wondered what Michael would say, though Michael's opinion would not alter Andrew's actions one way or the other. Except for Fairweather's eating like a starved wolf, Andrew could not see that the man had abused these folks' hospitality. If he left them feeling better for his coming, what was the harm? And far be it from Andrew to deny a similar comfort to Mrs. Nathan, who felt that a new home needed a minister's blessing. People who left everything behind them to come out and settle a wild new land deserved whatever consolation might come their way.

He had forgotten how many farms lay between San Felipe and the new place settled by the Nathan family. Fairweather insisted upon stopping at each one to extend his best wishes, inquiring if there was any spiritual need he might help satisfy. A ride that should have taken a few hours under normal circumstances stretched through that day and into the next. Fairweather resisted Andrew's efforts to push him along. "One does not rush the message or the messenger."

Suspicion gnawed at Andrew although the people along the way seemed to accept Fairweather without questioning his claim to speak for higher authority. He knew the Book backward and forward, it seemed. He must have done a lot of reading in it since Andrew and Michael had first encountered him on the trail to Texas. At that time Andrew had smelled a skunk when Fairweather spoke of Jonah in the lions' den. He seemed to have his stories straight this time, though Andrew by no means considered himself an expert on the subject.

He found the Nathans' roof finished and ready to be tested by rain. Mrs. Nathan was beside herself with joy when she saw Fairweather dismount. She recognized his calling by his black suit and the Bible which he took from his saddlebag before Andrew had a chance to introduce him. Bachelor neighbors Joe Smith and Walker Younts, who had helped raise the walls and work on the roof, were still hanging around. They probably enjoyed Mrs. Nathan's cooking too much to hurry back to their own places. Andrew suspected that both were also interested in the girl Birdy; their eyes followed her constantly. By Andrew's standards she was still underage, but scarcity on a frontier made girls a much-sought-after commodity. They tended to marry early. A rose hardly had time to blossom before it was plucked.

Lige Willet had gone home. Family men had responsibilities.

Andrew was surprised when Eli Pleasant walked out from the cool shade of the dog-run to shake his hand. Andrew said, "I thought you'd be gone to Michael and Marie's by now."

"Wasn't no hurry about it. These here are pleasant folks. I don't think I've et better since the time I set my feet under your mama's table back in Tennessee." Eli glanced toward the woman. "Miz Nathan is almighty tickled that you brought a reverend with you."

Andrew frowned. "I hope she won't find reason to regret it."

"Any reason she might?"

"His name is Fairweather. You've heard me and Michael speak of him."

Eli rubbed his chin, studying the minister speculatively from afar. "I don't remember you sayin' anything good. But maybe havin' a bad reverend is better than not havin' any reverend at all."

"I hope so. I never saw a black horse turn white before. I'm afraid a little rain might wash the paint off of this one."

"Then we'd better help him pray for sunshine."

Fairweather did his duties as if he were being paid. He blessed the new cabin, he blessed the family, he blessed the field and the livestock, and he blessed the big meal Mrs. Nathan set on the newly hewn pine table.

One of the Nathan youngsters let curiosity get the better of his manners. He asked what had become of the eye covered by the patch. Fairweather gave Andrew a quick glance across the table. "I once allowed myself to gaze upon wickedness, and the eye was taken for penance. You have two good eyes, my young gentleman. Take care that they look only upon what is worthy in the sight of the Lord."

"Amen," said Mrs. Nathan with a questioning glance toward the bachelors whose attentions had been devoted to her daughter.

The sound of horses' hoofs intruded upon the meal. Nathan got up and went to the door, casting a quick gaze upon his rifle over the new mantle but not moving toward it. "Three men have just ridden in with a dozen or so horses."

Andrew made his excuses to Mrs. Nathan and followed Nathan outside. Eli Pleasant trailed behind them. Fairweather did not pause in his good work at the table. Andrew recognized the Mann father and two sons he had met on the trail to San Felipe. They were riding better horses this time. The younger of the sons sat hunched in the saddle. As the horse turned, Andrew saw a bandage wrapped around the young man's arm. The father and the older son pushed the horses through the open gate of Nathan's pole-pen, dust swirling around them. The son stepped down from his horse and pushed into place the poles that served as a gate. Quenton Mann turned and raised his hand in greeting. He looked haggard and worn and worried.

"Any of these horses belong to you folks?" he asked.

Andrew stepped forward, and Mann recognized him. "Seen you down yonder a ways, didn't I?" He pointed his chin eastward.

Andrew nodded. "Looks like you found your horses."

"Ours and some more. Hoped you folks might know who the rest of them belong to."

Eli walked up to the boy whose arm was bandaged. He took hold of the bridle reins. "Son, you look mighty hard used. I see the blood in that wrappin'."

The father spoke for him. "He got an arrow in his arm. Me and Harlan, we pulled it out. Good lady named Willet on a farm over yonder cleaned the wound and wrapped it for him."

Alarm began to rise in Andrew. "You took these horses away from Indians?"

Mann demonstrated his story with much movement of his hands. "One Indian. He was holdin' them while the rest of the bunch was off somewhere, probably lookin' for more horses to steal. We come on him sudden and taken him by surprise, but he was quick as a panther puttin' that arrow in my boy's arm. I shot him before he could take another one out of his quiver."

"Kill him?" Andrew asked anxiously.

"Stone cold dead."

Andrew pressed, "What about the rest of the Indians?"

Mann shook his head. "We didn't figure it'd be smart to stay around and wait for them. We just gathered up all the horses there was and pushed them away from there as hard as they would run."

Eli asked, "You know what kind of Indians they was?"

"Got no idee. The one we saw was tattooed a right smart."

"Waco, more'n likely," Eli said.

Andrew's anxiety continued to build. He gave Eli a quick, searching look. The old smuggler's eyes were narrowed with concern.

Andrew said, "They'll be wantin' revenge for the one that was shot. If they follow the trail of the horses—"

Eli nodded. "They'll come to the Willet farm sure as hell."

Andrew found his hands shaking. "And it's just a short ways on over to our places, Michael's and mine. They could hit there just as easy."

Mann was apologetic. "We never intended to cause trouble for other folks. We just went to get our horses back. And I couldn't just sit there and let that Indian finish killin' my boy. I had to shoot him, don't you see?"

Andrew said, "We see, but I doubt them Indians will. Eli, I've got to hurry and warn Michael and Marie."

Eli's furrowed old face was solemn. "And I'll git myself over to Willet's as fast as I can. He's so easygoin' he may not realize the danger he's in."

Fairweather had sensed the excitement and wandered out to see what it was all about. "Anything I can do?" he asked.

Andrew said, "If you've really got somebody up there

who'll listen to you, you can pray for a bunch of innocent folks."

Fairweather told Eli, "Friend, I'll ride with you over to the Willet farm. If the Indians do come by, those good folks'll need all the fighting men they can get."

Andrew frowned. "I didn't think you were armed."

"I am armed with the power of the Word. I've also got a pistol buried deep in my saddlebag. One never knows when he may encounter a heathen."

"You'd be the one to know about heathens."

Andrew did not take time for good-byes. He quickly threw the saddle on his brown horse and put him into a run, leaving the pack horse behind. He looked back once. Eli and Fairweather followed far behind him, but he did not wait. Their trail was shorter than his.

He kept the brown horse in a lope as much as he dared, slowing him to a trot frequently to give him a chance to recover his wind. His imagination ran wild and free. Andrew had never been in an Indian fight or seen the aftermath of a raid, though he had heard about them often enough as a boy in Tennessee. Mordecai Lewis had been an Indian fighter, leaving home and family several times that Andrew could remember to join an expedition of rescue or revenge. His descriptions, when he returned, were graphic and terrifying. Those descriptions played through Andrew's mind now as he imagined himself finding Michael's cabin ablaze, Michael and Marie and the boy slaughtered. He left the longer trail that would have taken him by the Willet farm and cut straight across toward his own. In his anxiety he almost ran the brown horse to the ground. He forced himself to slow, though it was painful. He would be of no help to anyone if he killed the horse and could not reach the farm in time.

He kept watching for smoke. Once he thought he heard shooting, and he pulled the horse to a stop so he could listen. Now he heard nothing. He chastised himself. He had to put a bridle on that wild imagination.

The brown horse was lathered with sweat when Andrew pushed him at last over the final hill and saw Michael and

Marie's cabin below. Everything looked normal. The only smoke was rising from the chimney. He felt a little foolish as relief rushed over him like a tide. All those old Indian stories—he had let them run away with him.

Nearing the field, he saw Michael standing amid the corn, hoeing weeds. Andrew started waving his hat. Michael paused, started to go back to hoeing, then reluctantly walked out toward the fence to meet his younger brother. He offered no welcome. Andrew knew Michael still resented his taking the trip away from him.

Michael said, "You stayed gone long enough. Thought maybe you went all the way to Nacogdoches instead of to San Felipe."

Andrew felt a little tremor in his voice. "I might've stayed a little longer, but an emergency's come up."

"Emergency? What kind?"

"The kind that wear feathers in their hair."

Michael's resentment was quickly shoved aside. His eyes widened. "Where at?"

"Maybe here, before long. I think you'd better lay down the hoe and get up to the cabin. They'd make short work of you if they caught you out here in the open. They won't be as apt to rush a cabin that they know has got armed men in it."

Michael picked up a rifle he had leaned against the rail fence, and he left the hoe in its place. "How'd you come to know all this?"

Andrew explained it to him as he rode on up toward the cabin, Michael striding along beside him. Michael exclaimed, "You say Eli is in the country? I'd give a pretty to see that old man again."

"You will. He said he'd be comin' along. But right now he's over to the Willets', lendin' a hand in case the Indians come by there."

Michael said with concern, "We've never had any Indian trouble out here to speak of, a little horse and mule stealin', is all. Except for the Karankawas down on the coast, they ain't killed hardly anybody."

"We've never killed any of *them* before."

Marie had seen them coming. She waited on the dog-run, smiling her pleasure. "It is good that no one is angry now," she said, misreading the situation. "It is not good here when you argue."

Michael said, "Whatever argument we've got, it has to be set aside for a while. We have somethin' bigger to worry about."

Andrew said, "Don't you be gettin' scared, Marie, but there's a chance Indians may be comin' this way."

Marie looked anxiously toward the kitchen door. Little Mordecai came out. "How do, Uncle Andrew?"

Michael said quickly, "Mordecai, you'd best be stayin' in the cabin."

Marie gathered the boy into her arms. Andrew wondered if she ought to be lifting him in her condition, but it was not his place to say anything, and Michael didn't.

Andrew thought of something. "Where's your horse, Michael?"

Michael seemed surprised that he had not thought of the horse. "I saw him grazin' down by the river a little while ago." He pointed northeastward.

Andrew said, "I'd best find him and bring him up here where we can watch him. The reason the Indians are out and about is to pick up horses."

Marie put in quickly, "If you see the cow, Andrew—"

The boy said, "Indians? Are we goin' to see Indians?" He seemed eager rather than frightened.

Andrew swung up onto the brown horse and headed quickly for the river. From one day to the next, even one part of the day to the next, there was no telling where Michael's bay horse might graze. He was a free roamer. But he seemed to have a strong preference for one particular place downriver a mile or so from Michael's cabin. Andrew supposed it had something to do with the soil there, and the flavor or nutrients it put into the grass. He reined the brown in that direction, his senses keened. He was very much aware that the horse might not be the only thing he found.

He had traveled only a short way when the bay came running toward him. Andrew reined up, and the horse passed by him, eyes rolling in fright. The animal kept running, headed toward the cabin as if something were after him. Perhaps something was. Andrew's blood seemed to have ice in it as he held up a moment, staring hard in the direction from which the horse had come. He saw nothing. But a strong premonition made him shudder. He turned and followed the horse toward the cabin.

He remembered that Marie was concerned about the milk cow, but he decided it would be prudent to let the cow take care of herself. She was a creature of habit. Come milking time, she would amble in on her own. Indians had no use for cows except once in a while to butcher one for the meat, as they would do with a buffalo. They saw no pride of property in a cow.

The bay had entered the pen of its own volition and stood with its neck over the fence, watching Andrew's return. Instinct had made it turn to a place of safety when frightened. Michael was on his way from the cabin to the pen. He shut the gate behind the bay and waited for Andrew to ride up.

He asked, "What did you do to my horse? He came runnin' in here like the day we heard a big cat over in the timber."

"He ran by me the same way. I got a feelin' he saw somethin', and it wasn't a cat."

Michael asked no more questions. He bridled his bay horse, which trembled in fright. He patted the animal gently to calm it. "I been thinkin'—we'd better tie the horses up against the cabin, just in case. Worse come to worst, we can put them *in* the cabin."

"Might get a little crowded in there."

"Better crowded than left afoot."

Andrew was startled to see Marie walking toward the river with a bucket in each hand. He dropped his reins and hurried down to intercept her. "You've got no business leavin' the cabin. There's no tellin' where them Indians might be."

Calmly she said, "The buckets are nearly empty. Should they come and stay a long time, we will need the water."

"I'll fetch it. You better get back yonder to the boy."

It struck Andrew that many people, and not just women by any means, would be in panic at the thought of Indians somewhere near. Marie's mind was on the practical considerations. She said, "We will also need milk. You did not see the cow?"

"To tell you the truth, I didn't look none too hard."

She said pointedly, "If it were men who had the babies, you would know the cow is more important than the horse."

Andrew watched as she turned and walked back toward the cabin. In spite of the tension, he found himself chuckling.

If I ever find a woman for myself, he thought, *she'll have to be a lot like Marie.*

12

THE EMERGENCY took precedence over other considerations but did not eliminate them. Andrew was aware that Michael's resentment still simmered quietly beneath the surface. *Well, hell,* he thought, *if that's the way it's got to be, then it'll just be that way.* He went out to the dog-run and took a seat where he could watch most of three directions including the front of the cabin where they had staked the horses. Michael said nothing. He took up a position at the other side of the dog-run, his back to Andrew. He watched the opposite side of the cabin and westward, where the trees along the river stretched away into the horizon. West was his favorite direction, as it had always been their father's.

After a time Andrew was compelled to turn and look at him. By way of a peace offering he said, "You didn't miss much."

Michael only grunted.

Andrew said, "They've had aplenty of rain over east. The early-planted crops are lookin' good. May be late gettin' the rest of them into the ground, though. Mud."

Michael did not even grunt.

Andrew reflected that a certain amount of stubbornness went with being a Lewis, especially the oldest Lewis. It had been that way with their father. It would probably be that way with little Mordecai when he got old enough to assert himself over his younger brother or sister, whichever Marie turned out to be carrying.

He felt he ought to try once more to explain. "Like I told you, the shape Marie's in, I didn't figure you ought to be goin' off and leavin'."

"I'd say that's a decision for me and Marie to make."

"For you *and* Marie. Didn't look to me like you'd asked her one way or the other."

"If you'd go find you a wife of your own, you wouldn't have time to be tellin' me what-all to do about mine."

"I oughtn't to have to tell you. You ought to know."

"You don't understand how it is with me. Nobody could understand except maybe Papa. He was the same way."

"It got him killed, and left Mama a widow."

Andrew decided that further argument might only lead to a fight. He felt awkward, for over the years the two brothers had seldom traded cross words. He sealed off the subject by commenting, "Seems kind of hot, even for this time of the year." It wasn't really that hot, but it was something to say, better than silence.

Michael grunted.

Andrew decided to let silence prevail. He watched the line of trees that bordered the river on its easterly flow. That, he judged, would be the most likely point of approach should Indians come. They would hardly want to ride in from the open country that stretched beyond the field, for they would be seen far away. They would want to use the cover of the timber as long as possible, then, likely as not, come charging up from the nearest point, hoping to catch the Lewises unready. That was the direction from which the bay horse had come running. Andrew strongly suspected the raiders had tried to take the horse and he had run away from them. That meant they were probably down in that direction somewhere. He could only hope they were well on their way northwestward, back the way from which they had originally come. That would likely make them Wacos, as Eli had said, or possibly Tawakonis. From what Andrew had heard, these were kindred tribes which lived, hunted, and did some limited farming along the Brazos River far beyond the Texas settlements. It was claimed they were much less nomadic than, say, the Comanches, and even lived in lodges made of grass. They were not given to perpetual war as the Comanches seemed to be against the Spanish and the Mexicans, but they were not reluctant to raid and to fight against such other tribes as were considered enemies. That they had raided little in Austin's colonies was fortunate for the colonists. Like the Comanches, they were perhaps still trying to figure out just what kind of people these Americans were.

The Manns, father and sons, had shown them what kind of enemies the Americans could be.

Andrew sat for perhaps two hours, enough that his rump was beginning to feel sore and his back ached. Changing positions seemed not to help much. He got up and stretched, then walked a little to stir his blood into better circulation. He saw Michael's bay horse jerk its head around, its ears pointed eastward. Little Mordecai's spotted dog, which had appeared to be asleep beside Andrew on the dog-run, raised up and looked around.

Horsemen appeared on the rim of a hill, in the direction of the Willet family's place. Andrew felt a quick chill. His voice was husky. "Michael! You better come look."

Michael was there in an instant, peering in the direction Andrew's finger pointed. Andrew asked, "Look like Indians?"

Michael flexed his fingers nervously against the stock of his long rifle and was a minute in answering. "No, looks like white folks to me. Best I can count, there's eight of them."

With his fingers Andrew stretched the skin around the edge of his right eye, a trick he had found gave him a moment of improved vision, though to hold it long had an adverse effect. "If I'm not mistaken, one of them is Eli Pleasant. Looks like the horse he was ridin', anyway."

"Eli!" Michael exclaimed. Eli had always been good news.

Marie had heard their quiet speculation and ventured out onto the dog-run. But when the boy Mordecai tried to follow her from the kitchen, she shooed him back through the door. "Then the Indians are already gone, you think?"

Most of the riders stopped at the top of a rise. Only two came ahead. One was Eli Pleasant. The other—

Andrew had not found Michael in a mood for listening much, so he had not told him about the Reverend Fairweather. "That's Eli on the left," he said. "You'd best gird yourself up for a little kick in the belly when you see who's with him."

Michael recognized the man and whispered a word under his breath that he never spoke in Marie's presense. So far as Andrew knew, she would have no idea what it meant. He would like to think she had been sheltered more than that. "Fairweather! Or whatever his name is. How come somebody hasn't killed him by now?"

"Don't you be takin' a notion to do it yourself. He's got folks convinced that he's the holiest man since John the Baptist. I'm kind of wonderin' myself. Maybe he's changed."

"Only if you can change a wolf into a sheep."

Any other time, Eli Pleasant would have swung to the ground and pumped Michael's hand until his arm felt ready to come off at the shoulder. But he sat on his horse, his face grave. "You folks all right here?"

Michael responded to the old man's somber mien. Quietly he said, "We're doin' just fine, Eli. Mighty glad to see you." He walked out and extended his hand. He pointedly ignored Fairweather.

Eli took Michael's hand, but there was no joy in his eyes at their reunion. "I'd be tickled to see you too, Michael, if things was different. But them folks back yonder"—he jerked his head, indicating the direction from which he had come—"they ain't passed so well. There's been killin' done."

Andrew tensed, glancing back at the alarm in Marie's face. "Who's dead?"

"Lige Willet, that helped us raise the cabin for the Nathan family. It was done before me and the reverend got there to warn him. Willet was out plowin' his field, and they come upon him unawares. His boy Daniel was out there ridin' a pony I'd traded them. The Indians taken him along."

Marie asked urgently, "And what of Mrs. Willet? What has happened to her?"

"She's all right, except she's been left a widow. The rest of the family was close to the cabin. They seen what happened but was too far to help. They got inside and bolted the doors. The Indians come up close, but they decided not to go against the walls. They rode off takin' all the Willet horses, and the boy cryin' for his mama."

Andrew remembered the eager boy he had carried behind him on his saddle just a few days earlier. And he remembered the jolly face, the jovial stories told by Lige Willet. He felt like crying a little himself. He pointed his chin toward the horsemen who waited at a distance. "Who's that yonder?"

"Willet's bigger boy Zeb, and Mann and his oldest son, and Nathan and some others. We follered the Indian's trail. They didn't miss your place by more'n a mile or so. Probably crossed the river right down yonder, just beyond that rise where you couldn't see them."

Andrew shuddered. He hadn't seen them, but Michael's bay horse had. The Indians had been in too big a hurry to try to chase him down.

Michael said grimly, "We'd ought not to be standin' here wastin' time. I'll fetch me some powder and shot, and I'll be goin' with you."

Andrew saw Marie's face fall in dismay. He turned on Michael in a flush of anger. "No you won't. I'll go. You stay here and take care of your family."

Michael flared even more swiftly. "When're you goin' to quit tryin' to tell me what to do?"

"When you start doin' what you ought to without me havin' to tell you."

Michael glared, then strode toward his staked bay horse. Andrew started after him in long, angry steps. Michael took the reins. Andrew grabbed them up near the bit. "Marie needs you at home. So does that boy. You're not goin'!"

Michael's eyes narrowed, his cheeks flushed red. "Andrew, I ain't hit you since we was boys. But I'm fixin' to now if you don't turn aloose of my horse!"

Andrew only half heard Fairweather's voice. "Gentlemen, this is not a time for quarreling. There is a young boy yonder in the wilderness, crying out for rescue."

Michael grabbed Andrew's wrist and tried to twist it, to free the rein. Andrew fought back, shoving his brother up against the bay horse, which sensed the anger and began to strain heavily against the stake that held him.

Marie stepped between them, shouting as Andrew had never heard her before, "You will stop fighting, both of you. I will not have it. I will not!"

Andrew countered, "You can't stay here by yourself."

Eli declared, "She won't. They're gatherin' up all the womenfolks and young'uns from around here and takin' them to the Willet place. It's got the best protection. There'll be a wagon along here pretty soon to fetch Marie and the boy."

Marie said, "That is best. Mrs. Willet will need friends to be with her. There we will be safe enough."

Eli added, "The Indians appear to've already gone away from here anyhow. Probably tryin' to get back to where they come from as quick as they can."

Andrew backed away from Michael, but his blood still ran hot. He faced Marie. "His place is here with you. No tellin' when we might get back."

Marie touched Michael's arm and turned to look into her husband's face. "Michael's place is where Michael feels he needs to be. He will do what must be done. You are both needed, so go now. The boy and I will be all right."

Andrew felt a little chastened. He sensed that Marie did not really want Michael to go, but it was to be expected that she would back her husband. She would put on a brave face and make Michael feel that the idea had been her own. He would not leave this place carrying a burden of guilt.

She looked off toward the river and pointed. "The cow comes up to be milked. Her we will tie behind the wagon and take with us. There will be other children at the Willets' besides Mordecai. They will need much milk. But the chickens—the chickens will have to take care of themselves."

She walked into the cabin with Michael, her arm around him. When Michael came out in a minute with his powderhorn, a leather pouch, a sack of food, and one rolled blanket, she did not come with him. Michael did not look at Andrew, but he said to Eli, "She's busy gatherin' up stuff to be ready when the wagon comes. She'll give you a proper greetin' the next time."

There had been no greeting at all for Fairweather. He said, "God be with all who live in this house."

Michael gave him a surprised glance but made no comment. He set the bay horse into a long trot toward the riders who waited farther on. Andrew was busy tying his blanket behind his saddle and had to spur hard to catch up.

The other horsemen saw them leave the cabin and moved on down toward the river, passing out of sight. Michael altered his direction to compensate, for he had taken the lead without asking. The men were watering their horses when Michael, Andrew, Eli, and Fairweather reached them. The new settler Nathan was there, and the elder Mann along with the son Harlan who had not been wounded. The bachelor farmers Smith and Younts were there, and young Zebediah Willet, his face dark with pain and anxiety and hatred. He looked much older than the twenty or so that he really was. This country could age a young man fast.

Michael knew all of them except the newcomer Nathan, who quickly introduced himself. "It's a bad time, a bad time," Nathan said. "I had not thought to encounter Indian trouble. We had just gotten settled."

Andrew rode up beside Zebediah Willet and placed a heavy hand on the youth's shoulder. "I'm mighty sorry, Zeb."

The answer came in a voice strained almost to breaking. "I seen it, Andrew. I seen the whole thing. I was just too far off to be any help." Tears threatened in his eyes.

"There's no way we can bring back your daddy. But if there's any chance atall, we'll bring back your little brother.

Seems to me like you'd ought to go home now. You'd be a big consolation to your mother."

"I can't. If you'd seen them, if they'd carried off your brother, you couldn't stay home either."

Andrew glanced at Michael. "No, I reckon not."

Michael wasted no time. "This is their trail, I take it?" He nodded toward a mass of horse tracks on the riverbank.

Mann said, "They crossed here. Couldn't've been more'n maybe two, three hours, goin' by the sign."

Andrew flinched. That would have been about the time he had gone hunting Michael's bay horse.

Michael put his horse into the water. The Indians had chosen a fording place that required the animals to swim only a few moments before putting their hoofs on the riverbed. Andrew knew of a better place a little farther downriver, but he supposed the Indians were not that well acquainted with this part of the country. The Wacos' normal range was along the Brazos, not the Colorado. Michael turned once to see if everyone was following. Andrew pushed in just behind him. He glanced back. Fairweather, bringing up the rear, hesitated a minute before hitting the water on his big black horse.

Folks who talk about Heaven all the time are not usually in a hurry to get there, Andrew mused.

It quickly became apparent that this party had no real leader. Everybody was together by common consent, but sooner or later they would face a situation that demanded quick decisions; there would be no time to stop and take a vote.

Michael remarked to Eli, "They've sure left a clear trail."

Eli shook his head. "For now. They're wantin' to get as far from this place as they can, in a hurry. A little later on, when they think they've got time, they'll take the trouble to cover their tracks. Then they'll disappear like smoke. They'll be hell to trail unless we catch up to them before that."

Michael looked around to see if anyone would claim leadership. He pointedly avoided Andrew. Most of the men seemed to be looking at Eli, seemingly assuming that because he was by a wide margin the oldest, his experience would make him the logical choice. Eli felt the pressure and quickly demurred.

"Michael, these ol' eyes ain't as good as they was. But yours was always sharp, as I remember."

Michael hesitated, waiting to see if anyone would challenge his leadership or express a preference for someone else. No one spoke, least of all Andrew. Whatever his disagreements with his older brother might be in regard to family responsibilities, he had confidence in Michael's ability to carry this burden. Michael had more of their father in him than Andrew did.

Michael said, "Let's be gettin' on about the business, then." He turned the bay horse and led off at a trot. Andrew half expected someone to protest the slow pace, but no one did. This trail was so broad and plain that they could have followed it in a lope. But that abuse would run their mounts into the ground in a few miles. Even if they were fortunate enough to overtake their quarry before that, the Indians would probably outrun the pursuers' tired horses.

Andrew saw impatience in the eyes of young Zeb Willet, but the youth accepted the necessity of the slower pace without complaint. No one else spoke of a desire to push harder, though most probably wished they could. Andrew took the lack of argument as a promising sign; these were frontiersmen who knew what they were about, or at least were willing to put their faith in a leadership that knew what it was doing.

Andrew looked back once, wishing he could see the cabin, wishing he knew that someone had arrived with that promised wagon to take Marie and the boy to a place of greater safety. Like Zeb Willet, he had to accept some things on faith. If Michael was concerned—and Andrew thought certainly he must be—he gave no sign. He kept riding, his gaze shifting between the distant horizon and the tracks on the ground. Andrew could only guess what his brother was thinking. He thought it likely that Michael was remembering a time when he himself had been young—though not so young as the captive Willet boy—and had faced death in a strange land at the hands of an implacable enemy. Someone had come to Michael's rescue. It was time now, if it could be done, that Michael lead the way to the rescue of a boy much like the youth he once had been.

13

THE SUN dropped behind a thin line of reddening clouds to the west, then below the horizon. In the half light that lingered, Michael pushed the bay horse into a lope for the first time, trying to use whatever time remained. The pursuit would have to stop soon because of darkness, and the horses could rest then.

Though Michael had been in most ways a better woodsman and hunter than Andrew, it had been Andrew who excelled in following a track, whether of a tiny fox or rabbit or of a horse. Somehow this was one phase of their father's teachings that had come easier to Andrew than to his older brother. It had always scratched like a piece of gravel in Michael's craw that in this one occasionally vital area he was outdone. Andrew had been watching the tracks, the occasional scattering of horse manure, and gauging for himself how long they had been there. So far as he could tell they were keeping up with the Indians' pace but not besting it any. He did not voice his opinion to Michael. If Michael wanted it, he would surely ask for it. And to speak discouragingly in Zeb's hearing would be cruel.

Zeb occasionally lapsed into bitter self-recrimination. "Papa never was one to give much thought to the bad things that could happen, but *I* should've known. When the Manns brought those horses by our place, I should've guessed that the Indians would be trailin' them. I seen Daniel ridin' off on that new pony and could've stopped him. But I never once thought—"

Eli reined in beside the young man. He had a voice that could cut like a razor when the need arose, but it was soft and comforting now. "Ain't no more use in you blamin' yourself than for me to blame myself for tradin' your daddy that pony in the first place. You wasn't brought up in an Indian-fightin' country. Wasn't no way for you to guess what they'd do."

Zeb knotted his plow-hardened fists. His voice was raw. "I just wish I could kill them all! I will, if I get the chance."

Eli frowned. "I wouldn't be studyin' on that too much, boy. If a man lets hate get ahold of him, it robs him of his judgment. The only thing for you to be thinkin' about is gettin' your little brother back. Them Indians, they're just followin' their nature, like a wolf or a catamount."

"But Papa never done anything to hurt them. He never hurt anybody in his life."

"Just chance, boy. It's like a storm. He was standin' there when the lightnin' struck. Wasn't nothin' personal in it. And it didn't make no difference how good a man he was. To them he was just another white man, and a white man had killed one of theirs."

The elder Mann heard and looked back. He declared defensively, "I didn't kill just to be killin'. I killed to save my own boy."

Eli grunted. "Seems like there was bad luck all the way around. Been lots of people died in Texas just for hard luck. It's the damndest hard luck country ever I seen."

For others perhaps, but Andrew began to wonder if Michael considered this incident bad luck. Times, when Michael glanced around, Andrew saw exhilaration in his brother's eyes. This was Michael's element, this expedition across a new country; he was glorying in the adventure of it. Andrew remembered that look in his father, many times. And he remembered the sadness that always came into his mother's eyes because of it.

Darkness came. Andrew tried to guess how many miles

they had traveled. The last good look he had taken at the sign, he had doubted they were showing much if any gain on the Indians. Michael drew rein at the bank of a stream and waited for the others to come up even with him. "We'll lose the tracks if we go any farther tonight. All we can do is wait for daylight."

Zeb Willet demanded, "What do you think those Indians are doin'?"

Michael frowned. "They'll probably ride half the night, puttin' in all the distance they can. But they know their direction. They're not havin' to follow somebody's tracks."

"We know their direction too. They ain't changed it much. We could keep goin' the same way. Come mornin', we'd be that much closer to them."

"But like as not we'd stray off the trail, and we'd waste a lot of time tryin' to find it again."

"More time than we'll waste waitin' here for daylight?"

Michael had to shrug, for he had no answer to that.

Zeb declared, "You-all can stay here if you want to, but I'm goin' on if I have to go by myself."

Andrew pointed out, "You may be able to keep goin' all night, but your horse can't. What if you came upon the Indians with your horse all give out? Even if you got ahold of your brother, you couldn't get away with him. They'd run you down in a hurry."

Eli Pleasant seconded Andrew's statement. "There's a time to be bold and a time to be patient, son."

Zeb wavered but did not give in. Michael said, "We'll split the difference, Zeb. We'll stop here and rest a while; the horses need it. We'll fix ourselves a little supper, get some sleep, then be up and travelin' a long time before daylight."

Eli put in, "Them Indians'll stop eventually and take their rest. Might be we'd catch them by surprise in the early mornin'." He stressed the word *might*, so Andrew knew he thought it unlikely. Andrew considered the chance very remote that they would overtake the Indians this near the settlements. If this party caught up to them, it would almost surely be much farther up into the higher reaches of the Brazos

River, where few white men had yet traveled. But to voice that opinion would not help now. He kept it to himself, knowing that most of the men probably shared it.

Zeb Willet capitulated. "All right. But I'll be watchin' the stars. Two hours past midnight, I'll be travelin'."

Michael promised, "And we'll be with you. Let's water the horses. Then we'll build us a small fire low against the far creek bank where the Indians can't see it if any of them are hangin' back watchin'. We can all use a little supper."

Andrew had no provisions with him, for he had not been home. But the other men had brought bread and parched corn and some cured meat from the Willet place, and Michael had picked up a deer ham when he had gone into the cabin for his blanket, powder, and shot. He did not offer it to Andrew, however. Andrew ate a little from Miles Nathan's ration. They all drank a little parched-grain coffee.

Michael had avoided looking at Andrew, but he must have felt Andrew's gaze fixed on him. Defensively he demanded, "You been wantin' to say somethin'. Say it."

Andrew spoke quietly, for this was no one else's business. "I look at you and all I can see is Papa all over again, always ridin' off to some new country, lovin' every bit of it."

Michael frowned. "You think I like what happened back there to Willet and his boy?"

"No, but you like what's come after, the chase and all. You look like a man who's just been let out of jail."

"A man can't help bein' what he is."

"No. But I'd like it better if you didn't like it as much."

The horses were staked to graze atop the creek bank. Andrew took first watch, by the horses, while the other men rolled out their blankets and tried to fall asleep. Eli was snoring within a few minutes. Andrew had heard him say once that in his line of business he sometimes had to do without sleep for extended periods, so it was useful to be able to take as much of it as he could when the chance came. He looked at eating in the same way, something he had learned from his frequent association with Indians: eat all you can when you can, because there is no way of knowing how far away the next meal may be.

He listened to the sounds of the night, the insistent chirping of a bird, possibly calling for a mate with which to share a nest, a feeling Andrew knew also from time to time. He heard a wolf howl not far away, a call quickly answered from some distance. He felt an involuntary chill run up his back. He had no fear of wolves, but hearing them reminded him that he had ridden beyond the bounds of the colony he knew, into a part of the country he had not seen before. It had not looked different particularly, but knowing he had never been there imparted to it a sense of mystery. There was always a feeling that over the next rise, the next hill, might wait something totally alien.

Such a challenge was like strong drink to Michael; he thrived on it. But Andrew preferred the known to the unknown.

He heard a quiet voice. "Reckon them are really wolves?" Zeb Willet had come up to join him.

Andrew whispered accusingly, "You're supposed to be gettin' some sleep."

"You know I couldn't. I'd just as well stand all the watches. Even if I *did* close my eyes, I'd probably dream about what happened today. Maybe I'm even a little afraid to go to sleep because I don't want to see it all again. You think they're wolves? I've heard that Indians signal each other by makin' sounds like animals."

"Papa used to tell me the same thing. But I think those out yonder are just what they sound like. They're lonesome and tryin' to get together."

Willet was silent for a few thoughtful minutes. "I want you to tell me the truth, Andrew. What do you think are the chances we'll bring Daniel back?"

Andrew wished the young man had not asked him. But since he had, Andrew would not lie. "I'd say it's a chance, but not a big one. Like Eli said, they're not botherin' right now to try and hide their trail. They're movin' fast to get way off out into their own country. But once they feel like they've put enough distance behind them that they can afford to slow down, they'll cover their tracks. We'll have a hard time of it then."

"If we don't get Daniel back, what'll happen to him?"

"I've never had any experience with Indians myself. I hear that if a boy shows a lot of fight they'll sometimes take a likin' to him and try to make him into a warrior."

"He was fightin' them right enough. I could see that. I just wish I could've been down there to help him."

"Him, they just took prisoner. You, they'd've killed."

"Like they did Papa." Zeb's voice went grim, the hatred coming through again.

Andrew said sternly, "If you don't get some rest, you'll fall out on us tomorrow. You go back yonder and lay down."

Mann's son Harlan came, after a while, and relieved Andrew of his duty. Andrew lay down on the edge of his blanket, drawing the rest of it over him. He lay with his eyes closed, still hearing the wolves talking to one another in the distance. The last image that came to him was Marie's.

He felt a hand on his shoulder and came suddenly awake. Eli Pleasant said, "Best be gittin' up, Andrew. It's time."

He smelled the faint aroma of parched grain being boiled as a substitute for coffee, down below the creek bank. He arose, rolling his blanket. Remembering, he looked around quickly to be assured that Zeb Willet had not carried out his threat and ridden on. To his query, Eli said, "Zeb's down yonder fixin' him a little bacon on a stick. Wouldn't be a bad idee if you done the same. No tellin' when we'll eat again."

It was still just as dark as when he had given up his watch and taken to his blanket. He saw not a sign of light to the east except the brilliance of stars. He looked at the Big Dipper for the time and knew it was about halfway between midnight and daylight. "It don't take long to spend the night," he commented.

Eli grunted. "For a man in my occupation, this is the best time of the day."

Fairweather gave thanks for the quick breakfast they bolted down. So far as Andrew had been able to tell, Michael had not spoken a word to the man, nor did he give any sign that he intended to. Michael was long at remembering and short at forgiving. Fairweather had a lot to be forgiven for.

They saddled their horses in the light of the stars and by unspoken common consent followed Michael as he set the course in the darkness. He heard one of the bachelors, Walker Younts, express a worry that they were going back the way they had come. Some people never learned a sense of direction. Andrew's had always been good, and Michael's was even better. Andrew knew Michael was leading them the right way. He started to say so but decided that if Michael wanted to be defended, he could do it himself.

Eli whispered urgently, "You better hush up, Younts. Voices travel a long ways in the night."

Andrew wondered if Eli was concerned about the Indians or about Michael.

Daylight found them many miles farther to the northwest. But it also found them off the trail, the very fear Michael had expressed. He said, "It may not be far, but then again it might. We'll just have to split up and find it."

Andrew suggested, "Why don't I angle off to the northeast and Eli to the northwest? The rest of you can keep on travelin' the way you're goin' so you don't lose too much time. One of us is bound to find it." He saw that Michael was about to come up with an argument; he probably preferred to go himself. Andrew quickly turned off and started northeastward, not giving his brother time to change the plan. He looked back in a minute and saw Eli headed off at an opposite angle. Michael motioned with his hand, and the other men resumed travel in the direction they had begun.

Andrew put his reluctant brown horse into a fast trot, for he had more distance to travel than Michael and the main body. He had ridden perhaps half a mile when he came upon the trail, as plain as it had been last night. It still led northwestward. Andrew saw a slight rise in the ground ahead and put the brown into a lope. He stopped there, saw the rest of the men at a considerable distance and waved his hat, hoping they would see him. They did not at first, but he kept waving. Shortly they stopped. One man went riding off northwestward, probably to find Eli, while the rest rode toward Andrew. Michael, always in the lead, gave him a wordless glance, looked a moment at the tracks, then turned to Zeb Willet.

"I reckon you were right. I'd hazard a guess that we've gained on them a little."

Andrew doubted that, but he supposed Michael was trying to make Zeb feel better. God knew he had little enough to feel good about.

Fairweather said, "I prayed for the trail to be plain. The Good Lord hears the pleas of those who believe."

Michael gave Fairweather not a glance. Michael believed in the Lord, but he had no faith in Fairweather. He said, "We'll be ridin', then. Eli and Walker can catch up to us in their own good time."

The two riders were an hour or so in rejoining the others. Eli glanced at the tracks as he pulled up beside Andrew. "Reckon how far ahead of us they'd be?"

Andrew looked around for Zeb. He did not want the youth to hear. Quietly he replied, "The better part of a day, I'd make it. They've got to stop sometime, or we've got to do a lot of catchin' up." He tried to read Eli's eyes for some sign of the old man's thoughts. Eli was a woodsman, and his judgment in matters of this sort was better than Andrew expected his own ever to be. But Eli's eyes were half closed, hiding whatever thoughts lay behind them. Andrew took no comfort.

They came at length to a wide forest of pine and oak and a tangle of undergrowth that made travel slow for a while. The tracks indicated some confusion among the Indians as they picked their way through it. Andrew surmised that they had struck it in the darkness. The trail led to a spring-fed creek. Charred remnants of wood showed that the Indians had built a couple of small fires here. Andrew held his hand low over one set of ashes but felt no warmth. Carefully he dug his fingers in, hoping to find some remnant of heat to indicate that the fire had not been out very long. He was disappointed, for the ashes were cold.

Michael asked no questions. Andrew's face evidently told him all he needed to know. Michael said, "Looks to me like they slept here." Several patches of grass were flattened where men had lain.

Andrew saw many moccasin tracks. After a bit he found a few tracks much smaller than the others, tracks that indicated the heel of a boot or shoe. He beckoned Zeb Willet and pointed. "They still had the boy with them here."

Zeb knelt and placed his hand over one of the tracks, as if he might thereby feel something of his brother's presence. He looked up hopefully. "That's a good sign, wouldn't you think? I mean, if they've brought him this far without killin' him, chances are they don't intend to kill him at all."

Andrew glanced at Eli for support. Eli said solemnly, "Likely as not, they figure on tradin' him. These Wacos, they're tradin' Indians. They swap with the Comanches for buffalo meat and hides, and sometimes horses. They occasionally trade captives too. They're like some white folks I know; they'll trade in anything that'll fetch a profit."

Zeb's eyes narrowed. "They'd trade off my brother?"

"There's other Indians that might take him for a slave. There's white folks who don't care how they get rich. They might buy him and make him work for them. Boy that age, he'll forget in a few years where he come from. I've seen some that couldn't even remember their daddy's and mama's names. All the slaves ain't black."

Zeb's jaw was set hard and grim as he stared at Eli. "They won't do that to Daniel. I'll find him or die."

Andrew said, "Let's don't talk about dyin'. Let's just find him."

The country began to take on more of a rolling, hilly aspect, frequent thickly wooded patches interspersed with the open meadows. In these, the heavy shade from the trees prevented grass from growing, and the thick matting of old leaves on the ground sometimes showed little sign of the Indians' passing. More than once, Michael was stopped cold. Andrew and Eli would ride forward, quietly taking over the search for the trail without being asked. Andrew suspected Michael would not request his help unless it came to a matter of life and death. The rest of the men would hold back without being told, for they respected Andrew's and Eli's abilities as trackers. Presently either Andrew or Eli would find enough of a trace to show they were on the right path, and the pursuit would proceed.

Andrew found it remarkable that no evident friction developed between the men. The nearest thing to harsh words came from the elder Mann when his son suggested that they ought to turn back and see to the wounded brother they had left at the Nathans'. The father said sharply, "This trouble started with us, even if not by our intention. We'll stay and see it through."

The two young bachelors, Smith and Younts, rode close to Miles Nathan most of the time. First one and then the other asked him questions about his daughter Birdy. Nathan told them he was sure his daughter would appreciate their concern over her welfare, but she was much too young to show that appreciation in any tangible way. Andrew suspected he was wondering what kind of son-in-law one of them would make, a few years hence.

Fairweather rode in silence most of the time, just now and again requesting the Lord's favor when they encountered difficulty picking a path through one of the heavy thickets or tangled forests that blocked their way.

"This'll never be a fit country for civilized men," Quenton Mann declared. "I don't see how even the savage endures it."

Fairweather commented, "The Lord never meant for man to find life easy. He tests us at every turn to see if we are worthy."

Miles Nathan said, "This country is just waitin' for good men with axes and plows to come and make it blossom as the Lord intended."

Michael had spoken little, but he turned in his saddle and declared with an intensity that bordered on anger, "Lots of people seem to know just what the Lord wants without askin' Him. I ain't heard *Him* say to come in here and cut down His forests and plow up all the land. He must've had a purpose for it the way it is or He'd've made it different."

Nathan was taken aback. "I thought everyone understood that our mission in life as Americans is to go forth and tame the wilderness and bring it into the productive service of civilized mankind. That is why I brought my family to Texas."

Michael said curtly, "I never understood it that way atall. I like the looks of this country just the way it is."

Eli put in, "Then you'd better take a good look at it, because it won't stay this way long. I've seen it in other places: the forests go down, the houses go up, and the prairie goes under the plow. Almost makes me glad I'm such an old fart, because at least I've seen most of it the way it used to be. By the time you're my age there won't be none of it left."

"Progress," Nathan said. "Time does not stand still."

They came, in time, to a stream where the tracks seemed to disappear. They led off into the water but did not come out on the far side. Eli said, "Well, they've decided to start hidin' their trail. They probably figure they've put a lot of distance between them and the settlements, and they can afford the time to cover their tracks." Without waiting for Michael to make it official, he looked at Andrew. "Well, boy, I reckon it's a job for me and you. I'll go upstream. You go down."

Andrew glanced at Michael, who gave him no sign one way or the other. Andrew took the absence of a negative indication to be approval of sorts. As he turned downstream he heard Michael say, "Everybody had just as well rest their horses. We're apt to be here a while."

Andrew rode slowly, his gaze fixed intently on the north bank. He deemed it unlikely that the Indians would have turned south again, though that possibility could not be discounted entirely; they had a fox's cunning when it came to confounding their enemies. He had ridden a mile, perhaps nearer two, without seeing anything. Suddenly the brown horse jerked its head up and poked both ears forward, alert. Andrew drew rein and held his breath while he raised his long rifle up from his lap, ready.

For a minute he stood still in the stream, seeing and hearing nothing. Then a sound came to him, the sound a horse makes when it grazes, cropping off the grass. He held his breath again, listening hard. The sound continued, unhurried and undisturbed. Gently he walked the brown up out of the water and onto the north bank. He dismounted quietly, tied the horse, then crouched low and began making his way toward the sound. He kept to the timber, letting it screen his movement. He came in a minute to a small clearing. The first thing he saw was the disturbed ground leading up out of the stream. Someone had dragged a branch over the sand, obviously trying to rub away the tracks. But the surface had a brushed look and was still damp from the water the horses had dripped as they came up onto the bank. A few more hours and it would have been difficult, perhaps impossible, to see.

Andrew's blood went to ice. He stiffened, his hands cramped on the rifle. Forty feet ahead, a dark-skinned Indian boy sat leaning against a tree. For a moment Andrew thought the boy was looking at him. Then he realized the lad did not see him. He was asleep.

14

ANDREW PUZZLED over this unlikely development, catching an Indian asleep, his horse staked out to graze. This was a lad in his teens, not the full-grown warrior Andrew would have expected. And to find him this way! This was not the omnipotent Indian vigilance he had heard legends about as long as he could remember.

The boy appeared to be alone. He was dressed only in a breechclout and moccasins. A small leather medicine pouch was suspended from his neck. It moved up and down with the steady rhythm of his breathing. His face was heavily tattooed.

This was the closest Andrew had ever been to an Indian, not counting the tame ones he used to see back in the Tennessee settlements from time to time. He had to stare and wonder. A boy! That he had been a member of the raiding party seemed likely. Probably he had been left here to watch for pursuit. Had he been vigilant he would have heard Andrew coming and could have hurried forward to warn the others. But he was merely a boy, not a warrior grown. If the others had left him here as a test of his manhood, his qualification to become a warrior, he had failed the test. Eternal vigilance was too much to expect of such a youth. The ride had been long, and he had been tired. He had probably put forth his best effort to remain awake, but the demands of nature would not be denied.

Andrew pondered what he should do. Some men would simply kill the boy in his sleep and declare good riddance. They would say that a dead Indian boy would not grow up to kill settlers and prevent the taking of tribal lands that had been too long in the pagan service of savages. Certainly that would be the easiest thing, for the boy was vulnerable. But Andrew gave that notion no more than a moment's passing consideration. An alternative would be to take the lad prisoner. But what would he do with him once he had him?

He decided to do nothing except retreat and leave the boy lying where he was, undisturbed. He returned quietly to the brown horse, mounted, and rode once more in the direction from which he had come.

He found most of the men stretched out on the ground, taking their rest while they could. As Andrew rode up, Michael asked with his eyes. They had quarreled, and pride would not let him speak the question aloud.

Andrew nodded. "I found the trail. It's headed just about due north. Found somethin' else, too."

Zeb Willet came quickly to stand beside Andrew's horse. "Sign of my brother?" he asked eagerly.

"No, but I found an Indian boy asleep over yonder. I figure they left him to watch and see if anybody was comin'. He was just too give out to stay with the job."

Michael had to speak to him then. "What did you do to him?"

"Nothin'. Left him just like I found him."

"He'll flush like a quail when he sees us. He'll probably beat us to wherever the rest of them are goin', because he knows where that is and we don't."

Andrew frowned. "You know I couldn't just kill him."

Zeb Willet's face clouded with hatred. "*I* could."

Miles Nathan argued, "If we captured him, maybe we could get him to tell where they're takin' your brother."

Andrew argued, "How? I doubt that even Eli can talk the Waco language."

Michael said, "He can talk with signs, though. Just about all Indians can understand that." He turned to Joe Smith. "You'd better ride upstream and fetch Eli. We'll go on and see if we can catch that Indian. You-all find us."

Uneasiness stirred in Andrew. Likely as not somebody would become over eager and shoot the youngster. He argued, "That boy probably wouldn't tell us anything if we burned him at the stake. I know which way the tracks were goin'. All we have to do is circle north and find them. The boy don't need to know we ever even came by."

Michael seemed to give serious consideration to his argument, but some of the others did not wait. Zeb Willet got on his horse. Quenton Mann and his son followed suit, then Miles Nathan and Walker Younts. Nathan said, "It's a chance," and turned to go with the others.

Shrugging, Michael got on his bay horse. He jerked his head as a signal for Andrew to come along. Michael spurred out to circle the men and take the lead. He motioned for them to slow down, for they had put their horses into a lope. "He'll hear us comin' for a mile," he warned. The men eased their mounts to a walk, though Zeb Willet was reluctant. Andrew could see that the young man was keyed to a nervous pitch.

They had ridden a mile and more when Michael raised his hand to signal a halt. He turned, searching out Andrew. "How far now?"

Andrew pointed. "Just up yonder, past that bend in the creek." He looked around anxiously. "We don't have to kill him."

Michael was the only one who offered any acknowledgment. "We'll take him alive if we can."

They crossed over the stream to the north side and proceeded in a slower walk, the horses' hoofs making little sound on the mat of old decaying leaves and the thin scattering of grass upon the stream's higher bank. At length Andrew said, "We're gettin' close. I'd say maybe a hundred yards."

Michael nodded. "All right, me and you and Walker'll circle around past him, then come back on him from the other side. The rest of you give us a couple minutes, then come ahead. Everybody remember, we want to take him alive. You can't find out much from a dead Indian."

Andrew felt his pulse quickening as they made their arc, carrying them past the point where the boy should be. He heard a horse nicker. It could have been the boy's, or it could have been one of the others, becoming aware of the Indian pony.

Michael declared, "That spilled it. Let's go!"

They were too late. Before Andrew could see anything, he heard shouts, then the boom of a gunshot. The shouts subsided. He and Michael and Walker Younts broke out into the small clearing where he had seen the boy. The young Indian lay twisted on the ground, a small pool slowly spreading from beneath him.

Michael declared, "I thought I said—" He stopped then, staring at the elder Mann, bent over in his saddle. An arrow protruded from his leg, above the knee.

Zeb Willet exclaimed, "I had to do it. He put an arrow into Quenton, and he was goin' after him with a tomahawk. I had to do it."

Mann's son Harlan cried, "Paw!" He rode his horse up close and grasped the shaft of the arrow to pull it out. His father cried in pain and grabbed his son's hand, pushing it away.

Michael said, "We got to get him down off that horse and see what we can do for him." He dismounted quickly. Andrew and Walker Younts stepped to the ground and reached up to help Mann down from the saddle. Mann gritted his teeth but had to cry out in agony as he swung his leg over the horse. Andrew and Younts eased him to the ground.

Young Mann declared almost in panic, "Paw's bleedin' to death."

Andrew said, "He needs to bleed to wash away the poison. But that arrow's got to come out." He glanced around to see if anyone would volunteer.

Quenton Mann, cold sweat breaking across his face, looked up expectantly at his son. "It's your place to do it for me, Harlan. We're family."

Harlan trembled, eyes brimming with tears. "I can't."

Andrew said, "I'll do it, Quenton."

Mann's voice took on a stern edge, through the pain. "No,

Harlan'll do it. He's got the strength. He's just got to work himself up to it."

Miles Nathan took a small tobacco pouch from his pocket. "Here, Quenton. Somethin' for you to bite down on."

Mann took it. "Come on, son. Let's get it over with."

Harlan's shaking hands grasped the shaft. He closed his eyes for a moment, gathering his nerve, then jerked. Quenton bit down hard on the leather pouch but screamed in spite of that. Andrew thought for a moment that Mann was going to lose consciousness. Blood welled from the wound.

Harlan stared at the arrow shaft in white-faced dismay. Its bloodied end was bare. "The head didn't come out. It's still in there."

No one spoke for a minute. Quenton Mann shuddered in shock, his breathing rapid and heavy.

Michael said, "It's got to come out. It'll fester in there till the whole leg mortifies. He'll die." He brought a skinning knife out of its scabbard on his belt.

Harlan Mann protested, "You can't. You'll kill him."

"It's got to be done."

Harlan demanded, "Did you ever cut an arrowhead out of anybody before?"

Michael conceded that he never had.

The Reverend Fairweather stepped forward. "I have. Arrowheads, bullets. In my former occupation I was called upon many times." He took the knife from Michael's hand. "Somebody should build a fire. We need to cleanse the blade. While we wait, I shall consult with a higher power." He turned away, walking off to the edge of the timber and standing with his head bowed.

Michael stared at him in disbelief while Andrew and Younts quickly struck up a spark with flint and steel and built it into a small fire.

Zeb Willet had turned the young Indian over onto his back. The eyes were open and staring, but they no longer saw. Zeb said over and over, "I had to do it. I just had to."

Fairweather held the knife blade into the flames for a

minute, then said, "It'll take a couple of you to hold him." Andrew took Mann's arms, Younts the legs. Harlan held his father's hand.

Mann screamed when the blade entered the wound, and he almost burst free from Andrew's firm hold. Then he slumped, suddenly limp. Harlan cried fearfully, "He's dead."

Fairweather shook his head. "No, lad, it's just the Lord's mercy. He has allowed your father to fall unconscious so that he feels no more of the pain. It is no easy life He had given us on this earth."

The blood flowed freely, and Fairweather had to work by feel rather than sight. Andrew watched the one-eyed man sweat nervously as he probed, finding the arrowhead, almost getting it, losing it, then getting it again. Slowly, gingerly, he worked it upward with the tip of the blade.

"Hurry," Harlan cried. "He'll bleed to death."

"Hush, lad," Fairweather said. "Trust."

The arrowhead floated out on a sudden fountain of blood. Fairweather caught it in his fingers and held it up for all to see. He let the wound bleed a little more for cleansing, then said to Younts, "You'll find some bandaging cloth in my saddlebag. Fetch it for me, please."

Andrew looked at him in surprise. "You brought cloth to make bandages?" Such an idea had not even crossed his mind.

Fairweather replied, "Experience, young gentleman. One rarely ventures upon a mission of this kind without seeing the spilling of blood. My former life was not without its useful experience."

Eli Pleasant and Joe Smith rode up about the time Fairweather got the bleeding slowed. Fairweather said to Harlan, "Son, I have one more harsh duty to perform before I bandage this wound. I do not think you want to see it. Please, take your leave for a few minutes."

Harlan stared at him in doubt but accepted and walked away. Fairweather said, "Andrew, your powderhorn, please."

He uncapped it and poured black powder around and into the wound, then handed the horn back to Andrew. "Flint and steel, please." He struck a spark. The powder flared. Quenton

Mann went into a spasm and screamed again. Andrew smelled burned flesh and felt his stomach turn.

Eli edged up close to Andrew. He had lived a hard life and had seen many bitter things, but this sickened him too, a little. Andrew said tightly, "If it was me, I think I'd sooner just die."

Eli grunted. "You say that now, but if you was in Mann's place you'd want all the help anybody could give you. Whatever Fairweather may be otherwise, he knows about doctorin'."

Michael said, "Damned rough butcher, if you ask me."

Zeb Willet knelt again beside the young Indian. A tear ran down his cheeks into soft, youthful whiskers. He said in a breaking voice, "I thought I wanted to kill them all. But this is just a kid. He's not a whole lot older than Daniel. And I killed him."

Michael placed a hand on the youth's shoulder. "You wasn't given a choice. If he'd've killed you he wouldn't've sat up all night worryin' about it. Fortunes of war—"

Eli commented, "The boy was probably left behind to prove he could be trusted as a warrior. He went to sleep, which he shouldn't've done. But he put up a fight, so I guess he went out as a warrior sure enough."

Andrew looked at Quenton Mann, who had regained consciousness and was struggling not to lose it again. "Odd the way things turn sometimes. It was Quenton who killed an Indian down yonder and started everything to happenin'. Now, out of everybody here, it's him the kid puts an arrow in."

Miles Nathan remarked, "Three people dead, two wounded, one carried off. All for a few horses. Where's the sense of it?"

Eli declared, "There ain't no sense to it. That's just the way life is. But everybody wants to live it as long as they can. I expect Zeb's little brother is scared to death he's fixin' to lose his. We'd better be gettin' on about what we come for."

Harlan said, "Paw can't ride. And we can't just leave him."

Quenton Mann declared in a hoarse voice scarred with pain, "Like hell you can't. You have to. Just leave me a little food and my horse. I'll lay here till I get to feelin' better; then I'll start for home."

Harlan argued, "I'll stay with you."

"No, son, they'll need everybody. You'll go with them and tote your load. You've got my part to do now as well as your own. Go, and see that you do a good and proper job of it."

Joe Smith and Walker Younts dragged the Indian boy's body to the stream and caved off a section of steep bank to cover it.

Eli started dragging up dry deadfall timber and piling it where Mann could reach it. Nathan and Zeb helped him. Eli said, "That boy ain't buried very deep. The smell of him is liable to draw wolves. Come night, Quenton, if you ain't travelin' by then, you'd better build yourself a good fire to keep them away. They'll take the scent of your wounded leg and see you as meat."

Mann nodded grimly. "I'll be all right. You all go get that young'un back."

The men mounted their horses and prepared to go. Harlan hugged his father. As Harlan turned to leave, Quenton reached out and gripped his son's arm for a moment. "Go, son, and do your duty."

15

THE GOING was slow, and at times Andrew almost despaired. He remembered what Eli had said at the beginning, that a time would come when the Indians would seem to have disappeared. It was as if they had been swept up into the clouds. The trail, what there was of it, had grown cold. Often the searching party lost it and hunted for hours, finally finding some vague sign like horse droppings or old moribund grass stems bent and broken by hoofs. Andrew kept watching apprehensively a slow buildup of clouds to the west. Rain would wash away whatever little hope they still had of following the trail to its conclusion.

Andrew sensed restiveness in most of the party, even in Michael. Other men might already have admitted defeat and turned back. If any of these harbored such feelings, they were silenced by the driving determination in young Zeb Willet. The darker the prospects, the grimmer the set of his jaw became. Andrew was reminded of stout-hearted dogs back in Tennessee, trained to work cattle. They would grab a recalcitrant animal by the nose. The harder the cow fought, the deeper the dog's teeth bit in. The dog almost invariably won. Zeb avoided making a challenge of it, but he made it clear by his attitude that if the others turned back, he would go on alone.

Without exception, every man on this expedition came from a frontier heritage, a history of generation after generation moving farther out into the wilderness, each in its own time. That heritage was a driving force which impelled them onward now, not seriously considering abandonment of one of their own to continue a solitary quest that would probably result in his death. And somewhere out yonder, a frightened boy was probably looking back, wondering if anyone was coming for him. Everyone knew, and no one spoke of giving up.

The food they had brought was rapidly being depleted. There was no question of hunting, though they saw deer as well as smaller game, and on the open prairies now and again a few buffalo. The sound of a gunshot would racket far, they had no idea what the distance might be to Indian ears. They began stretching the food that still remained, eating berries when they found them. They paused to fish in the occasional stream they came across, usually with indifferent results. It was not a generous land to men who dared not use their firearms.

"Beautiful country," Michael enthused. "You ever seen prettier, Eli?"

"Mighty wild," Eli replied with reserve.

"That's what makes it so beautiful."

"If I was a younger man, maybe I could appreciate it more. And if you wasn't a man with a family—"

Andrew grinned. Eli could say it aloud without arousing Michael to a heated defense. Andrew could not.

Michael said only, "I wasn't talkin' about movin' here. I was just talkin' about the look of it."

"Somebody'll come along after us and settle. Then others'll come in behind him, and first thing you know it'll all look like San Felipe."

Andrew saw nothing wrong with that. San Felipe was a right nice place, with prospects. A hundred years from now there was no telling how big and important it would be.

The first sign that they might be nearing an Indian village was close-cropped grass and the tracks of many horses. Eli recognized the implications before Andrew did. In his smuggling operations he had often traded with Indian tribes in the region north and west of Nacogdoches. Eli knelt, careful about his rheumy knees, and examined the grass. Andrew dismounted and knelt with him, eager to learn.

Eli said, "They grazed their pony herd here yesterday or maybe the day before. They don't let their horses graze too far from the village. Afraid some other tribe'll run them off."

"Whichaway is it apt to be?"

Eli kept looking until he found the tracks moving in a definite direction. "They just loose-herded the horses to graze. But here's where they gathered them up and started drivin' them. Yonderway. Yonderway's the village. Where we find it we'll find a river or a creek, or at least a good clear spring. Indians are like the rest of us: they got to have water."

Andrew felt his pulse quickening. He looked up at Michael, still in the saddle, and saw exhilaration in his brother's eyes.

Zeb Willet said excitedly, "That's where Daniel is, then."

Eli held up his hand as a sign for caution. "Likely, boy, most likely. But where exactly? We got to know for certain before we can do anything. We can't just ride in there and tell them to give him to us. And if we get the camp stirred up, like as not they'll kill him out of hand just to keep us from gettin' him back. No, sir, we got to be as sneaky as coyotes about this thing. And patient."

"It's hard to be patient, knowin' we're so close to him."

"Your mama has already got enough to cry over. Let's don't be hasty and give her more grief." Eli studied the landscape. He pointed to a wood, lying half a mile to the east. "Michael, if you say so, we can hide ourselves over yonder till dark. We're out in the open here. There's always a danger some Waco'll come ridin' over the hill and see us."

Michael accepted the suggestion with a nod. Eli and Andrew remounted. Andrew kept looking back over his shoulder as they rode to the thicket, expecting any minute to see Indians appear. The riders made it into the deep shadows of the timber without being discovered.

Eli said, "Close as we are, we better not be buildin' a fire. The smell of smoke can carry a long ways."

Michael replied ruefully, "We got damn little left to cook anyway."

The men unsaddled their horses to give them a chance to rest. Zeb Willet did not. He trembled in excitement. "I can't just wait here, knowin' I'm so close to Daniel. I want to go scout around and see what I can find."

Michael said sternly, "You'll find an arrow, and we'll have to try and explain to your mama how come we lost both of her boys." He unsaddled Zeb's horse, leaving no room for argument.

Most of the men sat or lay down to rest. Andrew tried, but he found himself almost as nervous as Zeb. He studied the timber, a random mixture of almost every kind of wood he had seen grow in Texas. "Odd," he said to Eli, "how we'll go along and have long stretches of open prairie, and then we'll run into thickets like this on ground that otherwise looks the same."

Eli nodded. "Seems to be like that over the biggest part of Texas that I've seen. Must be the soil that makes the difference. Ain't always clear to the eye, but there's somethin' in part of it that likes to grow trees, and somethin' in other places that likes to grow grass. Me, I'm like the deer and the wild critters; I take it as it comes and don't ask for reasons."

"I'm wonderin' how far these woods reach to the north. You said the Indian village has got to be on a river or creek or somethin'. Reckon these woods reach to the water?"

"They might."

"And just about anywhere you find a river or a creek, you'll find timber. I was just thinkin' that if me and you was to follow this forest north, we might find cover to hide us all the way to the village."

"Nighttime, we won't need cover. The dark'll do that."

"But in the night we may not be able to see where they're keepin' that boy. If we would watch in the daytime, maybe we could see him and know where to go for him tonight."

Eli considered for only a moment, then pushed stiffly to his feet. "I've rested up already."

Zeb had been listening. "I'm goin' with you."

Andrew had rather he didn't, but he realized the young man

could not be denied. "You know the odds are against us. You know the woods may run out, or if they don't, we would watch that village all day and not see Daniel. I'm wonderin' if you're ready to handle that kind of disappointment without doin' somethin' that'll get you killed. Us too maybe."

"I'll be all right. You just give me a try."

Michael saw them saddling their horses and came to find out what they were about to do. Andrew did not answer. Eli explained, cagily making it sound like his own idea, for Michael would have rejected it had he known it was Andrew's. Michael said, "I'll be goin' with you."

Eli shook his head. "These other men look to you to lead them. With you gone they might get restless and do somethin' foolish. Besides, the fewer of us go, the less likely it is that we'll be seen." He swung into the saddle, giving Michael no time to think of a rebuttal. "You-all ready?"

Andrew and Zeb fell in beside him. "Ready."

They moved off quickly, leaving Michael standing there trying to think up reasons to counter Eli's explanation. They worked their way through the timber with some difficulty, dodging low limbs that threatened to drag them from their horses and briars that tried to snare and hold them.

Andrew said, "This'd be mean travelin' in the dark."

Eli responded, "In the dark we won't have to."

As Andrew hoped, the wood extended over the hill and down the other side. Without ever leaving it, they came in an hour or so to taller, bigger trees that lined a clear-running river. Eli glanced at Andrew. Words were not necessary, but his eyes said it: *Your hunch was right.*

They rode upstream, for judging by the horse tracks they had found earlier, that was where the village had to be. It was not necessary for anyone to say they had to be especially watchful or careful. After a little while Andrew heard something to the west and reined up, standing in the stirrups to listen. It came again, the distant barking of a dog, answered by another. Eli's gaze met his for a moment and confirmed his feeling. *We're getting close.*

Andrew began to watch Zeb with some apprehension. He

was still concerned that young Willet would forget himself and do something rash. But Zeb managed to contain whatever feelings might be building inside, threatening to burst into the open. Andrew touched his arm. "You goin' to be all right?"

Zeb nodded, not speaking.

They rode another hundred yards, then Andrew saw something move and made a quick gesture with his hand. The three riders drew into the heaviest timber they could see. A tattoed young Indian rode his horse down to the river and paused to let it drink. He carried a deer in front of him.

Eli whispered, "They'll have somethin' to eat in his lodge tonight."

Andrew's stomach growled, reminding him how little he had eaten. "I wish we were on friendly terms. I'd like some of that myself."

When the horse had drunk its fill, the Indian crossed the river and then followed its bank westward. Eli said, "Now we know the village is yonderway, and on the other side."

They heard more noise as they proceeded, more barking of dogs, the distant shouting of children at play. At length they spotted the pony herd, scattered at some distance on the south side of the river. So far as Andrew could see, it was being held by just two riders.

"Boys," Eli said. "That's a job they turn over to the young'uns to teach them how to be responsible. Unless they're lookin' to be attacked. In that case, they send the good warriors out."

"Then they're not lookin' for us," Andrew said, taking comfort in that. "They didn't expect anybody would ever trail them this far. Maybe nobody ever has."

Zeb declared, "Maybe nobody has ever had to try and follow a stolen brother before."

The smell of smoke began to reach them, becoming heavier as they rode slowly and watchfully. Sometimes it carried the scent of roasting meat, which only added to Andrew's discomfort. He saw then the round, grass-thatched huts which he had been told were a mark of the Wacos. Horseback tribes farther west used tepees, covered with buffalo hides, but these were Indians who stayed put, more or less, and built lodges for comfort and a degree of permanence.

Eli nodded toward a dense thicket and dismounted. Andrew and Zeb followed him as he led his horse there and tied him. Eli said, "From here, we'd best go afoot, and be careful as if we was rabbits prowlin' around a wolf's den."

The smoke seemed to drift into the thicket and settle there like fog. Andrew's nerves were drawn tight as a fiddle string. He studied Zeb, wondering if they had indeed made a mistake bringing the youth along. Zeb's eyes were wide with excitement. Beads of sweat were rising on his face. His whole body trembled. "Zeb, maybe you better stay with the horses."

"No. I've come to see, so I'll see."

They worked carefully through the wood, stopping often to listen for any change in the sounds, any sign of discovery. At the least, Andrew expected a loud reception from the village dogs. But the wind, such as it was, blew in their favor. It gave them the smoke, but it also kept their scent from reaching some sharp-nosed cur.

Eli was a couple of paces in the lead. He motioned quickly for Andrew and Zeb to drop, and he flattened himself to the ground. A moment later, two young boys appeared upon the creek bank, splashing their horses across with happy yelps and proceeding out of sight. They both looked about the age of the one Zeb had killed on the trail. Remembering young Willet's early declaration that he wanted to kill them all, Andrew worried. But though Zeb watched the boys with keen eyes, he gave no sign that he contemplated anything foolish. He had killed once; he seemed not eager to do it again.

Eli waited a couple of minutes to see if any more might be coming along. Satisfied, he pushed to his feet and went on. Andrew and Zeb followed, crouching to present as little profile as possible.

Presently Eli beckoned them to come up even with him. He had found a vantage point from which they could observe most of the village and yet be screened by the low, thorny vegetation. "It's a good place to watch from," he said. "I just hope there'll be somethin' to see."

The thing that caught Andrew's eye was a field, or perhaps a succession of gardens, in which corn grew much like his own at home, and melons and squash and the like. Several women stooped over the plants, pulling weeds. He thought he could enjoy one of those melons right now.

The village was a random scattering of grass-covered huts, their shape and general appearance reminding him considerably of beehives. The grass was sun-bleached, well-weathered. That, and the lush field, told him that though this might be a warrior society, these people were not nomads. Studying the huts, he realized they had one door to the east, another to the west. That could be useful information if they determined in which one the Willet boy might be held. He saw smoke curling from the tops of a few huts and wondered how the Wacos could have a fire inside without its catching the dry grass ablaze and sending the whole structure up in flames. He saw women scraping deerhides and cutting meat into strips for curing in the sun. Men lounged in the shade of the trees or the grass huts. Children played, rolling hoops made of willow switches, much like children in Tennessee, or around San Felipe.

Andrew looked in vain for sign of Daniel Willet. "Where *is* he?" he demanded after a long, silent wait. His voice had an edge of desperation about it.

"Patience," Eli counseled. "He's in one of them huts, I'm thinkin'. But which one, there ain't no tellin'. And we can't go pokin' in every one of them to find out. Just keep watchin'."

In the west, clouds built, dark and ominous. Much of the day Andrew had watched them and worried that a rain might come and wipe out the tracks. It did not matter now, for the tracks were no longer an issue. The clouds boiled up and covered the sun, and suddenly the air had a little of a chill about it. A distant rumble of thunder told him a spring storm was building to the west.

The rumble brought several men out of their huts to look. One hurried over to where some boys were practicing marksmanship with small bows. His hand movements suggested that he was giving brisk orders. The marksmanship contest broke up, and the boys scattered. Presently Andrew saw several of them start carrying firewood into the huts. He remembered the many times he had hurried to replenish the supply of dry wood for his mother in the face of a threatening rain. It struck him that in many ways these Indians were similar to his own people.

Zeb Willet grabbed Andrew's arm. In silence, he pointed, his face suddenly ashen. For a moment Andrew was puzzled, searching the village for whatever had caught Zeb's attention. Then he saw. Three boys had come out of a hut, followed by a man. The man wore only a loincloth, as did two of the boys. But the third wore shirt and trousers, ribboned and torn. That boy paused, looking back at the man in some confusion. The man pointed toward a pile of wood, then back to the hut. The two Indian boys shouted at the other one. At the distance Andrew could not distinguish their voices from others originating in the camp, but he suspected by their attitude that they were derisive.

Andrew glanced at Zeb. "Daniel?" he whispered.

Zeb nodded grimly. Movement in his throat suggested he was too choked to speak.

The boy reached down to pick up a stick. One of the Indian boys already had one, and he struck Daniel across the back. Daniel spun around, grasping his stick in both hands, swinging it hard. He connected against the Indian boy's head. The Indian boy went down. The other boy ran up and jumped on Daniel, knocking him to the ground. The two rolled in the dirt, punching at each other. The man stood for a minute, watching, then moved in to break up the fight. He pointed to the clouds in the west, then to the wood again. When Daniel stood back in an attitude of defiance, the man picked up the fallen stick and shook it threateningly at him. Daniel surrendered, after a minute, and began gathering wood. The boy who had been struck picked up another stick and moved toward Daniel with a vengeance, but the man cuffed him and put him back to the task at hand. The three boys carried an armload of wood apiece into the hut.

Eli grunted in satisfaction. "Well, at least we won't have to go knockin' on everybody's door tonight."

Zeb agonized, "I don't know how I can leave him down there another minute."

"You've got to. He's taken it this long. He can take it a few more hours. The boy's got a lot of fight in him."

Andrew said, "So've the Indians. Ridin' in there may be easy. Ridin' out could be a little meaner."

Eli grunted agreement. "If you come up with a better notion, I expect we'll all be ready to hear it. For now, though, I believe we've seen about enough. We better be gettin' back to the others."

16

ANDREW LET Eli and Zeb do the talking. He stood back and watched Michael's face as the old man and the young one described the village. Michael frowned deeply, listening. He asked, "Are you sure you can find the right hut? They'll look alike in the dark."

Eli said, "The one the young'un's in has another behind it, raised way up off the ground. They got food stored underneath. I hear tell they make the young girls sleep up there on the high floor with the ladder taken down so the boys can't get to them. I doubt as it works very good. In my day it wouldn't't've."

Zeb declared, "It don't matter how dark, I'll know which one Daniel is in. I'll feel it."

Michael gave him a glance that spoke more of sympathy than of belief. "I'd a lot sooner go by seein' than by feelin'." He looked back at Eli. "You said those huts look like beehives. They'll buzz like beehives too, the minute we go in there. We're apt to have the whole tribe down on us before we can get out."

Andrew felt a nervous itching along his backside. A vague idea had come to him as they were riding back along the river. He hesitated to bring it up for fear Michael would automatically reject any idea of his. But perhaps he could plant the seed and let Michael believe the idea had been his own.

"Eli," Andrew said, "somethin's bothered me about them grass huts. How can they build a fire inside without burnin' the place down?"

Eli explained, "They put the fire right in the middle, with stones around it and a hole in the roof for the smoke to go out. They don't let the fire get too big. One good spark could put them out of house and home in a minute."

Michael's eyes brightened. Andrew saw that the seed had sprouted. Michael turned away for a minute or so, staring off into the distance. Then he announced, "It just come to me how we can get their attention away from the hut where they're keepin' the boy. We'll set off a couple of huts on the far side. While they're all rushin' to try and stop it, we'll run in and grab Zeb's brother."

Eli said, "Seems to me like that's what Andy Jackson used to call a *dy*-version."

Miles Nathan declared, "Whatever you call it, it sounds good to me."

Zeb Willet said, "I'm with you, Michael."

Michael frowned at Andrew. "I'm surprised you didn't think of it yourself."

Andrew suppressed a smile. "I don't have your experience."

Michael looked to the west, where the sun had dropped below the horizon and a heavy cloud was rapidly bringing night's darkness upon the woods. A rumble of thunder shook the ground. He said, "If it sets in to rainin', that accidental fire is apt to be hard to start."

Andrew turned to the man with the eye patch. "Then, Reverend, looks to me like it's time you prayed for dry weather."

They waited for full dark. Lightning was flashing to the west when they started. Michael led them out of the timber, but only far enough that they could ride unimpeded by the tangle of trees and the clutching of briars. They were always near enough to the wood that they could quickly pull back into its protective cover. Andrew worried that the bright flashes of lightning might give them away if anyone was alert in the village, or guarding its perimeter.

Eli tried to ease his mind. "Indians don't seem to've ever

caught the white man's likin' for guard duty, unless they've got a strong feelin' there's an enemy about. Most of the time they don't bother with settin' up a watch. They just turn that over to the dogs and go to sleep."

The men fell silent. Though they rode in a body, each was alone with his own somber thoughts. In a while they reached the place where the village's horses were loose-herded on an open patch of grassland. Andrew watched for guards in the occasional flash of distant lightning. He saw none, but he knew there must be one or two, at least, preventing the horses from straying away in the night. They probably had little thought of attack by an outside enemy.

Walker Younts said, "This thing all started with the Wacos stealin' horses. It would pay them back good and proper if we was to run away with that whole herd. They'd be worth a fair dollar back in the settlements."

Michael replied, "They'd slow us down and get us caught up with. We're here to get that boy back, and nothin' else." He paused. "What's more, if we can get away without havin' to kill any more Indians, it'll help our chances. Kill one of them and they're liable to hound us all the way home."

Harlan Mann pointed out, "We killed and buried one already, the one that wounded Paw."

"They ain't missed him yet. Chances are they'll never know what come of him."

Reaching the river, the riders moved along its south bank until the smell of smoke began to mix with the pleasant hint of rain on the breeze from the cloudy west.

"Wind's still on our side," Eli noted quietly. "If we're careful, maybe we won't stir up the camp dogs."

The breeze carried a faint sound of singing. At least, Andrew guessed it was singing. To his ears it was discordant, unlike any music he had known.

Zeb worried, "I hope that's not a scalp song or somethin'. You don't reckon they're fixin' to burn Daniel at the stake?"

Eli reassured him. "I never heard of these Indians doin' such as that. If they intended to kill him they'd've done it at the start, like they done to your daddy." He pointed. "I expect this is a good place for us to cross the river. Village is right up yonder."

They eased into the water and let their horses drink. Done, they moved up over the north bank and halted. This was very near the spot from which Andrew and Zeb and Eli had watched earlier. Andrew could make out the vague outlines of many huts. Some had a faint glow from fires built inside, though most looked dark. A few outdoor fires made tiny pinpoints of light. Andrew studied the scene a minute, then pointed. "That's the hut where they had Daniel."

Zeb and Eli agreed.

Michael was silent for a time, concentrating his thoughts upon the village. "Where's the door?" It was too dark for him to see that kind of detail.

Eli said, "These huts have generally got two doors, one on the east and one on the west. The back door faces this side."

"Then we ought to be able to go in without havin' to be exposed to the center of the camp. Now, if somebody could sneak around yonder and touch off a couple of the huts on the far side, it'd draw the attention over that way."

Younts volunteered. "That's a good job for me and Joe."

Eli said, "I'll go and stand guard while they do the honors."

Michael accepted. "Try not to let anybody see you. It'll be better if they don't realize they've been invaded. Get the fires started, then h'ist your tails back to here. This is where we'll leave the horses."

Michael looked at Zeb Willet. "We don't want to make any mistakes in the dark and find out we've carried off some Indian boy instead of your brother. You want to go with me into the hut?"

Zeb nodded grimly. "That's the only way I'd have it."

Andrew declared, "Two won't be enough. I'm goin' in with you." His voice was firm. Michael frowned but did not disagree.

Fairweather said, "That still leaves three of us."

Michael yielded him a quick, distrustful glance, then said to Miles Nathan, "I want a good responsible man to stay here and hold onto the horses. If any of them was to get away from us, we'd be in a bad fix."

Nathan nodded assent. "You can depend on the reverend and me."

Michael did not seem to care whether Fairweather assented or not.

Fairweather said, "I will ask the Lord's hand to guide you."

Michael ignored him. Andrew, however, said, "We'd take that kindly."

Harlan Mann asked, "What do you want me to do?"

Michael said, "You'll go with us halfway and stand guard to make sure nobody cuts us off from gettin' back to the horses."

Andrew's pulse quickened as Michael dismounted. Michael said, "All right, Eli, you-all get started. We'll wait till the village is in an uproar, then we'll go in."

Eli beckoned Younts and Smith with his chin. "*Vámanos,*" he said, using Spanish without giving a thought to whether they understood. In seconds the three riders were swallowed up in darkness. Lightning flashed, but Andrew could no longer see them.

Michael handed his reins to Nathan. He looked at Andrew and Zeb. "No shootin' unless there's no way around it. We don't want to pull anybody's attention away from the fire."

Andrew could see Zeb's hands visibly trembling as he handed his reins to Fairweather. "Steady," Andrew said. "With luck, we'll be away from here pretty soon." But he could feel his own hands shaking a little, and cold sweat broke on his forehead. He stared at the quiet hut which they had targeted, and he wondered how many people inside might be inclined to fight. He wiped his wet palms against his trousers.

Michael gave him a critical study. "Maybe *you* better stay and help hold the horses."

Andrew retorted, "You won't have to be lookin' back, wonderin' where I'm at. I'll be in front of you."

"Not too far in front. That's like bein' by yourself."

Crouching, the three moved away from the river, closer to

the edge of the village. Somewhere to the north a dog barked, and other dogs picked up the call. Andrew was heartened to see that they aroused no particular interest among the villagers. One man stepped out of a hut and spoke threateningly. His dog stopped barking, but others did not.

Michael raised his hand. "Far enough. We'll wait."

The wait seemed an hour long. Andrew began wondering how long it would take three men to circle the village on horseback and start a fire.

Zeb was having the same thoughts. "Reckon they got caught?"

Michael said, "We'd be hearin' a lot of excitement. Things are pretty quiet."

Andrew could hear the singing continue from a hut somewhere away from the perimeter. He began to wonder if setting one of these grass structures afire might be more difficult than it sounded.

Then, on the far side of the village, flames began to lick up the side of a hut, and they burst suddenly atop a second hut nearby. A woman screamed, and children shouted. In the glow Andrew saw people running from the two huts. Within moments, excited voices were raised all over the village. Against the growing flames, he could see people hurrying in all directions. They poured out of other huts, some running toward the fires and some away. The west wind picked up sparks and then firebrands. A third hut began to burn.

Zeb raised up, ready to go. Michael touched his arm. "Wait a minute. We need to allow time for Eli and them to get back. When we leave this place, we'll want to be leavin' fast and not have to wait for nobody."

Andrew's mouth was dry. He was glad there was no need for words, because the tightness of his throat might not have let him speak. He sensed that Michael was counting under his breath. At last Michael whispered, "Let's go."

Andrew was two paces ahead when they reached the back side of the hut. He could hear children's voices inside, and a woman speaking excitedly. The man or men in the hut had probably gone to help fight the fires. At least Andrew hoped so. The door was of woven grass, much like the rest of the hut. He grasped it and pulled. It came free, without a hinge. He rushed inside and for a moment felt blind in the darkness. The interior smelled heavily of smoke. The only light was a faint glow of coals in a stone circle at the hut's center.

Zeb Willet cried out, "Daniel, where're you at?"

A surprised answer came in a boy's thin voice. "Over here!"

Andrew saw him lying on a blanket or a hide—he could not tell which. The boy tried to jump to his feet but could not. His hands and feet were bound, and he was tethered to one of the tree-limb braces that made up the hut's framework. A woman screamed. Other children cried out in their surprise and terror. A boy, larger than the others, rushed toward Daniel with a knife in his hand. Andrew tripped him and grabbed up the knife as the boy sprawled. He pitched it to Zeb and put his foot gently but firmly on the back of the boy's neck to hold him still.

Zeb rushed to his brother. The blade flashed a reflection from the coals as he severed the tether and swept Daniel into his arms.

Michael said, "Let's get the hell out of here!"

Andrew motioned for Zeb to leave first, carrying his brother. The woman dashed out the hut's front door, shouting, leaving the children behind. Andrew saw several pairs of bright eyes staring at him in fright from around the circular wall of the hut. He said, knowing they would not understand him, "You-all go back to bed." He lifted his foot from the bigger boy's neck.

Michael stood at the east door through which they had entered. He made an impatient motion with his hand. "Will you hurry the hell up?"

Andrew went out ahead of him, just in time to see an Indian man come running around the hut, grabbing at Zeb and the boy Daniel. Zeb turned quickly away, shielding his brother. Andrew saw a knife in the Indian's hand. He ran toward him, shouting a challenge. The man whipped around to face him. Andrew parried at him with the barrel of his rifle. The Indian stepped quickly aside, avoiding the thrust, then was on Andrew like a wildcat.

Caught off balance, Andrew tumbled and fell backward. The Indian was on top of him in an instant. Andrew let go of his rifle and used both hands to grab the Indian's wrist. The man was bigger and stronger. Inexorably, despite Andrew's best resistance, the knife blade was forced down toward his throat. He smelled the warrior's hot breath in his face. He felt the point bite into his skin.

A dark form appeared above him. Michael swung his rifle and struck the Indian a solid blow across the side of the head. The man went limp, and Andrew quickly rolled out from under him. He grabbed the knife from the loosened fingers. He considered plunging it into the Indian's throat, as the warrior had tried to do to him.

Michael said curtly, "I wish you wouldn't do it, but if you're goin' to, hurry up."

The impulse waned. Andrew struck the Indian's knife in his belt and picked up his rifle. "Wouldn't be any gain in it." He moved into a trot, following Zeb and the boy back toward the river where Nathan and Fairweather held the horses. Michael followed closely. Behind them, the village was thoroughly aroused, fighting the fires, trying to prevent their spread. So far as he could tell, no one except those in the hut and the one who had jumped him knew that outsiders had passed so near.

Harlan Mann fell in behind them, providing a rear guard.

Fairweather exclaimed as he saw the boy in Zeb's arms, "The Lord be praised."

Only then did Zeb pause to cut the rest of the rawhide thongs that bound his brother. Daniel clung tightly to Zeb's neck, but he did not cry.

Andrew asked, "Daniel, are you all right? They didn't hurt you?"

The boy declared, "They beat on me some, but I hit them back, every chance I got. The one you tripped, he was the worst. I'd like to go back and hit him with a stick."

Fairweather said quietly, "Vengeance is mine, sayeth the Lord. Be content, my young friend."

Daniel plainly did not understand what he meant.

Eli, Younts, and Smith rode up. Eli saw with satisfaction that the rescue had been made. He nodded toward the village. "They'll be lucky if half the place don't burn, the way the wind is gettin' up. I reckon they're too busy to be huntin' us for a while."

A bright flash lighted the entire village, and the ground shook to the power of the thunder. Michael said, "It's fixin' to rain, and that'll help them. We'd better be a long ways from here if they decide to come lookin'."

Zeb Willet mounted his horse, and Andrew boosted Daniel up behind him. Michael paused a moment to be sure everybody was in the saddle, then he heeled his bay horse into a run. The rest followed his pace. Their escape route led them past the horse herd. It would be easy to cut off several and drive them along, but Michael made no such move. Escape was the primary consideration now.

Daniel pointed. "My pony's out there. They stole him."

Eli said, "You just hang onto your brother and ride like an Indian. I'll git you another pony someday."

They ran the horses as long as they dared. Michael slowed his bay to a trot and looked back to be sure none of the party had fallen behind. Giving Zeb and Daniel a look of satisfaction, he smiled for the first time. "Zeb, I wish we could've taken time to get your horses back."

Daniel's arms were around his older brother. Zeb patted the small hands. "I've got what counts. For this, I'd walk the rest of my life."

Michael pulled around to Andrew. "Looked to me like you were havin' a little trouble back there with that big Indian and his knife. Did he cut you?"

Involuntarily Andrew's hand went to his throat. In the excitement he had put it out of his mind. It stung a little, where the knifepoint had driven into the flesh. "It was a long ways from the heart," he said. "It'll heal."

Michael grunted. "You didn't want me to come on this little sashay atall. I expect you're glad now that I did."

Andrew wanted to admit that he was. But he still felt that

he had been right. Michael's proper place had been with Marie. But where was the point in saying that now? He made no answer.

The rain started, suddenly and with a vengeance, lashing at them as the lightning split the night skies and thunder made the earth shake beneath the horses' feet. Andrew trembled at the chill and felt concern for the boy. But Zeb wrapped a blanket around his brother and kept riding. "After all he's been through," Zeb said proudly, "a little cold rain ain't goin' to bother him much. He's a fighter. Papa'd be proud—"

Andrew said, "He'd be proud of both of you."

The water ran in rivulets down the gentle hills. Eli looked back, then down. "Whatever tracks we left behind us, this'll wash them away. I doubt them Wacos'll come after us in all this rain. If they commence later, they'll have a hell of a time findin' a trace to start on."

The riders came to another heavy wood, where tall pines formed an almost solid canopy overhead. This did not stop the pounding rain from coming through, but it slowed the force. Michael said, "We'll rest the horses and wait out the storm."

Fairweather suggested they all kneel and offer up their gratitude for safe delivery from the hands of their enemies. Hats came off, even in the rain. Andrew thought the loudest *Amen* came from Zeb Willet.

The men huddled in sodden misery beneath the trees, the cold offset somewhat by the warm success of their venture. Andrew sat on his heels, his back against a pine, and listened to various ones recount their personal memories of the raid on the village. Younts said, "Ol' Joe here, he was so nervous he kept droppin' his flint. I thought he never was goin' to get a fire started."

"Ain't so atall," Joe Smith countered. "It was him that couldn't hold onto his flint. I got my fire started and had to go and help him with his. And I was the one had to blow on it to keep it goin'; he was plumb out of wind."

"*You* ain't never been out of wind," Younts declared.

Nathan Miles laughed aloud. "You-all both done yourselves proud," he said. Andrew suspected either one of them would be welcomed as a son-in-law, provided they didn't try to start soon. Birdy was young yet, even by frontier standards.

Michael said, "Everybody done themselves proud." He brought his glance painfully to the one-eyed preacher. "Fairweather, I'll always remember what you did to us years ago. But I won't forget that you held up your part here, and more."

Fairweather acknowledged the faint compliment. "I have never asked even the Lord to forgive me for my past life. I have only asked for mercy."

The rain stopped at daylight. The men had little food left except for some jerked venison. They gave that to the boy. The parched grain substitute for coffee was gone, but the wood was so wet they probably could not have started a fire to boil it anyway. Hungry, tired, chilled, no one had to say anything about going home. Michael tightened the girth on his saddle and mounted the bay horse. The other men silently followed suit.

Andrew was aware that they were retracing more or less the route they had taken on the way north. He guessed, but didn't ask, that Michael wanted to find the place where they had left Quenton Mann, to be sure he had managed to get on his horse and start home alone. They struck the river a little west of their original crossing and rode downstream. Andrew recognized the place where they had had their quick skirmish with the Indian boy. He knew the tree under which they had left Mann after the arrowhead had been removed from his leg. Mann was gone.

Harlan Mann nodded in satisfaction. "I reckon Paw got to feelin' stronger. He'll be home by now, with Maw takin' care of him."

The rain had washed away whatever tracks Mann might have created. The river was on a slight rise, its waters an angry brown. But it was no obstacle to men on their way home from a long and bruising expedition that had challenged their endurance. They crossed over and set out southeastward, the way they had come. Andrew guessed it was upward of noon when he saw a horse standing several hundred yards ahead of them, beneath an oak tree.

Michael held up his hand as a signal for everybody to stop while he tried to decide if a lone horse out there so far from civilization suggested any threat. "Anybody see somethin' that I don't?" he asked.

No one had anything to contribute. Michael proceeded after checking his long rifle and pouring fresh powder into the pan.

When they were within a couple of hundred yards Harlan Mann said tightly, "That looks like Paw's horse. Yes sir, I believe it is."

A little nearer, Andrew could see a man lying on the ground.

"Paw!" Harlan exclaimed, and set his horse into a run. The rest of the men followed but never caught up to him. When Andrew got there Harlan was on the ground, kneeling before his fallen father. He saw at a glance that the wounded leg had swollen far beyond its normal size, and blowflies had found it. The stench made his stomach turn.

Michael dismounted quickly and handed his reins up to Zeb Willet. Andrew did likewise. Eli stayed in the saddle but looked down sadly. "Is he dead?"

Andrew felt for the man's pulse. He saw Mann's eyelids flutter. Mann blinked a few times, trying to see. He picked out his son and painfully brought him into some focus. "Harlan?"

"It's me, Paw. I'm here."

"I tried to wait. But the leg—" His voice trailed off. "Tell your mama—"

That was all he managed to say. The pulse weakened gradually, and finally it was gone. Mann had waited for his son. Once Harlan had come, he had no strength left for holding on any longer.

Andrew said, "I'm sorry, Harlan."

Fairweather spoke a quiet prayer.

Young Mann bit his lip. "Will you-all help me put him on his horse? I'll take him home now."

Fairweather watched as Mann's body was tied securely to his saddle. He said, "I'll go home with you, son. Your mama will feel better if there's somebody to read the words over him right and proper."

The others sat on their horses and watched with bowed heads as Harlan and Fairweather started their solitary journey, angling almost due east toward the Mann home on the Brazos.

Nathan Miles mused soberly, "Two dead on our side and two dead on theirs. Kind of evens everything up, don't it?"

Nobody spoke for a minute. Finally Eli observed, "This Texas, it has a world of promise. But it sure asks a hell of a toll."

THEY WERE a tired, bedraggled, bewhiskered, and hungry group as they limped in finally to the Willet farm. Andrew's shoulders were slumped. His backside felt numb from the long, weary ride. They had managed to shoot one deer on the way back, a small doe that was more flavor than substance and certainly not large enough to satisfy everybody's need. They had given the boy the best of it.

During the trip he described his treatment as a captive of the Indians. Often he had been confused because he did not understand their language, and they tended to whip him when he did not respond as they wished him to. "Most of the time I didn't know what they wanted me to do. And even when I knowed, I acted like I didn't. The one you was wrestlin' with, Andrew, he acted like he was wantin' to make a slave out of me. One time when he hit me, I got ahold of his hand and bit him good."

His face saddened. "I never did know which one it was that killed Papa."

Zeb hugged his brother. "It don't matter anymore. Gettin' you home to Mama and them is all that counts now."

Fatigued though they were, the two young Willets seemed to gain new strength as they came in sight of the spread out, comfortable-looking log structure Lige Willet had built for his family on the farm which was to have been his home into his old age, a place to watch his children grow up and to raise the grandchildren who would have brightened his final years. Andrew felt a catch in his throat, looking at the place, at the field which Willet would never harvest again, at the young orchard from which he would never taste the fruit. It had always been a joy to come over here and sit a spell with the Willets and their brood. It would never be the same again. He felt the loss more now than when he had first heard of Willet's death.

He saw a number of horses being herded on grass a quarter mile from the house, guarded by two riders still unwilling to discount the threat of Indians. The horses belonged to the settler families who had gathered here for mutual protection. Several wagons stood near the shed. Lige Willet had not owned one.

The riders were seen long before they reached the cabin. More than a dozen people poured out onto the dog-run and into the open yard, waiting. Daniel cried, "Yonder's Mama."

Zeb could not restrain himself. He heeled his horse into a run, carrying him and Daniel in ahead of the others. Andrew blinked as he recognized Mrs. Willet, hurrying out to meet her sons. Zeb handed the boy down to her. She clasped him in her arms as if she would crush the life from him. Zeb slowly dismounted. When she looked up at him, he went to her, and the three of them stood there, holding to one another. At the distance Andrew could not hear if anything was being said. He doubted that words were necessary.

An excited crowd gathered around the Willet family, offering congratulations for the boy's return. Miles Nathan went to his own family, his wife reaching out for him. The two bachelors, Younts and Smith, gave their full attention to the Nathan girl, Birdy.

Andrew saw Michael's eyes brighten and a smile break across his whiskered face. Andrew followed his gaze, though he did not have to; he knew who Michael had been searching for. Michael put the horse into a trot and moved to meet Marie. She advanced beyond the others and stopped to wait for him. Andrew watched as Michael jumped to the ground and swept Marie into his arms. The boy Mordecai grabbed his father's legs and held tightly.

Only Andrew and Eli remained on their horses, on the edge of the crowd but somehow not a part of it.

Eli must have read the emptiness in Andrew's face. He said, "It's hard goin', sometimes, bein' a bachelor."

Andrew looked away, his eyes burning. He had never felt more alone.

PART III

THE

FREDONIAN
REBELLION

17

IN LATER years the incident would be remembered grandiosely as the Fredonian Rebellion, and some would claim it was the earliest glimmering of the Texas revolution against Mexico. It began with a brashly confrontational Kentuckian named Haden Edwards, one of many land *empresarios* who attempted to bring in American settlers and establish colonies in Mexican Texas after the pattern set by Stephen F. Austin. Most failed, but few did so with the bluster and bitterness and legacy of official mistrust that marred Edwards's brief career as an empire builder.

The fault was not his alone. Much of it was rooted in the inefficiency and carelessness of bureaucracy, granting him lands upon which others had prior claim, including Mexican citizens who had lived there for generations, peaceful Indians who considered it theirs by birthright, and even Americans who claimed squatters' rights by virtue of having survived years of futile efforts by the Spanish and Mexican governments to push them back across the Sabine River.

Andrew had little inkling of the future trend of events when he encountered Edwards's brother Benjamin that summer. He did not go often to Michael's cabin, for the rift that had broken between them had not healed. He would not have gone at all had it not been for his need to look in occasionally upon

Marie and the boy Mordecai. He kept himself busy on his own place and tried not to dwell upon the loneliness of it. Eli Pleasant had stayed only a little while, then drifted back toward Nacogdoches and his own place just across the Sabine in Louisiana.

One morning, working in the field, Andrew caught a movement on the horizon and stopped the blue-speckled ox. He wiped sweat from his forehead and eyes and squinted. He saw a lone rider, evidently a stranger, because Andrew did not recognize the mount. He knew every horse between here and San Felipe, just about, and could identify them from farther away than he could identify their riders. The horseman was coming from the direction of San Antonio de Bexar, the Mexican capital of Texas.

He's had him a right smart of a ride, Andrew thought.

He wondered at first if this might be Stephen Austin, for Austin often traveled to Bexar to conduct business with representatives of the Mexican government. But as the distance lessened, it was evident this was a larger man than Austin.

The rider was well-dressed for a man on the road, though dusty and trail-worn. He did not look at all like a farmer. Andrew took him for a lawyer. The man stared with much interest at Andrew's cabin, at his field, at the ox in the yoke. He spoke in a manner that indicated a better education than Andrew's. "I must say, I am glad to see sign of civilization. I had feared for some time I had lost my way."

"You're on the right way if you're headed for San Felipe," Andrew assured him. He strode forward and offered his grimy hand. "Name's Andrew Lewis. If you'll give me time to unhook the ox, I'll go with you to the cabin and fix us a bite of dinner."

The man dismounted and accepted the hand, dirt and all. "Benjamin Edwards. Perhaps you have heard of my brother, Haden Edwards?"

Andrew shook his head. "I don't get away from this place much. If you asked me who is the president of the United States, I might get it wrong."

"My brother is an *empresario,* like Stephen Austin. No, not like Austin—better."

It occurred to Andrew, now that he thought about it, that Eli had said something to him about an Edwards who was making a claim to land around Nacogdoches. If he remembered right, Eli had said there was trouble over the titles. But it would be impolite to bring up such a disagreeable subject with a chance passerby. He said, "The fare won't be fancy, but it'll be fillin'. I left a pot of beans on the coals this mornin'. And there's venison."

They went to the pens first, where he forked a little hay to the ox and slid a bar into place so the animal could not leave. If the visitor did not stay long, Andrew could get a lot more work done in the field before dark.

While he fried venison in the little fireplace, he asked about conditions in Bexar, a place he had always found somehow fascinating.

"Poorest town I ever saw in my life," Edwards replied distastefully. "Mexicans mostly, and no real cash money among the lot of them. They think poor and they live poor. What they need is some good American energy to bring that place to life."

Andrew shook his head in mild disagreement. "Always seemed an agreeable bunch of people to me. I've gotten along with them well enough."

He saw that Edwards's feeling was deeply held. It was bad form to argue with a guest, especially when he saw so few of them. He put the food on the table, asked a quick blessing, and told Edwards to help himself. Edwards fell silent, putting away two men's share of the venison, beans, and rough-ground cornbread. The trail from Bexar was long.

At last Edwards pushed his chair back from the crude table and rubbed his stomach in contentment. "Plain and humble fare, my friend, but filling enough to do me until I reach a better place."

"Glad you liked it," Andrew said with irony, for the visitor's mild disparagement had not gone unnoticed. The beans should have lasted Andrew three or four days. They wouldn't now. He said, "If your colony is up at Nacogdoches, what brings you all the way to Bexar and San Felipe?"

"The stupidity of government," Edwards declared sternly. "They gave us our grant, and now they say there is difficulty over titles. There are squatters on our land who resist our efforts to move them, and the central government has been no help. On the contrary, it has been a major part of the problem. I went to Bexar to apprise the authorities of the true situation and to let them know exactly where my brother and I stand." His face creased with remembered indignation. "I told them most forcefully that an agreement is an agreement. Sometimes, however, these Mexicans are like children. One must take a firm position with them, show them that an American is not to be trifled with."

Andrew felt a stirring of concern. Edwards's manner told him the man had done a lot of telling and very little asking. As little experience as Andrew had had with Mexican authorities, he knew their pride did not respond well to lecturing by a foreigner. Lecturing had never been Stephen Austin's style, one reason he had gotten along so well. He was a diplomat. Had he not been, no American would now be in Texas legally. And perhaps not illegally either. Stirred up, the Mexicans, like the Spanish before them, had a most severe manner of dealing with trespassers upon their ground. Somewhere up toward Nacogdoches, Mordecai Lewis's unmarked grave bore silent testimony to that fact.

Frowning, Andrew asked, "Just what was it you told the authorities?"

"I told them they had granted my brother that land, and if the central government did not expel the interlopers, we would do it ourselves without their assistance."

"The Mexicans don't appreciate bein' talked to like that."

"By the eternal, sir, they listened with rapt attention."

"I'll bet they did," Andrew said dryly.

Edwards stiffened. "You find fault with me, sir?"

"There's people in Mexico huntin' for any excuse to get rid of all us Americans that've taken up land on Mexico soil. Every time Austin deals with them, he acts like a man walkin' on eggshells. Feller like you goes to stirrin' them up, he's apt to make trouble for all of us."

"I did no more than stand up for my rights—mine and my brother's. If I stepped on any sore toes, they should not have been stuck out in the way. I am going now to San Felipe to apprise Mr. Austin of what has been done and said. If there is to be trouble, I shall expect him as an American to stand with us."

It was in Andrew's mind that Austin would not be pleased by this report. But Austin was plenty capable of speaking for himself; Andrew had no need to speak for him.

Edwards walked to the door and gave Andrew's farm a long study. "We have better land at Nacogdoches, and much closer to a civilized country."

"I've seen it," Andrew replied. Edwards could take any inference he wished from that. "I'm satisfied right where I'm at."

"And are you satisfied with Austin? He is much too thick with the Mexicans to suit me."

"I count him a friend of mine."

Edwards put on his hat. "Very well. Time will tell which of us is right. I am obliged for the meal, sir."

"Welcome any time," Andrew replied, though he hoped the next visit would not be soon.

He watched Edwards ride toward Michael's cabin and made a dry, humorless smile as he thought how much better meal the man could have eaten if he had gone there first and had sat at Marie's table instead of Andrew's. Well, he probably deserved about what he got.

He put the yoke on the ox and took him back to the field. He tried to put Edwards out of his mind but could not. He kept remembering Austin's concern over keeping friendly relations with the Mexican authorities. The American settlers in Texas could look to no one but each other for help if the radicals in Mexico gained enough influence to try to put them off of the land.

A few blustering bullies like Edwards could spoil the fragile alliances that held American Texas together and bring catastrophe down upon everyone.

18

EVER SINCE he had seen the surveyors, Isaac Blackwood had expected trouble. The Blackwood family had been squatters for generations, so they dreaded surveyors as they dreaded Indians. The lawyers would not be far behind, and eviction was sure to follow. It had been that way since Grandpap's time, way back in the Appalachians.

Finis had taken up his rifle to kill the surveyors, and Luke backed him, as always. Isaac had argued that missing men draw searchers, and it was hard to hide a killing, especially that of several men. Finis had maintained that they could throw suspicion onto the Cherokee Indians who lived in the general vicinity. Isaac had managed to convince him that the Cherokees were regarded as civilized, and the authorities in Nacogdoches would not long be fooled.

"All right," Finis had raged, flapping his stump of an arm, "but there'd better not be no striped-britches son of a bitch come and try to run us off of our place. I'll kill him deader'n a skint mule."

It wasn't much of a place to be run off from, Isaac thought. He said, "I don't know why anybody'd want to come here when there's so much better land to be had."

The Mexican soldiers who had captured them at the Lewis farm had conducted them first to Nacogdoches for examination by the civil authorities, then to the bank of the Sabine. The troops had waited in ominous silence while the Blackwoods swam their horses across to Louisiana. Isaac would have been content to squat on the Louisiana side, where the laws at least were American. But Finis had his hard head set on Texas and satisfaction from Michael Lewis. He could not do it sitting on the east side of the Sabine in Frenchman country. They had waited until nightfall, then sneaked back into Texas in the dark of the moon.

So now they bided their time at a place they had found abandoned on a small creek in a clearing in the midst of a heavy East Texas piney wood. Isaac surmised that some squatter before them had built the small cabin and had broken the ground for a field little larger than a garden. He had probably been driven out by Spanish or Mexican soldiers. Or perhaps simply by starvation. The field seemed to grow rocks better than it grew anything Isaac had planted.

It had one virtue, however: proximity to the Sabine River and quick escape into Louisiana in the event Isaac's brothers followed their natural propensities for mischief and a hasty departure for the United States became necessary.

He paused to lean on the hoe and wipe a sleeve across his face to stop the burning sweat from trailing down into his eyes. The tall, green cornstalks rustled around him, intercepting much of the breeze that might have blown cool through his half-soaked shirt. He looked about for his brothers. Luke sat in the shade beside the log cabin, sagging on a rough bench like a sack of cornmeal. He looked all tuckered out, but he was just lazy. He had spent perhaps half an hour helping Isaac hoe weeds out of the corn, then had quit the work.

Isaac did not see Finis anywhere, but he had a good notion his oldest brother was in the cabin, and not alone. Once Finis had found a woman who would tolerate him, he was rutting like an acorn-fed boar. They had discovered neighbors a few miles to the south, squatters like themselves who had no official sanction to be in Texas but probably were unwanted anywhere else. Or perhaps they *were* wanted, by one sheriff or another. Among their numerous brood was a plump and red-headed daughter Nelly, twenty years old, not much for looks but a fair-to-middling cook and housekeeper, and perfectly willing to take up with Finis Blackwood. Her folks had seemed relieved to see her go, though they had acted a little put out that no money went with the deal. They had made no fuss about the lack of clerical blessing. Mentally Nelly was on about the same level as Luke, certainly no bragging point. What made her attractive to Finis was that she seemed perpetually in heat.

Finis had first claim, but when he was in a better than average mood he lent her to Luke. When the two happened to be gone off hunting, Nelly would rub up against Isaac. Sometimes he resisted and sometimes he accepted her invitation. He was not proud of it. But he had been doing most of the work around here and getting damned little of the pleasure. Finis owed him.

With all the planting being done, it seemed a foregone conclusion that a crop would sprout one of these days, and nobody would know whose it was.

From the corner of his eye Isaac caught a movement at the edge of the wood. He paused only a moment before dropping his hoe and trotting to the end of the row where he had propped his rifle against a log. He saw three horsemen. They wore no uniform, so at least they were not Mexican soldiers. But strangers always had a way of bringing bad news.

First the surveyors, then the lawyers. It had been that way forever, seemed like.

He trotted to the cabin, shouting at Luke to wake the hell up and grab his rifle. He pushed open the cabin door and, as he expected, saw Finis on the bed, all tangled up with Nelly. "What the hell?" Finis grumbled. He was not embarrassed; embarrassment was not in him. He was simply irritated at the interruption.

"You better git your britches on and fetch your rifle. Looks like we got company comin'."

"Who is it?"

"I don't know. But you can bet they ain't here to bring us no money."

Nelly tried to cover herself with the blanket as Finis quit the bed. It didn't matter. Isaac had seen all there was, more than once. He went outside and took up a station in front of the cabin, rifle cradled across his arm.

Luke moved up beside him. "I can pick off one of them, and you can git another. Finis'll git the last one before he makes the timber."

Isaac frowned. "Shootin' at people is the way Finis lost that arm, or have you forgot?"

The three riders were not lawyers; they were too sun-browned and weather-creased to have spent their lives in a courtroom. But Isaac figured no lawyers would get out this far from the settlements anyway; they would send somebody who worked cheaper. These three had the dour look of lawmen Isaac and his brothers had encountered all over Tennessee, carrying out the orders of the landed gentry and merchant class.

The biggest among them leaned forward in his saddle, his gaze running from Isaac to Luke to Finis, who had finally come out with britches unbuttoned and no shirt or boots. The rider said, "You folks just passin' through here, I hope?"

Finis shook his head. "I was hopin' the same about you all."

"We represent Haden Edwards, who has permission of the Mexican government to settle eight hundred families. He has posted legal notice in Nacogdoches that all who have a prior claim are to present proof to him of their legal presence here or vacate the region immediately."

Isaac said, "We ain't seen it. We ain't been to Nacogdoches."

"I have a copy of his order if you want to read it." He reached into a saddlebag. Luke quickly hoisted his rifle to his shoulder. The man paused in ill-suppressed alarm. "I'm just goin' after the paper, is all."

Isaac said, "Stand easy, Luke."

Luke paid him no attention, looking instead to Finis. Finis said, "Let him, Luke. We can kill him afterwards."

The document looked official, but Isaac had never made much sense out of such things. Finis and Luke could not read at all. Isaac said, "A man can write down anything he wants to. That don't make it so. We found this place. Wasn't nobody usin' it. We claim squatters' rights."

The man gave him a long, cautious stare. "There's no such thing. You have no right to be on this property."

Finis spat, tobacco juice trailing back into his rough black beard and shining in the sun. "We got a right. We got it right here." He shifted his rifle to his shoulder and took aim at the man on the horse. "You want to come a little closer and see?"

The man glanced at the riders on either side of him for reassurance. Neither had moved. His face flushed a little. "Mr. Edwards is fully prepared to take the case to the Mexican authorities. You will find yourselves in court."

Finis grunted. "We been in court before. Ain't never been no judge's hammer come down as hard as the hammer on this rifle."

The horseman pulled up on his bridle reins. Isaac saw fear in his eyes, a fear that was more than justified. If Finis took it in his head to shoot, he would. He had never been one to dwell upon consequences. Isaac wanted to tell Finis to back off a little, but that might have seemed a weakening of their stand, giving strength to the visitors. He knew if Finis killed this one, he and Luke would have to finish the other two. They could not let any of the men leave here alive unless all three did.

The rider had trouble speaking. He finally managed, "Might I inquire you gentlemen's names?"

Knowing Luke would blurt it if he did not speak quickly, Isaac said, "It's Smith."

The man did not believe. "Half the squatters we've found are named Smith."

Isaac nodded. "We got a lot of kinfolks. Now, you-all have more than wore out your welcome. The trail you used comin' in here is the best one to use goin' out."

The three riders glanced at each other and seemed to agree that they had business elsewhere. The spokesman turned his horse half around before he declared, "There will be more to this."

Isaac said, "If I was you I'd forget how to find this place."

As the men rode away, Luke lowered his rifle, but Finis still held his aim, bracing the long barrel with his stump of an arm. Isaac reached out and pulled the muzzle toward the ground. He grunted at the effort, for Finis was surprisingly strong. Isaac had often wondered where he got it; certainly not from hard work.

Finis grumbled, "I got a mind to kill the son of a bitch. He ain't out of range yet."

"Then we'd have to leave anyway. What's the sense in that?" He knew the way to deflect Finis's attention from the three riders was to draw it to himself. He gave Finis a quick study from his tousled black hair down to his bare feet. "Hell of a sight you are. Wonder they didn't laugh theirselves to death."

Finis scowled. "Ain't nobody laughs at me. Not but once."

Isaac pointed his chin toward the tiny field. "The corn needs hoein', and I can't keep up with the weeds all by myself. Why don't you put the rest of your clothes on and come help me?"

"Ain't much I can do with one arm."

Isaac let sarcasm creep into his voice. "I expect Nelly'd disagree about that."

Finis looked quickly toward the cabin, as if he had forgotten she was there. "I'll be out directly. But don't expect me to do much." He went back into the cabin.

Isaac turned to Luke. "What about you?"

Luke's mind was not on the field. "Finis is with her right now."

Isaac shrugged with a sense of futility and let his gaze go back to the three horsemen, disappearing where the trail turned into the woods.

They would be back. Maybe not for a week, maybe not for a month. He wondered what he would do when they returned, for there would probably be more of them next time. Damned place wasn't really worth fighting over anyway. But fight he would, if it came to that, because he was a Blackwood. And he would probably lose. Because he was a Blackwood.

19

ISOLATION AND attention to what he considered more important matters kept Andrew Lewis from hearing much about the increasingly brittle situation around faraway Nacogdoches, or giving much thought to the little he heard about the growing conflict between old settlers and new ones the Edwards brothers brought in to place upon land others regarded as their own. The fall harvest kept Andrew busy, for he had no rich man's implements, no slaves, to help him gather the fruits of his summer's labor like he had seen on large places downriver. He gathered his corn crop the poor man's way, using a long, sharp knife as he slowly worked along row after row of ripened stalks. He hoisted each canvas bag upon the brown horse's back just before it became too heavy for him to lift alone, toting it up to his log shed for storage. At such a time he dreamed of acquiring a wagon someday. The produce of his garden likewise required hand labor—his own—for he had no money to hire help. Always before, he and Michael had combined their efforts for those tasks too large or too heavy for one man. But this time he did his work alone. The old quarrel still stood between them like a patch of briars. Neither knew how to take the first step to cut a path through the thorns without losing some of the Lewis dignity and pride.

Of more import was Marie's delivery of her second child. It

happened, appropriately, just as the crop harvest began. Andrew kept finding excuses to go to Michael and Marie's cabin to look in upon her, even if it was no more than whittling some sort of toy for little Mordecai. Michael would acknowledge his presence with a strained civility and find business elsewhere. The new neighbor, Mrs. Nathan, came over to provide midwife services. By the look of her, Andrew judged that she would be needing a return of the favor before winter was out. But her condition was no hindrance to her hustling and bustling about, ordering Michael and Andrew to the chores she needed done.

A woman of considerable stature herself, she kept worrying aloud about Marie's small size. "I had a cousin once, little bitty woman like Marie, married to a big strappin' feller like Michael is. Baby come, it taken after its papa. Too big for such a little woman. Died givin' birth, she did. Died hard."

Michael pointed out that this would be Marie's second; she had had no particular difficulty delivering Mordecai. But Mrs. Nathan kept talking about her cousin until she had Michael and Andrew both in a cold sweat. As the ordeal began, Andrew kept water boiling in a pot over coals in the fireplace while Michael held little Mordecai on his knee and tried to explain to the worried boy what was the matter with his mother and why they needed that bossy woman in the house.

Andrew poked nervously at the fire during the interminable wait, thinking of Mrs. Nathan's cousin and the thousand things that could go wrong. At last he heard a tiny cry from the bedroom, a cry that lasted but a moment. His mouth dry, Andrew stared intently at Michael and listened hard, fearful.

"Must be a boy," Michael said, his shaky voice betraying his own apprehension. "Lewis boys don't cry much."

Mrs. Nathan entered the kitchen, wiping her hands on a towel. She held the men in painful suspense a minute, then smiled. "Michael, she wants you to go in now. She'd like to show you your new daughter."

Michael stared at her as if he did not quite believe. "Daughter? You sure it's not a boy?"

Mrs. Nathan grinned. "After several of my own, I think I can tell the difference."

Andrew slumped, the tension flowing out of him. Damn Mrs. Nathan's stories. He wanted to grasp his brother's hand but waited in vain for a look that might seem an invitation. He took little Mordecai as Michael eased his son down from his knee. He said, "Lewis *girls* don't cry much either."

The boy had seen few other children. His had been a world of adults. All the talk had been about his getting a new brother to play with. He did not understand why he had been given a sister instead. "I don't know what we need her for anyway."

While Michael went in, Andrew held Mordecai and tried to explain that a little sister was just the same as a little brother except different.

"What do you mean, different?" his nephew wanted to know.

Mrs. Nathan was no help. She slumped exhaustedly at the table, drinking parched-grain coffee and smiling benignly at Andrew's stumbling efforts.

Michael came back into the kitchen presently, his rugged face aglow. Any momentary disappointment had already been put aside. "Marie wants Mordecai to come see the baby. You'd just as well come too, Andrew, long's you're here."

Marie was drawn and tired, but her black hair was freshly brushed, and her dark eyes were shining as she turned toward the tiny figure lying beside her. "Look, Mordecai. This is your sister."

The boy seemed less than impressed. "She looks kind of old."

Andrew ached to put his arms around Marie. He put them around the boy instead and said, "She'll get younger."

"She can't have my bed."

"Time she gets big enough to need it, I'll build you a larger one." His anxiety for Marie returned, for she appeared wrung out and frighteningly vulnerable. "The baby looks fine. But how about you? You've had us scared half to death."

"I feel like getting up from here and singing."

He touched her hand, then quickly drew away, but not before he saw a flicker of reaction in her eyes.

Michael sat on the edge of the bed, reaching across the

baby to hold his wife's hand. Little Mordecai looked with suspicion upon the new arrival. He crawled up on the side of the bed and drew close to his mother. She hugged him to give his assurance.

Andrew felt like a fifth wheel on a wagon. He withdrew to the door but paused to look back at the three people—four now—who were most of his world. "It strikes me, Michael, that me and you, we'll be Tennesseans as long as we live. And Marie'll always be from Louisiana. But them two little 'uns, they're born in Texas. What does that make them?"

Michael gave the question a moment's thought. "Texicans. They're the startin' of a whole new tribe."

MARIE WAS up the next day, getting around far sooner than Andrew thought she should. She took up most of her accustomed tasks, leaving little for Mrs. Nathan. Andrew waited for Michael to register disapproval. When he did not, Andrew admonished her, "Our mama always laid up for a couple, three days, takin' her rest. You oughtn't to be on your feet yet."

Marie acknowledged his concern with a soft smile, then shrugged it off. "I have been long enough in bed. There is much work to be done."

He said, "That's what Mrs. Nathan came here for."

Marie exaggerated a frown. "But she is in a delicate condition." She put an end to the discussion by pointing toward a wooden bucket. "I need some water, Andrew. Would you mind?"

Carrying the empty bucket down to the riverbank, Andrew wondered if Marie and Michael ever argued; he had never heard them. He thought it would be interesting sometime, for he could not conceive of either giving up to the other. If they were ill-matched in size, they were well-matched in wills.

They did not even have a proper argument over a name for the baby, though they had strong and differing opinions. Michael wanted to name her Patience, after his and Andrew's mother in Tennessee. Andrew thought that was a splendid notion, but he did not interfere. Marie, because of her French-

Spanish heritage, was torn between naming her Angeline, for a beloved French aunt who had graced Marie's childhood in Natchitoches but had died in a fever epidemic, and Cristina, from the Spanish side of her family. They compromised, joining the names and calling the baby Angeline Cristina Patience Lewis.

Andrew remarked, "Poor kid's apt to grow up slump-shouldered, carryin' the weight of such a name."

Marie kissed the baby on the forehead. "Most Spanish names are much longer."

Michael squared himself to his full six feet. "Just so she remembers that her last name is Lewis."

Being around Marie had been a constant reminder to Andrew of the emptiness of his own cabin. Now that she had the baby, the feeling was even more acute. Andrew found that he could abide being by himself only a few days at a time. Then he had to ride down to Marie and Michael's place, ignoring Michael's cool and calculated silence for a chance to talk with Marie a little and bounce the boy Mordecai on his knee. He would watch with a helpless hunger as Marie moved about the cabin, cooking supper in the fireplace, caressing her new daughter.

He had long sensed that Marie understood how he felt about her. In her relationship with him there was always a sisterly affection, but there was also a vague uneasiness, an invisible line which she had drawn and over which he dared not step. Her dark eyes would silently tell him when he came dangerously near that line, and he would back away.

The baby was about three weeks old when Marie broached a subject she had mentioned several times before. Michael was out at the shed milking the cow. Marie watched Andrew stack an armload of freshly cut wood beside the fireplace, then motioned for him to take a chair. Andrew argued that he had some more wood to be fetched in. But she nodded again toward the chair, trouble in her eyes. Andrew sat.

Marie pulled up another chair and stared at him for a silent moment before saying, "You'll very soon be finished with the harvest. There will not be much for you to do in the winter except trap, and pelts will bring but little money. I think a good idea would be for you to go away a while. See something different. Go visit Nacogdoches or Natchitoches."

He suspected what she was working up to. It would not be the first time. "You're wantin' me to bring home a wife."

"I did not say that. But if it be in God's plan, why not?"

If he traveled three thousand miles he would not find a woman who would measure up to Marie. He would never be free to tell her that, not in words, but she could read it in his eyes if she so chose. He said, "I've got mighty little to offer. It's a hard life for a woman out here so far from the settlements."

She shook her pretty head. "It is a good life. I am happy. Michael is happy. This country will grow, and our children will grow with it. Find the right woman, Andrew, and she will be happy too. You should have your own family. You should be raising your own sons of Texas."

Andrew frowned. He thought he could read her mind: if he had a woman of his own, perhaps he would be less drawn to Marie; perhaps the awkwardness they felt toward each other would disappear. With it, perhaps, would go the barrier that had arisen between him and Michael. But he was not ready. "Sometime, maybe. Not yet."

The trouble was strong in Marie's eyes. He thought they might even hold a touch of fear. "There is something else. Michael is restless again. He says nothing, but he stares to the west with that look, that look from his father. One day he will not be able to stop himself, and he will ride away to see what is out there. If he knows you will be here to watch over us, he will feel free to go."

Andrew nodded, thinking ahead of her. "And if I was gone, he'd have no choice except to stay."

Her black eyes begged him. "Please, Andrew. He might die out there as your father did, so far away that not even God would know where he was. I do not want him to go. But he will, if you do not."

Andrew rubbed his rough hands together and tried in vain to think of a good argument. It was useless. He would walk barefoot across a bed of hot coals if Marie should ask him to.

He said in resignation, "I remember your old daddy. A merchant to the core. He could sell an ox-yoke to a muleskinner. Looks like he raised his daughter the same way."

Michael returned from the cow pen, fresh milk steaming in the wooden bucket. Marie gave Andrew no chance to equivocate. She declared, "Andrew is going to make a trip. He is going back east to find a wife."

The warmth of embarrassment rushed to Andrew's face. "I'm just goin' to visit around a little, is all."

Michael set the bucket on the floor. Andrew saw momentary disappointment in his brother's blue eyes. Michael was realizing that Andrew's absence would force him to give up any notion of exploring, at least for now. The disappointment passed, after a bit. Michael did not speak directly to Andrew; he seldom did, these days. He said, "I been tellin' him all along that he needs somebody to share that cabin. I'm glad he's finally decided to listen to me."

Andrew glanced at Marie. She smiled with the guileless face of an angel come to earth. He said in resignation, "I always listen to good advice."

HE APPROACHED the journey without relish, feeling that the decision was not his own; he had been pressured into it. He kept putting it off until winter's cool breath was in the morning air. One day Michael came to him and said, "If you ain't goin', then I think I'll make a little ride out west a ways. There's some country I been wantin' to take a look at."

Andrew replied, "I was figurin' on leavin' tomorrow."

He packed the necessaries into a canvas bag and hung them off of the saddle, his blankets tied behind the cantle. The brown horse looked dwarfed beneath its burden, but it was more bulk than weight. Andrew gently pinched the baby's fingers, then hugged little Mordecai and Marie.

Michael watched him soberly and in silence.

Marie asked, "How far will you go?"

"Ain't figured, for sure. I expect I'll make a turn over by Nacogdoches, and maybe as far as Natchitoches."

Michael broke his silence. "You could go all the way back to Tennessee, see Mama and them."

Andrew shook his head. "Not until we can all go together and let Mama meet her grandchildren."

Marie said, "There will be some of yours by that time, perhaps."

Andrew frowned. "You-all are expectin' an awful lot of me. I tell you, I ain't lookin' for a wife. I'll be comin' back by myself."

Marie's eyes were wistful. "If you see my mother and father, tell them—well, you will know what to tell them."

"I'll tell them you're happy. That'd be no lie."

He gave Marie a brotherly kiss, feeling awkward about even that, then swung up on the brown horse. He started to pull away but glanced back. "I'll be comin' home by myself," he declared again.

He set out downriver, feeling as if he were being sent on a fool's errand. He had about as much business making this trip as a mule had going to a dance.

He stopped for a short visit at the Willet place, where he was pleased to see little Daniel looking fit and happy and none the worse for his experience with the Indians. He did not tarry long, because the memory of Old Man Lige Willet hung over him like a cloud. Mrs. Willet hugged him several times, telling him repeatedly how grateful she was for his part in bringing Daniel home. "I didn't do any more than the others," he demurred.

"All of you did more than Christian duty called for," she declared. "I pray for each one of you every night."

He stopped next at the Nathans' new cabin. Mrs. Nathan, her stomach pushing out more and more noticeably, wanted to know all about Marie and the baby. And she had advice for Andrew. "While you're a-travelin', it sure wouldn't hurt you none to keep your eyes open for a likely young woman. There's bound to be one somewhere just a-waitin' for an eligible young bachelor like yourself to come along."

Andrew figured she had been talking to Marie. Women saw romance in everything, seemed like.

Miles Nathan took a practical view of the matter. "Makes good business sense to me. Austin'd give you a right smart bigger grant of land if you was to come back harnessed up double."

"I'm just goin' to visit some old friends. Findin' me a life's companion never once crossed my mind."

"Be sure and sample her cookin' first. Beauty fades away"— Nathan glanced uneasily at his wife—"but good cookin' is a joy forever."

That kind of joy, at least, was in plentiful supply around the Nathan place. He noticed that Walker Younts was there, and Walker put away a hearty meal. But Andrew doubted that food was Walker's primary reason for coming. He was hanging on the girl Birdy's every word, every flutter of her eyelashes. Andrew wondered where Joe Smith was. He was not paying adequate attention to his interests if he was letting Walker steal a march on him.

Departing after eating more than good judgment would have suggested, Andrew carried some of the leavings at Mrs. Nathan's insistence so he could make another meal or two out of it along the trail.

She stood in front of her cabin and shouted one last bit of advice as he rode away. "Remember what I told you about my cousin. Find yourself a good sturdy woman that won't have any trouble bearin' babies."

He seriously considered bypassing San Felipe, the headquarters of Austin's colony. He figured he would probably get more matrimonial advice there, some of it like as not from Stephen Austin, still a bachelor himself and therefore probably an expert on someone else's need for a helpmate. Rumor was that Austin had seriously planned marriage himself to a likely young lady but had been too busy with his colony to invest the time and energy necessary to a successful courtship.

On reflection, Andrew decided a visit to San Felipe might be time well spent before he started the northward leg of the trip. Isolated at his and Michael's farms, he had heard but little of recent events. Nacogdoches and Natchitoches could both have burned to the ground or been wiped out by a fever epidemic without his knowing anything of it.

He was half surprised to find Austin there. The *empresario* was gone from San Felipe much of the time, traveling often to San Antonio de Bexar and even as far as Mexico City—on business for his colony. The wear was showing, for he appeared to have aged ten or fifteen years. His was a pace Andrew did not envy. It was probably easier being a farmer.

He found Austin distracted, seeming to pay little attention until Andrew mentioned that he planned to travel north to Nacogdoches. Austin's eyebrows went up. "Are you aware of the explosive situation which has developed there?"

Andrew shook his head, surprised. "No."

"The entire region around Nacogdoches seems on the brink of a revolt. Haden Edwards and his brother have tried to force old settlers as well as recent squatters from their land and turn it over to their own colonists. There has been a great deal of resistance and protest. Now the Mexican government has canceled the Edwards grant and ordered him to leave Texas. The last word I have is that he is resisting. He has even been recruiting Americans to join him and hold his colony by force if necessary."

Andrew whistled. "I'll bet the Mexican government ain't none too pleased about that."

"The situation reinforces those Mexicans who have opposed the American colonies. If it goes to an extreme, it could result in the eviction of all of us from Texas."

"You've got lots of friends in Mexico City. You can make them see that Edwards and his kind don't represent most of us."

"I try. But it may require us to do more than talk. It may require our joining the Mexican government in moving against the Edwards brothers."

Americans against Americans. The thought brought a bitter taste to Andrew's mouth. "It won't set well with a lot of folks."

"Neither would our eviction."

Andrew had gained the impression that those in Mexico who opposed allowing Americans into Texas were a minority voice, that a majority saw the American colonists as a stabilizing influence in a land but thinly settled and eternally subject to the terrors of Indian depredation. He had not given serious thought to what he would do—or what Michael would do—if anybody were to try to force them off of their land. Even the government of Mexico—

"Our roots are too deep now," he said. "We couldn't leave."

Austin's voice was grim. "When you remove a tree from a field, you do not dig it up by the roots. You simply chop it down. You have never seen anything of the Mexican army except a scattered few troops. You have never seen it as I have, deep in the interior of the country."

"Is it big enough to drive us out?"

"More than that. It is big enough to chop us to the ground and leave us lying in pieces. All it needs is the will, and a strong leader who hates Americans."

Andrew shuddered in premonition. He could see himself and Michael standing shoulder to shoulder in defense of their land, and being cut down like wheat under a scythe. "Anything I can do to help?"

"I receive only sketchy and contractory reports. You could quietly look around Nacogdoches and determine the true situation. That would help me decide upon our best course."

For the first time Andrew began to see a broader purpose in his journey beyond pacifying his brother and sister-in-law, and preventing Michael from going on the roam. This was a more sensible mission than looking for a wife.

Austin said, "My fervent hope is that the Edwards brothers will recognize their position as untenable and simply leave Texas. That would save all of us some grief."

Andrew remembered his brief meeting with Benjamin Edwards. He had not been impressed. "They're probably already gone."

"Let us hope so. That would be the best news you could send me." Austin brightened. "And while you are there—"

"You too?"

Austin shrugged. "Would that I had the time myself. There is not much comfort in this life for a bachelor."

BECAUSE NACOGDOCHES had become a gateway into Texas for American immigrants traveling overland, Andrew found the trail considerably better marked and worn than the last time he had ridden it. He met several travelers, occasionally one or two but more often small family groups, all wanting to visit a while and ask questions about Austin's colonies or others in the Texas interior. Andrew was glad to oblige, for he had little opportunity to see many people beyond his own small circle. And most of these immigrants brought real coffee.

He took the opportunity to ask them what they had seen or heard in Nacogdoches. The only agreement he found was that trouble was astir. What kind and whose responsibility it was varied with the teller of the story.

He remembered that the limited rural settlement in the Nacogdoches region, aside from scattered illegal squatters, was within a relatively short distance of the old Spanish fort town. The old Spanish royalist government had distrusted its citizens and actively discouraged settlement in isolated regions away from official scrutiny. That Mexico had finally turned to revolution and won its freedom from Spain was proof that the official misgivings had been well-founded.

He sensed that he was approaching Nacogdoches when he saw a dim trail leading off the main trace, meandering into the tall pines whose thick foliage sometimes blocked the sky from view. He followed it and came to a small farm. It was deserted. A few abandoned chickens, wily enough not to be caught by predators, scratched for food around and amid the gray ashes and blackened ruins of a log cabin. A couple of domestic hogs came out of a flattened log pen and grunted expectantly at him, wanting to be fed.

"What happened to your people?" he asked aloud.

Whatever, they had obviously departed in a hurry to have left even this little. People in Texas wasted not of the mite they had, for want was always close at hand.

Vaguely disturbed, he returned to the main trace and came, after a while, to another trail which circled around a dense piney wood and out of sight. He realized he was probably too far from Nacogdoches to reach there by night. Clouds boiling up from the east threatened a cold and rainy night. If he could find a farm and some friendly folks, he might at least sleep on a porch or under a shed, in the dry. He set the brown horse upon the track and in a few minutes was pleased to see a reasonably new cabin of logs, this one still standing. Livestock pens and a shed sat out beyond the cabin, and a small field beyond that, reaching to the edge of a pine forest so thick that he could not see twenty feet into it.

"Brown horse, you may even get a little hay tonight."

He saw a milk cow inside the pen, though the gate stood open. She was eating hay someone evidently had pitched onto the ground for her from a fenced-off stack just out of her reach. As at the other place, chickens scratched around the yard. But here he could see grain lying on the ground. Someone had just fed them.

"Hello the house!" he shouted. It was poor manners to ride up to a cabin unannounced. It could also be hazardous.

No one replied. He saw no sign that anyone was around. That seemed odd, the chickens and the cow having just been given fresh feed. He shouted again. The door stood half open, but no one moved or answered. He dismounted, looped his reins around a post, and walked up to the door. "Anybody at home?"

He looked back over his shoulder toward the shed, puzzled. "I'm comin' in," he said, and pushed the door the rest of the way open.

He saw a quick movement. In a dark corner a girl crouched, eyes wide with fright. She made a little cry and covered her mouth with her hands.

He raised his arms as a sign that he meant no harm. "Don't be scared," he said in the gentlest tone he could muster. His voice quavered a little, for he had been startled almost as much as the girl. "I didn't come to hurt you."

His eyes accustomed themselves to the darkness of the cabin, and he realized the girl was Mexican. She probably did not understand what he said. He struggled to repeat in Spanish. She still crouched against the wall, her eyes big and dark and frightened like those of a small rabbit caught in a corner. For a fleeting moment she reminded him of Marie.

Not for all the world would he willingly see Marie frightened this way. He began backing toward the door. He told the girl in Spanish, "It will be all right. I am leaving."

Something poked hard against the middle of his back. A man's voice declared in Spanish, "You will not leave yet. Raise your hands."

Andrew felt the breath go out of him. Even before he turned, he knew he would be facing a rifle. And holding the rifle was a young Mexican whose black eyes glittered with threat.

Andrew tried to speak but had to clear his throat. "You do not need that rifle. I am not here to hurt anyone."

"And you *will* not. Not tonight. You are my prisoner."

20

ANDREW CHILLED as he read desperation in the young Mexican's black eyes. A frightened man might squeeze the trigger without intending to. Andrew had to ponder his Spanish, for he had never used it enough that it came without an effort. "I am your prisoner if you say so. But I am not your enemy. Turn your rifle away from me, *por favor.*"

The young man seemed to consider the proposition, but Andrew could almost smell the fear emanating from him. The girl said in a frightened whisper, "Careful, Carlos. Careful."

Andrew's arms began to ache from holding them high. "I have to let my arms down. I will do it slowly."

"*Very* slowly," Carlos said, "and back away from me a little." The rifleman took a backward step of his own, far enough that Andrew could not easily grab the weapon. Andrew had no such foolish intention; it would probably get him killed.

He said, "I am just a traveler. I mean no one any harm."

Carlos seemed to want to believe him, but distrust was not easily put aside. The girl kept her back to the rough log wall, far beyond Andrew's reach.

The man demanded, "Where do you come from?"

"San Felipe de Austin."

"You swear you do not come from the *hermanos* Edwards?"

"I do not know the Edwards brothers." That was not entirely true. Benjamin Edwards had visited briefly at Andrew's farm some months ago. But it was no great stretch of the truth to say that he did not *know* him. "I am from Austin's colony."

Carlos stared hard, as if trying to see beyond Andrew's eyes and into his soul. The girl moved cautiously in a broad circle, trying to inch closer to Carlos while remaining well beyond Andrew's reach. Her first fear had eased, but her eyes remained suspicious. The young man asked, "What do you think, Petra?"

"He might be telling the truth. I do not want you to kill him."

"That might be safest."

"No. If he *is* one of them, they would stay after you like wolves until you are dead, perhaps until we are all dead. And if he is *not* one of them, the Father *Dios* would condemn us both."

Carlos demanded of Andrew, "If you are not one of them, why do you come into this cabin like a thief?"

"A thief would not shout three or four times, asking if anyone was here. And those people you are afraid of—I do not believe they would either."

The girl acknowledged with a nod. "He did call out. You must have heard him."

Andrew argued, "Look, my name is Andrew Lewis. I only wanted a dry place to sleep tonight." After this hostile encounter, he would as soon sleep in the rain.

The young man seemed almost convinced. "Do you know anyone who would speak for you?"

Andrew had spent no time around Nacogdoches. The only name that came readily was Lieutenant Elizandro Zaragosa. That brought a flicker of recognition to the young man's eyes. As an afterthought Andrew mentioned Eli Pleasant. "Eli lives on the other side of the Sabine, but he trades in Texas a lot."

Carlos's eyes narrowed. "You know the old man Pleasant?"

"I do." Andrew wondered if he had helped or hurt himself. Eli had many friends on the Mexican side of the Sabine River, but his various activities had left him enemies, too.

The girl moved closer, studying Andrew intently. He tried not to blink; she might take that for a sign he was lying.

She said, "The old man Pleasant has been good to us, Carlos."

In the gloom of the corner, where he could see little detail except her dark, fearful eyes, she had looked considerably like Marie. The light was better where she stood now. Andrew saw that the resemblance had been more than superficial. Petra was slight, like Marie, and her animated black eyes were much the same. Her complexion was a bit darker, more olive, than Marie's. He felt ashamed that he had given her a fright. He would not have wanted anyone to frighten Marie this way.

The tension began to drain from him, for he perceived in Carlos's eyes that the danger had passed. The rifle barrel sagged, pointing toward the hard-packed dirt floor. Carlos said, "I take you at your word that you are a friend of Pleasant."

Andrew tried to smile, but the tension had not drained that much. He raised his hand to chest level. "I have known him since I was that tall. I have not seen him in a few months."

"No one sees Pleasant unless he wishes to be seen. That is why he has lived to become an old man."

Andrew felt weakness in his knees after looking into that rifle barrel. He slumped into a rough-hewn chair. It struck him that the cabin had largely been stripped. He saw no pots, no pans, no utensils on a rough shelf over the table. A wooden bedframe had no blankets, no goatskin, no cornhusk pad. It was getting on toward suppertime, but the fireplace was cold.

"They must have looted this place."

The girl shook her pretty head. Her voice was sharp. "They would have. This was our own doing, to save all we could from the thieves. They would take our land and everything. But our father lived and died on this land, and our grandfather. The king gave it to them. Now come those American filibusters who say it is theirs."

Andrew could not help staring, for she looked so much like Marie. "I heard in San Felipe that the Mexican government ordered the Edwards brothers to leave Texas."

Carlos said, "The government is far away."

"It has soldiers in Nacogdoches."

"They are too few against so many. So we band together in

groups to protect ourselves and wait until the government does something. *If* it does something."

Andrew glanced from the man to the girl and back. "You do not look like a very large group to me, just you and your wife."

"My sister," Carlos corrected him. "This place is mine. We come here only to feed the chickens and the animals I could not take with me. Then we return to our family and our friends."

"Where are they?"

Suspicion flared again in the young man's eyes. He did not answer.

To repair the damage Andrew said quickly, "It is just as well that I do not know." He frowned. "South of here I saw a farmhouse burned."

The girl said sternly, "The land does not burn. It will still be ours when all these land-stealing *extranjeros* are gone."

Andrew warmed to the spirit in her voice, the angry fire in her eyes. It was what he would have expected from Marie. He wanted to distress her no longer. "If you are finished with me, I will be on my way."

Carlos asked, "To where?"

"To Nacogdoches."

Carlos's suspicion showed again. "What would you do there?"

"See what is happening, then report back to Stephen Austin. He is concerned."

"Do you think he would help us?"

"He wants no trouble with the Mexican government. I believe he will help you if he can." Andrew decided it was time to be riding, before Carlos took it in his head to disbelieve him again.

A distant rumble of thunder gently shook the cabin. The girl said, "You would be caught in the rain. Go with us. It is not far."

Carlos gave her a quick and questioning glance. She said, "I want to believe him. There may be someone who will know him and can say if he tells the truth. The old man Pleasant was with us last night."

Andrew brightened. "Eli? I would ride far to see him."

Carlos considered for a long moment before nodding. "All the work is finished here. We can leave now."

AT DUSK they broke out of the timber and came to a farm, a small open place in the midst of a dense pine forest. It was typical of many old Mexican farms he had seen in Texas; limited, providing for subsistence but nothing more. These were a people traditionally poor, used to little and asking little more of life than enough to eat and a place to live. Central to the farm was a cabin, the oldest part small and darkened with age. Additions had been made periodically, evidently to accommodate a growing family. Andrew saw a set of log corrals, the timber dark and sagging with its years, and a couple of sheds, all built of material cut and dragged from the woods which encroached upon the farm on all but one side and darkly threatened to overwhelm it.

He counted three wagons, which he assumed belonged to refugees. The place had some appearance of a military camp, for several tents clustered around the cabin. He counted three Mexican-style picket *jacales,* evidently put up to provide temporary shelter against the winter for some of the people banded together here. A couple of women cooked over outdoor fires. A light breeze drifted the pleasant aroma of pine smoke toward him, reminding him that he had eaten but little. From things Carlos and Petra had told him on the way, he knew Petra shared the old cabin with her mother, the Moreno family matriarch, and brothers and a sister younger than Carlos. Their father had been murdered by a Spanish loyalist officer many years ago, before Mexican independence. The rest of the people here, aside from the Morenos, included old Mexican settlers and some recent American squatters, assembled for mutual protection against a common threat.

Their situation reminded him of an occasion during his Tennessee boyhood when settlers had massed in the face of Indian danger. He remembered that he had worried more about the hazard of so many guns in the hands of careless people than about the Indians. The only casualty he recalled was a convivial leatherstocking—friend of his father Mordecai—who imbibed freely of corn whiskey and shot off his toe.

Andrew looked back over his shoulder toward the storm cloud. He could hear an occasional rumble of thunder and wondered if there was shelter enough for all these people to sleep dry. If they didn't, he couldn't ask to.

A tall, heavy-shouldered American of perhaps forty strode forward to meet the three riders. He carried no rifle, but his huge hands looked strong enough to provide a considerable persuasion. Andrew wondered if he might be a blacksmith by trade. "Who have you brought with you, Carlos?" the man asked in a Spanish better practiced than Andrew's.

"He says he is from the Austin colony at San Felipe. He says he knows the old man Pleasant. We wanted to see if Pleasant will speak for him."

The big man shook his head. "Eli is gone. He rode to Nacogdoches to see what is happening there." His dark gray eyes fastened upon Andrew with a measure of hostility. He shifted to English. "What's your name?"

"Andrew Lewis. Carlos has the right of it. I've got a farm out west of San Felipe."

"Maybe. Or maybe you're hopin' to get a farm out west of Nacogdoches by workin' for Haden Edwards and his bunch. You ever know an old feller called Tolliver Beard?"

The name sounded vaguely familiar, but Andrew could not remember why. "Not that I can recall."

The man looked back over his shoulder and jerked his head. Another who resembled him enough to be his brother walked out carrying a rifle. "You'll pardon us if we don't quite trust you to be tellin' us the gospel truth. We been lied to by several that was slicker'n goosegrease. Wouldn't be the first time that Beard has tried to send a spy into this camp."

The second man raised the rifle. He did not point it directly at Andrew, but was close enough. Andrew took a chill. He declared, "I've got nothin' to give you but my word. I can see that ain't enough. So I'll trouble you folks no longer and just be on my way."

The big man quickly stepped forward, grabbing Andrew's reins up close to the brown horse's mouth. "You've seen enough to have a good idea how many of us there is. Beard and the Edwards brothers would probably be tickled to know that. If you was to leave here, you just might go and tell them."

The man with the rifle moved in and motioned for Andrew to dismount. The muzzle now was aimed at Andrew's chest. But Andrew did not move from the saddle. It was in his mind that on horseback he still had a chance to cut and run. Afoot, he would be helpless.

The girl made a protest in Spanish. "Please! We think he tells the truth." She looked frightened, indication enough to Andrew that he also had reason to be. These people had been pushed hard, and they were strongly inclined to push back.

The girl pleaded, "We did not bring him here to be killed."

"You should not have brought him here at all. You have put this whole camp at risk."

Andrew said dryly, "Not as big a risk as mine. Why don't we just leave everything the way it is till Ol' Eli gets back?"

"We have no idea how long that might be. Eli does what he wants to, when he wants to. We may not see him for a week."

From beneath a shed a voice shouted, "Ain't you goin' to shoot him?"

Andrew thought he knew the voice. He wished he did not.

The big man answered, "Shootin' a man don't come easy."

"Depends. With some, it ain't hard at all."

The speaker stepped out of the shed's gloom and into the fading light of evening, his hands in his pockets. Andrew felt a mixture of apprehension and shame, as if he had foolishly stumbled into an enemy's camp.

Isaac Blackwood said, "What do you reckon, Andrew Lewis? Reckon I ought to tell him to go ahead and shoot you?"

Foreboding was like a knot in Andrew's stomach. "Wouldn't surprise me if you did, Isaac. Wouldn't surprise me if your brother Finis shot me himself."

The big man glanced at Isaac in surprise. "You know him?"

"Ever since back in Tennessee."

Andrew was not sure that such a statement from a Blackwood would be accepted as a recommendation; not if these people knew much about the Blackwoods. He said quickly, "We never was friends."

Isaac gave Andrew a long moment's contemplation. "Looks like you need a friend right now, Andrew. Even if it's just me."

Andrew had to swallow his resentment. "I'd be obliged if you'd tell them who I am." He sat in a nervous sweat, waiting for Isaac's words either to free him or to condemn him.

Isaac took his time, letting him stew. "What Andrew told you is the truth. He's got a farm in Austin's colony. Me and my brothers, we been there." He looked straight into Andrew's eyes without blinking. "Him and his brother Michael, they run us off. Said they'd shoot us if ever we come back."

The man who held the rifle let it sag to arm's length. The big man turned loose of Andrew's reins. He said, "I'm surprised that you'd speak up for him, then."

Isaac shrugged. "Surprises me a little too. But I guess in a time like this, all us Tennesseans got to stick together."

Andrew thought of his brother Michael, and how it would gravel him to learn that the Lewises owed a debt of gratitude to a Blackwood. He saw the big man wipe cold sweat from his forehead and realized the quandary he had been in. Andrew had sweated some himself. He dismounted from the brown and forced himself to extend his hand. "No hard feelin's."

The big man stuck his hand out. "And none with me." Andrew winced under the crushing strength of the grip. "Name's Simon Wells. Hope you'll pardon us for bein' suspicious, but that Edwards bunch burned out me and my family and my brother. If the Morenos hadn't taken everybody in, we'd all of us be in a bad fix."

Gratitude toward Isaac Blackwood did not lessen Andrew's misgivings. He could not believe the Blackwoods had any land to lose. "What are you-all doin' here, Isaac?"

Isaac's eyes were steady; he did not give an inch. "We'd found us a little place, me and Finis and Luke. That bunch out of Nacogdoches, they come up on the cabin while me and Luke was off a-huntin'. They taken Finis and Nelly by surprise. Time me and Luke seen the smoke and come a-runnin', the deed had been done. So we come here and joined up with these other folks that've been mistreated the same way."

Andrew wondered who Nelly was. "I reckon I owe you, Isaac."

"I reckon you do. But I ain't decided *what* you owe me. I'll think of somethin'."

Andrew had no doubt of that. He turned to the Mexican brother and sister who had brought him here. Her eyes reflected confusion; she had understood little or none of the conversation in English. She had seen only that the threat had passed. In Spanish he assured her, "It is all right now. This man"—he nodded toward Isaac—"knows me."

He saw doubt in her eyes. She asked, "You are friends?"

He suspected she had already formed an opinion of the Blackwoods. He said, "Not friends. But we know each other."

She gave him a fleeting smile that looked like Marie's. "I am glad you are not friends. That one seems not too bad, but his brothers?"

Andrew warmed to her. For a moment she was not a stranger named Petra; she was Marie.

Isaac puzzled. He did not know Spanish. "What's she sayin'?"

"She's just askin' if I'd like to eat supper with her and her folks."

Simon Wells arched an eyebrow.

21

ANDREW SAT on the cabin porch, listening to Simon Wells recount the settler's grievances against the Edwards brothers, but his primary attention was not with Wells. He watched the girl Petra move about the cabin, helping clean up after a simple family meal to which she and her mother had invited Andrew. He had shared it with Petra, Carlos and his wife, two younger brothers named Ramón and Felipe, a sister named Juanita, and the old *señora*. The Moreno family had eked out a living in the region for generations, farming in a small way, raising a few cattle. The oppressive final years of the Spanish government had been a brutal trial, taking the life of Petra's father, forcing her brothers to assume the burdens of manhood years too early. Many of their relatives had been driven into exile in Louisiana because of their real or imagined opposition to the crown. To have endured all that, only to be subjected again now to possible loss of their venerable land claims, had been a cross they were unwilling to bear without stiff resistance.

Wells conceded, "We can't rightly blame the Edwards brothers for all of it. Way I've been told, Haden Edwards spent a lot of time and money and work down in Mexico earnin' the right to bring settlers into this part of the country. But the Mexican government is new and big and clumsy. One part ain't got the first notion of what another part is up to. One side grants rights and another takes them away. They don't trust each other, and it's sure as hell they don't trust Americans."

Andrew could hear Petra and her family in the cabin, speaking Spanish among themselves. Some of the talk was so rapid that its meaning was lost on him. He pointed his chin toward the door. "There's the biggest trouble of all: we don't understand one another. Us Americans, we come out of a different upbringin'. We get throwed together with the Mexican people, and all anybody can see—them or us—is the differences. It was probably a mistake for us to've come into their country in the first place."

"But we're here now," Wells said firmly. "This is our home too, and we ain't noways about to leave." Wells stopped talking. He seemed to wait for Andrew to make some comment, but Andrew was silent, watching through the door. Wells turned to see Petra kneeling before the fireplace, poking up a blaze. "There's good folks amongst these Mexicans, even if we don't always understand each other."

Andrew grunted agreement.

Wells smiled. "Some don't hurt the eyes none either."

Andrew felt a little like a boy caught at mischief. "She just reminds me of somebody, is all."

"You a bachelor, Lewis?"

"Never had a chance to be otherwise. Livin' way out past the settlements don't allow for much social life."

Wells said, "My wife's Louisiana French. But if I was a young bachelor in Texas I might be lookin' to marry a likely Mexican girl. It'd set a man up better with the government."

"I'd be more concerned about how I set up with the girl."

"But if you had the girl and the government both feelin' generous towards you, it'd be like a double patch on your britches, wouldn't you say?"

Petra rose and turned, her eyes catching Andrew looking at her. She smiled self-consciously and turned quickly away. His face warmed.

Wells studied him. "She was scared to death that me and my brother was fixin' to shoot you."

"The same idee crossed my mind."

"We wouldn't have; that was all bluff. I had a feelin' she'd've walked in front of the rifle to stop us."

Andrew blinked. "Why?"

Wells shrugged. "I ain't been married but twenty years, and that ain't near long enough to figure them out. But I'd guess she's took a likin' to you."

"She don't talk English, and my Spanish is barely passable."

"There's worse things in this world than havin' a woman that can't talk to you."

"I didn't come here lookin' for a wife."

"I wasn't either, when I met mine. But a man that don't grab a good opportunity when he sees one is liable to sleep in a bachelor's bed the rest of his life. It can get godawful cold here in the wintertime."

Andrew pushed to his feet. He removed his hat and stepped into the doorway. Petra smiled Marie's smile, and watched him with Marie's dark eyes. He said in Spanish, "I am grateful for the good supper. Now I will be saying good-night."

Petra said, "But you will stay until the old man Pleasant comes back?"

"No, I will be going on to Nacogdoches in the morning. Austin will be waiting to hear from me."

Petra's smile left her. "I—we thought you might remain with us a while."

"I wish I could. It would be a great pleasure."

"At least you will visit us on your way back to San Felipe?"

"I will look forward to it."

Petra started to extend her hand, glanced uneasily at her watching mother and drew it back, clasping both hands at her waist. "As we will."

Andrew stepped backward onto the porch, nearly stumbling over a rough-cut board.

Wells said, "Careful, Lewis, or you'll lose your balance."

Andrew could have told him he already had.

He hoped the storm cloud might go around, but it did not. The thunder became louder, and lightning flashes told him he had better hunt for a dry place to sleep. He found the first shed already sheltering all the men who could crowd beneath it. He dreaded the second because he had seen Isaac and Luke there. But he saw no choice other than to bed down in the rain.

Isaac watched impassively as Andrew brought in his blanket and sought out a place on the ground not already taken. "Careful. You might get contaminated, breathin' the same air as us Blackwoods."

Andrew frowned. He saw only Isaac and Luke. "Where's Finis?" He thought it a good idea to know the whereabouts of all three.

Isaac jabbed his thumb in the direction of a canvas-covered wagon near the shed. "Him and Nelly, they got their own accommodations."

Andrew had seen Nelly, an amply fleshed girl who did not seem to have all of her buttons sewed on tight. "Where'd you-all manage to steal a wagon?"

Luke took offense and stepped menacingly toward Andrew, but Isaac caught his brother's arm and pulled him back. "You Lewises always did look for the worst. We figure we had the wagon comin' to us. Them fellers that burned us out, some of them was travelin' by wagon. We convinced them it'd be good for their health to walk back to Nacogdoches."

Andrew conceded, "I can see a certain justice in that."

Isaac smiled thinly. "Glad we can agree on somethin'."

Andrew was a long time in going to sleep. He had little concern about Isaac, but it was worrisome lying so near Luke, who had never been known for good sense. Grunts and groans, both male and female, emanated from the wagon. They were disturbing to say the least of it. After a time Andrew complained to Isaac, "Don't Finis know everybody hears, or does he just not give a damn?"

Isaac said in a resigned tone, "I hope you don't have any notions about makin' them stop. You'd have to fight Nelly as well as Finis."

Andrew turned over in his blankets and tried to block the couple from his consciousness. But they made his thoughts drift unwillingly to the girl Petra, and sleep was as elusive as a doe in the woods.

NACOGDOCHES HAD grown in recent years, since Mexican independence had encouraged many of the refugees from Spanish oppression to come back, and since American colonization had turned the piney-woods town into a resting place and supply point for overland travelers bound toward Austin's and other colonies. It was still dominated by an old stone building which had variously been courthouse and military headquarters in Spanish times. But a great many new buildings had gone up, mostly of logs because timber was plentiful and required little haul. Horses and cattle grazed around the outskirts. Andrew's eye was caught by the numerous wagons, and he wondered if all the newcomers were so rich.

As he rode up the street it was apparent there was some unusual excitement in the town. Men gathered in small huddles, talking earnestly, some of them shouting, some arguing, most seeming to be having themselves a high old time. Several staggered, obviously drunk. One man waved a bottle and whooped loudly with almost every uncertain step.

A large man in a long black coat clutched a Bible and protested at the top of a voice that Andrew found familiar, "Awaken, brothers. This is no time to indulge ourselves in drink and debauchery. It is a time to counsel with the Lord, to beg Him for His guidance and mercy."

If anyone besides Andrew heard him, no one gave any sign.

The man turned, and Andrew could see the black patch over one eye. The other eye lighted with recognition, and he hailed Andrew. "Welcome, my young friend. You seem sadly out of place here among the Philistines."

"Howdy, Fairweather. How's the collections comin'?"

"I subsist. That is all I ask for. That is about all this land provides for anyone."

"Looks like a lot of excitement in town."

"The devil has found many idle hands here for his workshop. Were I you, I would not tarry any longer than it takes to water your horse. Seeds of violence are being sown here today. The harvest will be briars and thorns."

Andrew frowned. "What seeds are they plantin'?"

"Seeds of sedition, of rebellion. They are declaring themselves independent of all law except their own. I am about to depart this wicked place before God and the Mexican government hurl down a thunderbolt and destroy it. I would strongly advise that you leave with me."

"I can't, not yet. I've got a job of work to do."

"Then watch yourself. You could find more trouble here than you found in that Waco village." Fairweather turned and walked toward the stone building, his large Bible tucked under the arm of his black coat.

Andrew saw a dozen or so men clustered around a flagpole at the front of the old structure. He watched two of them raise an unfamiliar flag of red and white. It was not Mexican, not Spanish, not American. He rode the brown horse up closer. On the flag he made out the words "Independence, Liberty, and Justice." As it reached the top of the pole, men cheered. Some waved their hats, and a couple fired rifles into the air. Fairweather raised the Bible above his head and exhorted them to prayer, with the same lack of results as before.

Two buckskin-clad men came up and stood beside Andrew's brown horse, watching with much interest the commotion around the flagpole. One held a long rifle, the other a jug. The man with the jug said, "Never seen it to fail. Try to celebrate a happy occasion and a preacher'll show up to sour the whiskey."

Andrew asked, "What's the happy occasion?"

The man with the rifle looked up, his face furrowing. It was a young face, stubbled with whiskers. His gray eyes held a challenge. Andrew thought perhaps he had seen the man before. He immediately took him for one of those who turn mean when they get drunk. The red veins in his eyes made it appear likely that he was drunk a lot. "You don't know? Where you been, anyway? The moon?"

"It seems that far. Where I've been, you don't hear much. What's that flag?"

"Why, my friend, that's the flag of the Republic of Fredonia. This community has just declared its independence from Mexico and the United States and the whole damned world!"

"That don't sound legal."

"Anything's legal if you can make it stick." The man patted the rifle's long barrel. "We're the boys that can make it stick."

"There's Mexican troops stationed here. What're they goin' to say about it?"

"Ain't enough of them to say anything. If they was to try, we'd hoe them down like weeds in the field. We'll be sendin' them packin' pretty soon, back to Bexar. And hell, we may decide to go down there and take Bexar too." The whiskey was loud.

The other man unstoppered the jug and raised it for a long drink. He passed it to the rifleman and laughed. "Here you go, Jayce Beard. Better oil up your goozle some more before you start marchin' off to Bexar. It's a fur piece."

Beard. Andrew had heard the people at the Moreno place speak the name. He thought he had heard it somewhere before, as well. He studied the face, and he remembered. This was the young ruffian who had angrily bumped into him one day in front of Stephen Austin's office in San Felipe. An older man had been with him, his father. What had been his name? Tolliver, that was it. Tolliver Beard.

Jayce's Adam's apple bobbed up and down as he held the jug high. He wiped the back of his hand across his mouth and lifted the jug toward Andrew. "Better have a snort, moon man. The celebration is a-fixin' to commence."

Andrew shook his head. "If I was you, I'd wait and see what the Mexicans say before I celebrated too much. And I expect Stephen Austin will have some notions on it too."

"Stephen Austin has got nothin' to say about it. Haden Edwards tried to get him to help us, and he wouldn't raise his hand."

"He may raise it now."

The man with the rifle began to frown deeply. Suspicion crept into eyes glazing from the whiskey. "I thought you just now rode into town. How come you to know so much about what Austin's goin' to think?"

"I can guess."

The other man's face had clouded. He pushed in close beside Andrew's left stirrup. "Where'd you come from, stranger? Louisiana?"

Andrew considered lying to them but decided against it. When he had to lie to such as these, it would be time for him to slink off into a hole. "I just came up from San Felipe."

"Then you're a spy!" shouted Jayce Beard. "A damned stinkin' spy!" He turned and yelled to the men at the flagpole. "Come a-runnin', boys. We got ourselves a spy!"

Andrew tried to pull the brown away, but the man with the jug grabbed the reins and held them. Andrew saw three or four men come running from the direction of the stone building. He tried to bring up his rifle, but someone grabbed its barrel. Rough hands gripped him and began trying to pull him down from the saddle. He struggled to hold on, to spur the brown and break free. He felt himself being dragged off the horse's left side. He clutched at the pommel but could not hold it against all that angry strength. Falling, he kicked his left foot free so it would not hang in the stirrup and perhaps break his ankle. He struck the ground with an impact that took the breath from him. He felt himself being dragged between two log buildings.

He heard Fairweather's voice. "Gentlemen! Gentlemen! I implore you not to resort to violence. It is an abomination in the sight of the Lord." No one paid any attention to him.

"What we goin' to do with him, Jayce?" someone demanded.

"Take him to Ben Edwards and see if he wants to hang him. But we're fixin' to stomp on him a little first."

Jayce had uncommon strength as he hauled Andrew to his feet. His breath was foul. He pushed Andrew up against a log wall and drove a huge fist into his stomach. Andrew lost what little breath he still had. He tried to shout a protest, but the cry was choked off in his throat by another blow. He bent and felt a fist strike his face, driving him half around and slamming his head against the log wall. He tasted blood warm and sticky and tinged with salt. He sensed more than saw the men gathered around him, two or three joining Jayce and his friend at the beating, others cheering them on. Lightning flashed before his eyes, and he felt himself trying to retch.

Gradually he seemed to go numb, hardly feeling the blows to his ribs, his stomach, his face. He sensed that he was sinking to the ground, that he was looking at the men's boots from close up.

He heard an angry roaring voice and saw a tall, angular shape pushing between the men semicircled around him. He felt a boot strike him in the ribs, but the impact was dull, without pain. He saw the quick movement of a long-barreled rifle and heard it swish as it swung with a mighty force. He expected it to crush his head open, but it did not. He heard a cracking sound and a cry of pain. A man sprawled on the ground beside him. Through a red haze he recognized the bloody face of the man called Jayce. His eyes were rolled back.

He heard that angry voice again. "Now the rest of you-all had better step back, because I'm just on the point of losin' my temper." The voice had the crackle of age, but it carried an authority that would make a prudent man stop and take notice. Andrew sensed that his antagonists were backing away.

The voice raged, "You there, drag that son of a bitch away before I take a notion to hit him again. And any of you wants a taste of what's in this barrel, you just make a false move towards me or that boy."

Apparently their curiosity was limited, for nobody made any such move. Someone grabbed Jayce's feet and unceremoniously dragged him off through horse droppings that happened to be in the way.

The voice demanded, "You, preacher, you fetch that brown horse over here. And you two, you lift that boy up onto him. Careful now, you hear me? I'm fixin to get mad in a minute. When I get mad I even scare myself!"

Andrew felt strong hands raise him up from the ground, then lift him into the saddle. He tried to find the stirrups. Fairweather guided first one boot into place, then the other.

"All right, now, back away from him, all of you."

Andrew blinked. He could see the men, though they seemed to sway backward and forward. It was like looking at them through a fog. He got a grip on the pommel of the saddle, for this would be a poor time to fall to the ground. The preacher took the reins at the bit and led the brown horse out into the dirt street. Andrew dimly saw the tall man climb stiffly upon a horse of his own, then turn back and take the brown horse's reins. Andrew blinked his eyes clear. There in front of him, gaunt as an old wolf but defiant as an old badger, sat Eli Pleasant, ten years older than Methuselah and still as tough as the first time he had ever shaved.

Pleasant said, "Thanks, Fairweather, for comin' and fetchin' me." To Andrew he said, "I declare, seems to me like I am everlastin'ly havin' to come and drag you Lewis boys away from trouble. Between you and Michael, you've probably worried ten years off of my life."

22

ANDREW FELT his throbbing eyes swelling shut. After a while he could see through little more than a slit in his left and less in his right. He clung painfully to the saddle, knowing that if he loosened his hold he would fall like a sack of corn. Old Eli rode in front, setting an easy, plodding pace, leading Andrew's brown horse. Andrew was apprehensive over possible pursuit, but Eli showed not a whit of concern, humming a discordant little tune that grated on the ears. He had probably thrown a healthy scare into that bunch with the crazy-old-man look in his eyes, his raspy voice carrying a threat of hellfire that the preacher Fairweather might have envied. If any of the crowd were personally acquainted with him, they had probably counseled the others that Eli Pleasant was a good man to leave alone. He was a quiet old codger when things went his way, but he could be aroused to fight like a sore-footed bear. He had survived long years in the outlaw country of western Louisiana, making his living smuggling goods in both directions across the border at considerable risk to life and liberty. He was not one to be intimidated by anything or anybody small.

Eli's voice was gentle now. "We're fixin' to come to a little stream, just yonder a piece. You'll feel better when you've got all that blood washed off of your face."

The water was freezing cold. Its first rude shock set Andrew to trembling. But it eased the fever in his battered face, at least temporarily. He could see a bit better, too.

Eli fetched a bottle and bade Andrew take a long drink from it. It warmed him all the way down, though Andrew knew its warmth was but temporary. When it passed he would probably be colder than ever. Eli eyed him critically. "You ain't pretty. I wonder what you done to get them boys back yonder so riled up."

"They thought I came here to spy for Austin."

"Did you?"

Andrew considered a moment. "I wasn't lookin' at it in quite that way."

"If you was in their boots, how would you look at it?"

"Like they did, I reckon. That don't make me hurt any less."

"Always try to look at a thing through the other man's eyes. At least you'll have a better idee what to expect from him. Come on, we'd best be goin' if we don't want to ride all night."

"Where you takin' me?"

"To some friends of mine. Same place I carried your brother Michael the time he was wounded and your daddy killed. They're pretty good at takin' care of hurt folks. They've had a-plenty of practice with their own."

As the sun went down, the evening turned cold. Andrew hunched painfully in the saddle, shivering. In the darkness, with his vision impaired by the swelling, he had no idea what direction they traveled.

Eli talked on. "Them boys in Nacogdoches ain't ready to start listenin' to reason; they're havin' too much fun. But they'll wake up some mornin' with their heads hurtin' and their stomachs all soured, and they'll know it ain't no easy thing to run your own country. I'd say the hell with them, except they're liable to get Mexico riled up and spoil Texas for all of us. I'll bet there ain't a hundred fifty, maybe two hundred Fredonians if you was to put them all in one wad. The Mexicans just need to set back a little while, then come marchin' in some mornin' when the boys are sick of one another. Like as not, there won't even be no fight to it."

Andrew grunted. He feared Eli was not taking his own advice, that he was not seeing the incident through the Mexicans' eyes. "I've got to get the word back to Austin."

Eli sniffed. "The shape you're in, you'd be to New Year's gettin' there. The news'll reach Austin in due time."

"But I promised him—" Andrew realized he was making no headway with Eli. The old man was selectively deaf; he heard only what he wanted to hear. Andrew felt his body slowly going stiff, the soreness settling all the way to the bone. He gritted his teeth and resisted complaint until finally he lost his grip on the pommel and felt himself sliding forward over the horse's shoulder. He tried in vain to make his numbed fingers grasp the brown mane. He struck the ground with a dull thump. The impact hurt all the way to the ends of his fingers and toes.

Eli dismounted and knelt. "World's come to a hell of a pass when a Lewis can't even stay on a horse. Bust anything?"

Andrew groaned. "Feels like everything's busted."

"Got to give them boys credit: they don't settle for halfways. We'd just as well make a dry camp. Looks to me like you're used up. Next time you go to talk politics, you'll first take the measure of them you're talkin' to."

Andrew offered no argument. Eli staked the two horses while Andrew struck flint and steel, trying to spark a fire in a wad of dry grass. He hurt too much, and Eli had to complete the job. Andrew rolled up in his blanket and tried to get warm as the blaze slowly built in a small pile of deadwood. Eli voiced regret over not having anything to fix for supper. That was the least of Andrew's concerns; his jaw was too sore for chewing, and his stomach was too riled to accept food if he could have forced it down.

Eli said, "I wasn't worried about *your* supper; I was thinkin' about mine. I ain't et since breakfast."

Andrew huddled close to the fire, trying to absorb all of its warmth. He said, "The one that started it all, I heard somebody call him Beard."

"That was Jayce Beard. He's got a mean streak in him but damned little sense to go with it. Tolliver Beard, his old daddy, is the one you really got to watch. He's just as mean but a right smart faster in the head. It's his notion that he can take over a fat lot of land under Haden Edwards's new rules. And he's got the determination to do it if somebody don't put a stop to the Fredonians. I know that old bastard from Louisiana. He's like a dog that, once he gets ahold of a bone, he don't turn it loose."

The cold and the constant hurting kept Andrew from going to sleep for a long time. He hoped the two men Eli had struck with his rifle barrel were feeling a similar misery. When he finally managed to nod off, his dreams carried him to Marie's kitchen, warm and snug and smelling of a hot supper cooking on the hearth. He played with little Mordecai and watched Marie rock the baby in a cradle Michael had built. He could not tell if Marie was talking French or Spanish or English; he only knew that her voice tinkled like a silver bell.

Once his dream altered a little. Instead of Marie, he saw the girl Petra. Then it was Marie again, or perhaps not. He found he could not tell them apart.

He awakened to see a cold winter sun rising in the east, all light and no heat. Half frozen, he shivered and tried to sit up. He made it on the third attempt. Through a blur he watched Eli saddling the horses.

Eli studied him critically. "Your face is speckled with blue welts, and them eyes appear to be swollen nigh shut. Do you feel any better than you look?"

"Damn little," Andrew admitted. He struggled slowly to his feet, swaying. Eli led the brown horse up to him, and Andrew steadied himself by leaning against the saddle.

Eli gave him a careful boost up. "I've seen beef hangin' on a hook that looked better'n you do. Wouldn't surprise me none if you've got a rib or two broke. But we still need to ride a ways if you can make it."

Andrew gritted his teeth. "I can make it."

He soon reconsidered that declaration of confidence, though he was determined not to retract it. Every step the brown horse made was like the blow of a Fredonian's fist. Andrew broke a dry twig from a tree and stuck it between his teeth, clamping down on it when he felt like making a cry. He did not want Eli to see the extent of the pain. It had been part of Mordecai Lewis's teaching to his sons that a man never complained; he took whatever was his lot and made the best of it.

Andrew began recognizing landmarks. He sensed Eli's destination long before they reached it. His swollen eyes made out the shape of the log cabin, the nearby sheds, the wagons and tents and *jacales* close around. "I've been here," he said. "Some of these folks thought I was a spy for the Edwards brothers."

Eli chuckled. "I never thought about it before, but all you Lewis boys have got an honest face. That's more'n enough to make folks suspicious in a country like this."

Word of their coming preceded them. People emerged from the tents and sheds to watch their approach. Andrew saw the three Blackwoods standing beside their wagon. Finis had his one arm around the waist of the plump girl Nelly. Her startled gasp at the sight of Andrew's face told him how bad he looked. Finis hollered at Eli, "Did you do that to him all by yourself, old man? I'd've been glad to come and help you."

Eli ignored him, and Andrew tried to. That was difficult, hearing the pleasure in Finis's voice at Andrew's misfortune. Finis declared loudly, "I swear, Andrew, this is the first time I ever thought you looked good."

Luke Blackwood laughed.

Andrew had no strength to respond, but he mentally set Finis's remark on a back shelf in his memory, to be called up for review at some appropriate time in the future. He sensed someone following him and turned his head painfully. Isaac Blackwood trailed him afoot. Isaac's two older brothers stayed behind.

Several people had come out onto the tiny porch of *Señora* Moreno's cabin. The girl Petra made a small cry and hurried forward, lifting her skirt so she could run. She spoke to Eli as she passed him, then stopped beside Andrew's horse. "What has happened to him?" she demanded in Spanish.

Eli replied that Andrew had disagreed with some men in town over a matter of politics and had failed to persuade them to his line of thinking.

Petra called for her brothers to help her lift Andrew down from the saddle. Carlos gently edged her aside and took hold. Andrew managed to swing his leg over the horse, but he would have fallen had the strong hands of Carlos and Ramón not held him. He swayed drunkenly and bumped hard against the brown. The animal shied away from him, almost making him fall despite the efforts of the Moreno brothers. Isaac Blackwood lent them a hand.

Andrew wanted to tell him to go back to his brothers Finis and Luke, but at the moment it was expedient to accept help from any quarter. At least Isaac was not laughing at him.

Isaac said, "Must've been some of the Edwards people."

"It was," Andrew managed.

"Some of the same ones that burnt us out, I expect. Same ones that've got all these folks forted up here. What're we goin' to do about it?"

Eli put in, "Andrew tried talkin' to them. You can see how much good that done."

Isaac said tightly, "I was thinkin' about somethin' stronger than talk."

Andrew took a quick though blurry look at the people gathering around, eager to know what was happening. "There's a way too many for this little bunch to whip."

Isaac shook his head. "I know we can't do that, not without some extra help. I was just wonderin' how we might go about gettin' that help."

Andrew said, "Austin."

Isaac asked, "What about Austin?"

"Austin has got to know what's happened. I've got to go and tell him."

Eli snorted. "I didn't think I'd even get you *this* far. It'll be some days before you go anywheres."

Andrew grudgingly admitted to himself that Eli was right. "Then you go tell him."

Eli shrugged. "Not me, boy. Austin never did approve of

my business activities. Was I to go down into his bailiwick, he just might take it in his head to turn me over to the Mexican authorities in Bexar. It'd tickle them to have me for their permanent guest."

Petra cried out, "Are you men going to keep him standing out here all day? Bring him into the house."

Isaac said quickly, "Austin's got no quarrel with me. I'll go. What you want me to tell him, Andrew?"

Andrew stalled. Surely there must be somebody here more responsible than a Blackwood to carry the message; Simon Wells, perhaps. But Isaac allowed him little chance to argue. He took Andrew's right arm, and Carlos took the left. Together they half carried Andrew into the log cabin. Isaac kept talking. "This ain't no time for holdin' old grudges. Me and my brothers, we got an interest in this thing too. Even bigger'n yours, because there ain't nobody burned you out yet. Now, what is it Austin needs to know?"

As they eased him onto a rough wood-frame bed with rawhide stretched beneath a cornshuck mattress, Andrew reluctantly told what he had heard about the declaration of a Fredonian republic. "If Austin can get word to the Mexican authorities about it before they learn from their own people, maybe it'll help keep them from seein' us all as rebels."

Isaac declared, "I don't much give a damn what the authorities think; they're a greasy-lookin' lot to me. But I'd admire to see them land thieves in Nacogdoches get their due for what they done to us. So I'll carry your message to Austin." He turned toward the door but stopped. "Never thought me and any of you Lewises would ever take the same side in a fight. It'd spoil Finis's supper for a week if he was to know I done you a favor, Andrew. So if he asks, you tell him you tried to stop me but couldn't."

Andrew *would* have stopped Isaac if he had known how. He tried to raise a protest with Eli, but Eli had already gone back out the door and was talking earnestly to Isaac, telling him what he knew of events in Nacogdoches.

The last thing Andrew saw was Petra's sympathetic eyes as she laid a damp cloth over his face and gently told him to lie still.

A SMALL blaze in the fireplace made the cabin pleasantly warm. Andrew gradually lost his chill and drifted off to sleep, though the pain momentarily awakened him every time he moved. When at last he came fully awake, he knew by the faded light that the weak winter sun was almost gone. He opened his eyes as much as he could. The blurred images confused him at first. He thought he saw Marie sitting in a handmade wooden chair. That made no sense; there was no reason for her to be here.

"Marie?" he asked incredulously.

Petra's voice told him he was mistaken. "Who?"

He blinked, trying to clear his vision. "Sorry. I woke up and thought you were somebody else." He realized he had spoken in English. He repeated in Spanish.

She said, "You slept a long time. Do you feel better now?"

He was not sure. He tried to raise up, but he felt as if he were bound by rawhide. Every muscle in his body seemed paralyzed. He lay back, defeated.

She touched his face with her small, warm hand. He remembered old times at home in Tennessee, when he had been ill or hurt, and his mother's hands felt as if they had a healing power. Petra's touch was like that, soothing, strengthening.

She said, "Your face is still fevered. Now that you are awake, I will bring another wet cloth. That will draw out some of the pain and the heat."

He could have told her that her hand had the same effect. He said simply, "Thank you."

He felt with his right hand and confirmed what he already knew, that his face was swollen and cut and sore in a dozen places. He felt his nose, wondering if it might be broken; it hurt enough. Those damned Fredonian patriots might have killed him if Eli Pleasant had not shown up. He doubled his fist in remembered anger but quickly relaxed it when a sharp pain jabbed his knuckles.

Petra brought the wet cloth and carefully laid it across his face. Her hand rested a moment on his cheek before she drew it away.

He felt a cold draft as the wooden door opened, then closed. His eyes were covered, but he could hear boots scuff across the packed-earth floor. Eli Pleasant's voice was solicitous. "Girl told me you finally come awake. For a while I was afraid we might have to organize a buryin' party."

"You may yet. There's a whole army of little demons hammerin' away inside of me."

"Naw, it takes a heap of killin' to put a Lewis under the ground. Remember, I've seen some mean ones try."

"They might've done it this time if you hadn't been there. I owe you, Eli."

"I'll mark it down in my ledger. Someday when I'm an old man I may want to come and live with you."

"Someday? You're already old enough to've helped raise George Washington. You can come and live with me now; I'd be obliged for your company."

"You don't need an old man sharin' your cabin. What you need is a young woman. Have you taken a good look at that girl Petra?"

"My eyes've been swollen to where I can't hardly see."

"When they get unswelled, you open them good and wide. Was I a couple years younger, I'd be interested in her myself."

"Everybody keeps tryin' to get me harnessed up. I don't remember hearin' that *you* ever got married."

"I never stood up in front of no preacher, but a man is meant to share his blessin's. How do you think I learned to talk Spanish so good, and French too?" Eli paused. "Your Spanish could stand some improvement, boy. While you're laid up healin', you ought to work on it. I got a feelin' that girl'd be a willin' teacher."

"I'll be up and leavin' here as soon as I can."

"What for? Austin'll be bringin' help, more'n likely. You'd just as well stay here and wait for him. Besides, if that bunch in Nacogdoches decide to do mischief out thisaway, these folks'd need all hands. They could use a Lewis's help."

Andrew mused, "I hadn't thought of it like that. You'll be here too, won't you?"

"I'm fixin' to go back into Nacogdoches. Takin' care of you made me run off and leave some unfinished business."

"That bunch that jumped me, they'll know you. No tellin' what they might do."

"Ain't no swamp rats got the guts to bother Ol' Eli. Ol' Tolliver Beard has knowed me from way back. He knows I got some rowdy friends that'd stove their heads in. Besides, in Nacogdoches I can see what's goin' on. Out here, all I can do is guess."

Andrew was still trying to argue with him when he heard the old man's feet shuffling across the floor. Eli had never been given to lengthy arguments. He just went ahead and did what he wanted and let the devil take the hindmost. He acted as if he had Lewis blood in him.

Andrew shivered from the chilly draft as Eli went out.

He heard Petra's concerned voice. "Are you cold?" Her hands pulled the blanket up tighter around him, and they stayed longer than was necessary, touching his shoulders.

"I am all right," he replied in Spanish. He considered a moment. "Did you hear what Eli said?"

"He spoke in English. I do not understand English."

"He said my Spanish is not very good."

"It could be better," she admitted ruefully.

"I could improve it. But I need someone to talk with."

"When you first awakened you called me by someone else's name. Marie. Your wife, perhaps?"

"I am not married."

"Your sweetheart?"

"I have no sweetheart."

"But the way you called her name—perhaps she is someone you *wish* were your sweetheart."

"Nothing like that. Marie is married to my brother. When I saw you, I thought you looked like her; that was all."

He thought he heard her release a pent-up breath. Her voice sounded like a smile. "Ah—then, Andrew Lewis, I think I would like talking with you—to improve your Spanish."

She did not get the chance, not for a little while. He felt the cold air again as the door opened. He recognized Finis Blackwood's sullen tone. "Andrew Lewis, what did you go and talk my little brother into doin'?"

Andrew could not see him; the damp cloth still covered his eyes. "I didn't talk him into anything."

"Well, he rode off for the south and said he was carryin' a message to Austin. Your message. What right you got to be sendin' a Blackwood off to do your errands?"

"Fact is, I told him I didn't want him to go. I wanted somebody else."

The tenor of Finis's voice began to change. "You mean he went agin your wishes?"

"He did. I'd've rather had anybody go besides a Blackwood."

Finis was silent a moment, thinking it over. "Well now, that puts a whole different complexion on it. You don't trust a Blackwood to do anything right, is that what you're sayin'?"

"That's about it."

Finis chortled in triumph. "Then damn you, you're fixin' to see somethin'. He'll deliver that message to Austin and do it better'n you could've. He'll show you high and mighty Lewises."

He left the door open as he went out. Petra hurried to close it and returned to Andrew's bedside. "I do not wish to speak against your friends, but that one I do not like."

Andrew smiled, though the effort was painful. It pleased him to know she was a good judge of character.

23

PETRA BROUGHT Andrew some of the family's meager supper from the cooking place on the hearth in the next room. Though he tried, he managed to put down only a little of it. Petra worried, "How can you live if you do not eat?"

"Maybe tomorrow," he said apologetically.

She set the spoon in the plate and the plate in her lap. "It seems strange. I remember when the old man Pleasant brought another Lewis here a long time ago, just as he has done for you. Your brother had been shot by the federal soldiers. I was only a girl then, and had much fear because I had seen their officer murder my father. But my mother and brothers said we should take care of Miguel Lewis because we were all on the same side.

"We won that fight. Now you are here, and we are on the same side in another."

"You'll win this one, too."

She touched his hand. "With your help. That is why you must get well."

Some time after dark, Petra's brother Ramón—younger than Carlos—came into the tiny room and undressed, folding back a blanket on the other small bed.

Andrew felt a twinge of guilt. "I have taken someone's place here."

"Felipe. You are in Felipe's bed."

Felipe was a third brother, the youngest.

"Where will Felipe sleep?"

"Out there." Ramón jerked his head toward the door. "Under a shed."

"He will be cold. I am not so badly hurt that I should force Felipe to sleep outside."

"It will be cold in here too, once the fire dies out. Do not concern yourself. Felipe and his friends will tell wicked stories half the night. He will not notice the cold."

"I do not like being a burden."

"We did not consider your brother a burden. His enemies were our enemies. The men who hurt you would do the same to us if they could."

Despite the reassurance, Andrew lay awake a long while after Ramón had begun snoring. As the cabin's chill closed in and he pulled the blanket tightly around him, conscience made him think of Felipe lying out yonder under a shed, a raw winter wind cutting him to the bone. That was above and beyond hospitality.

Next morning, sore and aching, Andrew arose when Ramón did. With some difficulty he managed to get into his clothes, waving off the young Mexican's offer of help. Gingerly he felt his face, knowing it was still puffed and discolored. He asked, "How do I look?"

Ramón grimaced. "You do not want me to tell you."

Andrew nodded. That was answer enough.

Ramón broke into a knowing smile. "If I were you, I would lie in bed and let my sister wait upon you. It is not a privilege she often gives to anyone, certainly not to Felipe or me."

"I am not an invalid."

"One should accept blessings whenever they come. We do not receive many in this world."

Petra, her short, stocky mother, and a sister younger than Ramón were in the cramped area which served as kitchen, eating place, and sitting room for the Moreno family. Petra's dark eyes widened with misgiving when Andrew stepped into the small room. "You should not be up," she declared.

"I am all right."

"You should look at yourself. No, you should not. The shock would be bad for you."

"It is better that I am up and moving. People die in bed."

Petra insisted, "Ramón, talk to him."

Ramon shrugged. "I cannot hold a rifle on him."

Señora Moreno said, "He is a grown man. You will learn that grown men do not listen well, especially to good advice."

Ramón grinned at Andrew. "I told you Petra enjoys being nurse to you. You should not be so eager to give that up."

Petra blushed. "Ramón—"

Younger brother Felipe, fourteen or fifteen years old, walked in from outside, blanket wrapped around his shoulders. He shivered from the cold.

Andrew said, "Look at Felipe. Next she will have to be nurse for *him*. I have been a burden long enough."

Petra's eyes softened. "But you are not, Andrew Lewis. We are glad to have you here."

Andrew thought Felipe looked less than enthusiastic. His face was a chilled blue. "I will not take Felipe's bed another night. I will find a place for myself."

Petra glanced at her mother for support. "There is no need. We can make room here somewhere. Perhaps in the kitchen. It has often served for sleeping in the past." Her eyes pleaded. They had the same look as Marie's when Marie had asked him to make this trip so Michael would be obliged to remain at home.

He demurred. "The inconvenience—" It was much more than the inconvenience. The way Petra's fingers clutched his arm—

After breakfast he went outside. Several young men huddled around a fire just beyond one of the limb-covered sheds. A couple of them moved to make room for him. A chunky young bachelor farmer whose name he remembered as Dick Johnson rubbed huge hands together briskly. "You don't look too good, Lewis. Was I you, I'd stay in that nice warm cabin as long as I had the chance. I do believe this was the coldest night we've had."

Andrew asked, "Where'd you sleep?"

Johnson pointed his chin toward the shed. "Another night like this and we're liable to all freeze to death. Then Ol' Man Beard and the Fredonians can just walk in and take everything."

Andrew stared toward the several flimsy picket-style *jacales* various ones had built for shelter. "If three or four of us worked together, it wouldn't take long to build somethin' like that."

A man named Pete Bradley frowned. "And live like a Mexican?"

"They're warmer'n *we* are."

Johnson rubbed his hands again. "Well taken. How do we start?"

Bradley said with misgivings, "I don't believe us Americans can build one. It takes a Mexican to rightly do that."

Andrew had visited in a number of these crude *jacales* around Bexar. Their walls were of upright pickets, the lower ends of tightly fitted branches set into a shallow trench, the tops tied together, the roof a thick set of branches topped by sod. The walls were mudded inside and out to turn the wind. There was even a mud fireplace, poor to look at but functional. A tentative shelter at best, a *jacal* was nevertheless better than sleeping cold beneath an open-ended shed.

He found the exertion helped draw out the soreness and speed the healing process. The black-and-blue marks gradually faded from around his eyes, along with the swelling. He remembered that when anyone among the Lewis children had complained about the burden of labor and asked what they were going to receive for it, their father Mordecai would declare, "Work is its own reward. It clears the mind and heals the body and makes a man wise."

Andrew had always harbored reservations about the wisdom gained by working endless rows of corn, chopping out weeds with a hoe, but he had accepted the rest of the axiom.

Carlos and Ramón gave advice and often pitched in to help with shovel or ax or mallet as the *jacal* began to take shape. Despite his dark predictions that the work would come to naught, Pete Bradley put his thin back into the project. A wiry young man, in contrast to Dick Johnson's fleshy build, he seemed never to tire. And never to stop worrying about failure.

Somehow the pair, Johnson and Bradley, reminded him of the two young bachelors, Younts and Smith, who were courting Miles Nathan's daughter in the Colorado River settlement.

Finis and Luke Blackwood idly watched with a superior air. Finis taunted, "Won't be nothin' but a damned hovel. Fit for Mexicans, maybe, but not for a white man."

He changed his mind when he saw it finished and found it snug and warm and dry inside. He loudly declared that he and Luke could build a better one. Finis contributed mostly orders and ill temper; Luke did the sweat labor. After they finished the structural work they put too much heavy earth cover on top against the advice of Carlos Moreno. Finis declared that he had never met a Mexican who could tell him anything worthwhile.

A hard rain added the weight of all the water that soaked into the sod. About dusk it brought the *jacal* crashing down upon a surprised Nelly and Finis and Luke. Hefty Nelly shook clenched fists and told Finis her opinion of him and all his ancestry while rain washed rivulets of mud out of her hair. He, in turn, cursed Luke with a magnificent command of Tennessee backwoods maledictions. Luke, having no one to whom to pass it on, picked awkwardly through the wreckage, trying to rescue his soaked blankets.

Andrew thought it was probably the first time he had laughed since he left the farm on the Colorado for his ride to Nacogdoches.

Petra was more inclined toward sympathy. Standing on the small porch, watching the Blackwoods chase each other aimlessly through the rain, she said in a half-scolding manner, "It is a shame to laugh at the misfortunes of others."

That only caused Andrew to laugh the more. "Not when you know the Blackwoods." His laugh was contagious, for her frown turned unwillingly into a faint smile. She hurried into the cabin, but not before he heard her break into laughter.

Her laugh was like music. It reminded him of Marie's. His own laughter ended, and he began to feel hollow inside.

It was a long way back to the Colorado River.

THE MEN who had gathered for mutual protection at the Moreno farm had established a military-style schedule of guard duty to help prevent any surprise attack by the Fredonians. After a couple of days of mending, Andrew insisted that he take up his share of that responsibility. Pete Bradley was dubious about his beginning so quickly. "It won't work," he predicted. "Shape you're in, you might not stay alert. Might even fall asleep, like Luke Blackwood does. Takes one man to watch out for Luke and another to watch out for whoever might come."

"I can tote my own load," Andrew insisted.

Dick Johnson accepted Andrew's offer without voicing any reservations. "Me and you can stand watch together. I like your sand, Andrew Lewis."

Andrew suspected Johnson wanted to be on hand to add his own weight in case Andrew was not up to the responsibility. But he accepted the man's friendship with gratitude. "Dick, if you ever get tired of these piney woods, I'll be glad to put in a word for you with Austin. There's good land to be had along the Colorado."

Johnson shoved his hand forward. "Couldn't ask for no better'n that."

Pete Bradley worried, "I hear you can't grow nothin' down there, hardly."

After some days Andrew began to feel that all this guard duty was wasted. The nearest thing he saw to outside intrusion was a few white-tailed deer poking their way out beyond the edge of the woods to browse late in the evenings. By day, those refugees who had left livestock elsewhere would ride out to see after them, making it a point to be back before dark. They always went well-armed. Carlos was among them, usually taking Ramón to help him. Since their scare with Andrew at Carlos's place, Petra had not been going. She said that was Carlos's choice, not hers. But she appeared content to remain at the home place. It seemed to Andrew that almost every time he looked around, she was somewhere within sight, hanging clothes on a line, feeding the chickens, gathering the eggs, sweeping the ground in front of the cabin. And she always had that smile—Marie's smile—when he caught her looking at him.

It warmed him, yet made him vaguely uncomfortable. In an odd way that he could not comprehend, he felt disloyal to Marie. It did not help to remind himself that Marie belonged to his brother and always would. He tried to look away from Petra's smile, but that too was difficult.

Half of the men were away seeing after their livestock the morning old Eli Pleasant came spurring in. Andrew, sharing a casual guard duty with Dick Johnson on the trail that led toward Nacogdoches, saw Eli coming and walked out to meet him, dropping his long-barreled rifle to arm's length. He perceived a basic contradiction between Eli's calm face and the fact that he had run the horse until it was lathered with sweat despite the winter chill. But Eli seldom let anything excite him much, at least not in a way that it showed.

"Welcome, Eli."

"I may be welcome," Eli declared, "but I doubt as them behind me will be. You-all better be gettin' yourselves ready to receive company." He delivered the message with about as little emotion as if he had announced that the west wind was getting up.

Dick Johnson's ruddy face quickly became agitated. "How many's there goin' to be?"

"Enough to go around," Eli replied casually. "I hope all the men are in camp."

"They're not," Andrew admitted. "Half of them are gone out to tend their stock."

"Them that's left had better get up on their tippy-toes, then," Eli said. "Them Fredonians ain't far behind me. Ol' Tolliver Beard is in the lead of them. He's got it in his mind to take this place for his own."

Andrew said, "We'll rouse up all that's here."

Eli nodded his satisfaction. "Reckon you could rouse up a cup of coffee for me? And a bite to eat wouldn't hurt my feelin's none. I left a mite too early for breakfast."

Johnson stayed to watch the trail while Andrew went to the Moreno cabin with Eli. Eli's message brought anxiety to Petra's eyes. "What will we do, Andrew?" she asked urgently.

"Stop them," he replied, not giving her time to ask more questions for which he would have no answer. He turned the old smuggler and his appetite over to the mercies of Petra and her mother. He beat a piece of steel bar against a big iron ring hanging from the edge of the porch, a device *Señora* Moreno had used for years to call her menfolk in from fields and pasture. In a minute Andrew counted just five men standing anxiously in front of him. He regretted that two of those were Blackwoods; a man had to accept what he could get in a pinch. The womenfolk gathered too, standing beside or behind their men. Andrew tried not to betray his uncertainty as he relayed the message Eli had brought.

"How many's there goin' to be?" demanded Simon Wells, whose brother was among those gone to see after their own affairs.

"Fifteen to eighteen, best Eli could tell. He didn't stay around to call the roll."

Pete Bradley's gloomy face went into deep furrows. "That's two apiece, just about. Looks hopeless to me."

"Depends on how much you think of your homes."

Bradley said gravely, "They'll whip us, maybe kill us."

"There's one way to avoid that. Everybody could hurry up and pull out before they get here. Just turn it over to them without a fight."

Simon Wells stiffened. "The odds is poor, but they ain't impossible."

Andrew could see anger building in the men's faces, and courage, too. They glanced at one another, borrowing determination.

Wells said sternly, "Andrew, your farm is down in Austin's colony. But ours are here, and we ain't leavin'."

"Then what're we standin' here talkin' for? Let's get out yonder and fix for company."

The men scattered to tents and *jacales* and sheds for their rifles and ammunition. Shortly they were back, faces flushed with excitement as they took count. There were Simon Wells and the youngest Moreno boy, Felipe. There were Finis and Luke Blackwood. There was lean Pete Bradley, who shared a *jacal* with Andrew and Dick Johnson. Johnson waited out at the guard post on the trail. With Andrew himself, that made seven.

Eli stepped from the door of the Moreno cabin, a cup of parched-grain coffee in his hand. "I got nothin' better to do," he mumbled around a mouthful of food.

Eight. Andrew frowned at Eli. "You sure? Things might get awful uncomfortable for you in Nacogdoches if you help us."

Eli shook his head. "The string's about to play out on them boys. I figure Austin and his bunch are apt to be here pretty soon. Any business I got in Nacogdoches can wait a while."

The women embraced their men and cautioned them not to get themselves shot up. Andrew saw deep concern in their faces, but he was pleased that he saw no panic. Petra started to reach toward Andrew, then stepped back. "Be careful," she whispered. He did not hear the words; he read them on her lips.

As they hurried up the trail to join Dick Johnson, Andrew waited for somebody to assume the leadership. No one took hold of the reins. "All right," he demanded after a short wait, "we've got to have a plan."

Bradley declared fatalistically, "I don't see where a plan'll make up for the way they got us outnumbered. They're goin' to whip us anyway."

Simon Wells countered, "You're right, Andrew. What's your plan?"

Andrew felt a quick annoyance. They had been sitting here for weeks expecting just such a contingency, and they had no plan designed to meet it. They had a far greater stake here than his; in fact, he could argue that he had none at all. Yet they expected him to lead them. He almost wished Michael were here.

He looked around hurriedly for a place to set up a line of defense. "We've got to take all the advantage we can to offset their numbers."

Wells looked at the others, then back at Andrew. "If you have an idee, let's hear it."

Andrew looked to Eli for help, but Eli just stared back, his eyes calm and trusting. "You're ol' Mordecai's son. I expect you can handle it."

Andrew wished he could be that sure. He felt like a pack mule under the sudden and heavy burden of responsibility. He wondered if he could carry it. "We need to scatter out where we can give ourselves some good cover. Just up yonder there's a fair amount of timber fallen down alongside the trail."

Felipe volunteered in Spanish, "It fell in a twisting wind last year. We were afraid we would lose the cabin also."

Andrew said, "That's damned little of a plan, but it's all I've got."

Eli grunted. "It'll serve." His long legs began striding toward the fallen trees, their leaves and needles just brown remnants lying beneath the dried and skeletal branches. The other men followed him. Andrew quickened his step to catch up to Eli. It occurred to him that he could not have moved so easily a week ago.

Eli gave him a long glance. "I still see a blue mark on your face. Otherwise, you look like you've healed up."

"It's been long enough."

"Good nursin' probably didn't hurt you none. You thought any more about that girl?"

That Andrew had thought a good bit more about her than he wanted to was none of Eli's business. "We got more important things to be thinkin' about."

"Them boys from Nacogdoches'll come and go in a little while, but a good woman'll stay with you."

They reached the place where Andrew thought they could put up the best defense. He waited a moment, glancing first at Simon Wells, then at Pete Bradley, waiting to see if anyone would assume some leadership. No one did. He pointed to one side of the trail, then the other. "Let's scatter out behind that deadfall stuff, about half of us on one side and half on the other, to where we'll catch them between us. Maybe it won't even come to shootin'. But if it does, let's be careful we don't hit our own people on the opposite side of the trail."

Bradley fretted, "If they was to rush by, we couldn't stop

them all. Most of them'd get on past, and they'd be down there amongst the women and children before we could reload to fire a second shot."

Andrew said, "I figured to hold them right here."

"How? The trail is open."

"Time comes, we'll close it."

Eli's face twisted. "I already rescued you Lewis boys once apiece. You fixin' to make me do it again?"

"I hope not. But we've got to let them see that our intentions are serious."

As Eli had told them, they did not have long to wait. Andrew heard the sound of horses' hoofs from within the woods, where the trail bent out of sight beyond the outer fringe of timber. The others heard it too. They knelt behind their protective piles of downed trees to present little target. Andrew remained on his feet. As the riders burst into sight in the fringe of pine and scrub he knew they spotted him instantly. He took a rough count; seventeen or eighteen. One more or less didn't make much difference. He saw several rifles pointed at him. The pit of his stomach felt as if it carried thirty pounds of lead, but he forced himself to stand still. When the lead riders were thirty or forty yards away, he stepped out into the trail and set his feet solidly upon the ground, a little apart. He thumbed the hammer back and cradled his rifle in his arms.

The horsemen reined in. Several formed a solid line, facing Andrew. He hoped they could not smell his apprehension. *He* could. It was like the nose-tingling smell lightning sometimes left in a spring thunderstorm. He gripped the rifle hard to keep his hands from trembling.

He heard himself say, "You fellers ain't welcome here." The voice did not sound like his own. He thought he should have said something more authoratative, like, *Stop or I'll shoot!*

He picked a blocky, gray-eyed, gray-bearded man in the center as the probable leader. The dour old man confirmed his judgment by demanding, "You ain't one of the Mexicans who claims this place. Your face ain't brown enough."

Andrew's gaze swept quickly over the men in the front line,

the ones he thought most likely to move against him first. He recognized Jayce Beard, who had led the beating in town. He discerned some facial resemblance between Jayce and the older man who led the party. The gray-haired one was the Tolliver Beard he had been hearing about, the one he had encountered once in San Felipe.

Andrew was pleased to see a long dark streak across Jayce's nose and cheek where Eli's rifle had clubbed him.

"Mornin', Jayce," he said. "Remember me?"

Jayce had already recognized him. He scowled bitterly. "You're that spy we caught. If you don't move out of our way we'll finish what we started."

Andrew's words spilled without conscious thought on his part; he did not know where they came from. "Might cost you considerable. Ain't much free in this life."

The gray-haired Tolliver Beard was impatient. "I'll handle this, son." He focused his attention on Andrew. "We have come to claim this property. We find the title faulty and the claim null and void under the laws of the Republic of Fredonia."

"I'm a farmer, not a lawyer. Seems to me like generations of plowin' and plantin' mean more than a piece of paper."

"We are not here to bandy words. We have come to take this property. We will do so peacefully if possible. We will use force if we must."

Andrew drew a long breath of winter morning air. It seemed to steady him. "Well now, Mr. Beard, you might be able to do that. Then again, maybe not. Before you start tryin', I feel like you ought to meet some folks who don't agree with you." He glanced to the lefthand side of the trail, to the pile of deadfall timber there. "Felipe Moreno, would you stand up?"

Felipe did, slowly, raising an old musket that probably had originated in Spain.

Andrew said, "That's Felipe. He's the youngest of the Moreno family who own this land. That gun he's got there, they call that an *escopeta,* I believe. Ain't much to look at, but it can blow a hole in a man big enough to let the wind whistle through him." Andrew turned to the other side. "Simon Wells, I wish you'd show yourself."

Wells rose. His long rifle was pointed at Tolliver Beard. The hard look in Wells's eye told Andrew that he had encountered Beard before.

Andrew said, "Now, Simon, he's got a wife and family down yonder. I don't know how many of you fellers are family men, but those that are, you know a man don't stand back and let somethin' happen to his family without he puts up a fight."

Andrew switched his attention back to the left. "Dick, would you and Pete please stand up? I want to introduce you." They complied, their rifles aimed into the riders. Andrew said, "I saw Dick Johnson shoot four squirrels the other day. Hit all four of them in the head so as not to spoil the meat. But there was five squirrels in all. He flat missed one of them. Maybe you'll be lucky, and he'll miss again.

"Pete Bradley, now, he don't claim to be a great shot. Says he has to get close. But he's close now, wouldn't you say?"

Tolliver Beard's face gradually flushed. His voice went deep, but Andrew thought he detected a slight rattle of uncertainty in it. "There's twice as many of us as there is of you. You couldn't get us all."

"That's a fact," Andrew admitted. "Best we could do would be to get half of you. You sure you want to find out which half?"

The men from Nacogdoches began to stir uneasily. The rest of the defenders rose up on both sides of the trail. They had the horsemen boxed. One of the invaders said, "Beard, I don't like this one bit."

"Shut up. Can't you see he's tryin' to bluff us?"

Andrew said, "Sure, I'm tryin' to bluff you. If we all fired a volley, half of you would still be alive to go on down yonder and take over the camp. Trouble is, you don't know which ones that'd be. I can only guarantee that you won't be amongst them, Beard. And neither will your little boy Jayce."

Jayce said, "Papa, we goin' to stand here and let them do us thisaway? We can take them." It was probably imagination, but Andrew thought the bruise on Jayce's face had darkened with his anger. His eyes were getting a little wild.

Andrew said, "I haven't finished introducin' everybody yet.

You probably wouldn't like them—I don't—but there's the Blackwood boys over yonder, Finis and Luke. Finis ain't too good a shot. He tried to kill my brother one time but hit my uncle instead. He'd probably miss whichever one of you he aimed at and hit somebody else. You never can tell about Finis."

Several of the Nacogdoches men began pulling their horses around. Tolliver Beard called out to them in anger, "We come here to do a job. You ain't fixin' to let him scare you off, are you?"

They didn't answer him, but five started riding away. Two more watched them uncertainly, then turned and set out after them in a trot. Andrew sucked in another long breath and slowly let it go. He found his hands still sweaty on the rifle, but they were steady now; he did not have to grip so hard.

He waited until Beard got through mumbling under his breath, then said, "That changes the odds some, but there's still more of you than there is of us. Three or four of you might still make it through to the camp."

Jayce was sweating now despite the winter's cold. He had spotted Eli Pleasant among the defenders. He tugged at his father's coatsleeve and pointed. "That's the old man everybody's been tellin' about, the one who laid that rifle over my head. He ought to be amongst the first ones we get, Papa."

Tolliver Beard said grittily, "That's Eli Pleasant. He can shoot the wings off of a bumblebee. If you've got a lick of sense, you'll leave him alone."

One of the Fredonians who remained said, "Looks to me like we'd better leave them all alone, Tolliver."

"You goin' yellow on me too?"

"Not yellow. But I can't help wonderin' what good a piece of this land is goin' to do you if you're buried under it, and some of us layin' there with you."

Beard's eyes blazed. "Get out of here, then. Get the hell away from me."

The man did not tarry long. "I'm obliged you see it my way. Anybody comin' with me?"

Four of them did.

Andrew waited to see what Beard might do. Beard stood his

ground. Andrew said, "I believe you might want to take another count."

Beard began to slump. When he dropped his gaze to the ground, Andrew knew he had won. He relaxed a little.

Jayce Beard cried, "Papa, you ain't fixin' to give in! We come here to take this land away from those damned Mexicans, and by God we're goin' to take it!"

Andrew tensed again. He did not like the wild look in Jayce's eyes. He said, "If you-all want to go catch up to your friends, I guarantee you none of us will shoot at you. But stay here another minute and I can't promise what anybody'll do. Especially Finis."

Tolliver Beard said in resignation, "Come on, son."

Jayce gave Andrew a gaze that could have burned bark from a tall pine. "You son of a bitch!" His hand moved, and Andrew instantly brought the muzzle of his rifle into line with the man's chest. Jayce screeched like a panther and came spurring, a pistol in his hand.

Tolliver cried, "No, Jayce! Come back!"

But Jayce drove straight at Andrew, his right arm extended, the pistol leveled at Andrew. Andrew caught one quick breath, then pulled the trigger. He saw the powder flash in his rifle's pan, then felt the hard shove against his shoulder and watched the black smoke billow. Jayce's pistol went off. The ball smacked harmlessly into the earth, for Jayce was already falling from his horse. He pitched to the ground almost at Andrew's feet. Andrew held his breath, his mouth dry, his heart pounding. He made no effort to reload the rifle.

Tolliver Beard sat a moment in shock and dismay, then cried, "Jayce! Son!"

That brought Andrew out of his trance. He drew a deep breath, choked a little on the remnant of powdersmoke, then knelt and felt for a sign of life in Jayce. He found no pulse.

He looked up at the old man. He said in anguish, "I didn't want to do that."

Beard's voice was thin and raspy. "He's dead?"

"He oughtn't to've rushed me. I didn't go to kill him."

Jayce's horse had run by Andrew. Felipe Moreno caught it

and brought it back. He bent down and confirmed Andrew's finding. "He is dead," he said in Spanish.

The other men from Nacogdoches held back. It had probably sounded easy in town; just go out and throw a scare into those people and run them the hell off. A gunfight had not sounded like much over a bottle of whiskey. But it was different now in the cold light of a winter sun, one of their own lying here dead in a small pool of his own blood. The Fredonians looked on from a safe distance, stiffened by shock.

Tolliver Beard rode slowly forward. He was careful not to make a threatening move with his rifle, because the settlers' rifles were all aimed at him. They would cut him to pieces if he showed a real threat to Andrew. He said thinly, "Jayce was headstrong, but he didn't deserve bein' murdered."

Defensively Andrew said, "I didn't murder him. I shot him because I had to."

The man's eyes brimmed with tears. "Would you kindly lay him across his horse so I can take him home?"

Andrew put his rifle down against a weathered log and, with Felipe's help, placed Jayce across his saddle. The horse did not like the burden. Andrew handed the reins up to the old man.

Beard's eyes had taken on fire. "What is your name?"

Andrew told him.

Beard said, "I got a boy to bury, and the mournin' to do. But I'll be seein' you again, Andrew Lewis. And they'll be buryin' you the way I've got to bury my son." He turned and led the horse away. The other Fredonians parted to give him room, then closed around him. Shortly they had disappeared into the tall pines.

Andrew felt as if he had a thousand needles sticking into his flesh. Eli Pleasant handed him his rifle. He said, "Wouldn't hurt if you keep that loaded from now on."

"He won't be comin' back right now."

"But he *will* be comin' back sooner or later, or layin' in wait for you someplace. I told you, I know that old man. He's swore to kill you, and he'll do it or die tryin'."

"One killin', and that has to lead to another? I didn't want any of this." Andrew looked at his hand, trying to see the blood. There was none, but he was sure he could feel it anyway. He rubbed the hand against his leg as if trying to get rid of it. He wanted to cry out, but he held it back. He turned, his eyes afire, and started down toward the cabin.

24

DICK JOHNSON remained behind to watch the trail. Like Pete Bradley, he had no worried womenfolks to report to. The rest walked back toward the cabin and the tents and the *jacales,* where they could see the women and children waiting in the open yard, fearful for what the gunshot might have meant.

Andrew felt sick at his stomach. He wanted nothing so much right now as to be back home on the Colorado, to put this incident as far behind him as he could.

Most of the men had little idea how he felt; they were too jubilant over their turning back the Fredonians. That a man had died seemed not to matter a great deal. That man, after all, had been a land thief, on the other side.

Pete Bradley was almost dancing in unaccustomed euphoria. "I knew we could do it!"

Simon Wells said with admiration, "Andrew, that was mighty slick, the way you counted us off one by one and bluffed all that bunch."

Andrew did not feel like talking, but he replied, "I learned that from my brother Michael one time. No matter how many people a man has got with him, he feels all alone when he looks at a bunch of rifles and knows one of them is probably pointed straight at him."

Felipe, youngest of the defenders, hurried ahead to give the first account. By the time the others reached camp, the women had a fair picture of what had happened.

Petra stood with hands clasped just under her chin. As Andrew neared, she took a couple of steps forward, her dark eyes soft with sympathy. "You are all right, Andrew?"

He stopped. He came near calling her Marie by mistake. "I killed a man," he told her painfully.

"I know." She extended her hand. "Come. Come into the house. I think I can find you some whiskey."

He followed her. *Señora* Moreno followed both of them, but only with her eyes. She remained outside with her youngest son Felipe.

In the cabin, away from the others' sight, Petra turned. She threw her arms around Andrew and buried her face against his chest, sobbing in relief. "Oh, Andrew, Andrew. I was so frightened for you."

He stood awkwardly, not knowing what to do with his hands. So he let nature tell him, and he put them around Petra.

HE SHARED a meager supper with the Moreno family. Through the meal he tried not to see but could not escape the tug of Petra's gaze. He gave up after a bit, pushing the food aside. His stomach was still in turmoil. He excused himself from the table to walk outside and wrestle with his confusion in the chill of dusk. Shortly Petra came out onto the small porch, a thin shawl over her shoulders. Her eyes searched, lighting when they found him. "Where are you going, Andrew?"

"Just walking a little, taking some air."

She came down into the yard to join him. "I would like to walk with you."

"Where?"

"It does not matter. Along the creek, or up the trail."

Reason warned him to find an excuse, but reason left him when he looked into the dark eyes so much like Marie's "People might say it would not be proper."

Her eyebrows arched. "You would not do anything improper, would you?"

"Would you want me to?"

She slipped her arm beneath his. "I might."

Señora Moreno came onto the porch. She watched them with concern but made no move to follow.

They walked arm-in-arm beneath a darkening winter sky. A bend in the creek took them out of sight of the cabin and camp. Large trees on the bank extended their branches almost far enough to intermingle with those on the other side. Petra asked, "Do you have such a pretty creek on your farm?"

"I have the Colorado River. It is much wider. The trees cannot reach across."

She said, "I have not seen even the Sabine River. I never have been far from this place in my life. Where you live, does the land look much like this?"

"It's sandier. The trees are not so tall, and in most places not so dense. I think we get less rain than you do."

"I get tired of the rain sometimes, and the mud. I wish I could see your country, Andrew. It must be beautiful."

He shrugged. "Any place looks good if it is yours."

Her fingers tightened on his arm. "You look good to me, Andrew. I wish I could know you were mine."

He wished he knew some way to answer. He mumbled something that made no sense.

The air had turned from a light chill to very cold. She shivered and drew closer to him. He said, "We should go back."

"I wish I never had to go back. I want to be with you. Put your arms around me and I will be warm enough." Turning, she raised her own arms.

He hesitated, then embraced her. Her arms went around him, and she pressed her face against his chest. He bent to rest his cheek against the top of her head, her soft hair. He felt her body convulse and sensed that she was sobbing.

"Petra." He touched her face with his hand, trying to lift her chin so he could see her. He felt the wetness of a tear.

"No," she protested quietly, "do not look at me now. I feel foolish, crying like this. But I keep thinking how easily you might have been killed."

"I wasn't. There is nothing to cry about."

"It is not the first time I have cried for you, Andrew. You have not known—"

"I have known," he said uneasily. "But you shouldn't. There is no reason."

"There is reason. I love you, Andrew."

"You don't even know me. I have not been here long enough—"

"I know you. I feel that I have known you all my life. I feel that I have waited for you since I was a little girl. Can you not feel something like that for me?"

He floundered, trying to find an honest answer that would not bring pain. "I do, but not the kind of feeling you need."

"Do you find me ugly, Andrew?"

"No. I find you very pretty. But love has to come from more than that."

She clung fiercely. "I would go anywhere with you, Andrew. I would do anything you want of me, just to be with you. There would not even have to be a priest if you did not want that."

"I would not shame you, Petra. If I felt that strongly, I would want a priest too. But—" There was no painless way to tell her. "Do you remember the day I awoke and mistook you for someone else? There *is* someone else. Yes, I am drawn to you, Petra, but it is because you remind me of her. The feelings I have for you are not honest, because when I look at you I see her. When I hold you, I am holding her. You deserve much better."

"I would be content with that, if that was all there could be. But there could be more. I could teach you to love me."

Holding her, he felt a rising warmth, an intoxicating desire to take her, here and now. He brushed his cheek against her face and found it almost hot to the touch. He felt light-headed, as if he had been drinking. He sensed that he could lay her down upon the dry grass, and she would not resist. In the heat of the moment he toyed with the temptation, nearly crushing her in his arms. But the moment passed, and reason forced him back from the edge. To do such a thing to Marie would be unthinkable. And Petra, to him, was another Marie.

He pulled away from her as far as she would let him, for she still clung to his arms. "What is the matter, Andrew?"

"Nothing. For just a minute there—We had better go back before we make a bad mistake."

Her eyes brimmed with tears. "It is my fault, Andrew. I have made a fool of myself. I will not do it again."

She squeezed his arms once more, then broke free and ran back toward the cabin. He followed, confused and frustrated but grateful that he had found willpower to retreat.

She brushed past Eli Pleasant with her head down, giving no sign she had seen him. Eli stared after her, then turned toward Andrew, the question in his eyes.

Andrew said shakily, "Don't ask me, Eli. I wouldn't want to lie to you."

"Wouldn't do no good if you tried. It don't take a man of education to read what you've both got writ all over you."

"Don't be jumpin' to any notions, Eli. Ain't nothin' happened."

Eli glanced toward the cabin, where Petra had closed the door behind her. "Pity. Looks to me like she'd've been ready, and you too."

"But I ain't proud of it. Any other pretty girl'd affect me the same, like as not. I just ain't been around enough of them to know for sure. And I figure she ain't been around many men, outside of family. She's put me up as a hero or somethin'. I never been a hero in my life."

"Waitin' around for true love to find you, you'll keep sleepin' cold and all by yourself. True love probably don't even know where Texas is at. Take what's offered to you and don't ask too damn many questions. I never did."

"It wouldn't be fair to her."

Eli shrugged and turned away. "Then you'd best pray for Austin and his bunch to turn up quick and give you a reason to leave here."

ANDREW DID not go so far as to pray for that eventuality, but Austin turned up anyway, three days after the encounter with the Fredonians. The approach of a large armed force aroused apprehension among many in the Moreno farm encampment, fear that the Fredonians might be returning in massive strength. Though he did not dismiss that possibility, Andrew thought the direction, from the southwest, was unlikely for invaders out of Nacogdoches. He saddled his brown horse and rode out warily, hoping to identify the riders at a distance that would not put him in peril. He determined that they were a mixture of civilians and Mexican soldiers. Fredonians would not be traveling with the military, except perhaps as prisoners.

Relieved, he rode boldly on. He soon recognized Isaac Blackwood riding at the head of the column, guiding it toward the Moreno farm. Beside Isaac rode Stephen Austin, and beyond him a dark-skinned Mexican officer whose dusty but braided uniform bespoke considerable rank. Following, Andrew was pleased to see, came a long column of armed Texas colonists and, separately, what appeared to be a couple of companies of Mexican soldiers. Most slumped wearily in their saddles; the road had been long. Several rifles were brought to bear on Andrew as he approached. He held his breath until Austin and the officer sent back orders for their men to stand easy.

Isaac Blackwood nodded at Andrew but did not extend his hand. He said dryly, "Well, Andrew, I see my brothers ain't killed you yet. I hope you ain't killed them."

Andrew flinched at the bitter memory. "No, I didn't kill *them.*"

Austin shook Andrew's hand. He looked thin and tired, but that was nothing new. "It is good to see you, Andrew. I assume things here are as Isaac Blackwood represented them."

Andrew gave Isaac a brief study but withheld judgment. "I don't know what he represented, but the Fredonians sent a bunch out three days ago to try and take this place."

"I would assume you did not yield it to them."

"We—I—had to kill one of them. They ain't tried again." Andrew's gaze ran down the long, strung-out column, making a rough count. "Goin' to be hard to catch them by surprise. A bunch like this won't be easy to hide."

Austin nodded. "We have not tried to make a secret of our

coming. We want them to know. If they are not of strong resolve they will have time to retreat to Louisiana, and we will have no need of a fight."

"And if they are resolved to stand on their ground, you've got enough men with you to push them off of it."

"That is our reasoning. Will you go with us into Nacogdoches?"

"I reckon that's what I've been waitin' here for."

"Very well. Isaac has told me about the Moreno farm. We will camp there the night to rest the men and horses, then proceed in the morning." Austin scrutinized him closely. "Isaac spoke of injuries. You appear well mended."

"Us Lewises have always been fast menders."

Austin smiled. "Which reminds me, there is another Lewis with us, somewhere down the column."

Andrew stiffened. "My brother Michael?"

"The same. I think you will find him with one of the soldier companies."

"Soldier companies!" Andrew was surprised, for the sight of soldiers always seemed to upset his brother. Soldiers much like these had slaughtered his father and the Tennesseeans who had come to Texas with Mordecai and Michael a long time ago.

Austin said, "He has been riding with an officer, an old friend, I believe."

Andrew nodded. "That would probably be Zaragosa."

"Yes. A good and honorable man, from what I know of him. Proceed, Isaac."

Andrew pulled out of the line of march, nursing a growing resentment. His initial relief at seeing Austin and the column had turned sour. He waited to let the column pass by him rather than ride down to meet Michael. Any pleasure he might take in seeing his brother was more than counterbalanced by his strong old conviction that Michael belonged at home on the farm with Marie and the children. He had no business coming way to hell up here on an adventure that had some potential for leaving Marie a widow. Andrew's rising anger was near a boil by the time he spotted Michael riding beside the officer, Lieutenant Elizandro Zaragosa, and a younger Mexican soldier Andrew remembered seeing on the Colorado the day the Blackwoods had come to call.

Michael recognized his brother and pulled out of the column, trotting his horse until he reached Andrew. He seemed about to extend his hand, which surprised Andrew a little, then he withdrew it, which was no surprise at all.

"Well, little brother, looks to me like you're in one piece after all, far as I can see."

Andrew's voice was crisp. "What the hell are you doin' here? The only reason I came myself was that I tried to make you stay home with Marie where you belong."

Michael's eyes flared in quick response to Andrew's challenge, but he seemed to try to hold the anger from his voice. "Now wait just a minute, little brother. I knew why you came up here. Believe me, I taken it to heart. I didn't want to leave Marie, but she insisted. Isaac brought word that you was hurt, and she was anxious about you."

Andrew was dubious. "She sent you?"

"She sure as hell did, or I wouldn't've come. You don't seem to know, Marie's a grown woman, and strong. She takes care of herself mighty good. When she says *go* and really means it, I go. And another thing, I taken her and the young'uns over to stay with the Nathan family till I get back. Miz Nathan's fixin' to have her baby. Marie and the young'uns are as safe there as at home. Probably safer. You think I'd just go off and leave them?"

"Wouldn't be the first time. You sure you didn't come here just because you saw this trip as some kind of a lark?"

Michael's face twisted with pain. He turned in the saddle and looked back toward the approaching Mexican troops. "You think I enjoyed it, bein' amongst all these soldiers? I've had a cold chill all the way. Every time I look at them I remember what happened to Papa. But I gritted my teeth and came on because of you. And because Marie wanted me to."

Andrew's anger began to ebb. "Maybe I spoke too quick."

Michael gave him a critical study. "You sure them fellers didn't club you across the head and addle your brains a little?"

The last of Andrew's resentment faded away. "I wouldn't be surprised." He extended his hand, and Michael took it.

Zaragosa rode up smiling, his teeth very white against several days' trail growth of black whiskers. He greeted Andrew in Spanish and said he was glad to see him looking so well; he had thought he might find him otherwise. He turned to the young soldier who rode with him. "This," he said, "is Corporal Diaz. He speaks much better the English than I."

Diaz nodded with a quiet reserve, not offering to shake hands. Andrew thought he saw distrust in the dark eyes. He chose not to force the issue by extending his hand and pressuring Diaz into shaking with him. *What did I ever do to him?* he thought.

Michael asked, "You got any brothers, Elizandro?"

"Several. They are far from here."

"Kind of wish right now that I was far from here myself. I come all this way to rescue my brother from God knows what, and he jumps into the middle of my back."

Zaragosa seemed uncertain, afraid he had blundered into a family argument. "He does not seem to have drawn any blood. And did I not see you shake hands?"

Andrew said quickly, "We did. It was nothin'. Let's just forget about it."

Michael agreed. "We can't be fightin' amongst ourselves. We'll likely face the Fredonians tomorrow."

Andrew noted, "Austin hopes they'll pack up and leave town before this column gets to Nacogdoches."

"That'd be a pity. I ain't had a good fight in so long, I was almost glad to see Isaac Blackwood."

Zaragosa put in, "I hope Austin is right. I have seen enough trouble, enough fighting, to last me forever."

Michael frowned. "That's an odd thing for a soldier to say."

"Who knows better than a soldier what the cost of blood is?"

Andrew shuddered. "There's others that know."

SUCH A large column would have swamped the Moreno farm had it attempted to camp around the cabin. Austin and the

Mexican commander selected a place down the creek, where the men could attend to their necessities without concern over the sensibilities of the women. Andrew took Michael up to the cabin. "You recognize this place?" he asked.

Michael said gravely, "I wouldn't forget it if I lived for a hundred years. Was it not for those kind folks, I'd've been dead a long time ago."

Michael stared with interest at the tents and temporary *jacales* the refugees had put up. Andrew saw his brother's face twist at sight of Finis and Luke Blackwood standing beside their wagon. Isaac was already there. Finis held his good arm possessively around Nelly's expanding waist.

Michael demanded, "Where'd a snake like Finis ever find him a wife?"

"He hasn't married her."

"He'd better, the way her stomach's pushin' out. How'd the Blackwoods come to be mixed in here with decent folks?"

"These people couldn't afford to be choosy. They needed all the help they could get."

"I'd've been choosier than *that*."

"You'll have to admit that Isaac took it on himself to go to Austin and tell him what was happenin'."

Michael's eyes narrowed. "Not out of pure human kindness. He was workin' on somethin' for himself—and his brothers."

Andrew missed a step. "What?"

"You'll remember that Austin wouldn't let them stay in his colony the first time they tried. He didn't like their looks. You reckon he could refuse them now? He's obligated."

Andrew felt suddenly foolish. "I never thought about that."

"Just goes to show which is the smartest of us, little brother. It was the first thing that came into my mind."

Señora Moreno waited on the porch. Petra stood beside her, hands clasped nervously at her waist. When Andrew's gaze met hers, she quickly looked away, pain in her eyes.

The older woman did not wait for Michael to be introduced. Recognizing him, she stepped down from the porch and opened her arms. She hugged him tightly, tears on her cheeks. Michael responded with embarrassment at first, then melted into the spirit of the reunion. He struggled with his Spanish. "I have never forgotten your face, Mrs. Moreno." His voice quivered. "I owe you my life."

The dark-faced woman backed away and looked up at the tall Michael Lewis with approval. "You owe God your life. We are but His servants. You grew into much of a man, Miguel." She glanced at Andrew, then back to Michael. "I see much of your brother in you."

Michael tried to break the solemn spell with a forced smile. He glanced at Andrew for help with his Spanish. "Tell her I can't help it. Our old daddy marked us all."

Señora Moreno declared, "You will have supper with us, both of you." It was not an invitation; it was a command. Andrew was about to decline as gracefully as he could, for he knew how uncomfortable it would be, sitting at the table with Petra. But Michael spoke quickly, "Of course we will."

Michael turned his attention to Petra. He bowed in a style brought from Tennessee and enlarged upon after exposure to the courtesies of Mexican people in Texas. His Spanish was slower and more awkward even than Andrew's, but he managed to work his way through it. "I remember a little girl. She looked at me with fear and stayed behind her mother."

Petra avoided Andrew's eyes, concentrating her attention on Michael. Her voice was subdued. "I had not seen an American before. And your wound frightened me. I thought you would die, as my father had died. I am glad you did not."

Michael said, "So am I."

Petra let herself glance for just a moment at Andrew. He met her gaze, and she looked away again. Michael seemed to notice, for he looked from one to the other with a question he did not put into words.

He went through an emotional reunion of hugs and *abrazos* with the Moreno brothers, Carlos and Ramón, one of whom long ago had helped Eli Pleasant with the wounded Michael while another had gone up the trail to watch out for Spanish soldiers. Felipe stood back. He had been too young to remember much.

Someone mentioned Eli's name, and Michael demanded,

"Where is that old reprobate? I have looked forward to seeing him."

Carlos shook his head. "The old man Pleasant did not wish *Señor* Austin to see him. There is some difference between them. And he is not much liked by the military. He said he remembered some business left unfinished in Louisiana."

Lieutenant Zaragosa came in a while, along with the young soldier Diaz. They both received a warm welcome from the Moreno family. Zaragosa had done what he could to shield them from persecution as rebels in the final years before freedom from Spain. Diaz had grown up not far from here; his family had fled into Louisiana to escape that same persecution.

The visit lasted long after supper. Andrew sat back and let Michael do the talking for both of them. Not once did he catch Petra looking at him. Now and again he felt the strong gaze of Diaz, however, and he puzzled over the young soldier's hostility.

As Andrew and Michael walked in darkness toward the *jacal* Andrew had been sharing with Dick Johnson and Pete Bradley, Michael said, "Grand folks, the Morenos. Grand people."

Andrew knew the problem his brother sometimes had in dealing with Spanish and Mexican people; the ghost of Mordecai Lewis always seemed to stand between them. "It doesn't bother you that they're Mexicans?"

"They had nothin' to do with what happened to Papa. The same officer who killed him murdered their daddy too."

Andrew could only nod agreement, for his mind lagged behind, in the Moreno cabin.

Michael said, "That girl Petra— There's somethin' about her— All night long I had the feelin' she looks a little like somebody. I just can't figure out who."

Andrew almost stumbled. He looked back once and swallowed. "I guess just about everybody looks like somebody else."

25

EVER THE pessimist, Pete Bradley worried aloud all the way to Nacogdoches. "They won't give up without a strong fight. There's some of us ain't comin' out of this alive."

Dick Johnson finally got enough of it. He said, "Maybe you'll be lucky, Pete, and just get shot in the head. That's the only place in your body that a bullet won't penetrate."

But there was no fight, hardly even a scuffle. The arrival of Colonel Ahumada and Stephen Austin's column in Nacogdoches was anticlimactic, as Austin had hoped. The Fredonian movement had dissolved ahead of it. Those loudest in their denunciation of Mexican authority retreated across the Sabine into Louisiana. Most others who had attached themselves to the Fredonian cause met the troops without hostility or arms and expressed a hope for leniency and understanding. As the column marched into the old Spanish town, most of the populace cheered, relieved to see the last of the abortive rebellion. The most pressing concern for the military was the Cherokee Indians, some of whom had allied themselves with the Fredonian movement out of frustration over the government's slowness to follow through on promises of secure land grants. To reassure the Cherokees, Ahumada dispatched an old filibuster named Peter Ellis Bean, survivor of a Spanish massacre not unlike the one which had taken Mordecai Lewis.

Virtually the only blood spilled was that of two Cherokee leaders who had taken up the Fredonian banner. Their chief put them to death as a show of loyalty to the government of Mexico.

To Lieutenant Elizandro Zaragosa that seemed more extreme than justice called for, given the evident hopelessness of the Fredonian cause from the beginning. But he could not recall when anyone over the rank of colonel had ever asked his opinion.

"A pity," he told the young corporal Diaz. "This has been a farce, too ridiculous for anyone to have to die over it, don't you think?"

Diaz shrugged. As an enlisted man, he was unaccustomed to having anyone over the rank of private ask his opinion. "One never knows why the Indians do what they do."

Diaz was riding with Zaragosa and a small detail of troops from house to house as interpreter to be certain none of the army's orders were misunderstood by the English-speaking settlers. A one-eyed preacher named Fairweather rode with them, trying to ease any lingering apprehensions the people might have, and explaining in his own way that the government meant no harm to those who meant no harm to *it*. Diaz was a little dubious about having the minister along, for he was Protestant, and the law decreed that the only religion here be Catholic. But Zaragosa was a realist. The Americans would come nearer listening to one of their own. Besides, from what Zaragosa could ascertain, Fairweather held no real authority to preach. He had no diploma, no church sanction, nothing but a big black Bible and an ease with words. For all Zaragosa knew, the man might be a charlatan. But at least he seemed to help in this situation; the Americans listened to him and understood what he said.

It appeared to Zaragosa that Americans understood what they chose to understand. They pleaded ignorance when the message went against their pleasure.

Diaz agreed with a dark frown that betrayed his antipathy for the entire race. He could speak freely in Spanish, for Fairweather knew only English. "They understand more than they admit, these Americans. They are a selfish and scheming lot." That he had lived among them while his family was exiled in Louisiana, avoiding persecution by the Spanish royalists, had left the young man unaccountably bitter, the lieutenant thought.

Zaragosa said, "One does not condemn the many for the sins of a few."

"The many envy the few. They would all do the same were they not fearful for their lives and their possessions. They put much value in possessions, these Americans. And they would possess all that belongs to someone else if they were but given the chance to take it."

"Did they ever take anything from you?"

"Much. Those blackguards in Louisiana set upon us soon after we crossed the river. We thought we were safe because we had left the Spanish soldiers behind us. We did not know that worse waited on the American side. They took the little money we had, and our horses."

Zaragosa said, "You were in the neutral strip. It has always been infested with outlaws; ours as well as theirs."

Diaz shuddered. "My sister was a girl much like the Moreno's Petra. They carried her away screaming."

Zaragosa felt a chill. He had not heard this before. "Did you ever find her?"

"Much later, in Natchitoches. She wandered there when they were done with her. She was working in some American woman's household. She did not want us to see her. She was with child. From which of those demons, it was impossible to know." Diaz clenched his fist. "God was merciful. When time came for delivery, He took both her and the child."

Zaragosa nodded his sympathy. "I understand."

"The Americans did not understand. They saw we were penniless and without hope, so they put us to work in the fields like their black slaves. They worked us hard and paid us little and fed us even less. My father was much ashamed. He said it would have been better had we died fighting the Spanish. But he died in a cottonfield, carrying a sack with the black men. I came back to Texas and fought the Spanish so what was left of my family could return and live where they belonged, in peace."

Zaragosa wished for an adequate way to express his compassion. But he also had to express his reservations. "Surely you must have known a man named Guadalupe Lucero. Like you, he fled to Louisiana because the Spanish hellhound Rodriguez put him on the death list. Rodriguez murdered some of Lucero's kinsmen like the old Moreno, trying to make them betray Lucero. I was there. I saw. Lucero lived among the Americans, but he did not hate them. He had many friends like the Lewis brothers, Michael and Andrew. He did not confuse the good with the bad."

"I have no wish to offend you, sir, but I have seen that you count the Lewises as your friends also."

"They once saved me from Rodriguez. I was privileged to return that favor."

"You may one day regret that you did, sir. They may seem to be your friends now, but a time will come when they will see you only as another Mexican to be robbed of whatever they wish to take from you."

"I cannot believe that."

"Why are we in Nacogdoches, sir? We are here because some Americans decided to take land that belongs to Mexico. They will try again. They will keep trying until their numbers are so large that they overwhelm us. Then they will take it all: Nacogdoches, San Antonio de Bexar— Who knows? They may go all the way to Mexico City."

Zaragosa vigorously shook his head. "There are many good men among them. They will not let that happen."

"It will happen. And when it does, your friends the Lewises will be there with the rest, seizing whatever they can take." Diaz's eyes pinched with resentment. "Did you not see the one named Andrew, and the way he looked at the girl Petra? And did you not see her eyes? I think he has already taken her, as those others took my sister."

"Imagination," Zaragosa countered briskly. "The Lewises are not that type."

"They are Americans. We have seen only the beginning.

They will yet take everything we have. As soldiers we will have to fight them. And we will probably lose."

Zaragosa shook his head. "I will not be fighting ever again, at least not as a soldier. I am going to leave the army and become a farmer."

Diaz said with regret, "That would be a waste, sir."

"Not to me. I am separated too often from my family. My father-in-law is sickly and asks me to take over his farm. My wife wants me to do it. I have given it much thought."

"We will need you, sir, when the fight comes."

"There will be no fight, Diaz, not with the Americans."

"They are not like us and never can be. We are not like them and should never wish to be." He looked at the minister Fairweather with eyes that betrayed his hostility. "Yes, lieutenant, we will fight."

LIKE AUSTIN, Andrew was gratified that they had not had to fight to enter Nacogdoches. He sensed that Michael harbored a little disappointment, however, for a good scrap would have capped this little venture away from the boredom of the farm on the Colorado River. Andrew had to smile when Pete Bradley cockily declared, "Cowards, the lot of them. I figured they'd turn tail and run when they seen us comin'."

Dick Johnson called Bradley's hand. "I thought you said they were liable to kill us all."

Bradley vigorously shook his head. "When did I ever say that? You must've been listenin' to somebody else."

Andrew was relieved that a diligent search of the town revealed no trace of old Tolliver Beard. Like many of the others, he evidently had fled eastward into Louisiana, from whence he had come.

Michael was not quite so pleased. "It'd've been better if we could've caught him. I'd feel a lot better knowin' he was in a Mexican prison someplace and not roamin' around out yonder somewhere waitin' for a chance to kill you."

"It's a long way from Louisiana to the Colorado River. He won't know where to find me."

"The Blackwoods found us, didn't they?"

The two older Moreno brothers had joined Austin's column, leaving younger brother Felipe behind to watch over the rest of the family. Carlos and Ramón rode with Andrew and Michael, Johnson and Bradley now, carrying their search through the town and out into the countryside. The Morenos' main interest had been in finding Tolliver Beard and impressing their disapproval upon him in some memorable way. They accepted failure philosophically. Ramón said, "Your brother is right, Miguel. We seek after birds that have flown the nest, while we are tied to the ground."

Carlos spoke what was truly on his mind. "There is nothing more for us to do here. I would like to go home."

Carlos was a married man with responsibilities. Andrew thought Michael should feel the same way. He looked hopefully at his brother. "Ramón's right. Marie'll be wonderin' and worryin'. You'd ought to be gettin' home to her."

Michael's eyes softened at mention of his wife's name. His righteous indignation seemed to fade. "We ought to go tell Austin before we take our leave."

They found Stephen Austin looking very concerned for a man who had won a victory without firing a shot. The *empresario* sat in the old stone fort building, frowning over a lengthy report he was writing. Though the papers were upside down from his side of the table, Andrew could see that Austin was composing in Spanish, probably giving a full report to the authorities in Mexico City. He smiled at the Lewis brothers, seeming to read their minds. "You have my permission."

In truth, they did not need it. Neither was an enlisted member of the militia. But Andrew said, "Thank you." He nodded toward the papers spread in front of Austin. "At least you can tell Mexico that the whole thing was a little of nothin'. It wouldn't've raised a wave in a coffeepot. Most of the people around Nacogdoches are glad to see the Fredonians go. The Americans who've settled in Texas are a faithful lot."

Austin's face pinched with concern. "I know that, and you know it. But except for Colonel Ahumada, the officials of Mexico have not seen it themselves. I am afraid they will read a great deal more into this little insurrection than was ever here. Those who have always distrusted us will tell them the worst. And I fear the officials will be inclined to listen to them."

"But in the end they always listen to *you*."

"Up to now," Austin said darkly. "Up to now." He looked beyond Andrew and Michael to the door, to the four men who waited outside. "The Morenos will be going with you?"

"Yes, sir. I expect the people camped around the Moreno farm will be packin' up and leavin' for their own homes. Carlos and Ramón want to be there to tell them *adiós*."

Michael said dryly, "And they'll want to be there when the Blackwoods leave, to be sure they don't take away more than they brought with them."

Andrew felt he should probably salute or something, inasmuch as Austin was an officer of the volunteer colonist militia, but he did not know how. He said simply, "Come see us when you can," and started for the door.

Austin called, "Andrew, Michael, there is one thing more."

Andrew turned. He did not like the reluctance he saw in Austin's thin face.

Austin said, "Michael, you mentioned the Blackwood family. I have already gathered that you and Andrew have no great love for them."

"You have good eyes, sir."

"Nevertheless, I owe Isaac Blackwood a debt for having come to report to me about the Fredonians. So I gave him a letter for my assistant Sam Williams in San Felipe. The Blackwoods will receive a grant of land."

Andrew swallowed. "Not close to ours, I hope."

"The choice is theirs."

Andrew saw steel come into his brother's eyes. He gritted his teeth and grabbed Michael's arm, hustling him out of the room before he could say something he might someday regret.

Michael trembled with anger. "He don't know what he's done."

"He did what he thought he had to do."

Michael's body was rigid as he mounted his horse. He kept

a stony silence and avoided looking at anybody. Dick Johnson arched an eyebrow and asked, "What's got into him?"

Pete Bradley said, "Must've been bad news. Ain't but little happens around here that ain't bad news."

Carlos and Ramón were too polite to ask questions. Michael took the lead as they started upon the trail that led southward from town. At length he grumbled, but not loudly enough that Andrew could understand.

"What did you say?"

Michael kept his gaze fastened upon the trail. "Just said I'm sorry for all the times I had a good excuse for shootin' a Blackwood and didn't do it."

Carlos took the lead, for he was a married man whose wife awaited him anxiously and would be demonstrative in her relief that nothing unpleasant had befallen him. Pete Bradley and Dick Johnson argued good-naturedly about which had been most apprehensive. They still reminded Andrew a lot of the bachelors Younts and Smith. Michael was moody and silent, brooding about the Blackwoods. Andrew found himself riding along with his head down, thinking about Marie, about Petra; sometimes it was hard to know which image came into his mind.

Ahead, from down the trail, he saw a flash. In the split second before the rifleball snarled past his ear, he recognized Tolliver Beard, smoking rifle braced against a heavy pine tree. Then, before anyone seemed able to react to the surprise and begin to move, Beard was on his horse and racing away through the pines. Andrew sat, frozen.

Ramón and Carlos, Johnson and Bradley went spurring into the timber after Beard. Michael reached out and grabbed Andrew's shoulder. "You hit?"

It was a moment before Andrew was able to answer. His mouth was suddenly bone dry. "I'm all right. Just taken me by surprise, is all."

"That the man we all been huntin' for?"

"He is. I reckon he decided not to go to Louisiana."

Michael said gravely, "It don't look that way." He checked the powder in his rifle's pan.

For a few minutes Andrew could hear the sound of horses moving in the forest, plunging through the underbrush. Then the woods went quiet. There were no shots, so nobody had caught up with Beard. Andrew regained composure enough to step to the ground, where he might make less of a target if Beard circled back.

It was the better part of an hour before the four men returned empty-handed. Dick Johnson said apologetically, "We seen him once or twice, way off in the timber. Never got close enough for a shot. Last we seen of him, he was movin' in the direction of Louisiana."

Pete Bradley worried, "But he won't go there. He'll come back, Andrew. He'll come back and kill you, sure as hell. Maybe kill all of us."

Michael Lewis gave Andrew a long, concerned study. "I think it's high time we got back to our own part of the country, little brother."

ANDREW DREADED stopping at the Moreno farm because he did not know what he could say to Petra that would not add to the hurt he had already caused her.

The six horsemen found the refugee camp breaking up. A few families had already gone. Felipe Moreno came to the shed to greet his brothers as they unsaddled their horses. He was disappointed at the report that they had not been able to exact retribution upon Beard or his followers.

Andrew missed the Blackwoods' wagon. Felipe said, "They were the first to leave."

Michael asked, "Did you count your chickens?"

Felipe grinned. "I watched them load their wagon. There was almost a fight between Finis and Simon Wells over the rightful ownership of a saddle. Everyone knew it belonged to Simon. Isaac made Finis leave the saddle here."

Andrew observed, "Isaac is pretty honest, for a Blackwood."

Michael snorted. "He just knew they couldn't whip the whole camp."

The older Moreno brothers walked toward the cabin. Carlos's wife hurried out to throw her arms around him. Mother Moreno hugged Ramón. Petra came out onto the porch, her gaze touching gratefully upon her brothers, then searching out Andrew. Her eyes held to his for a moment, until he flinched and looked away. When he glanced up again, she was hugging her two brothers who had ridden away to war. She and the rest of the family—except Felipe—were grateful they had not found one. Felipe had wished for blood.

Johnson and Bradley went down to their *jacal* to start gathering up their few possessions. Andrew and Michael stood back from the old cabin, not intruding upon the Moreno family's reunion. Petra pulled away after a minute and came down from the porch. She walked toward Andrew, her dark eyes steady. She stopped two paces short of him.

"I am glad to see you, Andrew. I am glad no one was hurt."

"Petra—" He stammered in confusion. He had expected her to cry, or to shout at him, or simply to turn away in silence. He had not expected this calm, controlled reception.

He said, "We'll be riding on, Michael and me."

"But you will take bread with us first."

He floundered, trying to find words. "We had better not. It's a long way back home."

Michael put in, "Much too long for us to leave here on an empty stomach. We accept your invitation, *señorita*, with thanks."

Andrew could have kicked him.

Señora Moreno said, "Petra, we must start cooking. These hungry men must eat." Petra gave Andrew a moment's quiet and inscrutable study, then turned and followed her mother into the cabin. Andrew watched the door and felt somehow empty.

Michael said, "That girl still makes me want to think of somebody. I just can't figure out who."

Andrew started to tell him she looked a little like Marie, but he was not sure how steady his voice would be. He decided to let Michael figure it out for himself. "I'll go and water the horses," he said.

The meal was punishment to Andrew. He had to sit across

the table from Petra and try not to look at her, for seeing her stirred feelings of guilt. He excused himself from the table as soon as he could and walked out to the corral where the horses had been unsaddled and given a little grain. He bridled and began saddling the brown. Hearing footsteps, he turned, expecting to see Michael. Petra stood at the gate, watching him.

While he tried to think of something to say, she took the initiative away from him. "I'm sorry," she said.

He blinked, surprised. "*You're* sorry? It's me who has something to apologize for."

"No, I threw myself at you. I had no right. I have had a few days to think about it and to see that I have caused embarrassment to you."

He stood slump-shouldered, trying to come up with a response.

She said, "I just wanted to let you know I am ashamed of myself. I promise you nothing like that will happen again."

Before he could speak, she walked back toward the cabin. She met Michael, who tipped his hat and turned to look at her a moment before coming on down to the corral. He gave Andrew a quiet study before saying, "Seems to me like you're in an almighty hurry to leave here."

"I thought you'd be in a rush to get home, with Marie waitin' and all."

"I reckon. But I have time to tell folks a decent *adiós*."

"I've said my good-byes. If you're ready, let's ride."

"You sure you ain't leavin' anything undone?"

"Nothin' I can think of."

Riding away, crossing the creek, he stopped once and looked back at the cabin. He thought he might see Petra standing on the porch, watching, but she was not there. He hunched a little and spurred to catch up to Michael.

They rode south in silence a while. At length Michael said, "As I recollect, you was aimin' to come back from this trip with a wife."

"That was your idea, and Marie's, not mine."

"Maybe so, and not a bad idea, either. Couldn't you find a suitable woman?"

"I got kind of busy."

"Not *that* busy. You was at the Moreno farm a right long time. Seemed to me like I seen somethin' in that Petra girl's eyes whenever she looked at you."

Andrew swallowed. "You've got too much imagination."

"Or maybe you've got none atall." Michael gave him an accusing look which Andrew tried to ignore by calling attention to the fact that a little green was beginning to show at the base of the old dry grass. Spring would be coming pretty soon.

Michael was not so easily distracted. He said, "I finally figured out who that Petra girl reminded me of."

Andrew thought, *She looks like Marie. You ought to've seen that from the first.*

Michael said triumphantly, "I don't know how you missed it. She looks a little like our sister Heather, back in Tennessee."

THEY ANGLED across the country, bypassing Austin's San Felipe because they had no particular business there. They crossed the Brazos River and in due time struck the Colorado at a ford a little way below the Nathan farm, where Marie was supposed to be. It was not a river that could be crossed just anywhere a man wanted to unless he was prepared to swim. And it was a little swollen, indicating that rain had fallen upstream, a harbinger of a favorable spring season.

"Water looks cold," Michael said, standing his horse on the bank and looking at it.

"A little muddy too," Andrew agreed. It often was, in varying degrees. That was why it bore as a name the Spanish word for "reddish."

Michael dismounted and began peeling off his clothes. "Then our dirt won't hurt it much. I ain't goin' home to Marie without I bathe first. She's got notions about such as that. Comes from the French side of her, I reckon."

Andrew dropped his roll on the ground and sought out a chunk of Marie's lye soap, made in a washpot behind her cabin. It had been used sparingly on this trip because the winter weather had not been conducive to bathing often or long. It was good for removing dirt, but sometimes it took skin too. He pitched the soap to Michael, who caught it, took a deep breath, and stepped out into the edge of the river. He let out a whoop. "Cold, did you say? It may be comin' spring out on the land, but it's still winter in the water."

Andrew finished stripping to the skin, then plunged in. The initial shock was enough to take his breath; but once he had shivered away the first chill, the water became bearable. Michael handed him the soap. He shaved the best he could with the cold river water and the lye soap, and without a mirror. His face burned as if he were peeling the skin from it. He suspected he probably was, in places. Done, he handed the razor to Michael and climbed out of the river, shivering while the wind dried him.

"Hell, ain't it?" Michael declared, "the things a man'll do for a woman?"

Andrew thought of Petra Moreno. "You'd know better than I would. I don't have one."

"Your fault, not mine."

Dressed, they crossed over the shallow ford. Michael grinned in anticipation. "Marie'll be tickled to see us. She'll put the big pot in the little one tonight. I've been hungry ever since we left the Morenos' place."

Andrew took that for a favorable sign. Maybe Michael had the roaming worked out of his system for a while.

"Can't hardly wait to see the young'uns," Michael exulted. "Till you get some of your own, little brother, you can't know how they pleasure a man."

Andrew frowned. He didn't see much chance for having any of his own, not in the near future.

They were all keyed up for a reunion at the Nathan place, but they were disappointed. Miles Nathan met them in the yard and invited them into the cabin to see the new Nathan baby. Andrew noticed that the two bachelors, Walker Younts and Joe Smith, were sitting together on a rough bench in front, staring glumly off toward a meadow. There the girl Birdy walked with a boy who appeared to be nearer her own age, or at least not so much older as Younts and Smith. Squinting, Andrew recognized Zeb Willet.

Nathan grinned. "The path of true love is indeed a thorny one, full of pitfalls."

Mrs. Nathan was already at the fireplace, fixing something for the family to eat. She said, "Michael, your Marie is a fine midwife. I just wish you'd look at my new baby girl."

Michael tried to show a great interest, but his disappointment showed more. "Where'd Marie go?"

"Home. There was some folks come by in a wagon and offered her a ride, so she tied her milk cow on behind and went with them. Said she had a heap of work piled up and waitin', and a garden that'd soon need plantin'. You-all are stayin' for dinner, aren't you?"

Michael said, "Couldn't eat. Ain't hungry. Much obliged, but we'll be ridin' on."

Andrew was gratified to see his brother so eager to return to Marie. Maybe it would be a while before he got restless enough to want to leave again.

Other times, coming home after a long trip of solitary exploration, Michael had gone in nervously, guilty about having left, guilty about having stayed so long. For this trip he had had a solid excuse, and no apologies were necessary. He was singing as they came upon a roan cow with his brand burned on her hip. She pulled away distrustfully from the horsemen, but not before Andrew saw that her sides bulged. Michael observed happily, "Looks like she'll be freshenin' pretty soon." The Lewis fortune was growing, one crop, one calf at a time.

Andrew nodded. "Looks to me like you've got just about everything a man could want."

They rode up over a small roll in the land, and Michael's cabin came suddenly into view, half a mile away. "Come on, Andrew," Michael chortled. "I can already taste that cornbread."

Andrew saw a wagon sitting near the double cabin. It was covered with canvas. "Looks like you've got company."

Michael nodded, puzzled. "Reckon who it could be? You don't suppose some of our folks from Tennessee—?" He tapped his spurs against his horse's ribs.

Approaching the cabin, Andrew began to suspect that he knew the wagon. He decided not to voice his suspicions. If he was right, Michael would find out all too soon.

He was right. He saw a man on a wooden bench leaned back against the log wall, lazing in the sun. The man got up and slowly stretched himself, then strode forward. He had only half of his right arm.

Finis Blackwood said, "Welcome home, Michael Lewis."

26

MICHAEL DISMOUNTED stiffly. His jaw was thrust forward belligerently as he confronted Finis Blackwood. "I've run you off of this place once already, Finis. What're you doin' here?"

Finis was looking more like his shiftless old daddy every day, Andrew thought. His beard was black and unkempt and showing traces of tobacco juice. He had old Cyrus Blackwood's half contentious, half whining way of meeting a challenge. "Why now, it was your missus herself that invited us to stay. We wasn't figurin' to impose, but when she seen Nelly's delicate condition, she wouldn't have it no other way. Good woman you got there, even if she does talk a little funny."

Andrew found dark humor in Finis's description. Nelly was indeed pregnant, but hardly delicate.

Michael said firmly, "I'll expect you to be gone in an hour, Finis, and I never want to see you on my land again."

"Well now," Finis replied, his back stiffening a little, "might be you'd want to ask your missus about that first. Strikes me as a woman with notions of her own, she does."

A boy's voice cried, "Daddy!" Little Mordecai hurried out from the open dog-run, opening his arms for his father. Michael turned away from Finis and leaned down to catch his son, sweeping him up into his arms. He and the boy hugged each other fiercely.

Andrew watched, wishing.

Marie stepped out then, wiping her hands on a rough home-spun cotton towel. "Michael!" She started to run to him as Mordecai had, then glanced at Andrew and Finis and caught herself. Andrew felt suddenly guilty, feeling that he was compromising the couple's rightful joyous reunion. Michael embraced his wife while still holding onto the boy.

"How's the baby?" he asked.

"Fine. She's fine. It is good you have come home."

Michael turned, staring balefully at Finis. "I'd sure have to agree with that. You know who this man is?"

She had to know, for the Blackwood family had often been discussed around the Lewis family hearth, along with droughts and grasshoppers and fever epidemics. She said, "They are in need. Nelly is in the hope."

Michael responded dryly, "Damned little hope, tied to such as Finis. Did she tell you they ain't even married?"

Finis put in, "We're married, Michael. Found us a preacher named Fairweather and done it all proper and legal. Man gets more land if he's got him a wife."

Andrew had to turn away and grin. He doubted that Fairweather's services carried any legality; he was self-ordained. But that was a problem for the Blackwoods to work out. And Austin.

Michael said sternly to Marie, "I told Finis to pack up and be gone from here before dark."

Marie pulled back to arm's length. Her voice took on a strength she had always possessed but did not often bring into the light. "And I told him they could stay until they get a cabin up."

Michael protested, "Maybe you just don't realize what kind of people they are."

"A woman in her condition should not live in a wagon; *that* I realize. Until they have a cabin, she will stay with us." Her tone carried a finality that Andrew would not have wanted to argue with.

Evidently Michael did not either. He turned resentfully upon Finis. "You've got yourself some land already?"

Finis nodded, triumph in his eyes. He raised his good hand and pointed eastward. "Yonder, a ways down the river and on the other side."

Andrew took some little comfort in the fact that they would at least be across the river.

Michael glanced at Andrew, his eyes flashing anger. "I thought Texas was far enough away—"

Finis gloated. "We'll be your neighbors again, Michael, just like back in Tennessee."

"You may live here, but you'll be no neighbor of mine, not in a hundred years." Michael lifted the boy up onto one shoulder. "I'm goin' in and see the baby."

Marie said, "She's not in the bedroom. I let Nelly have that, and Finis. We sleep in the kitchen."

"Damn!" Michael declared, and stomped into the cabin.

Marie stared after him, her dark eyes a little hurt. They reminded Andrew of Petra's.

He said, "Hello, Marie. Remember me?"

She gave him a sisterly hug. "I am sorry, Andrew. It was not as I wished. I did not know he felt so strongly."

"You know now." Andrew watched as Finis retreated to the bedroom side of the double cabin. It was discomforting to think of him and Nelly profaning that place which had been graced by Marie and Michael's love.

Marie glanced in that direction a moment, and Andrew wondered if the same thought had come to her. She probably would not admit it, but she might have found reason by now to regret her hospitable nature.

He said, "The sooner the Blackwoods are off of this place, the better."

"I could not turn the poor woman away."

"We can't run them out of the country. I reckon they've got a legal claim to stay. Best thing to do is to get some of the neighbors over and raise them a cabin as quick as we can. Till we get that done, I'll give them the borrow of mine."

"I could not ask that of you, Andrew."

"I'm doin' it on my own. I don't want to see an argument come between you and Michael."

"And what of the argument between *you* and Michael?"

"We sort of lost it somewhere along the way. Did you really send him along with Austin, to see about me?"

"I did."

"You're too generous a woman, Marie."

She smiled. "And you are a generous man, Andrew Lewis, to give up your cabin to the Blackwoods."

"I'm just hopin' to keep Michael from doin' murder. I'll bring my stuff over here and sleep in the shed."

"When the Blackwoods leave, you can sleep in the kitchen."

That would not give Michael and Marie the privacy they needed, especially since Michael had been away a while. "The shed'll be fine."

She smiled again. He suspected she understood his reason. "For you and Michael, I will fix a big supper tonight."

"I'd be much obliged."

She started to turn away but stopped to study him thoughtfully. "I had hoped you would not come back alone."

Looking at Marie, he remembered Petra and felt a tug of regret. "A man can't force some things. They've got to come natural or not at all."

She touched his hand, and warmth arose in him. But as he looked into her lively eyes he found he was seeing Petra, not Marie. She said, "Sometimes nature needs help."

She left him standing there awkwardly holding the brown horse's reins. He heard the sound of wood chopping out behind the cabin. He tied the horse to a post and walked around to the back. There he saw Isaac Blackwood, ax in hand, cutting pine logs and branches into firewood. A goodly supply was neatly stacked near the cabin.

Andrew asked, "Did you cut all that yourself, Isaac?"

Isaac turned, wiping sweat from his face onto his sleeve. "Not all of it. There was already a little here when we come. I figured I'd ought to do somethin' to help earn our keep."

Andrew wondered. This was not like the Blackwoods he remembered, certainly not like Finis or Luke. It was the first time the middle brother had come to mind. He asked, "Where's Luke?"

"Down by the river, tryin' to catch some fish. He never was much of a hand with a choppin' ax."

Or anything else, Andrew thought. He pointed. "That's my cabin you see up yonder. I'm goin' to lend you-all the use of it till you get a cabin of your own put up. Or maybe two cabins, seein' that Finis and Nelly are married now. It'd be kind of awkward, all of you sleepin' in one."

"Wouldn't be the first time." Isaac frowned. "Nelly may not look like much, and she's not as smart as some, but she's a woman. We're goin' to do right by her. She's goin' to be a mother bye and bye."

"To Finis's baby."

"Maybe. But I'd like to think it just might be mine." He rubbed his arm across his face. "That surprise you, Andrew?"

"Can't say as it does. I'd think the young'un'd have a better chance in life bein' yours than bein' his. But how'll you ever know?"

"I'll know. I'll look at it, and I'll know."

Andrew bent over and reached for a piece of wood. "I'll be carryin' this into the kitchen for you."

ANDREW MADE a horseback round to the nearest neighbors, including the Willet family, the Nathans, the bachelors Younts and Smith, and set a day for them all to gather at the Black-woods' place to raise a cabin. He knew he should be breaking out his field in preparation for the spring planting, but it was more important to get the Blackwoods out of his cabin and far enough away that he did not have to look at them often. He and Michael and Isaac felled and trimmed trees, dragging them up to the site where two cabins were to be erected. Finis pleaded helplessness because of his crippled condition. Luke did not plead at all; he just went to the river and fished.

The saving grace in the whole situation was that the claim was a full three miles downriver and on the opposite side. The river was a barrier of sorts, psychological if not physical, so maybe the Blackwoods would not venture too often to its south side. Andrew and Michael agreed that Marie had better take a close count of her chickens every day for a while. There had always been plenty of four-legged varmints skulking around, looking for a chance to grab them, but the Blackwoods introduced a new dimension to the need for vigilance.

Michael was in a dark mood while they prepared for the cabin-raising. "It goes against all that's sacred and holy to be puttin' forth this amount of sweat for such people as that," he complained to Andrew. "But Marie wouldn't have it no different. I hope the day don't come when she regrets that kind heart of hers."

"That's one of the things that makes her special," Andrew replied. "Maybe you don't know how lucky you are to have her."

"I do know. Otherwise I'd be doin' somethin' else than choppin' timbers for the Blackwood family."

Cabin-raising was usually the occasion for a community party in colonial Texas, and some effort was made in that direction for the Blackwoods. The womenfolk brought food, and some made new clothes for Nelly to wear during her indisposition. The men brought their building tools, their teams, and somebody brought along some bad whiskey that had never seen Kentucky. Finis and Luke got a lot more interested in the whiskey than in the building project, and they became considerably more of a hazard than a help. Isaac stayed sober and did much of the heavy lifting. By dusk, two cabins were standing where there had been but grass before. There would be much finishing-out to do, but the major work was done.

Normally it would have been time for everybody to cut loose and celebrate, but Finis and Luke got into a terrible row that ended with each of them trying to beat the other's brains out. Watching disgustedly, Andrew thought it a hopeless cause; neither had enough brains that anybody would notice if they *did* get knocked out. At least now he should be able to move back into his own cabin, though he might have to let it air a couple of days first. He had noticed a long time ago that horses hated to move in where hogs had moved out.

THERE WERE times, usually when he least expected it, that a sudden violent image would explode in his brain, and he would find himself confronting the memory of the day he had been forced to shoot Jayce Beard. He would awaken suddenly in the middle of the night, shouting at Jayce to back away. He would find himself in a cold sweat, shaking.

He began to understand how old dreams of a Spanish massacre could still sometimes haunt his brother Michael. Always, after the image of Jayce, he saw the vengeful eyes of old Tolliver Beard, and heard Beard's promise to kill him.

It was a long way to Nacogdoches, and farther even to the Louisiana line. He felt some safety in that distance. The old man had tried once to kill him and had missed. Chances were he had given up and had gone back to Louisiana to nurse his grief, Andrew told himself. But Michael had a colder view of the world and its violence, for he had seen more of it than Andrew.

"From what I heard about that old man, he meant what he told you," Michael warned. "It might be a week, it might be a month, it might be a year, but the day'll come when you'll look up and see him. And you'd better not let him catch you unprepared."

As Andrew had stayed close to Michael earlier, when they had reason to fear the Blackwoods, Michael kept close to Andrew now, watching always for a stranger. They worked together as they plowed their fields, as they handled their few cattle, as they hunted wild game for the table. A rifle was never far from reach by one or the other.

Andrew wearied of the watchfulness and was inclined to forget, but Michael was not. And one day as they were planting corn, Andrew saw Michael stop abruptly, his attention riveted to the east. Sweat ran into Andrew's eyes and stung them, so he had to wipe them clear before he made out the vague shape of two horsemen.

"That wouldn't be Beard," Andrew said. "There's two of them."

"He might've brought help," Michael replied, stepping across the plowed rows and picking up his rifle that he had leaned against the rail fence. Andrew had left his own weapon at the end of the field. He set out in a trot across the soft ground to fetch it.

By the time he had retrieved the rifle, Michael had joined him, waiting by the fence on the lower side. A rail fence always made a good rest for a rifle if a man needed to take careful aim.

But Andrew saw no threat. In fact, one of the riders was slumped forward in the saddle, as if hurt or sick. The other began waving his hat and hollering, long before he was in good hearing range. Andrew turned his left ear to the sound but could not make out the words. When the two riders were close enough, he recognized one. "It's Isaac Blackwood. The other one, I can't tell."

Michael sucked in a long breath. "It's Eli Pleasant. It's Eli, and there's somethin' the matter with him!"

He vaulted over the rail fence and hurried toward the horsemen in a long-legged stride that Andrew found impossible to catch up with.

Eli was bleeding. He had his right hand pressed against his chest, but blood seeped out between his bony old fingers. His grizzled face was ashen.

Michael reached him first, grabbing the old man as he seemed about to slip out of the saddle. He steadied Eli on the horse, then turned furiously upon the other rider. "Isaac Blackwood, if you-all've done this—"

Isaac quickly shook his head. "I was out a-huntin'. I heard a shot and found Eli on the ground. I wanted to take him to our place—it was closer—but he wanted to come to you."

Eli raised his head. He seemed to have trouble seeing, because he looked at Michael and called him Andrew. "I had to come tell you. It's Tolliver Beard."

Andrew felt the bottom drop out of his stomach. "He's here? He shot you?"

Eli nodded. He tried to say something more, but the words were unintelligible.

Michael said desperately, "Let's get him to the house. He'll die sittin' on that horse."

Andrew bit his lip. To him, it looked as if Eli would die no matter where he was. He took the reins while Michael swung up behind Eli to hold him in the saddle. Isaac motioned for Andrew to get onto his dun horse, behind him.

Michael called for Marie, and she was waiting at the dog-run as they rode up. Andrew slipped off of Isaac's horse and helped Michael lift Eli carefully down from the saddle. The old man gasped as he was moved. Marie's face whitened, but she held the bedroom door open while the brothers carried Eli in and laid him gently on the bed. She shooed the boy Morde-cai back to the kitchen so he would not see.

Michael said desperately, "I'll need a sharp knife, and hot water and some cloth for bandages. We've got to get that bullet out of him."

Eli raised his hand as if to wave Michael off. "Too late for that," he said. "He put it in too deep." He grimaced in pain, and cold sweat broke across his forehead. For a moment Andrew feared he was gone. But Eli opened his eyes. He blinked, trying to see. "Which one is Andrew?"

Andrew said, "I'm here, Eli."

"He's come for you, Andrew. I heard, and I tried to get here first. But we run together out yonder—"

Andrew's throat tightened. He had a hard time speaking. "You oughtn't to've, Eli. We've both been watchin' for him. He wouldn't've caught us by surprise."

Eli rasped, "Missy—where's Marie?"

"Here, Eli."

"Seen your papa. Your mama too. They said tell you—" He began to cough blood.

Marie took his hand and held it tightly. "It's all right, Eli. You don't have to talk now."

Eli quit coughing. Andrew took a cloth and wiped the blood away from his mouth. Eli tried to focus on him. "Watch him, Andrew. He's a mean old man. He'll—"

The voice trailed. For a moment Andrew heard nothing except Marie's quiet sobbing. Then Eli spoke once more. "You Lewis boys—you're goin' to be the death of me yet."

With that, he was gone.

Michael folded the old hands carefully across Eli's chest. Andrew wiped the blood from Eli's face the best he could, then pulled the boots from Eli's feet.

Isaac stood back quietly. He had known Eli but briefly at the Moreno farm. He said, "I'll go tend to the horses and leave you folks with him for a spell."

Nobody replied, so Isaac walked quietly out the door and onto the dog-run. He stopped dead still. Something about his manner made Andrew look up.

"Andrew!" Isaac said, his voice a little strained. "He's out here."

Andrew knew before he asked. "Beard?" He felt that cold chill in his stomach again.

"I expect so. He looks like the description. He's just standin' out here beside his horse, like he's waitin'."

Michael said in a low voice, "Let him wait. I can draw a bead on him from the window."

Andrew gritted his teeth. He picked up his rifle and checked the load. "No. I've got to do this myself. It was me he came for. It was me Eli died for. It's for me to finish."

He gave his brother and Marie a long study. He saw raw fear in Marie's eyes. He said, "Isaac, you'd better come back in here."

Isaac complied. He said, "He's got a look in his eye that I've seen in a bear's, just before he charged. He's got a rifle, and he looks like he knows how to use it."

Andrew glanced once more at Eli. "I know he does."

He took a deep breath and stepped out onto the dog-run, rifle in his hands, in a ready position.

Old Tolliver Beard's eyes were as Isaac had said. They were like eyes Andrew had seen in a boyhood nightmare.

Beard's voice was deep and grim. "I've come to have my vengeance, Andrew Lewis. Blood for blood. Are you prepared for eternity?"

Andrew made no answer; his throat was too tight. No answer would have changed anything.

The old man betrayed himself. He narrowed his eyes just before he brought the rifle into position to aim. That was edge enough for Andrew. He leveled his own rifle, saw the man's broad chest over the sights and squeezed the trigger. He saw the flash of the pan just before Tolliver's rifle belched fire. He saw Tolliver stagger backward.

Something struck his head with the force of a sledge. He felt as if his brain had exploded. He was driven back, stumbling, falling hard upon the ax-hewn floor of the dog-run.

27

ANDREW'S RETURN to consciousness was slow and painful. His first awareness was that his head ached as if someone were driving a hammer against his skull. He drifted in and out of vague dreams in which he relived the shooting of Jayce Beard, and he saw the vengeful old man standing in Michael's yard, cursing him, raising the rifle to his shoulder. The dream would fade, and he was back at the Moreno farm, sitting with Petra or walking with her along the creek, holding her and not wanting to let go. Then Petra would disappear and Jayce would come again, with the hard-eyed old Tolliver Beard. Andrew would go through the shootings once more. Sometimes he saw Eli Pleasant, sometimes he didn't. There was something strange about Eli—

He sensed that these were only dreams, but they were so real that he went through the rush of all the old emotions as each came and went and transformed into something else. He became aware of light, eventually, and slowly opened his eyes. He found his vision was blurred. Something seemed to be crushing his head. He raised his hand and found a bandage there. He saw the vague, thin figure of a woman sitting in a chair, and he was back at the Moreno farm, as he had been after the beating in Nacogdoches.

He called, "Petra?"

The woman rose and came to his side, and he realized he was lying on a bed. The voice said, "It's Marie." A hand touched his cheek. "You do not need to move. You just lie there." Through a haze he could see her move to the light, where he discerned the fuzzy outline of a door. She called, "Michael!"

The voice was Petra's, or seemed to be. But why would Petra be calling for Michael? His confusion frustrated him. How did he get back to the Moreno place?

Michael spoke then. "You finally comin' alive, little brother? Me and Marie, we began to wonder if you ever would."

"Marie? What is Marie doin' at the Moreno farm?"

"This ain't the Moreno place. It's our house, mine and Marie's. That shot kind of churned your brain, looks like."

Andrew closed his eyes, for the light hurt them. Gradually it began coming back to him, a little here, a little there. He remembered about Tolliver Beard.

"Beard!" he exclaimed. "What happened to Tolliver Beard?"

Michael said, "He's dead. You got him square through the heart. The way it looked to me, you fired a second before he did. Your bullet hit him just as he pulled the trigger. Else he'd've shot you plumb center instead of layin' a bullet up against your skull."

Andrew could not remember that part of it. He remembered the old man bringing his rifle around. He thought he remembered himself, squeezing the trigger; he wasn't sure.

Michael's voice was grim. "At least you paid him for Eli."

Eli. Andrew had forgotten. Eli was dead. Old Eli, friend of their father. He had saved Michael's life, and probably Andrew's as well, pulling him away from that mob in Nacogdoches. Now he was dead. Painfully Andrew said, "Nothin' would ever pay for Eli."

He opened his eyes again, though the light hurt them. He could discern Michael standing over him, Marie by his side. Or was it Petra? Everything was so blurry he could not tell. "My eyes. Somethin's wrong with my eyes."

Michael said, "I'm not surprised. That rifle ball cut a crease along the side of your head. It was bound to affect somethin'. But you've got the hard head that comes with bein' a Lewis. It'll probably be all right in a day or two."

Andrew tried sitting up. The pounding intensified, and he had to drop back upon the pillow. Marie's voice spoke. "You lie still now, Andrew. You should not too soon get up." The words were English, so this had to be Marie. Petra did not speak English.

He said, "First time in my life I didn't know where I was at."

Marie said, "Or who was with you. You called me Petra."

Odd, he thought. That other time, he had been with Petra, and he had called her Marie.

He said, "Michael, we got to do somethin' about Eli."

"Isaac has gone to fetch the neighbors so we can give him a fittin' funeral. I thought we'd bury him up on that hill yonder where he can watch over us. Wasn't for him, we wouldn't none of us be here."

"What about Tolliver Beard?"

"We'll bury him on the other side of the river, where we don't have to look at the place, and a long ways from Eli."

Andrew remembered something Eli had said after Quenton Mann's death. He said huskily, "Texas. It sure does take a toll."

HE WAS unable to walk up the hill for the funeral. Young Zeb Willet put him onto his own horse and rode double with him to the place where neighbors had dug the grave. There was no preacher, so Miles Nathan delivered the eulogy. Michael stood beside Andrew so Andrew could lean upon him for support when his legs weakened. His vision was better but still blurred. He saw Marie as if she were wearing a veil, and she looked for all the world like Petra Moreno.

Days, Michael was in his field, planting. Andrew felt he should be at his own place, doing the same, but he lacked the strength. That blue-speckled ox would be getting fat, not having to work. Then one day all the neighbors came back together, and they stayed long enough to plant a good part of Andrew's field for him. They had no sooner finished than a good rain began, assuring that the seeds would sprout.

Texas. It could take away with one hand, but it could turn around and give so much with the other.

Until his strength returned, Andrew remained with Michael and Marie and the two children. Earlier, he would have liked nothing better than to be close to Marie this way. Now, somehow, things had changed. He could look at Marie without wishing she were his. He looked at Marie and saw someone else.

One day he watched Marie hanging out the family's clothes on a line Michael had strung for her. His vision had cleared; it had returned to normal now, except when he looked at Marie. Finished with the clothing, she walked up and stood before him with a willow basket in her hands.

She asked, "Do you think you can ride a horse?"

"I suppose I could. Why?"

"Just now you watched me, but you did not really see me. You looked beyond me, to somewhere else. Somebody else."

He felt a stirring of surprise. "I didn't know it showed."

"Always it has shown, ever since you came home from Nacogdoches. I was not sure, but when you called me by that girl's name, then I knew."

"Petra?"

"Petra. Michael has told me about her. You are a sick man, Andrew Lewis. You will not be well until you go and get her."

"I hurt her, Marie. She might not come."

"I think she will come. I think all you must do is ask her. Must I get Michael to put a saddle on your horse?"

Andrew pushed to his feet. "I reckon I'm strong enough to saddle my own horse."

HE LEFT at daylight. The first day's ride found him still weak, and he had to stop several times to rest. The second day he did better, and the third day he stopped only because the brown horse needed rest. He found himself pushing the animal harder and harder with each day that passed.

The pine trees seemed taller and denser. His excitement

built as he remembered landmarks that told him he was getting closer to Nacogdoches. He came, finally, to the narrow road leading into the timber that hid the Moreno place. He put the brown into an easy lope, a pace he had resisted until now. He broke out of the timber and saw the sprawling cabin, the shed, the corrals. He saw the field, where Ramón and Felipe were working their oxen. They recognized him and waved, and they halted their plowing. Andrew waved back but did not stop, for he had not come to see Ramón and Felipe.

He saw her then, in the garden, wielding a hoe. The old mother was there with her. It was *Señora* Moreno who saw him first and pointed. Petra turned, her dark eyes wide with surprise and joy.

Andrew swung down and almost leaped over the rail fence in his eagerness, but he managed to get control. He tied the horse and walked to the open gate. *Señora* Moreno came out to meet him. She gave him a hug, looked back with a smile at Petra, then walked toward the cabin without once turning to see.

Andrew stopped and stared at Petra from a full two paces. "Petra. You do not know how beautiful you are."

She blushed and looked down self-consciously at the stained old dress she wore for the garden work. "You should not surprise me so. I must look terrible, so dirty and all."

He moved a step closer. "You are the most beautiful sight I ever saw in my life." He wanted to reach for her, to sweep her into his arms, but there were things that had to be said. "I made a mistake, Petra. I told you that when I looked at you I kept seeing someone else. Well, I have seen her now, and when I looked at her, all I could see was you. All I wanted was to come back and see you again."

"So now you see me, all ugly and dirty. Is it worth so long a ride?"

"It will be much shorter going back, because I will be taking you with me."

She stared at him with some trepidation. "I would like that, Andrew. But one thing is bothersome: you are American, I am

Mexican. Some people say the two are much too different; life together may not be easy."

"*Texas* is not easy. But it is worth the struggle."

She came to him, and he took her into his arms. She said, "Then let us make the struggle together."

COMING NOVEMBER 2007

A saga of early Texas by one of
the greatest Western writers

ELMER KELTON

THE

REBELS

SONS OF TEXAS

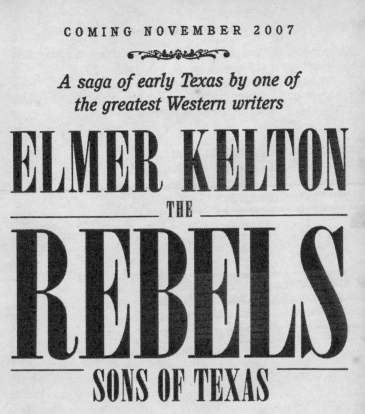

Against the bloody backdrop of the Texas War of Independence—
the battles of Gonzales, San Antonio de Béxar, Goliad, the Alamo,
and San Jacinto, the Lewis men and their families join such
rebels as Jim Bowie, James Fannin, Ben Milam, Juan Seguín,
James Butler Bonham, William Barret Travis, and David Crockett
in wresting Texas from Mexican rule.

"If there's an heir to the Louis L'Amour legacy, it's Kelton."
—*Booklist* on *Ranger's Trail*

ISBN-13: 0-978-7635-1526-7 | ISBN-10: 0-7653-1526-2
A Forge Hardcover | www.tor-forge.com